BY ALISON WEIR

FICTION
SIX TUDOR QUEENS

Katharine Parr, The Sixth Wife
Katheryn Howard, The Scandalous Queen
Anna of Kleve, The Princess in the Portrait
Jane Seymour, The Haunted Queen
Anne Boleyn, A King's Obsession
Katherine of Aragon: The True Queen

The King's Pleasure
The Last White Rose
The Marriage Game
A Dangerous Inheritance
Captive Queen
The Lady Elizabeth
Innocent Traitor

NONFICTION
ENGLAND'S MEDIEVAL QUEENS

Queens of the Crusades
Queens of the Conquest

The Lost Tudor Princess: The Life of Lady Margaret Douglas
Elizabeth of York: A Tudor Queen and Her World
Mary Boleyn: The Mistress of Kings
The Lady in the Tower: The Fall of Anne Boleyn
Mistress of the Monarchy: The Life of Katherine Swynford,
Duchess of Lancaster
Queen Isabella: Treachery, Adultery, and Murder in Medieval England
Mary Queen of Scots and the Murder of Lord Darnley
Henry VIII: The King and His Court
Eleanor of Aquitaine: A Life
The Life of Elizabeth I
The Children of Henry VIII
The Wars of the Roses
The Princes in the Tower
The Six Wives of Henry VIII

The Passionate Tudor

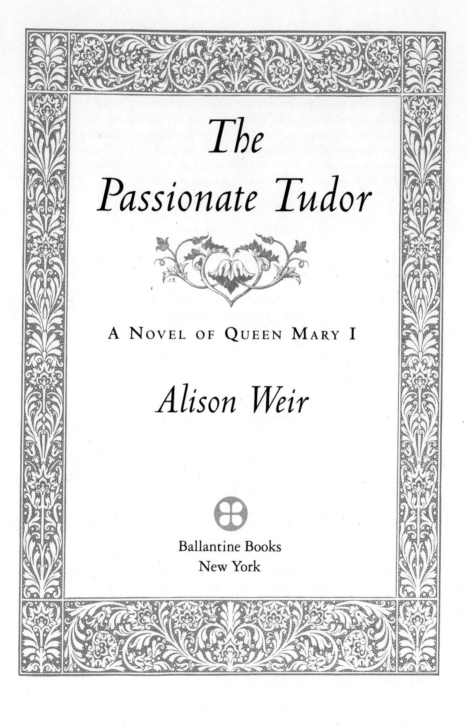

The
Passionate Tudor

A Novel of Queen Mary I

Alison Weir

Ballantine Books
New York

Published in the United States by Ballantine Books, an imprint of Random House, a division of Penguin Random House LLC, New York.

BALLANTINE is a registered trademark and the colophon is a trademark of Penguin Random House LLC.

Originally published in hardcover in the United Kingdom as *Mary I: Queen of Sorrows* by Headline Review, an imprint of Headline Publishing Group, a Hachette Company, London.

LIBRARY OF CONGRESS CATALOGING-IN-PUBLICATION DATA
Names: Weir, Alison, author.
Title: The passionate Tudor: a novel of Queen Mary I / Alison Weir.
Description: First edition. | New York: Ballantine Books, 2024. |
Includes index.
Identifiers: LCCN 2024004962 (print) | LCCN 2024004963 (ebook) |
ISBN 9780593355107 (hardcover; acid-free paper) |
ISBN 9780593355114 (ebook)
Subjects: LCSH: Mary, Queen, consort of Louis XII, King of France, 1496-1533—Fiction. | LCGFT: Historical fiction. | Novels.
Classification: LCC PR6123.E36 P37 2024 (print) |
LCC PR6123.E36 (ebook) | DDC 823/.92—dc23/eng/20240202
LC record available at https://lccn.loc.gov/2024004962
LC ebook record available at https://lccn.loc.gov/2024004963

Printed in the United States of America on acid-free paper

randomhousebooks.com

2 4 6 8 9 7 5 3 1

First U.S. Edition

Book design by Virginia Norey

This book is dedicated to my fellow historians,
Sarah Gristwood, Julian Humphrys, Michael Jones, and Nicola Tallis
And in memory of Derek Malcolm

The Spanish and English Royal Houses, 1525-1527

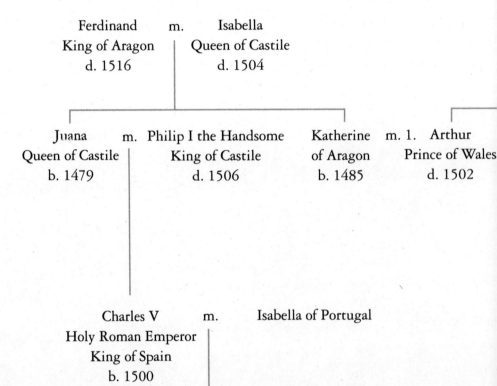

Ferdinand   m.   Isabella
King of Aragon | Queen of Castile
d. 1516   d. 1504

Juana   m.   Philip I the Handsome   Katherine   m. 1.   Arthur
Queen of Castile   King of Castile   of Aragon   Prince of Wales
b. 1479   d. 1506   b. 1485   d. 1502

Charles V   m.   Isabella of Portugal
Holy Roman Emperor
King of Spain
b. 1500

Philip of Spain
b. 1527

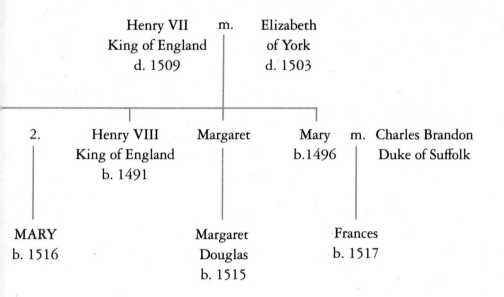

Henry VII m. Elizabeth
King of England of York
d. 1509 d. 1503

2. Henry VIII Margaret Mary m. Charles Brandon
King of England b.1496 Duke of Suffolk
b. 1491

MARY Margaret Frances
b. 1516 Douglas b. 1517
b. 1515

PART ONE

The King's Daughter

As to the Princess my daughter, she is the King's true child, and as God has given her unto us, so I will render her again to the King as his daughter, to do with her as shall stand for his pleasure. Neither for my daughter nor any worldly adversity, nor the King's displeasure that might ensue, will I yield in this cause to put my soul in danger.

—Katherine of Aragon

Chapter 1

1525

Mary's earliest memory was of a glittering ceremony at her father's court when she must have been very tiny. She could recall nearly tripping over her silk skirts, grasping her mother's hand as they greeted some very important strangers. She had been aware that it was her special day and that she was the center of everyone's attention. She could remember the whole court bowing to her as she toddled past, and later the roar of that great golden giant, the King her father, as he threw back his head and laughed heartily, brushing back a tear, at something she had said.

"You asked the French ambassador if he was the Dauphin. 'If you are,' you said, 'I want to kiss you,'" her sainted mother told her, one February afternoon seven years later, still smiling at the reminiscence. Mary loved to see her mother smile. It brought a radiance to her face, made her almost beautiful, although she was very old and often looked tired and sad.

Mary knelt upon the cushioned window seat beside her and peered through the diamond panes of the casement at the palace gardens below, where she could see the Queen's maids playing tag, cheered on by some young, gaudily dressed gentlemen.

"Is it true that I was going to marry the Dauphin?"

Mother smiled. "Yes. You were set to be queen of France, but God had a greater destiny in store for you."

"Yes—I am going to be the Holy Roman Empress—and queen of Spain, as well as queen of England!" Mary fingered the gold brooch on her velvet bodice that bore the legend "The Emperor," which she wore always to honor her betrothed. "When will I go to Spain?"

"Not for a long time yet, I hope," Mother said, picking up her embroidery. "When you are old enough to be married."

"Lady Salisbury says that girls can be married at twelve," Mary persisted. "I'm nine now."

"I was fifteen when I came to England to be married to your uncle, Prince Arthur," Mother said. "Twelve is too young. And you are small for your age. You still have a lot of growing up to do."

Mary heard the relief in her voice and suspected that her mother was dreading their parting as much as she was. While part of her relished the prospect of her glorious future, she hated the thought of leaving England, her parents, and everything she loved and knew, because it would be forever, unless she was very, very lucky. Look at Mother: she had never been back to her native Spain in nearly twenty-five years. Already Mary could imagine the despair of homesickness . . .

"When he was here, the Emperor Charles asked your father if you might go to Spain immediately," Mother told her. Mary drew in her breath sharply. "He said you should be educated as befitted a future empress and queen of Spain. But your father said that if Charles searched all Christendom for a lady mistress to bring you up after the manner of Spain, then he could not find one more perfect than myself, for I have such an affection for Charles that I would bring you up to his satisfaction. And Charles, bless him, had to agree. I was so relieved, because I felt you were not strong enough to risk a sea voyage or acclimatize yourself to the air of another country. I was remembering my own terrible voyage to England and how ill I was for six years after my arrival. And I was a lot older than you."

She smiled at Mary and stroked her hair. "When the time comes, we will make sure that you sail to Spain at the most clement time of year. You will love Spain, Daughter. I had the happiest childhood there. After my parents drove out the Moors and reclaimed the land for Christ, my sisters and I grew up in the great palace of the Alhambra at Granada. It is a beautiful place with fair courtyards and fountains. This future is what I want for you; I have always prayed that you should find happiness in the land of my birth. Never forget that you are half Spanish!"

"Never!" Mary declared, and begged the Queen to recount the oft-told tale of the deeds of her noble grandparents, the renowned Spanish sovereigns Ferdinand and Isabella.

"Isabella was a great queen, as you will be one day," Queen Katherine said. "You will rule England, with Charles beside you, and Spain and the Empire too."

Mary found it impossible to imagine the extent of the vast territories over which her future husband held dominion. Spain, the Low Countries, Germany, Austria, parts of Italy . . . He was the mightiest prince in the world.

She had met him once, three years ago, when he had come to England for their betrothal. She had been six then, and greatly in awe of the tall, grave-faced young man with the ugly jaw—a jaw so misshapen that he could not fully close his mouth. Yet he had been courteous to her and taken such a kindly interest in her childish concerns that she had felt overwhelmed with gratitude to the King her father for making such a great marriage for her. She had not quite understood then what it would mean for her. Yet she had been aware, young as she was, that her mother was overjoyed that there was to be no French match for her daughter; France was the ancient enemy of Spain, and Mother's hatred of the French was no secret. Her joy had known no bounds when she saw her beloved child affianced to her nephew, her sister's son.

And there, Mary knew, lay a tale, one Mother was reluctant to recount. She had spoken just once of her sister, Queen Juana, and then only to say that the poor woman was ill and confined to a convent.

It was Reginald Pole, the son of Mary's beloved governess, Lady Salisbury, who had enlightened her. Reginald was a clever young man who seemed to know everything—and so he should, for the King had paid for him to have a very expensive education—and Mary adored him, hanging on his every word; it had ever been so, for as long as she could remember; he was like a big brother to her. One day recently, after her lessons had ended, he had pulled up a chair to her desk and they had spoken of Christopher Columbus, who had discovered the New World under the patronage of Ferdinand and Isabella, and then the talk had led to more recent history. Reginald had explained that Queen Juana ought to be ruling Spain, but could not because of her madness.

"Madness?" Mary had echoed, horrified.

Reginald seemed reluctant to elaborate. "I fear I have said more than was proper to you, my lady Princess. I thought you knew the truth."

"I know some of it," she told him, aware that she would have to confess the lie later.

"Then you will know that she was confined in a convent and that her son Charles rules in her stead."

"But what did she do? How did people know she was mad?"

"By her behavior. Her husband died. He was known as Philip the Handsome, and she loved him to idolatry. His death unhinged her. She would not give up his body for burial, not for months. They had to prize her away."

Mary shuddered.

"Queen Isabella's mother was mad, too," Reginald said.

"No, she wasn't!" she protested, bewildered. There was an awkward pause.

"They're all mad in the Spanish royal family," he grinned, with that twinkle in his eye that showed he was teasing her. "Take care, my lady Princess, that you don't fall victim to the curse, too!"

Mary had thrown a cushion at him for that, and chased him around the schoolroom until her tutor, Dr. Fetherston, had come and shooed him away, scolding him for encouraging indecorous behavior in his precious charge.

"It will be time for your music lesson soon," Mother said, pushing a loose tress of red hair back under Mary's velvet hood. "When you have practiced, you must play for me. I love to hear you play."

"Will my lord father be there?" Mary asked, sliding off the window seat. More than anything, she craved his approval.

"I hope he will visit us this afternoon before Vespers," Mother said, sounding wistful. Father did not come as often as he once did. He was so busy, weighted with the burdens of state. It was fortunate that he had Mary's godfather, the mighty Cardinal Wolsey, to help him. But if Father was an often absent figure, Mother was always there, a constant loving presence in Mary's life. That was why it was hard to imagine a future without her.

Mary slid off the window seat, curtseyed, and danced off to her music lesson. She spent an hour practicing on the virginals, then sped back to the Queen's apartments to play the song she had learned.

"Walk!" Mother admonished gently. "Ladies do not run."

Mary curtseyed and set up her virginals on the table. She was just about to begin when the door opened and the King was announced. And there he was, her great and glorious father, larger than life and glittering with jewels. He pulled her up from her curtsey and spun her around. "And how is my little princess today?"

"Happier for seeing you, Sir!" she cried, kissing him heartily. How handsome he was, how dashing! Where Mother was all gentleness and comfort, he represented pleasure and excitement. He was one of the most powerful princes in the world, and everyone jumped at his command. Never had there been a king so popular, so loved.

He set her down and bent to kiss Mother. Then they sat together as Mary performed for them, both beaming with pride and applauding her when the last note had died away. She smiled at them, secure in the warmth of their love. She had never been in any doubt that they doted upon her. Others looked after her daily needs, as was proper for a princess—her first lady governess had been Lady Calthorpe, and then there was Lady Bryan, who had been replaced by dear Lady Salisbury—but her parents were at the center of her world. Father had always delighted in showing her off to visiting dignitaries, sweeping her up in his arms and carrying her around, bursting with pride. Mother told her how she used to jump forward in her nurse's lap when she caught sight of him. As soon as she had learned the basic courtesies, she had been allowed to take part in court festivities and pageants. At four, she had been deputed to receive foreign envoys and play the virginals for them.

"Dance for us, child," Father bade her now, and she rose and executed a perfect pavane as Mother strummed a lute, smiling.

"Excellent!" he pronounced. "You twirl so prettily that no woman could do better, eh, Kate?" Mary thrilled to his praise.

The next day, she looked for him, but he did not come. Nor did he come on any other day that week. Mary sensed that Mother was as disappointed as she was, but Mother would never criticize Father or complain about him, so strong was her love for him. Instead, she took evident pleasure in Mary's company, and in prayer. Her strong faith was the guiding light and principle in her life, and she spent hours on her knees in her chapel. She had instilled in Mary a devout love for God and a deep-seated piety. Mary loved the rituals of faith, the rich hues of the stained-glass windows, the statues of the saints glittering with gems, the serene face of the stone Virgin in the chapel as She cradled Her Child, and the jewel-encrusted crucifix that stood on the altar. She loved the mystery of it all, held her breath when the Host was elevated and miraculously became the actual Body of Our Lord, received it with awed reverence. She was rarely happier than when sharing these precious hours of devotions with her beloved mother—unless it was when Father joined them, and the choir of the Chapel Royal sang for them with voices that seemed more divine than human.

Mother had impressed on Mary that she was a very special little girl, and very lucky, for Father had decreed that she should have a fine education and grounding in all subjects appropriate to a princess. Her first tutor had been Dr. Linacre, whom she had liked very much, but he had died last year, and then Mother had brought in Master Vives to advise on a replacement. He was a Spaniard with advanced views on female education and an excellent reputation as a scholar. Father's great friend, Sir Thomas More, who sometimes came to dine with Mary's parents, said he was the best teacher in Europe.

Master Vives had written a special treatise for Mary's guidance. It was he who had recommended that the King appoint as tutor Dr. Fetherston, a gentle, devout man who had been Mother's chaplain.

"Between ourselves," Dr. Fetherston had confided to Mary when he arrived for her first lesson, "I think Master Vives's curriculum is a little demanding for such a refined young lady, although I applaud his emphasis on studying the Scriptures and the classics, and we shall make merry with that, my lady Princess. But I am an advocate of the carrot rather than the stick. Master Vives believes that if any pupil does not work hard, they should be whipped. He thinks that girls especially should be handled without cherishing, for—he says—cherishing mars sons, but utterly destroys daughters. You need not worry about that! I find that praise is far more effective than chastisement."

Mary adored Dr. Fetherston, not only on account of his tutoring, but because of his kindness, his warmth, and his love for humanity. Under his tutelage, she worked hard and made remarkable progress. Father and Mother were delighted to see it. She did especially well at Latin, which Master Vives himself taught her; she was determined to give him no excuse to whip her and was grateful when Mother stepped in to help with her translations.

She thrived on the myths and fables from the ancient authors of Greece and Rome, read with horrified fascination the story of Patient Griselda, which Master Vives considered improving for a young lady, and was enthralled by the stirring histories of more recent times; but she was disappointed when Master Vives banned all light reading, arguing that romances put silly notions into girls' heads. Terrified lest he confiscate her book of tales of King Arthur, she hid it under her bed, praying that no one would find it there, and felt guilty for having resorted to such a wicked deception.

One morning in March, Mary was summoned from the schoolroom at Bridewell Palace to attend the Queen and was surprised to find both parents waiting for her in Mother's privy chamber, which overlooked the River Thames and the Blackfriars' monastery.

Father looked jubilant. "There is wondrous news from Italy, Mary. You will remember that the Emperor declared war on France? Well, he has won a resounding victory at Pavia and King Francis has been taken prisoner. When the messenger came today, it was like the Angel Gabriel announcing the birth of Our Lord!"

"God be praised!" Mother murmured.

"Our great enemy is muzzled!" Father declared.

"I am glad to hear it!" Mary cried. "What a valiant prince the Emperor is!" She had an idea. "May I send him a present to congratulate him?"

"That would be a very pretty gesture," Father beamed.

He summoned his jeweler and Mary chose an emerald ring. Father had it dispatched to Charles with a loving message she had written, and in due course Mother came to her chamber to show her a letter of thanks that Charles had sent her. He would wear the ring for her sake, he wrote.

"He is still asking for you to be sent to Spain," Mother told her, and Mary froze, terrified at the imminent prospect of being torn away from her parents and England and everything she loved. "Don't look so worried," the Queen said, squeezing her hand. "Father is adamant that you shall not go until the appointed time." Mary sagged with relief. Reprieved! But for how long? What if Charles persisted? Father might not want to offend him with repeated refusals.

Then, one day, she heard Father telling Mother that Charles had demanded payment of her dowry as an act of good faith.

"The answer is no," he said. "It is not due for another three years. And I am determined that Mary shall not go to Spain until then." Another uprush of relief. Three years! It was an eternity.

But Charles did not give up. From things that were said or overheard as the months went by, Mary gathered that he was still demanding either his bride or her dowry—and Father was still refusing.

She heard other things too. Maids tended to gossip, and often it seemed they thought that children had not the understanding to comprehend what they said. Mary had no idea what Mother being "past the ways of women" meant and did not like to ask. But it seemed to be a matter of some importance and linked to something else she overheard mentioned: the succession. It was a word that seemed to be increasingly on people's lips nowadays.

"Why do people talk about the succession?" she asked Reginald Pole during one of his rare visits to court.

He suddenly looked uncomfortable. "For various reasons," he said. "You might ask your tutor."

She did, but Dr. Fetherston was equally evasive. He told her to ask the Queen. Mary balked at that. Instinctively, she knew that the subject would not be welcome.

Chapter 2

1525

Something was happening in the presence chamber at Bridewell. Mary could see the crowds of courtiers from her window, queuing to get in.

Dr. Fetherston looked up from his marking. "What is it, my lady Princess?"

"I don't know." Mary stood up and leaned out of the open casement. The June air was warm on her face. "I think there is some important ceremony taking place. Could we go and see it? Please?"

Dr. Fetherston hummed and hawed.

"Please, sir! I have finished my book."

"Oh, very well!" The tutor rose. "I will escort your Highness."

The press of people in the presence chamber was very great, but the ranks of courtiers parted to let Mary through, making reverence as she passed. The air smelled of sweat and unwashed linen; not everyone was as fastidious as her father wished them to be. Dr. Fetherston spoke to someone, then turned to Mary. "An investiture is about to take place. The King is creating new nobles."

She stood with him by the great doors as the trumpets sounded and the King and Queen entered from behind the dais. Father was wearing his purple and ermine robes of estate and looked very hot in them on this simmering day. He smiled as he seated himself beneath the canopy of estate.

As Garter King of Arms, the royal herald, stepped forward, a scroll in his hands, a procession entered the chamber, passing closely by Mary. Mary recognized her cousin, Lord Roos, who looked so much like Father, and Sir Thomas Boleyn, an important courtier who was brother to her old governess, Lady Calthorpe. Behind them walked a small boy of about six, a golden-haired child who carried himself with a regal bearing. Mary had never seen him before, but her gaze took in the fact that he was richly appareled like a prince. She heard indrawn breaths around her and sensed Dr. Fetherston stiffening.

The lords stepped forward in turn and knelt before the King as their patents of nobility were read aloud. Then the boy came forward and dropped to his knees. Mary saw her father pat his head and place a long mantle of crimson velvet about his slight shoulders.

The herald announced that Henry Fitzroy was created duke of Richmond and Somerset.

Who was this Henry Fitzroy? Why was Father giving him two royal dukedoms? And why were people murmuring and exchanging glances—and staring at Mary and the King and Queen?

Dr. Fetherston's rotund cheeks had gone a deep shade of pink. "I think it time that we resumed our lessons," he murmured, and led Mary away through the throng. She heard someone mutter that Henry Fitzroy was also to be made a Knight of the Garter, while another said he'd heard that the boy had also been appointed Lord High Admiral. So many honors for one small child! It did not make sense.

"Who is Henry Fitzroy?" she asked once they had emerged into the gallery.

"Alas, your Highness, I am not the person to ask." The tutor looked embarrassed.

"But you know everything," Mary countered.

"Some knowledge is not mine to impart," he replied, and would say no more.

*   *   *

When Mary visited the Queen that afternoon, she was dismayed to find her downcast. She had been going to ask her about Henry Fitzroy, but thought better of it. Once she had told Mother about her day, not mentioning the investiture, the Queen sent her to find Lady Salisbury.

Her governess was waiting for her in the nursery. Making it clear that there was to be no ceremony, she held out her arms and Mary went into them, glad of the comfort.

"Be seated, child." Lady Salisbury's pale, gaunt features were set in a sad smile; her eyes were gentle. "Her Grace asked me to talk to you about what happened today. She feels it is time you knew the truth."

Mary suddenly felt fearful. The truth? About what?

"Henry Fitzroy, whom you saw raised to the peerage today, is your father's son," the governess said.

Mary was puzzled. "But my father has no son. All my brothers died."

"He has no son with your lady mother. But some years ago, one of her maids-of-honor bore him this boy outside wedlock. Because he is a king's son, Henry Fitzroy has been ennobled."

Mary did not understand. She knew nothing about how children were born, only that God sent them to married people, who were supposed to love each other and be true unto death. How could her father have been unfaithful to her mother? He loved her; he often said so. No wonder she was sad. Mary felt indignant on Mother's behalf, because this public ennoblement must have been deeply humiliating for her. And yet she could not, would not, criticize her father. There must be some mistake. Why would he treat her mother like that?

Lady Salisbury was watching her with eyes full of concern. There was so much Mary burned to ask, yet she feared to hear the answers.

"Is Henry Fitzroy my brother?" she asked.

"He is your half-brother, and he is bastard-born. It is you who are the heir, Mary. You will be queen of England one day. A bastard cannot inherit. Bearing that in mind, you will do as her Grace wishes and show kindness to Henry Fitzroy if ever you meet him. He is but a child and in no way to blame for the sin of his parents." She patted Mary's hand. "I would not speak of this to your lady mother. She has had enough to bear for one day. And do not think to judge your father; that is for God alone to do."

Mary returned to the Queen's chamber. She kissed her mother and knelt down by her chair, her hands delving into the sewing basket for the bookmark she was embroidering. They sat together in silence, with so many unspoken words lying between them. Presently, Mother ventured a word of advice about Mary's choice of stitches, and showed her how to fashion a French knot, and once again they fell into their easy mode of conversation.

Then Lady Salisbury arrived to take supper with them. Afterward, the two women sat by the empty hearth, and Mary retreated to the far end of the chamber and curled up in the window seat with one of Mother's books, hoping she would not notice that it was a romance. Fortunately, she was deep in conversation with her friend; it seemed she had forgotten that Mary was there. Mary could not hear everything that was said, but her ears pricked up when Mother's voice hit an unusually passionate note.

"I can do nothing," she said. "I am obliged to submit and have patience."

Lady Salisbury laid a comforting hand on her arm. "Little pitchers . . ." she said.

Mother turned to Mary. "Go to bed, child."

"But it's still light," Mary protested.

"Do as you are bid," Lady Salisbury commanded.

"You can take the book with you," Mother said, smiling.

Mary slid off the seat and knelt for the Queen's blessing, then left the room, closing the door softly behind her. The antechamber was deserted, for once. She bent to listen at the keyhole to see if she could learn more. She knew it was wrong, but she had been unsettled by the revelations of the day.

The women were talking in low voices, but loud enough for her to hear them.

"He is being brought up like a royal child," Mother was saying, "and he keeps the estate of a great prince. He might easily, by the King's means, be exalted to higher things."

"I cannot imagine . . ."

"His Grace is desperate for a son to succeed him. He knows I am past the ways of women. It is in his mind to have Henry Fitzroy declared legitimate by Act of Parliament and name him his heir. Today's ennoblement was but a preamble to that, I am sure. Probably he thinks to test public opinion."

Mary was horrified, and so, it seemed, was Lady Salisbury. "But there is no precedent for the succession devolving upon a bastard," she cried. "The people of England will never accept Henry Fitzroy as king. They will not see the right of the Princess set aside."

"I fear that my husband is prepared to go to any lengths to ensure a male succession." Mother sighed. "I have reminded him many times of how my mother, Queen Isabella, ruled successfully, and how well other women govern—look at the Regent of the Netherlands!— but he heeds me not. He says the English will not tolerate rule by a queen, that it is against Nature. It is an entrenched view, and not even his dread of civil war can overturn it."

Mary was trembling. For as long as she could remember, she had been told that she would be queen one day. Now it seemed that her father had plans to displace her. She burned with the injustice of it. He loved her; how could he do that to her? She knew she could be a queen like Isabella and those others who wielded power beyond the sea. If the Emperor trusted his aunt to rule the Netherlands for him, why couldn't Father trust her, Mary, to rule England?

Ear pressed to the keyhole, she heard Mother say that his throne was based on firmer foundations than his father's had been, yet he still felt insecure on it. "Saving your pardon, good Lady Salisbury, he feels threatened by those of the old royal blood."

"He sees me as a threat?" Lady Salisbury was of the House of York, the niece of the late King Edward, Mary's great-grandfather—and she had four sons, which might explain why Father felt threatened.

"Never. He says you are the saintliest woman in England," Mother assured her.

"But none of my kin have designs on his throne," Lady Salisbury protested. "His Grace has ever been a good lord to them."

"It cannot be denied that some of your kinsmen have plotted

against him," Mother said, "but that is all in the past now; the traitors were dealt with. Still, the King fears what might happen were he to die and leave no son to succeed him. How would a nine-year-old girl fare in such a perilous situation? Who would stand up for Mary? My husband believes that factions would form and there would be another civil war, like the late wars between Lancaster and York. That, he says, is why he needs a son. And as I cannot give him one, I am in no doubt that he is looking to legitimize Henry Fitzroy."

Mary felt sick. Her world was crumbling about her; there were no certainties anymore. She could not bear to hear the rest of the conversation. Tiptoeing to the door, she slipped out of the Queen's apartments and ran down the spiral stair to her own. Reaching the sanctuary of her bedchamber, she shut the door on her maids, threw herself on the bed and wept her heart out.

One hot August day, Father burst into Mother's chamber as Mary was playing the virginals for her. Flushed with rage, he threw a letter on the table.

"Is there no faith in the world?" he shouted. "Sometimes I think I'm the only prince with any honor left!" He glared at Mother. "The Emperor has declared that, as he has received neither his bride nor her dowry, he considers his betrothal null and void—"

"No!" Mother cried, looking horrified. "Henry, you must do something to make things right. Charles's friendship is so important, to us and to England. Think what his rejection will mean to Mary! She has grown up knowing that she will be his Empress. She loves him. There must be something you can do, or Wolsey—Wolsey is clever at diplomacy."

"Kate, if you had let me finish, you would know that there is nothing to be done! Charles has found a richer bride—your own niece, Isabella of Portugal. She has a dowry of a million crowns, far more than I can offer with Mary. What's more, she is of an age to bear children, and very beautiful." He was pacing up and down in his fury.

"I have always dreamed," Mother said brokenly, "of England and Spain being united. It has been my dearest wish that Mary would marry into Spain. This is dreadful. I cannot believe it!"

"And I cannot credit that Charles could be so perfidious!" Father barked. "Wolsey warned me, but I would not heed him, as I know him for a Frenchman at heart." He sat down, seething, then looked at her challengingly. "Wolsey wants me to make a new treaty with France, and I tell you I have a mind to do it!"

Mother looked alarmed. "Henry, please don't make a hasty decision. Wolsey wants you to abandon the Emperor; he has not forgiven or forgotten being overlooked in his bid to become pope."

"What can the Emperor offer me now, Madam?" the King asked, his temper flaring again. "This isn't about Wolsey. It's about maintaining a balance of power in Europe. If Charles wants his freedom, he can have it, but it will come at the price of my signing a new treaty with France, and then he had best look out!"

"Please, Henry, listen to me!"

"Hold your peace, Kate! You are in no position to make demands."

Mother pursed her lips. "Your interests are my interests, Henry," she said, rising to face him. "I would never say or do anything to your detriment. I am heartily sorry that Charles has done this terrible thing. But it was no fault in me, and I pray you not to judge me guilty, even though he is my nephew. Were I to see him now, I would give him a piece of my mind!"

"Would that I could see him now!" Father growled, and turned to leave.

"Am I not to marry the Emperor after all, Father?" Mary asked, bewildered.

"No, child, and you may consider yourself fortunate! I will not give my daughter to a prince whose word cannot be relied on!"

When he had stalked out, Mother put on her most reassuring smile, although Mary knew she was shaken by the news—and thought it had been unkind of Father to act as though this was all Mother's fault.

"Do not think too badly of Charles, Mary," the Queen soothed. "Sometimes there are complicated political circumstances that have to be taken into consideration. He is twenty-five and needs an heir.

My niece Isabella is of an age to bear children, and I suspect that pressure has been put on him. You must not take this personally, child. The marriages of princes are dictated by policy." For all her brave words, there were tears in her eyes, and Mary was painfully aware that Mother's hopes for her had been cruelly shattered. She felt ashamed, because all she could feel was relief that they would not have to be parted after all.

The next day found Mary playing in the Queen's privy garden. To cheer her, Lady Salisbury had helped her to make some paper dolls, using pattern books of clothing that had been sent to Mother from Italy. Now Mary was sitting in the little summer house with them all laid out on the table in front of her, a beaker of cordial to hand, for the August heat was fierce.

She could hear Mother and Lady Salisbury talking as they sat in a shady arbor a few feet away, apparently thinking she was out of earshot. They were commiserating over Mary's broken betrothal.

"I had so longed to see England and Spain united in friendship," the Queen lamented. "Mary could have had no higher destiny than to be Empress."

Mary thought she could have no higher destiny than to be queen of England—unless that horrible Henry Fitzroy usurped her right. How she hated him! She could not even bring herself to utter his name.

"I understand what a great sadness this is to you, Madam," Lady Salisbury sympathized. "And to our dear Princess, of course."

"The worst of it is that the Cardinal, I am sure, has persuaded the King to seek a new alliance with France; King Francis would welcome him with open arms as he needs a strong ally, being stuck in that prison in Madrid. Wolsey was ever the friend of the French, and he has not forgiven or forgotten the Emperor's failure to help him become pope."

"How likely is it that the King will ally with France?"

"It is a certainty." There was a long silence, then a strangled sob.

"Do not distress yourself, Madam," the Countess said gently.

"You think I have not cause? Barren as I am, I have become of no importance in this realm. And as for Mary . . . Lady Salisbury, my husband is even contemplating marrying his bastard to her."

"But she is his half-sister!" Lady Salisbury sounded as shocked as Mary felt. Marry that insufferable, jumped-up brat? She'd die first! "Of course, his Holiness will never grant a dispensation."

"Stranger things have happened," Mother said darkly. "Oh, if only Mary could be wed to your Reginald!"

If only indeed! Mary could not imagine anything better.

"I have told the King several times that it would be a popular match, a second union of Lancaster and York," the Queen went on. "And Mary adores Reginald. He would make the perfect husband for her."

"It was my dearest wish too," his mother said wistfully.

"But he will not listen. I said, if there is one way to avert any threat from your kinsfolk, that is it. But he says he will not have his daughter marry a commoner."

"A commoner with royal blood, who is the great-nephew of kings!"

"No matter. My arguments fall on deaf ears. So now we will just have to hope that there is no new plan to marry Mary to France. I do not think I could bear it. At least she does not have to go to Spain now. I was dreading the parting. But it would be so much worse if she was going to my country's deadly enemy."

"It may not come to that," Lady Salisbury said. "Just be grateful she is here with you now."

"I thank God daily for it," Mother replied.

The following day, Mary received a summons to the Queen's privy chamber. When she stood before her, she could see that her mother had been crying, yet she wore her usual sweet smile.

"Daughter, there is to be a change in your life. You are your father's heiress and must learn how to govern England. You have never been formally created princess of Wales, but his Grace has now decided that you should follow the custom and go to Ludlow Castle on the Welsh border with an honorable council to learn how to be a great queen."

Mary was both pleased and perplexed by the news. Pleased because it showed that Father really did mean her to be his heir; perplexed because the Welsh border seemed a long way away.

"Will you be coming with me?" she asked.

Mother swallowed. "My place is with the King," she said, her voice hoarse. "But you will have Lady Salisbury to look after you, and we will keep in touch by letter. Rest assured, I will be watching over you from afar, just as I do here, and Cardinal Wolsey and I are drawing up a special set of instructions for Lady Salisbury, to ensure that everything is perfect for you." There was a catch in her voice.

"But I don't want to be apart from you." Mary struggled to control herself, to be the serene princess she had been brought up to be.

Mother's smile was bright. "You will like living at Ludlow. I lived there myself when I was married to Prince Arthur. The castle is set in beautiful countryside, and there will be lots of distractions. Now, you must be a brave girl and do as the King your father wishes."

There was nothing more to be said.

Mary lived under a cloud of dread as the day of her departure drew nearer. She felt increasingly sick at the thought of saying farewell to her mother and being dragged away from everything loved and familiar.

Inexorably, the days passed. Now her traveling chests were packed and her retinue stood waiting in the courtyard. It took all her might to resist clinging to Mother as she bent to kiss her farewell. Father was in a hearty mood, lifting her up and nuzzling her nose, yet she sensed that he too was putting on a brave front. She made herself climb into the cushioned litter and held on tightly to Lady Salisbury's hand as the procession moved forward, taking her away into the unknown.

"God bless you, Mary!" she heard her mother cry. "God have you in His keeping!"

She was overawed by the sight of the massive stronghold at Ludlow. With its high towers and stout walls, it looked like a castle out of legend. After days on the road, the long, wearisome journey was finally over, and she was, in truth, glad to have arrived.

Lady Salisbury had been very kind, holding her close as she wept for her mother, distracting her with riddles and word games, and pointing out the sights as they passed. Mary had not realized that her father's realm was so vast or so beautiful, even as she yearned to be back at Richmond or Greenwich or Hampton Court, that fine palace that the Cardinal had built for himself, but given to Father in a grand gesture earlier in the year.

Once they were installed in the luxurious, spacious lodgings in the castle, and the bustle of unpacking was over, Lady Salisbury ordered that a good supper be served and then sent Mary to bed, for she was nearly asleep.

From the next day, Mary had barely a moment in which to miss her old life. She was dressed as a princess should be and taught how to comport herself with dignity. Her lessons with Dr. Fetherston immediately resumed, and she was set numerous exercises in Latin and French. After dinner, Lady Salisbury took her for long walks around the gardens and the castle precincts. Then there were more lessons, although the governess warned Dr. Fetherston that they were not to fatigue her charge. When they were over, Mary practiced on her virginals. Supper, like dinner, was an elaborate affair. The food was beautifully cooked and appetizing, and she was expected to make merry conversation with Lady Salisbury and the household officers who ate with them. Afterward, there was a little time for playing with the young girls who had been specially selected to be her companions. By the time she got to her bedchamber, she was more than ready for bed, and too tired even to weep into her pillow.

Mother's hand was apparent in everything. Mary was served with reverence and respect; her chambers were kept sweet and tidy; and everything was done for her comfort and happiness. Homesick she was, but it was bearable, and she knew that the weeks would pass quickly until Christmas, which she was going to spend at court. She was praying that she could prevail on her parents to let her stay there.

Her courage almost failed her when the Queen's letters arrived, as they did regularly. It distressed Mary to read that their separation troubled her mother, too. But she was full of praise for Mary's progress, on which she had clearly received full reports, and wrote that it was a great comfort to her that her daughter was keeping up her Latin and perfecting her italic hand. Mary's eyes blurred with tears when she read the familiar handwriting.

Yet there was nothing for it but to endure and have patience. She was learning what stoicism was. And time was flying by as she counted down the days until their reunion.

Mary was overjoyed to see the towers and pinnacles of Greenwich appear in the distance. Ahead lay two whole weeks with her parents.

It was wonderful to be swept into the arms of her father and then enfolded in Mother's loving embrace. How she clung to them, forgetting her dignity before the watching courtiers. It did not matter. The King and Queen were clearly delighted to see her, and everyone was beaming at them.

The golden days passed in a whirl of merrymaking, dancing, feasting and caroling. There were games of blindman's bluff and hide-and-seek, and gifts on New Year's Day. And then came the moment Mary had been dreading, the time to say farewell, with only the prospect of a long journey and a bleak January before her.

"Do not weep," Father said. "You will be back at court for Easter. It will not be long."

Chapter 3

1526

The short, cold days found Mary huddled before the fire, completing the work set by Dr. Fetherston. When the snow came, she wrapped herself in furs and ran out to play in it, but skidded on the ice and fell over, hurting her knee, which put paid to that. Cooped up indoors, her only consolations were her music and her books. Thankfully, Dr. Fetherston and Lady Salisbury had agreed that Master Vives's rule about reading could be relaxed, and Mary was allowed to absorb herself openly in the tales of King Arthur.

In the spring, she felt her spirits lift, knowing that she would soon be with the two people she loved most. Mother wrote that she was longing to see her and that the weeks could not pass quickly enough.

But to Mary's horror, a concerned Lady Salisbury brought the news that there was a fearsome outbreak of plague in London and that the King had forbidden her to leave Ludlow. There would be no going to court for Easter. How she wept!

She was desperate to be with her parents, and fearful for them. It was dreadful, being cut off from the life that should be hers. But Mother's letters exhorted her to be patient and apply herself to her studies. *Remember, Daughter, that we never come to the Kingdom of Heaven but by troubles,* she wrote. Dr. Fetherston reminded Mary how important it was that she sit with her council and learn how to govern, especially since she would have the rule of the kingdom one day. She did her best to interest herself in the affairs of Wales and the Marches, even as she struggled to understand the politics. Lady Salisbury devised games and pastimes to distract her and enliven her leisure hours.

Days became weeks, and the weeks turned into months. Nothing was said about her going to court for Christmas, and she began to fear that the plague was still about and that she would have to stay at Ludlow. But then, in November—oh, joy—came the summons, and Mary danced around her chamber, throwing her favorite gowns on the bed, ready for packing. She could barely focus on her lessons, and in the end, Dr. Fetherston gave up and pulled out a chessboard.

She had been away for a year, and in that time her parents had subtly changed. Father was his usual ebullient self, yet she sensed an inner tension in him. Mother had aged. She was forty-one now, but looked older, and there were lines of sadness around her eyes. Yet, as ever, she showed a smiling face to the world, and she could not contain her happiness at seeing Mary.

"How you have grown!" she kept saying. "You are so accomplished for your age. The Ludlow air has done marvels for you." So many people commented on how Mary had blossomed and how beautiful she was. Much of it, she knew, was flattery; courtiers liked to win favor. Nevertheless, it made her peer into her mirror with greater scrutiny. Was she beautiful? Did rosy cheeks, a snub nose, wide-set eyes and a determined chin make for loveliness? She doubted it. She might have grown, but she was still small for her age and a touch too slender. But she was graceful and had that cloud of glorious red hair, which Lady Salisbury declared was as beautiful as any ever seen on human head.

Christmas was gloriously festive. Mary was thrilled when Father led her out to dance with him before the court. Every eye was upon her as she twirled in her silver dress, and Mother was standing by, smiling radiantly at them.

Alas, such golden days could not last. Mary knew that after

Twelfth Night, she must return to Ludlow. She begged to be allowed to stay at court, but Father was adamant.

"Your place is at Ludlow, Daughter. It is fitting that the heir to the throne resides there. We are pleased with the progress you have made and wish it to continue. And you may come back to court for Easter." Schooled to obedience, Mary dared not plead further, but that night she wept into her pillow.

1527

By Easter, Father had inexplicably changed his mind.

"You are to return to court for good," Lady Salisbury informed her. Mary stared at her, hardly daring to comprehend—and yet it was true. She flung her arms around her governess. "Oh, I am so happy!"

"His Grace writes that you are to remain at court and complete your education under your lady mother's supervision."

There was, of course, another joyful reunion with her parents at Greenwich Palace, and Mary was relieved to hear that Master Vives had returned to Spain and that dear Dr. Fetherston would be in sole charge of her education.

Father and Mother were delighted to hear how well she had progressed since Christmas.

"The Princess," Dr. Fetherston told them, as they sat in the schoolroom looking at her exercise books, "is proficient in speaking and writing Latin and French; she knows Spanish and Greek and is well read in theology and history."

"I see she has translated a Latin prayer of St. Thomas Aquinas into English," Father said admiringly, patting Mary's hand.

"Your Highness should show their Graces how well you play the virginals," Dr. Fetherston invited. Mary seated herself and launched into a new piece she had learned; then, at the tutor's bidding, she took her lute and performed on that.

Her parents were gazing at her in admiration. They clapped when she had finished. "You have become an expert, Daughter," Father complimented her.

"Her Highness practices daily. We have to get new strings regularly." Dr. Fetherston smiled. "She sings, too, like an angel."

Mary flushed at his praise; she knew it was not wholly deserved, for her voice was unusually deep for a girl. Still, when prompted, she sang, choosing one of her father's songs, "Pastime with Good Company," which pleased him no end. "You have far exceeded our expectations, Mary," he said. "Dr. Fetherston, we owe you a debt of gratitude. You have done wonders."

"You have proved—if proof were needed—that girls benefit as much from a good education as boys," Mother chimed in. At that, Father's demeanor changed.

"I must leave you, I fear," he said abruptly. "Mary, your lady mother wishes to speak with you."

Once they were alone in Mary's bedchamber, the Queen seated herself by the fireplace. "You must not mind your father," she said. "He is well pleased with you, but he has many cares of state to preoccupy him."

Mary knelt at her feet, still unable to believe that she was back with her beloved mother. Yet she could see that she looked drawn.

"Mary, I wish to talk to you about your marriage," the Queen said.

Her marriage? This was news to her.

"You will have heard that King Francis was released from captivity last year. Understandably, he is seeking your father's friendship, and he has offered himself as a husband for you."

Mary was shocked. She did not need to be told that her mother was not happy at the prospect of a French marriage.

"Please tell me that my father's Grace said no," she blurted out.

Mother laid a gentle hand on her shoulder. "On the contrary, he is eager for the alliance. Or rather, the Cardinal is."

"But I don't want to marry the King of France!" Mary cried, forgetting her duty. "He is far too old, and I hear he is of loose morals."

"Where did you hear that?" Mother asked sharply.

Mary did not like to get her gossiping maids into trouble. "Just servants' talk," she muttered.

"One can only hope that his reputation has been exaggerated. Be assured your father would not give you to a man of bad character. And many men are older than their wives. Royalty must not let personal considerations sway them when making marriage alliances."

The Queen spread her hands as if to show that she had had no choice but to agree to this match.

"But you always said you wanted me to be happy." Mary could not hide her misery. "And I do not want to go to France."

Mother stroked her hair. "I do want you to be happy, more than anything, dear child, and I know Father will do everything in his power to ensure that King Francis treats you well."

"Yet you don't want this alliance, surely? Can't you stop it?"

The Queen's expression was sad. "I wish I could. But I have no influence these days. The Cardinal rules all. My views do not count. To be truthful, he sees me as the enemy. He knows I have no love for the French."

"But Father will listen to you?" Mary was desperate.

"I will tell him how you feel, although I fear it will make no difference. He is convinced that this alliance will profit England. And he has not forgotten the Emperor's perfidy, as he calls it. No, Daughter, I fear you must resign yourself to a future in France."

"But I will be queen of England? How will I rule my realm from France?"

"King Francis will rule it for you, as your husband."

Mary fought back tears. Was that what Father really wanted for England? Would he actually see his kingdom handed over to the French? Could someone not talk him out of it? And what of her right to rule? She'd be better off marrying Henry Fitzroy!

She saw now why she had been summoned back to court. A French embassy was on its way to England to discuss her betrothal; great preparations were being made, and she was to be paraded before the envoys like a prize cow in a market. In a mad moment, she contemplated telling Father that she had no desire to wed King Francis, but every time she saw him, her courage failed her.

"It may not be as bad as you fear," Mother soothed her, as she watched Mary's maids dressing her in a gorgeous gown of cloth of gold in which to be shown off to the foreigners. "They are discussing whether you should wed King Francis or his second son, the Duke of Orléans, who is not much younger than you."

Mary thought about this as she graced the jousts at Greenwich or picked at her food at the lavish banquets held in honor of the visitors. If she married the French prince, she might be able to make her life in England and, in time, reign with him as her consort. And if she liked him, things might not be so bad after all.

She was aware that the King, the Cardinal, and the envoys were engaged in long private talks about the alliance. She was present when the French delegation had an audience with the Queen and watched her mother receive them cordially, as was her duty, but she was sure they went away with the impression that there was only one alliance that would satisfy her—and that it would not be with France.

But Mother had been right. Her views did not count. In May, Mary was dismayed to learn that her father had ratified a treaty that provided for her marriage to King Francis or the Duke of Orléans. She was to go to France in three years, when she was fourteen.

"It will be Orléans," Mother told her soon afterward. "King Francis has to honor his betrothal to the Emperor's sister, your cousin Eleanor; it was one of the terms of his release from captivity." That came as something of a relief, enabling Mary to put on a braver face during the celebrations at court. Mother was graciousness itself as she presided with Father over the feasts and festivities. And the King, of course, insisted on leading Mary in the dancing, having commanded her to wear a Roman-style gown of cloth of gold and crimson taffeta and be laden with enough precious stones to dazzle the sight of the beholders. He was so keen to display her charms to the Frenchmen that, at the banquet that followed, he pulled off the jeweled garland she wore on her head and let fall her tresses, to the evident admiration of all.

"Her Highness is the pearl of the world!" the envoys declared.

But the celebrations were brought to an abrupt end when news came of the sacking of the holy city of Rome on 6 May by mercenary troops of the Emperor, who was campaigning in Italy. Mary was as appalled as everyone else to hear of the atrocities that had been committed. Although she was aware of Mother ensuring that the grimmer details were kept from her, she could judge just how terrible the sacking had been from the shocked reactions of others. Father was clearly horrified, especially when he heard that the Pope was now a prisoner of the Emperor. He took it almost as a personal affront. Mary had rarely seen him so beside himself. When she looked back later, she realized this had been the beginning of his madness.

For that was the summer her father changed. Not only was he unusually preoccupied, but he was also fiercer in his demeanor. His visits to Mother became rarer and rarer, and the Queen grew tense and often looked near to tears. Something was wrong, but Mary had no idea what it could be. Everyone said she was imagining it, but she could not be convinced. She sensed that her household knew things she didn't. When she entered a room, conversations ceased. And then she began to be aware of the name Anne Boleyn being whispered.

Anne was one of Mother's maids-of-honor, a slim, dark-haired young woman who seemed to attract the attention of a lot of court gallants. It seemed she had been involved in some sort of scandal. Mary longed to know what it was.

"Why are people talking about Anne Boleyn?" she asked Lady Salisbury.

"What do they say?" The governess's tone was a little sharp.

"Nothing to speak of. I just keep hearing her name mentioned."

"Well," Lady Salisbury said, suddenly smiling, "I daresay it is because she gets herself noticed. It's those French fashions she wears, and the manners and accomplishments she learned at the French court. She attracts attention to herself."

That explained it. Mary hurried off to her lessons and gave Anne Boleyn no further thought.

1528

One May morning, Mother appeared in Mary's chamber. She had seemed tense and anxious of late, as had Father, and Mary had been worried, for neither seemed very happy. She had overheard people speaking of something called "the King's Great Matter," but always they had fallen silent when they saw her, so she had no idea what it could be.

Mother sat down. "Your father is very worried," she said. "Cases of the sweating sickness have been reported in London. It's this hot weather that's causing it."

Mary now saw why her parents had been preoccupied. She could remember the previous outbreak of the sweat, two years before. It was a terrifying disease that struck at rich and poor alike with frightening speed. You could be merry at dinner and dead by supper. She shivered, despite the heat.

"What are we to do?"

"The King is considering the best course. For the moment, we are safe here at Greenwich. But you must keep the windows closed and not go outdoors. I know it's hot, but we must protect ourselves."

Mary tried not to worry, but the news struck fear into her. The epidemic was spreading at an alarming rate. Thousands were perishing in London, and Father could not hide his terror; he had a horror of illness and death. When he learned that one or two had sickened in the court, he gave the order to move to Waltham.

"Lady Salisbury, make ready with all speed. Do hurry!" Mother urged, eager to be gone and get Mary away from danger.

When they arrived in the crowded courtyard, Mary was astonished to see Anne Boleyn standing with Father in the midst of a small throng of courtiers and household officers. While everyone else seemed impatient and on edge, Anne was laughing. It seemed odd that she should be there with the King.

Mary glanced at Mother, but the Queen was smiling as she made her way to where her litter stood waiting. Only when she reached it did she pause, looking in Father's direction. Anne Boleyn was still there, still smiling.

Mother turned to Mary. "Get in, child. We must be on our way."

At Waltham, they did not stay in the great abbey, but at a nearby house called Dallance. When they arrived in the Queen's lodgings, Mother sent Mary off to have her lesson with Dr. Fetherston in the hall; whatever happened, her normal routine was to be preserved.

On her way downstairs, Mary passed a window and noticed her father and Anne Boleyn below in the garden, engaged in a lively conversation. Her eyes widened when she saw Anne tap him on the chest, her laughter ringing out.

Suspicion flowered. Had Father fallen in love with Anne? Was she the reason why Mother was so sad these days? Surely not! Father loved Mother; they were devoted to each other. No, Mary reasoned: he could not possibly see anything in Anne, with her sallow skin and narrow face. They were probably just sharing a jest.

As the sweat raged, the King reduced his household again and again, and kept moving to one safe house after another. Mary was sent to Hunsdon in Hertfordshire, one of his smaller residences, with her governess and her tutor.

"The air is wholesome there," Mother explained. "I hate to see you go, Daughter, but it is best that you stay deep in the country where the atmosphere is unpolluted."

Reluctantly—and fearfully, for no one, even kings and queens, was safe from the pestilence—Mary said her farewells and set off for her new abode. She found much of it under scaffolding, for Father was having it refaced with fashionable brick, and had ordered a moat to be dug, but the workmen had been laid off when the sweat came, and all labor had ceased. Propped against the walls inside were new stained-glass windows depicting coats of arms, ready to be installed. When they were finished, the royal apartments off the great gallery would be sumptuous. For now, the house had been aired and sweetened, and Mary's rooms were comfortably furnished. There were worse places to wait out the epidemic.

Mother wrote regularly. Her longing to be with her daughter came across loud and clear. Her letters were full of advice on how to keep safe. Homesickness was a continual ache in Mary. She yearned to be with her parents again. Her constant prayer was that they would all emerge unscathed from this dreadful visitation that God had seen fit to send to England. She wondered why He was so displeased. What could have merited it?

One afternoon, when lessons were over, Dr. Fetherston suggested that she might like to take her embroidery into the garden, for it was a warm day. She wandered along the gravel paths, enjoying the heady scent of the flowers in the railed beds, and found a shaded seat by one of the few walls that were not encased by scaffolding. Humming to herself, she took up her tambour and began stitching.

Presently she could hear the voices of Lady Salisbury and Dr. Fetherston through an open window just above her.

"Why did God spare her and take so many other blameless souls?" Lady Salisbury was saying.

"The ways of the Almighty are sometimes unfathomable," the tutor sighed.

"If the sweat is a punishment on the King for pursuing his Great Matter, then God could easily have taken the woman to Himself and resolved the situation!"

Mary could not credit what she was hearing. Why would God want to punish Father? And what was his Great Matter? More to the point, who was the woman who clearly had something to do with it? The memory of Anne Boleyn's laughing face came instantly to mind.

Lady Salisbury sounded near to tears. "Cannot God see what this is doing to the Queen, who has been the most loving and faithful of wives? All this nonsense about Leviticus! Every learned doctor she has consulted has told her that it does not apply in her case. The issue is not whether her marriage to Prince Arthur was consummated, but whether she bore him a child, which she didn't. So there was no impediment to her marriage to the King. He has been led up the garden path by Wolsey and Anne Boleyn!"

Mary was shocked to have her suspicions confirmed.

"I think his Grace's doubts of conscience are genuine," Dr. Fetherston argued. "Scripture warns that a man who marries his brother's wife shall be childless. With only one daughter, that is how he sees himself. And let's face it, Anne Boleyn or no Anne Boleyn, he needs a son, and the Queen cannot give him one. I think he truly believes he has offended God by an incestuous marriage and that God, in His wrath, has denied him sons."

"But he has misunderstood the laws of Scripture—deliberately, I fear."

"The Queen may be distressed—"

"May be? She is in grief!"

"Yes, but the Pope is in fear of the Emperor, and the Queen is the

Emperor's aunt, so he is unlikely to grant the King the annulment he desires."

"And in the meantime, my beloved mistress has to endure this hell of waiting. She does not deserve this. The people love her. If they knew what was going on, they would not tolerate it. No one should tolerate it! Why can his Holiness not just pronounce in her favor?"

"Because he needs the King's friendship."

"It's an impossible situation. I have no idea how much longer I can keep the truth from poor Mary."

Mary did not catch Dr. Fetherston's reply. The voices faded, a door banged, and all was silent again.

Dropping her tambour, she stood up on shaky legs and walked almost blindly along the path, trying to make sense of what she had just heard. She could hardly believe that her father was trying to divorce her mother. No wonder Mother had looked sad lately. It was wicked, wicked! Trying to stem her tears, she kicked at a stone, needing to take her anguish out on something.

Where was Anne Boleyn in all this? Had she had the sweat and recovered? Would that she had died! It sounded as if she was scheming with the Cardinal to oust Mother. Mary could hardly believe it. Wolsey was her godfather; he would surely never do anything to hurt her? It was this Anne who had come along and wrecked everything! She must have cast an enchantment on the King—and on the Cardinal! Mary's passionate heart burned with hatred. What did Father see in her? She was evil. No decent woman would plot to steal another woman's husband!

Weeping now, she sank down on the grass, her shoulders heaving. It was as if she had lost the father she loved. Who was this strange man who was trying to split their family asunder? If he wanted to be rid of Mother, what of her, his daughter? Did he not care if she suffered as a result? He, who was supposed to love and protect her? Her duty was to love, honor, and obey him, not only as her father, but also as her sovereign. Yet how could she do that when he had shown he had feet of clay and was planning to do the greatest injury ever to her mother and herself?

How long she knelt there sobbing, she did not know. When the storm passed, she rose and returned to the bench, taking up her needle and stabbing the tambour with it, imagining that she was plunging a dagger into Anne Boleyn's treacherous heart.

Misery soon gave way to a burning anger. She was the Princess of England, its future queen, and she would never permit anyone to disparage her. Her pride would not allow it.

It would soon be suppertime. She could not go indoors just yet. Everyone would see that she had been crying and they would want to know why. And she knew she could never bring herself to explain. She would not diminish herself or her parents in any way. If she said nothing, the horrible Great Matter might go away.

With the coming of autumn, the sweat abated, but Mary stayed at Hunsdon. It was safer, Mother assured her. The Queen's letters from Greenwich and Bridewell were cheerful and full of news, as if she knew that Mary felt cut off from the world. But maybe, Mary wondered, that was the whole point of her being there, to keep her unaware of events that would distress her. Yet she was desperate to know what was happening. She had heard nothing more about the Great Matter or Anne Boleyn, and was beginning to dare to hope that the storm had blown over.

Her hopes were heightened when she was summoned to court for Christmas. Father was his old genial self, in high good spirits, as proud and loving a father as ever. When Mary was with her parents, there was no sign that anything was amiss, and she began to hope that all was well again.

But on the very first evening of her visit, as she made her way to the watching chamber for a feast, she suddenly encountered Anne Boleyn, sweeping around the room as if she owned it and attracting the attention of all. Father's eyes were riveted on her, like those of a man possessed. Mary boiled inside as she watched the courtiers fawning on Anne, felt murderous at seeing her ignoring Mother, who was sitting patiently at Father's side, enduring all for his sake. Worst of all was when Anne turned and looked dismissively upon Mary as if she was of no consequence and merited only the sketchiest of curtseys. Not to be borne!

When they played hoodman blind, fox and hounds, and ninepins,

Mary could only seethe at the woman's presence. She stayed close to her mother and found it hard to be nice to her father, even though he was doing his best to make merry with her.

Then came Holy Innocents' Day, when Mother took Mary aside and sat her down.

"I think you may have heard something about what people are calling the King's Great Matter," she said gently.

Mary swallowed. "Yes, my lady." She could not lie.

"You must not worry about it," Mother enjoined. "Your father has certain doubts about the dispensation given to us by Pope Julius, but Pope Clement is looking into the matter, and has sent a cardinal—Cardinal Campeggio—here to try the case in a special court with Cardinal Wolsey. I have no doubt that everything will soon be sorted out, and that your father's conscience will be set at rest."

Mary could not stay silent a moment longer. "But my father wants to marry Mistress Anne Boleyn." It was not a question.

Mother stared at her, dismay in her eyes. "If the Pope finds our marriage invalid, then the King must marry again, and he has told me that he wishes to ensure that Mistress Anne has it in her to be a good queen."

"But she is not royal—and she is not very nice."

"Not very nice?"

"She scants her respect to me! And to you! I hate her!"

Mother was again taken aback, and Mary realized that she had never spoken so venomously in front of her. But she did not regret it. It was only the truth!

The Queen took her hand and squeezed it. Her face was full of grief and compassion. "We must be charitable toward her, for the King's sake."

Mary's anger flared. "My lady Mother, I cannot, even to please you. She is a wicked woman, trying to steal my father away from you."

"Mary!" Katherine grasped her shoulders. "Never let the King, or anyone else, hear you say things like that. You owe him respect. Soon, I pray, all will be well, and Mistress Anne will be forgotten."

Mary hugged her, wanting to believe it. "I understand. May I go and play with my new puppy now?"

Chapter 4

1529

Mary stayed at court until the spring. Sometimes she longed to be gone, because the place was alive with gossip, and she did not want to hear it. It was terrible knowing that her parents' troubles were being chewed over and speculated on, and she was horrified at the scurrilous talk about her father and Anne Boleyn—not that she understood a lot of it. There was no escaping Anne, who was queening it over the court, evidently confident that she would soon be married to the King, so Mary kept as far as possible to her apartments or her mother's, and strove to be a comfort to her. Not that Mother ever complained. She had the patience of a saint! And she was firm in her resolve.

"I am your father's true wife. and I will never say or do anything to jeopardize your title of princess or your right to the succession," she declared to Mary, again and again.

It was only after the King had said something that particularly upset her that Mother finally confided in her. As they sat by the fire one evening, she dabbed at her eyes with her kerchief, unable to conceal her misery. "You are thirteen now, Daughter, and old enough to be told what is happening. You should know that I have been threatened. Your father says I do not care for him, when nothing could be further from the truth. He complains that I am too merry, too richly dressed, and that I should be praying for a good end to this Great Matter rather than presiding over entertainments at court. Heaven knows, I do pray! I spend hours on my knees in chapel."

"I know you do." Mary knelt and took her mother's hand.

It was as if a dam had burst and released a flood of emotions in Mother. "He is so suspicious of me! He says that by riding out and acknowledging the cheers of the people, I am inciting his subjects to rebellion. He thinks I am involved in some mad plot to kill him and the Cardinal. He even had the Council write to warn me that if it could be proved I had any hand in it, I must not expect to be spared, since they felt in their consciences that his life was in danger. They said I was a fool to resist the King's will, and that they had urged him to separate from me entirely—and to take you from me."

Mary was appalled, chilled to the marrow. Her mother was trembling. How dare they treat her like this! She was a good woman and had never wished anyone harm, even Anne Boleyn. Unlike herself! It was awful for them to be at loggerheads with the King—not that she herself had ever dared to confront him. She knew he would never dream of her opposing his will and defending the cause of her beloved mother, who had been shockingly treated by anyone's standards. Yet she would stand up to him if it came to it. She would show him that she possessed all the courage and spirit of her grandmother, Queen Isabella!

Mother put an arm around her. "My dear child, if they do take you away from me, I want you to know that it is not of my doing. If I have put on a brave face and dressed well and ridden out, it is because that is what a queen should do. One must never parade one's griefs in public. As for this mysterious plot—well, it is pure fantasy! Your father knows in his heart that I would never wish any ill to befall him. I love him."

"They will not part us, will they?" Mary could not bear the prospect of another long separation, especially one with no end in sight, and shuddered to think of what it might mean for her mother. "Surely Father will not allow the Council to proceed against you? They have no grounds."

"It is but a bluster, I am sure. A warning not to defy the King.

They think to bully me into submission, make me agree to enter a nunnery so that he can be free to remarry. Well, I have said, time and again, that I have no vocation. If only the Pope would rule on the matter and put an end to this uncertainty."

"Hopefully, Cardinal Campeggio will rule on his behalf when the court sits."

"Alas, Mary." The Queen shook her head. "I fear there will be more delaying tactics, and I cannot expect impartial justice when the court is sitting in my husband's realm and Cardinal Wolsey is the other judge. He would see me gone with a click of his fingers. No, I want the matter decided in Rome."

"And you think his Holiness will find for you?"

"I have no doubt of it!"

Mary had wanted to stay at court and support her mother, but with the court case looming, both her parents thought it best that she be sent to Hunsdon. It was hard to say farewell to the Queen, knowing that she was leaving her to an uncertain fate.

When she went to say goodbye to the King, she found him with the Cardinal.

"Mary!" Father exclaimed, as ebullient as ever. "Let us hope it will not be long before you are back with us."

Yes, she thought bitterly, but in what circumstances? Would the cardinals have ordered him to return to her mother? Or would she be returning to a court bereft of its Queen?

Lowering her head so that Father would not see how angry she was with him for the misery he was putting them through, she knelt for his blessing. When Wolsey bade her a fond farewell, she noticed that his florid, fleshy face was wan and haggard. So he was dreading the hearing, too. Probably he feared Father's displeasure if the verdict went against him. There would be no winners in this case.

At Hunsdon, feeling very cut off from the world, Mary waited anxiously for news. Lady Salisbury was as kind and protective as ever, but she was missing her son Arthur, who had died last year of the sweating sickness, and Reginald, who had gone to Italy to pursue his studies at the King's expense, for he was planning to enter the Church. Mary thought it sad that her father had frowned upon a marriage between them, for she was certain that she could have loved Reginald as a husband. But once he had taken holy orders, he would be lost to her forever.

His mother was proud of her son's vocation, but fearful for him, too, for, from the safety of Italy, Reginald had openly called Anne Boleyn a Jezebel and a sorceress, leaving no one in any doubt as to his opinion of her.

Lady Salisbury was suffering agonies of anxiety. "I am sure he is right and that she is responsible for the whole lying affair," she said, as she and Mary discussed the matter one night at supper, there being no secrets between them now. "But I wish he was not so outspoken in his views. I fear he may have to remain abroad now, for he has rendered his position in England insupportable and shown himself ungrateful. After all, the King has paid handsomely for his education. It is wrong to bite the hand that feeds you."

"And yet Reginald *is* right!" Mary declared, leaving half her food untouched.

"Alas, dear child, it is not enough to be right when might can prevail. I fear that many people are facing a crisis of conscience over this Great Matter. All we can pray for is that the cardinals will resolve it."

Mother's letters were less frequent than Mary would have liked, and to begin with they told her very little. She seemed reluctant to commit much to paper, probably for fear that her writings would be used to compromise her. Mary remembered her saying she was convinced that Wolsey had placed spies in her household.

One day, Lady Salisbury came into the schoolroom, where Mary and Dr. Fetherston were working on a French translation.

"I have received a letter from Lady Exeter," she said. Mary looked up keenly. The half-Spanish and forthright Lady Exeter was a good friend to Mother and indignant at the way she was being treated.

Lady Salisbury sat down. "She has sent me an account of what has taken place at the Blackfriars." That was where the court was sitting. "The King and Queen were summoned into the court—can you imagine it? Such a thing has never been heard of in England! But your lady mother did not sit upon her throne. Oh, no! She made her way around the court and knelt before the King and made the speech of her life! She begged him to spare her the court proceedings, for she said she would get no impartial justice in England. She swore that she came to him a true maid, and that she had always been a true wife to him. When he did not answer, she committed her cause to God, then departed, ignoring calls for her to come back. The crowds outside cheered her heartily."

"They cannot rule in my father's favor after that!" Mary cried.

"They may declare her willfully disobedient to the court's authority, and proceed without her," Dr. Fetherston warned. "The case must still be heard."

Mary's heart sank.

If it had not been for Lady Exeter, who cared not a fig for the Cardinal's spies, they would not have had any news. Dr. Fetherston had been right: Mother had been declared willfully disobedient. The cardinals were hearing the case in her absence, which didn't seem fair to Mary. And the weeks were dragging by. Apparently, they were calling witnesses. On her knees in chapel, praying for a happy outcome, she wondered who these witnesses were and what they might have to say, and why it was taking such an age for a ruling to be given. Hadn't they all waited long enough? It was two years since her father had asked Rome for an annulment. Did not his Holiness understand how grievously the Great Matter was overshadowing their lives? With a stroke of his pen, he could have put a stop to it long since. But, as Dr. Fetherston repeatedly reminded her, the case was not as simple as that.

Mary began to sense that Lady Salisbury was withholding some details from her. When she walked into a room and saw the governess slip a letter into her pocket, she challenged her. "What are you keeping from me? I must know!"

Lady Salisbury's fair cheeks flushed. "Alas, child, some of the testimony given in court about your mother's first marriage is too indelicate for your tender ears. It is not fitting for you to hear it. More to the point, it is superfluous to the matter being debated." Her thin lips pursed disapprovingly.

Mary sank down on a settle, wondering what her governess was talking about. She knew very little about what passed between married people, only that there was something mysterious about it, which, she supposed, she would find out when she married herself. Although when that might be, given her uncertain future, she could not know. She wasn't even sure if she was still betrothed to the Duke of Orléans.

"Lady Salisbury," she asked, "if my parents' marriage is annulled, will I be deemed baseborn?" Baseborn, she knew, was when you were born outside lawful wedlock, and it was a shameful thing to be, for it meant that your parents had sinned and you had no rights of inheritance.

The governess sat beside her. "That's very unlikely," she said briskly. "If your father and mother married in good faith, not being aware of any impediment to their union, then you would be deemed legitimate. And they did marry in good faith, never doubt it. Pope Julius had granted them a dispensation."

Mary was instantly relieved, but something struck her forcefully. "So my father is saying that Pope Julius was wrong to grant it. But I thought the Pope was never wrong, for he is the mouthpiece of our Lord Jesus Christ."

Lady Salisbury hesitated. "The King has indeed called the authority of the Pope into question. I think that is one reason why Pope Clement is unwilling to reverse the decision of Pope Julius. A lot of people are concerned about the effect of this Great Matter on the Church, especially now that the wicked heresies of Martin Luther are gaining ground."

Mary had heard a lot about Luther, none of it good. Dr. Fetherston had told her of the former German monk who believed that the Pope had too much power, that the Church was corrupt and venal, and that salvation was gained through faith alone and not good works. Worse still, he denied most of the seven sacraments. But his heresies had attracted many followers, even in England. They were called Protestants, and they were wicked heretics, infecting the faithful with their unorthodox, wrong-headed views.

Lady Salisbury lowered her voice. "I have heard it said that Anne Boleyn and her family are Lutherans."

Mary's loathing for Anne intensified. "That would not surprise me! We can only pray that she does not corrupt my father with her heresies! She should burn for them, but of course she will get away with it. She does as she pleases, and my father lets her!"

The governess was regarding her with compassion. "We must pray that she will see the error of her ways. Do not let her distress you, child. Soon, mark my words, the King will have to send her away."

"I long for that day!" Mary breathed.

When Lady Salisbury appeared at supper one warm, muggy day in July, Mary knew that she had bad news. It was apparent from her demeanor, her defeated look. She braced herself for the worst.

"They have ruled for my father?" Her heart was thudding alarmingly.

"No, dear child. In view of your lady mother's appeal, the case has been revoked to Rome for a decision."

"That means more delays!" She could not face another agony of waiting. "Why can they not give a decision now?"

"Because, Mary, this is not just a matter of Scripture, or the authority of the Pope. You must not forget that his Holiness fears to offend either the Emperor or the King."

"But surely, in delaying, he offends both?"

"I think he fears the Emperor more. I know, I know. It is not fitting that the Pope, who is Christ's vicar on earth, should have regard to political considerations. But he is a prince like any other, and I fear he is a timid man."

"It seems to me he is compromising the Church at a time when it most needs defending," Mary observed bitterly. "My father is supposed to be its defender—he wrote that book condemning Luther's heresies. But now he seems bent on undermining all it stands for."

Lady Salisbury shook her head sadly. "Your mother writes that the King is angry. His wrath has fallen on Cardinal Wolsey."

"Good! The Cardinal has made himself my mother's enemy, and mine—he, who is supposed to be my godfather!"

"There may come a time when we must pity him. Whatever his faults, he has always served the King faithfully, never sparing himself. I have long suspected that his heart was not in this Great Matter, especially after he realized that your father meant to marry Anne Boleyn. She loathes him, and I'll wager she will now seize this opportunity to bring him down."

Mary thought about this. "So you think he worked for an annulment because he felt he had no other choice?"

"I do, whatever the Queen your mother believes. I think that secretly he was on her side."

Lady Salisbury had been right. Lady Exeter wrote that, once his anger cooled, the King had made it plain that he was willing to forgive Wolsey, but Anne Boleyn had intervened and made certain that there would be no reconciliation. The Cardinal had been banished from court and was now on his way to York, where, as archbishop, he was to attend to the needs of his flock.

"That will be a change for him," Dr. Fetherston said tartly, as he packed up books ready for Mary's long-awaited move back to court. "It's about time he remembered his spiritual duties."

Mary thought the Cardinal had got off lightly, given Anne Boleyn's enmity. She hoped he would be left in peace now.

She was longing to be back with her mother, but half dreading returning because she could not stomach seeing Anne Boleyn flaunting herself. But in the emotional moment when she fell into the Queen's embrace at Greenwich, she knew that this was where she should be.

Father was affectionate enough, which made her glad she had never confronted or criticized him in any way. She wanted everything in her world to be perfect, as it once had been, when her parents were being loving toward each other. Clearly they were making an effort to put on a show of unity, if only for her sake, and no one seemed to want to talk about the Great Matter. She could almost believe things were returning to normal.

And then she saw Anne Boleyn, decked out like a queen and surrounded by fawning courtiers. Bristling, Mary acted as if Anne was beneath her notice, studiedly ignoring her, and Anne never acknowledged her presence. Mary tried not to look when she saw her father hanging on Anne's every word or looking at her with lustful longing. She felt sick. As far as she was concerned, the Witch, as she now thought of her, did not exist.

The Emperor had sent a new ambassador to England.

"His name is Messire Chapuys, and he says he has been instructed to look to our interests," Mother told Mary. "He is a lawyer from Savoy and a great scholar. I feel he will be a true friend to us."

When Chapuys next came to pay his respects, the Queen insisted on Mary being present. The ambassador kissed her hand with the greatest reverence. "It is an honor to meet you, my lady Princess," he told her. He had a sensitive face and his eyes were kind. Of course, he was quite old, about forty, she reckoned, but he had a certain charm and great courtesy. "Your Highness's steadfastness, piety, virtue, and learning are renowned throughout Christendom, and I hear that you are universally adored by your father's subjects."

Mary blushed. "I thank you, my lord ambassador."

Chapuys was regarding her with feeling. "I know these are troubling times for your Highness and the Queen your mother, but you may rest assured that I will spare no effort to help you both in any way I can."

"I am most grateful, Messire," Mary said warmly. "Anyone who supports my lady mother is a friend to me. I will accept no one for queen except her."

"Brave words, my lady Princess," the ambassador said.

"You should know that Messire Chapuys is being watched," Mother said. "He cannot visit me as freely as he would like. Alas, the King fears that I will persuade him to incite the Emperor to war—which is the last thing I would ever do!"

Mary was stunned. That it had come to this! Someone was dripping poison into Father's ear—and she had no doubt who it was.

"But I will endeavor to get messages to your Majesty," Chapuys assured the Queen.

When he had gone, Mary was aware of feeling strangely com-

forted. Here, she knew, was someone who could be relied on to be
steadfast and true, someone who would fight for their rights. The
Emperor had chosen well. They had found a champion at last.

It was Christmas Eve. Mary stood with her parents, watching the
Yule log being hauled into the great hall and placed on the hearth,
where it would burn throughout the festive season. Around them,
there was much mirth and good cheer, but her father seemed to take
no pleasure in it. He was in a prickly mood, doubtless because Anne
Boleyn had gone home for Yuletide, and still there had been no word
from Rome.

Mary saw Chapuys among the courtiers. He smiled at her and
gave a little bow. The few times she had encountered him, she had
felt again a sense of being safe and protected, and now, always, she
looked for him in the court.

Suddenly, he was at her side with a plate of sugar suckets. "Allow
me to be your server!" he invited, offering them to her. "It's Christmas, and your Highness should enjoy it!"

Yes, it was the season when the normal order of things was completely overturned, when servants became masters, rules were dis-
obeyed, and even Father had to bow to the edicts of the Lord of
Misrule. Maybe she would be allowed to dance with Messire Chapuys.
She would like nothing better. She took a sucket and smiled at him.

Wishes did not always come true. When the dancing began on
Christmas Day, she watched as some ladies boldly invited the gentlemen of their choice to partner them. Mary yearned to invite Chapuys,
but was too nervous of seeming forward or incurring her father's
displeasure. So she remained seated by the Queen, her feet itching to
be dancing.

Chapter 5

1530

It was spring again, and Mary was in Essex, at Beaulieu, one of her father's most luxurious properties, preparing to return to court. Beaulieu was beautiful, with oriel windows, ornate royal lodgings, and eight courtyards. She loved the place, but she had hated being apart from her mother. Yet the King had ordered her to go there, and even before she left court, people had been saying he had sent her away to punish the Queen for thwarting his will. Evidently, he had heard the gossip and feared a backlash of public opinion, for within a short time he had summoned Mary to Windsor to be with the Queen, then left them there together to go hunting with Anne Boleyn, making no secret of it. Mother had been overjoyed to see Mary. "My dear child!" she cried. "Let me look at you! You are growing up so fast. Every time I see you, there has been a change." It was true. Mary was fourteen now, still small and slight, but filling out with the first curves of womanhood. She still retained her childish prettiness, but she was finding it hard to be sweet and charming when she felt so nervous all the time, and fearful of what might happen next.

They spent that first day together in the Queen's chamber in her lodging in the Upper Ward, catching up on their news. Mother asked Mary about her lessons, her daily life at Beaulieu, and whether she had been diligent at her devotions. She was evidently pleased with Mary's answers, but Mary wanted to talk about more important things.

"My lady Mother," she said, as they sat sewing with the Queen's ladies, "I have been worried about you."

"There is no need to worry about me," Mother said briskly. "I am very well."

"But my father's Grace is still trying to put you away," Mary blurted out.

"We are both waiting for the Pope to pronounce sentence on our marriage," the Queen replied gently. "I am sure he will do so soon. There is nothing to worry about. Your father and I are perfect friends, as ever."

"But he is always with the Lady Anne." Mary was on the verge of tears. "I cannot believe that he has brought that witch here with him."

"Do not let it upset you," Mother soothed. "One day soon, his Holiness will speak, and then his Grace will return to me and the Lady Anne will be sent away."

Seeing Mary looking doubtful, the Queen made a visible effort. "He will only marry her if he is forbidden to return to me, which is what he wants, of course; yet he does not realize what is best for the health of his soul, and for this kingdom. And as it is unlikely that our marriage will be annulled, do not fret about it. Now, let me hear how you play on the virginals!"

Mary bit her tongue. Mother was a fool if she really believed that. But she was a dutiful daughter, so she said nothing.

As she was playing her lute, the King arrived. She rose and curtseyed dutifully, then knelt for his blessing. He swept her into his arms.

"How does my dear child?" he asked, kissing her.

"I am well, Sir. I trust that your Grace is too."

"That was an excellent performance," he complimented her. "I could hear it as I approached." He sat down next to the Queen. "How are you progressing in your studies, Mary?"

It was a pleasant interlude—almost like old times. He stayed for an hour and was even merry with them. And when Mary moved to Hunsdon in July, he visited her, and they dined together in her privy chamber.

As soon as the fruit and comfits had been served, he waved the servants away. "I fear I have seen too little of you of late, Daughter," he said. "It is a matter of great regret to me. I would not want anything to come between us."

"I have always loved and honored you as my father, Sir, and I always will," Mary said carefully.

"Yet I fear there are those who have infected you with their obstinate opinions," he replied, and she could hear the steel in his voice, see his expression harden. "I know you are aware of the Great Matter that overshadows us all, and you should also know that I have been assured by many learned doctors that my marriage to your lady mother is of doubtful validity. They have urged me all along to have the case tried. I don't know what others have been telling you, but you must understand that I do not pursue this cause lightly, and that it is a righteous one. I cannot have it said that your mother and I have lived in sin these twenty years and more."

Mary could not think what to say. She sat there, unable to finish the cherries on her plate, and wished she were anywhere else.

"You are strangely quiet, Daughter. Do you not have an opinion?"

"Alas, Sir," she stammered, "I am no doctor. I do not know what to think, and the matter touches me too nearly for me to see things clearly." She summoned up her courage. "But I have heard contrary opinions about the Great Matter . . . Father, why are you doing this to us?"

His temper flared. "I see you have your mother's obstinacy. What she refuses to see is that God is punishing us for our sinful union. All your brothers died soon after birth. Eight children she's borne me, and only you have been spared to us. Can you not see the hand of God in that, Mary, sense His displeasure? I cannot continue any longer in this state of sin! You must understand that."

She was sobbing now, unable to control her feelings. "And where does the Lady Anne Boleyn come into this? How could you forsake a great princess like my mother for her? She is not worthy of a crown!"

"Enough!" Father snapped, his face red with fury. "You will not speak of her so disrespectfully."

"She shows no respect for me!" Mary cried. "I am your heir! I fear she would have you divorce me too and deprive me of my birthright."

The King's voice was icy. "I see that your mother has failed to bring you up to a proper awareness of your duty to me. And no doubt Lady Salisbury must take part of the blame. That family make no secret of their views on my Great Matter—and after all I have done for them. Watch your tongue, Daughter, and mend your opinions, or I shall see that these pernicious influences are removed from your life."

He rose, almost upsetting the chair in his angry haste, and stumped out, leaving Mary in anguish. She could not believe he would go so far as to separate her from Mother and dear Lady Salisbury. It was just bluster, surely? But what would she do if she were cut off from them completely? She could not bear to think of it. She wished, how she wished, that she had held her tongue.

She confided in Lady Salisbury, who looked faintly alarmed, but agreed that it had probably been Father's anger and frustration talking. She wrote to her mother, who counseled her to have patience and show herself a dutiful, obedient daughter at all times, adding a gentle reproof for having spoken to her father and sovereign so boldly. And then she counted the days and weeks, praying for a summons to court.

During this time, her monthly courses started. Lady Salisbury explained, without fuss, that they signaled the beginning of her childbearing years and that she was now of an age to be married. But who would want her? Mary wondered. Did King Francis still mean to marry her to his son, with her legitimacy in doubt? Because despite what her governess had said, the matter had yet to be determined.

Many a night found her weeping into her pillow, longing to be back in the safe haven of her childhood, when she had been adored and cherished by her parents, and they had loved each other, and there had been no Great Matter blighting their lives. How she yearned to know again that security, and to live once more in a world where the faith she held so dear, the faith her mother had instilled in her, had been held by all. She did not belong in this new world, with its uncertainties and its encroaching heresies.

Early in December, her low mood plummeted when she heard of the death of Cardinal Wolsey. Lady Salisbury broke it to her. "Lady Exeter says his enemies united to bring him down. You can guess who is most likely to have been behind it."

Mary could. Anne had no doubt been biding her time, waiting for an opportunity to present itself.

"It seems that the Cardinal had been working secretly on your lady mother's behalf. He was accused of treason, and the Earl of Northumberland was sent to Yorkshire to arrest him—he whose betrothal to Anne Boleyn the Cardinal broke years ago."

"He had a lucky escape," Mary muttered.

"Indeed. And I perceive the hand of the Lady Anne to be clear in this, suggesting she has never forgiven the Cardinal. It would explain her hostility toward him. Heaven knows why she is so vengeful, seeing she now has hopes of a far better marriage."

"It will be no marriage!" Mary hissed, shocked at Anne's vindictiveness. "What happened to the Cardinal?" Since Lady Salisbury had spoken kindly of him, she had felt more warmly toward her godfather, remembering his kindnesses to her and his loyal, indefatigable service to the King. And now that she knew he had seen the rightness of her mother's case all along and had lately even risked all to support her, there was a great lump in her throat and tears welled in her eyes.

"He was escorted south under guard," Lady Salisbury went on. "He probably knew that his destination was the Tower."

"But my father would not have had him executed, surely? A prince of the Church?" It was unthinkable. His cloth would have exempted and protected him.

"One would hope not!" the governess exclaimed. "I suspect he would have faced a long imprisonment." Mary wondered if Anne would have countenanced that, or if she would have demanded his head. "He was not a well man, and by the time they reached Leicester, he was clearly dying, so they took him to Leicester Abbey, where God, in His mercy, took him to Himself."

Mary crossed herself. It was tragic to think of that old man, abandoned by the King he had loved and served, worn out by a lifetime of work and the burden of failure, dying alone in the custody of his captors. "I will pray for him," she said.

When, after long, anxious months out in the cold, she received the summons to join the court at Greenwich for Christmas, she understood that she was forgiven. Her father's welcome was as warm as ever.

"I have missed you, sweet child," he said, crushing her against his jewel-encrusted doublet.

"And I have missed you, too, Father." She was not referring just to the months of separation. She was thinking of the man he used to be.

Mother was as loving as ever. It was heartening to see her in her rightful place by Father's side, gracing the festivities. But Anne Boleyn was clearly determined to make her presence felt; it galled Mary to see the courtiers still dancing attendance on her and flocking to her apartments, when the rightful Queen was all but left alone. Mary pursed her lips when she saw the Witch flaunting herself or making the barest of reverences to Mother and herself. Rage consumed her.

When they were alone one morning in the Queen's chamber, Mother regarded her with concern. "You look troubled, Mary, and you have lost weight."

"Do you wonder?" Mary burst out. "How can I be happy when I see what is going on here and how we are slighted? I detest her! She is a wicked woman. How can my father do this to you, Madam?"

"Hush, child! You must not speak of him so, and you must be charitable toward the Lady Anne for his sake."

"My lady mother, you have the patience of a saint!" Mary cried. "I cannot be like you, however hard I try." She was struggling to stem the tears.

Mother said nothing. Even now, she never criticized Father—at least not in front of Mary. But on Christmas Day, Mary had the strong impression that they had quarreled. Father was evidently feeling very sorry for himself, and he barely spoke to Mother. This black mood continued throughout the twelve days of festivities. Even at Twelfth Night, when the King and Queen sat enthroned together and there were masques, games, and a great banquet, he would not stop grumbling about the interminable delays in Rome and how badly the Pope had used him. In the end, even Mother gave up trying to get him to show a little mirth for Mary's sake.

That night, she came to Mary's bedchamber. "You must not worry about Father. He is like a man possessed, but I am sure that this madness will pass and that his natural virtues and goodness will win through in the end. Would that I could have him with me for just two or three months, as we used to be, I know I could make him forget all about a divorce."

Mary forced a smile. Bless Mother, she always liked to see the best in people, and her love for Father was such that she was blind to his cruelty. But Anne Boleyn was clever. She would never allow him to spend much time with Mother, and he was so in thrall to her that he had no idea he was being so evilly manipulated.

I 5 3 I

Reluctantly—for she did not wish to leave Mother in such an unhappy situation—Mary obeyed the King and moved to Hunsdon in the new year, back to the daily round of lessons, prayers, and recreation, although it was too cold to be walking out in the gardens this winter. Instead, she spent much time on her knees in chapel, praying that God would move her father's heart to do the right thing.

In February, she was struggling with a Latin text when Lady Salisbury burst into the schoolroom. "I beg your pardon, Dr. Fetherston, but there is news from London and you, Mary, should hear it. The King has assumed the title Supreme Head of the Church of England."

"But the Pope is head of the Church," Mary faltered, unable to believe her ears. "How can my father be its Supreme Head?"

"How indeed?" Dr. Fetherston echoed, clearly stunned.

"Lady Exeter writes that he has browbeaten the clergy into agreeing to it, and they did so only under protest. Archbishop Warham and Bishop Fisher at least insisted that the title be amended to Supreme Head *as far as the law of Christ allows.*" Lady Salisbury looked ashen.

"It allows nothing of the sort, I am certain," the tutor muttered. "So does this mean that the King has turned his back on the Pope?"

"No, surely! He would not go so far."

"Which does not mean to say that it does not herald something more serious, should things not go his way." Dr. Fetherston clamped his mouth shut and turned to Mary, who was regarding them with alarm. "Forgive me, your Highness. I should not have spoken so vehemently."

"No matter," she faltered, realizing that she was shaking. "I am as shocked as you are. I cannot bear to think about it. My father is Defender of the Faith; how can he slight his Holiness in this way? He cannot be Supreme Head of the Church of England—it is just not possible—"

"Nevertheless," interrupted Lady Salisbury, recovering herself a little, "it would be wise for us to keep our opinions to ourselves. If the Queen is watched, we may be, too."

Mary bit her tongue. There was so much that she was bursting to say.

In March, she began to feel ill. She could not keep down any food and felt so sick that she dared not leave her bedchamber. Lady Salisbury ordered her to bed and consulted the household physician. He bled Mary to balance her humors, tested her urine, and prescribed an infusion of wormwood, mint, and balm. The wormwood, he insisted, was to be taken in small quantities, for an overdose could be poisonous. Lady Salisbury herself took to the still room, raided her chest of dried herbs and made up the potion.

Mary lay in bed feeling wretched and longing for her mother.

"I wish she was here," she wept, as Lady Salisbury took away yet another covered basin of vomit and murmured soothing words.

"I know she would come if she could," she said, and Mary guessed she was holding something back.

"Then why doesn't she?" she sobbed.

The governess hesitated. "She writes that she has begged the King your father for permission to visit you, and he agreed that she might see you if she wanted, and also stay here. Dear child, you must understand that if she did that, he could say that she had left him. She dare not risk that happening, for it could prejudice her desire to safeguard your rights—and you can rest assured that she will do that with her own lifeblood, if need be."

That made Mary weep afresh. Father had put Mother in an impossible position, and it seemed he had done so deliberately. Did he not realize how much she herself needed her mother with her? How was she to get well when she felt so miserable?

Her illness lingered. For eight days, she had kept no food down. She had lost a lot of weight. The doctor was visibly concerned.

"What the Princess needs, I cannot prescribe for her, and I will write and tell the King so!" he declared in the middle of March. Mary held her breath. Surely Father would act now?

A week later, when she was forcing herself to take a spoonful of food now and then, Lady Salisbury entered her room, smiling. "Mary, dear, the King has sent orders that you are to be carried by litter to Richmond Palace, where the Queen's Grace will join you."

Mary cried again at that, but this time for joy. And when she finally reached Richmond, after a long and wearisome journey, she was overjoyed to find herself in the sanctuary of her mother's arms. It was all the physick she needed.

Mother could not hide her dismay at how ill she looked.

"We have done everything we could," Lady Salisbury assured her, her long face drawn and tired, for she had had little sleep these past days and nights.

"I am sure you have. But I am here now."

She stayed with Mary, feeding her tiny portions of heartening broth and fish poached in almond milk with her own hands. She read to her, the fables and stories and romances that young girls loved, which Master Vives had deplored; she watched over her while she slept, bathed her face and hands and combed her hair. Gradually,

Mary began to improve, until there came the joyous day when she was well enough to get out of bed and take a few wobbly steps.

Afterward, she lay down to sleep, exhausted by the effort, but feeling safe and much happier. Through the open door, she could hear her mother and her governess chatting softly in the outer chamber.

"She has had a lot to cope with," the Queen said. "The troubles between the King and me must cause her great anxiety. I have seen it with my own eyes."

"I agree, Madam. She loves his Grace and yourself equally, but it is clear to me that her sympathies lie with you. She often says she longs to see you and comfort you in your trouble. I know that she also worries about her future and about what is happening to the English Church. She has become very devout, and I believe she finds much solace in prayer."

"She has always been a pious child. I am glad she finds comfort in religion at this time."

"So am I, Madam. It is as if it represents the security she knew when she was little, before all this happened. She keeps harking back to those days. She worries about you all the time."

Mother sounded very emotional. "My dear friend, when the subject comes up again, please assure Mary that I am as cheerful as may be, and that I have good friends to support me. Tell her to continue as she is, and to trust in God that all will be well, as I do. And, as ever, see that she gets plenty of good food and fresh air, and keeps busy, so that she does not have time to dwell on her troubles. I, for my part, will stay with her as long as I can."

By April, Mary was much better, sitting up in her chair and taking light meals. The doctor was very pleased with her.

"The Princess will make a full recovery," he informed Mother.

"God and all the saints be praised!" she cried. "I have been so worried." She turned to Mary. "Dear child, you know I would rather stay here with you, but now that you are much restored, I must return to court. I dare not be away any longer than I have to, and who knows what has been going on in my absence? I will go tomorrow, much as it tugs at my heartstrings, and leave you in the loving hands of Lady Salisbury. It is for the best, believe me."

"I wish you didn't have to go," Mary mourned, clinging to her.

"So do I, Daughter; so do I. But I will ask your father if you might visit the court, so hopefully we shall see each other again soon."

When she had gone, Mary's spirits sank, although she held on to the hope that she would be back at court soon. Her recovery was almost complete, much to the doctor's satisfaction, but then she began to suffer painful, irregular courses and debilitating headaches.

"It's your age, child," Lady Salisbury assured her, but that did not help when Mary was tormented by cramps and migraines. "This is all a reaction to the trouble between your father and mother," she soothed, unusually outspoken for once. "Your loyalties are cruelly torn. No child should be placed in such a horrible position."

The governess had hit the nub of the matter, Mary felt. She was perpetually torn: she loved her father, but her first loyalty now was to her mother. She missed them both dreadfully—missed the mother she adored and the father she had once had. In her loneliness and grief, she found solace in the hours she spent in chapel, offloading her miseries, praying that the Church would triumph over heresy, and beseeching the Almighty for a speedy ruling from Rome.

When Mother wrote and broke the news that she was not to be summoned to court, it was a dreadful blow. Of course, she could guess why, and cursed Anne Boleyn for being such a pernicious influence on her father. Now her prayers were for him to relent and permit her and Mother to be together. And this time, God was listening, for in July, Mary was instructed to join the court at Windsor. Immediately, her monthly pains abated and the headaches vanished. Joyfully, she assisted her maids with the packing. When she set out on her journey, England had never looked lovelier; everything was in full bloom, the sun cast a golden light on green fields and dappled trees, and a light breeze rustled the leaves.

Father's greeting was loving enough, and his concern for her health genuine, but Mary sensed a new fierceness in his manner, barely suppressed. She supposed he was angry because of the long silence from Rome. It had been nearly two years now; what was the Pope thinking of? Certainly he was doing the Church no favors by his procrastination. And now, Lady Salisbury had told her, Father was canvasing the views of the universities on his Great Matter. What good that would do she had no idea.

Mother shook her head in despair when Mary raised the subject as they sat in the garden beneath the Round Tower. "I believe he thinks to bolster his case with learned opinion. But for every doctor who supports him, I can show you two who disagree." It was unlike her to venture a criticism, but there was a new brittleness to her.

"Mary, you must be wondering why you could not come to court before now," she said suddenly, looking distressed. "Things have not been good between your father and me. Some weeks ago, he sent a deputation from the Privy Council to wait on me at Greenwich. They pressed me to withdraw my appeal to Rome. I refused. I also denied the King's supremacy. I said that the Pope is the only true sovereign and Vicar of God, and the only person who has power to judge in spiritual matters. But I also told them that I love your father as much as any woman can love a man, and that I would not have borne him company as his wife for one moment against the voice of my conscience. I declared again that I am his true wife, and I told them to go to Rome and argue with others than a lone woman!"

Mary was inwardly applauding her. "That was very brave of you!"

Mother nodded. "When the bishops tried to dispute with me, I cut them short, saying I meant to abide by no decision save that of Rome. Afterward, Messire Chapuys told me I had confounded the deputation. Yet I dread to think of your father's reaction. I have not seen him since. He is always out hunting with the Lady Anne."

So Mary had heard. Her heart burned with hatred for that woman—or rather that witch, for surely she had cast a spell on him.

To everyone's relief, Father took the Witch to Hampton Court for a few days, and there was a welcome respite from all the tension. Mary and her mother went for long walks in the great park and the Queen attempted to cheer her with music and dancing in her chamber. One of her maids-of-honor, a pleasant, pale-faced young woman called Jane Seymour, was trying to improve her skills with a lute, and Mary took pleasure in teaching her a new and quite demanding piece of music.

"You have mastered that well, Mistress Jane," she said. "Shall we dance a pavane?"

"I should be honored, your Highness," Jane said, as the Queen signaled for the musicians to begin.

The pavane, with its two beats to a step, was challenging, and Jane clearly found it hard to maintain a slow, stately pace. Always she wanted to go faster.

"No!" Mary cried, tossing back her long red hair. "You must stay in time!"

Jane tried again, and still managed to stay ahead of everyone else. In the end, they all collapsed in giggles. It was heartening to see Mother laughing.

As the days passed, Mary began to relax more and enjoy the company of the maids-of-honor, playing blindman's buff in the deserted galleries and tag in the gardens. But when Father returned with Anne Boleyn, Mother forbade her to leave her apartments. Mary was all too aware that he was flaunting his mistress in the court beyond the door, and her happy mood evaporated.

The court was full of the bustle of preparations for the King's annual summer progress, and Mary glumly expected to be sent back to Hunsdon. Her parents were due to leave Windsor for Woodstock in the middle of July, and that day would soon be upon them, but no order had come.

On the morning they were meant to depart, Mary joined her mother for Mass and then for breakfast. They had been sitting there for a short while when the Queen laid down her knife. "Do you not think it is quiet here, ladies?" she asked. It was true. There was none of the commotion and noise that was normal when the court departed on progress, no running feet or shouts from below. Mother rose and looked out of the window, then gave a little gasp.

"The wards are empty," she said.

Mary and the other ladies crowded around her, peering through the casement. There was no procession forming, no sight of any carts or sumpter mules.

"Maybe I am mistaken, and it is not today," Mother said. "No one tells me anything these days." She gave them a weak smile, and sent her chamberlain, Lord Mountjoy, to find out when the court was leaving.

He returned looking decidedly uncomfortable.

"Madam," he informed her, "the King left for Woodstock very early this morning."

Mother nodded and continued with her breakfast. Mary could not help feeling upset that her father had left without saying goodbye, and concluded that this was some new ruse of Anne Boleyn's, intended to slight and discourage the Queen.

Dinner was almost over when an usher in the King's livery was announced. He bowed to Mother, but addressed the wall beyond her shoulder.

"Your Grace, it is the King's pleasure that you vacate Windsor Castle within a month and choose some house of your own to go to," he said, and swallowed nervously. "You may remain here until the time comes for the Princess Mary to return to Hunsdon."

Mary did not immediately understand the significance of the order—until she saw her mother's face, and then she knew. He had left them, without even saying farewell, and this time it was for good. They had been abandoned without a word. He had not even waited for the Pope to speak. The enormity of it took her breath away. She watched, bewildered and speechless, as her mother struggled to preserve her composure, then reached out and squeezed Mary's hand. "Go where I may," she said, "I remain his wife, and for him I will pray."

"I am to go to Easthampstead, in Windsor Forest," the Queen informed Mary, on a hot August afternoon, "and you, Daughter, will not be sent to Hunsdon after all. Your father has ordered you to leave for Richmond."

"Why can't I go with you?" Mary asked plaintively.

"Because you must obey the King's will in all matters and give him no cause to doubt your loyalty and obedience."

"Mother, you are a saint!" Mary retorted. "How can you accept these cruelties so patiently?"

"Because it is my duty as a wife to do my lord's pleasure, as it is yours as his daughter."

Mary shook her head, utterly baffled. Father did not deserve such unquestioning loyalty.

She was glad that so many of the Queen's attendants had chosen to accompany her to Easthampstead, especially Jane Seymour, of whom she had become fond these past weeks. There was no doubting where Jane's loyalties lay.

The parting was worse this time, because there was no knowing when Mary would see her mother again. She feared that Father was separating them as a punishment for Mother's refusal to agree to an annulment. That certainty deepened when, on arriving at Richmond Palace, she was informed—to her great grief—that she was forbidden to visit her mother, as was Lady Salisbury, who feared that the Queen's other friends, including the redoubtable Lady Exeter, had been banned from seeing her as well.

In other respects, life went on as normal. Mary kept great state as princess, pursued her studies, and took her small pleasures with Lady Salisbury and her maids, making music, dancing, and playing cards. Her courses continued to plague her, obliging her to spend at least two days in bed each month, with a hot brick wrapped in flannel pressed to her belly; and she was so nervy these days, subject to all kinds of fears and fancies. As always, Lady Salisbury did her best to allay them and instill some common sense into her, but it seemed to Mary that one anxiety was invariably replaced by another. If she was not troubled by a strange lightheadedness, she was fretting over some vague bodily symptom, or riddled with guilt, feeling she had not done enough to defend her mother. Sometimes, she wanted to run away from herself. If it was not for the comfort of her faith, she would have been lost indeed.

Neither she nor her mother was invited to court that Christmas. Father sent her to keep the season at Beaulieu. His messenger informed her that she was not to communicate with her mother or

Messire Chapuys. She broke down at that, for never had she or the
Queen failed to exchange gifts at New Year, and the thought of poor
Mother all on her own was more than she could bear. The thought of
Chapuys made her weep even more. Mother's letters had left her in
no doubt that that reassuring, caring man with the kind eyes had
been indefatigable in his support of them both. Mary wished she
could see him and pour out her troubles to him. He would help and
comfort her, she knew it.

Chapter 6

1532

The January winds were bitter and there was frost on the ground as Mary and her retinue approached the More. It was a wonderfully welcome sight, not only on account of the weather, but also because Mother was waiting there to receive her. Father had finally relented and allowed Mary to visit her.

"He must be anxious to placate the people," Lady Salisbury had said, tartly, when the order came. "There has been much comment about his keeping you apart." It came to Mary that public opinion could make a difference. The King's power might be absolute, but the goodwill of his subjects was essential to maintaining it. When she was Queen, she vowed, she would do everything in her power to court that goodwill.

She had traveled in some state from Beaulieu, and the people had come running and slipping on the ice to see her and call down blessings as she rode by on her palfrey. She had scorned the litter; the prospect of seeing her mother seemed to have banished her chronic aches and pains. But it was so cold, and she longed for the comfort of a roaring fire and that dear lady's arms. When they clattered through the gatehouse and the grooms came running across the courtyard to take their mounts, Mary hastened indoors and raced up the stairs to the Queen's lodgings. And there she was, her beloved mother, holding out her hands, her tired face radiant with love. Mary clung to her, painfully aware that she had aged in the months they had been apart and that she had lost weight. It struck her forcibly that Mother would not always be there for her and that they should make the most of this gift of time together. How long it would last she had no idea.

They spent a week cocooned in the warmth of the Queen's chamber, talking, playing cards, and making merry, as if all was as it should be. Sometimes Lady Salisbury joined them and gave Mother news passed on by her sons, Henry, Geoffrey, and Reginald; it was all the news the governess got these days, cut off as she was in Mary's household, and with Lady Exeter unable to send her any; but it was better than nothing.

The women had not brought up any contentious matters, but Mary could not stop herself from voicing her loathing of the Witch. "I hate that woman for what she is doing to you," she burst out, lying snuggled up to her mother in bed. "I hate what is happening to the Church and the evils that are befalling this realm!"

"Hush," Mother soothed. "Forget them. Let us enjoy this quiet time together." She picked up the book they had been reading and turned to a new page.

When a week had passed, Mother bade Mary attend her. "You are to go home to Beaulieu tomorrow, Daughter."

"No!" Mary cried. Was this all the time they were to be allowed? She had hoped that she might spend her sixteenth birthday next month with the Queen, and even stay longer than that. She clenched her fists, devastated by the news. "Surely I don't have to leave so soon?"

"Alas, that is what your father has decreed. I fear it suits him best to keep us apart. It has been intimated to me that now you are growing older, he fears we might intrigue with the Emperor against him."

"It would serve him right if we did!" Mary cried.

"Child, have you taken leave of your senses?" the Queen gasped, shocked. "Have you forgotten your duty to the King? It would be treason! It is different for me. If, as he maintains, I am not his wife, then I am not his subject and cannot be deemed a traitor if I appeal to a foreign power for aid—which I would never do, of course, because I am his true wife. But you are not only his daughter, but also his subject. If you were overheard saying such things, it would go ill for you and give your father a justifiable pretext for keeping us apart for good."

Mary shrank into herself, chastened. "I would not risk that for the world. But we are alone here, with only you to hear me."

"Walls," Mother said ominously, "have ears. I fear that this new man in power, Thomas Cromwell, who has evidently replaced the Cardinal as the King's chief adviser, is having us watched. Beware of your tongue, Mary, and never utter anything remotely compromising."

Their parting the next day was especially painful, as neither knew when they would see each other again. Mary rode to Beaulieu in abject misery, heedless of the cold that penetrated beyond the leather curtains of her litter. They had had so little time together. She was sure that Father was punishing Mother for defying him. But could he not understand how much suffering he was inflicting on her, his daughter?

She tried to find pleasure in everyday things: in books, music, and in the company of dear Lady Salisbury. She reminded herself that she lived in a grand house, with servants and every material thing she could wish for. Compared to many, she was extraordinarily fortunate. Yet none of it compensated for the absence of her mother, or the loss of her past happiness. And always she was reminded of her sadnesses by the pains and anxiety that now never left her.

Father visited her from time to time. She suspected he came to satisfy himself that she was a dutiful daughter. She made sure that she gave every appearance of that; never again would she speak out as she had before; she would give him no cause to be displeased with her. And then she felt guilty that she was not championing her mother as she ought. Round and round in tortuous circles her mind went.

Father's visits were a trial because of the unspoken things that lay between them. Mother was never mentioned. He was faultless in his courtesy, as interested in her academic progress as ever, and affectionate when the mood took him. Yet there was a reserve about him, an edge to his manner; he was not a happy man. She supposed that he had much to make him angry and frustrated.

Once, after her household had moved to Hunsdon for the summer, she forgot her resolve, and when he tried to win her around to his point of view, she told him, weeping, that she could never consider herself baseborn. He left, seething at her defiance. Again, she told herself she must not anger him. But it was so hard to keep her feelings in check.

Over the months, his visits became more infrequent, and he grew ever more distant. Mary would be left wondering if she had offended him, and fret for weeks, but then he would come back, giving the lie to her fears.

One September afternoon, after he had departed for the court, having bidden an awkward farewell, Lady Salisbury received a letter from her son Henry Pole, who was a member of the King's household. Mary heard her intake of breath as she read it.

"Is something wrong?" she asked, anticipating some new crisis. It was how she was these days, always expecting the worst.

Lady Salisbury raised troubled eyes to her. "I'm not sure if I should tell you, but I fear I should, for your own safety. It may be nothing, just the rantings of an evil woman, but we should be on our guard."

"What is it?" Mary cried, really alarmed now.

"Henry writes that it is said at court that the King dares not praise you in the Lady Anne's presence for fear of provoking her temper, and that he keeps his visits to you as brief as possible because she is so jealous. When he was in attendance on his Grace last week, Henry heard her with his own ears saying that she would have you in her train and might one day give you too much dinner, or marry you to some varlet."

Mary felt as if she had been punched.

"It may just be bluster," the Countess said. "But Henry is concerned because there was a recent attempt to poison Bishop Fisher, and there has been speculation that the Boleyns were behind it."

Mary had no doubt that Anne was perfectly capable of putting her threats into effect. She shuddered. "Is there no end to the Witch's malice? What have I ever done to her?"

"You have supported your lady mother. And, simply by existing, you pose a threat to the children she hopes to have. You have prior right to the succession."

"I fear she may bear a son—for he would take precedence, if my father ever succeeds in marrying her. Not that I would acknowledge him!" Mary declared hotly.

"Let us hope that her threats are just the outpourings of a nasty and frustrated shrew," Lady Salisbury said. "Nevertheless, we must be vigilant. I will have all your food tasted before you eat it."

That night, Mary could not sleep. Grim vistas of the future were opening out before her. The relatively safe world she inhabited seemed safe no more. At a stroke, her father could separate her from Lady Salisbury, just as he had separated her from her mother. She could see herself being forcibly carried to court and made to serve her bitter enemy, and living in terror of poison, for there would be no one to protect her. Not even Father, she feared—he was too besotted with the Witch to see anything bad in her.

From Henry Pole's next letter, which arrived when they were preparing for the day's lessons, they learned that Anne had been created Lady Marquess of Pembroke in a glittering ceremony at Windsor.

"It's a scandal, that woman being raised to the peerage in her own right!" Lady Salisbury fumed, angrily banging Mary's books down on the table. "The last person to have that honor was me, a lady of high blood, not some jumped-up harlot!"

"It's an appalling scandal," Mary agreed, yet it was dawning on her that this might not be such bad news. "But do you not think it significant? Maybe my father has grown tired of her, or realized that he can never marry her. Maybe this is her reward for being his mistress."

The governess paused for a moment, thoughtful. "You may be right. There was something in Henry's letter." She drew it from her pocket. "Yes. Many present at the ennobling noticed that the title was granted to Anne and her heirs male—not, as is usual, to her *legitimate* heirs male."

"That's against all the laws of the peerage," Mary cried, outraged. "A bastard cannot inherit."

"The King can ennoble whoever he likes. Look at Henry Fitzroy! But you may be right, Mary. He could well be making provision for any bastard she might bear him and securing a comfortable future for them."

Mary's heart leaped with hope.

That hope was dashed when she heard in October that Father had gone to Calais to meet King Francis and taken the Witch with him. So he had not discarded her after all. He had probably ennobled her to make her fit to be presented to his brother monarch.

Lying sleepless that night, Mary could not stem her fears. She had heard that Dr. Thomas Cranmer was to replace old Warham as archbishop of Canterbury. Warham had cautiously upheld Mother's case until he died, but Henry Pole had described Cranmer as a religious radical, a creature of the Boleyns, and the man who had suggested that the King canvass the views of the universities on his Great Matter. Cranmer could prove a very dangerous influence indeed. Henry Pole feared that the universities had been bribed with huge sums to pronounce the royal marriage invalid, and it seemed that most had spoken in Father's favor.

But, Mary tried to reassure herself, their declarations weighed nothing against the authority of the Pope. Only he had the power to rule in such cases. Heaven only knew why he had delayed for so long, but he must surely reach a decision soon. She prayed it would not come too late, because she felt in her bones that something ominous was afoot. The portents were not good.

1533

In February, on Mary's seventeenth birthday, a messenger wearing no livery arrived at Hunsdon, where she had spent her second Christmas without her mother. She saw the man when he came into the hall, where she was directing the rehanging of a tapestry. The steward sent him to Lady Salisbury's lodgings; later, she learned that his name was Master Hayward.

When Lady Salisbury joined her for dinner in the privy chamber, Mary could see that something was wrong.

"I hate to have to tell you, but the word at court is that the Lady Anne is with child," the governess said.

"With child?" Mary echoed.

"I fear so. I have had a secret communication from Lady Exeter. She fears that some wickedness may be afoot."

"But the Pope has not spoken! What can they do?"

"Given that your father has made himself Supreme Head of the English Church, I would not be surprised at anything," Lady Salisbury said despondently.

Mary felt like howling; she was a dam fit to burst. She could only pray that it wasn't true, that this so-called pregnancy was just mere gossip.

"Does my mother know, do you think?" All her instincts were to protect that dear soul from such distressing news.

Lady Salisbury shook her head. "I have no means of knowing. Lady Exeter wrote that her Grace is still not allowed visitors or any contact with the outside world. I do not even know where she is."

Mary did weep at that. What had Mother ever done to deserve this?

In April, the weather was warm enough for Mary to take her books into the garden and work on her translations there. She had not been sitting in the sunshine for long when Lady Salisbury came hurrying toward her along the graveled path.

"Mary!" She looked utterly dismayed, and Mary braced herself to hear the worst. The Pope had ruled against Mother! Or she herself was to go to court and serve the Witch—or, worst of all, Mother was dead.

The Countess sank down on the bench beside her, out of breath. "I have heard from my son," she gasped. "On Easter Sunday, the Lady Anne went in procession to Mass as Queen, wearing royal robes of crimson velvet and attended by sixty maids-of-honor."

Mary felt faint. Her vision blurred and there was a jolting sensation in her head.

"No! No!" she cried. "Surely his Holiness cannot have ruled in Father's favor?"

"He has not ruled at all!" Lady Salisbury's eyes flashed. "If he had, it would have been triumphantly announced. As far as anyone knows, the King has committed bigamy."

Mary glanced nervously about, fearful that someone might be listening, but there was no one. She felt sick to her stomach, appalled that her father had gone so far.

"If it's any comfort, most people were as shocked as we are. Henry said some looked as if they did not know whether to laugh or cry, and there was much whispering. Several made obeisance as that woman passed by, but others just stared."

As well they might! How dare the Witch parade herself at court, wearing a crown to which she had no right? Mary's blood boiled. If Anne had been present, she would have plunged a dagger in her heart or strangled her with her bare hands.

Spring flowered in glory, as if in mockery, but Mary could take no pleasure in it, bowed down as she was in misery, and in fear of what might happen next.

On a glorious May day, Dr. Fetherston set up a table in the garden, and began testing her on the finer points of rhetoric. It was then that she saw the horsemen approaching, with outriders wearing the royal livery. As they rode up to the house, she recognized some lords of the Privy Council, men she had known for years, who had made much of her in happier times. Dread filled her heart. What did they want with her?

Dr. Fetherston was clearly wondering the same thing. "You had best go and find Lady Salisbury," he urged. "We will receive them together."

The councillors were waiting in the great hall when Mary finally entered, sweating in their fine gowns and gold chains. It was a relief to see them doffing their caps and bowing to her. Somehow, she found the courage to address them. "This is an unexpected pleasure, my lords."

The Duke of Suffolk, her uncle by dint of his being married to Father's sister, her Aunt Mary, stepped forward. He was a florid, hearty man, much like the King in looks, and greatly trusted by him. "My lady Princess, we come on the King's business, and we are instructed to inform you that the Archbishop of Canterbury has pronounced the King's union with your lady mother to be null and absolutely void, and contrary to divine law. He has also found his Grace's marriage to the Lady Anne Boleyn good and valid."

Mary was shaking with outrage. "Has his Holiness ruled on the matter?

"The Pope has no authority to dispense in such a case," Suffolk replied, looking embarrassed.

"And who has told you that?"

"It is the opinion of the divines in the universities, and of his Grace of Canterbury himself."

Mary drew herself up to her full height. She was the Princess of England, heiress to the throne, and she had had enough of their nonsense.

"I fear they are all mistaken, my lord Duke, even my lord Archbishop." And one day, she vowed inwardly, Cranmer would be called to account for his wickedness. "The Pope is the only authority in such cases, and I assure you I will accept no one for queen except my mother."

"Your Highness, I beg you to reconsider. You would not wish to incur the King's wrath, I am sure."

Anger flared. "My mother is the King's true wife, and I will never say otherwise."

The Duke of Norfolk, that self-seeking old martinet, stepped forward. "Then in future, Madam, you are forbidden to communicate in any way with the Princess Dowager, as your mother is now to be titled. You will not be allowed to see her until both of you come to your senses."

"May I not write a last note to her?" Mary asked, fighting back tears.

"You may not."

"Very well," she said. "But if you think to intimidate me into submission, you are very much mistaken. My mother is the true Queen, and I will never call her Princess Dowager. And I will never acknowledge the Lady Anne as Queen."

"On your own head be it, then," Norfolk barked, and with that the deputation bowed—less deferentially this time—and walked out.

Three days later, a letter came bearing the Queen's seal. At first, Mary thought it was from her mother, but when she opened it, she saw that it was from the Witch.

She would not read it, she resolved. She wanted nothing to do with the woman. Yet she could not help herself. She had to know what was in it.

It was cordial enough—an olive branch, or so it seemed. Anne had invited her to court. If Mary would honor her as Queen, it would be a means of reconciliation with her father, who was most displeased with her.

So they meant to bribe her into submission!

Seething with fury, she dashed off a reply, her pen flying across the page. She knew of no queen of England save her mother, she wrote, but if Madam Boleyn—she would give her no other title—would intercede for her with the King, she would be much obliged.

Anne's next letter was not so friendly in tone, but it was another invitation to court.

Again, Mary rebuffed her. Only after the messenger had departed did she begin to fear the consequences.

There were no more invitations. The next she heard, from Lady Salisbury, was that Henry Pole had overheard Anne publicly threatening to bring down the pride born of Mary's unbridled Spanish blood. Battle had been engaged, and if Anne was determined to give no quarter, then Mary would be more than a match for her.

There had been no word of Mother, and there was no means of obtaining any. Mary spent hours on her knees praying for her and calling on the Holy Virgin to comfort her in her great tribulations. She had no doubt, though, that the Queen would stand firm.

Desperate for news, she wrote a letter to Messire Chapuys, and asked Lady Salisbury if Master Hayward, Henry Pole's messenger, could take it to his master. She waited in suspense for a reply, fearing what might happen if the letter was intercepted. Days passed, and there was nothing.

But then Master Hayward arrived at Hunsdon, and in his scrip he carried a sealed packet for Mary, which he silently handed to her when only Lady Salisbury was present. Inside was a letter from Chapuys!

She took it to her bedchamber to read in privacy. It told her what she needed to know.

Mother had borne the news of Cranmer's judgments bravely, as Mary had known she would. She had taken a pen and scored through the words "Princess Dowager" on a document she was supposed to sign to acknowledge that she was no longer Queen; and she had done it with such vehemence that the nib had torn the parchment. She had declared stoutly that she was the crowned and anointed Queen and the King's true wife, and so she would always call herself. When reminded that Queen Anne was now the rightful queen, she had retorted that all the world knew by what authority it had been done, and declared she would abide by no judgment save that of the Pope.

Mary's heart swelled with pride and admiration. It was heartening to know that adversity and cruel treatment had not crushed her mother's spirit, and that she remained strong in her convictions, even in the face of relentless cruelty. For the lords had delivered an ultimatum from the King. If Mother persisted in her obstinacy, he might withdraw his fatherly love from their daughter. Mary blanched at this, feeling as if she was dying inside, but the Queen had remained resolute and said she would not yield for her daughter's sake or anyone else's, notwithstanding the King's displeasure. Warned that she was putting herself in danger of her father's anger and its consequences, she had replied that not for a thousand deaths would she consent to damn her soul or that of her husband.

Chapuys reported that Father was furious at her mother's defiance and had sent her farther away from court, to the Bishop of Lincoln's palace at Buckden in Huntingdonshire, where she was being treated as a prisoner.

Mary dropped the letter and wiped the hot tears from her eyes. She grieved for her mother, longing to comfort her in her trials. It was heartening to know that Chapuys was doing his best to help them both, but he had warned that he could not write to her very often, as it was too dangerous. But he would do all in his power to alleviate their sufferings, as the Emperor had bidden him, and as he himself was determined to do, for he could not stand by and see injustice done.

What a marvelous man he was; the kind of man Mary might one day want for a husband. But Chapuys was a mere ambassador, she a princess, so she must not let her thoughts stray in that direction. Besides, he was in holy orders. If things had been otherwise, she might well be married now to some great prince. Her marriage was in her father's gift, and she was supposed to be betrothed to the Duke of Orléans, although Heaven knew if he or anyone else would want her now, with doubts about her legitimacy hanging over her. Cranmer had not ruled on that, she realized, and she doubted he would have ruled in her favor anyway. He was Anne's creature.

As the summer passed, Mary was aware that the time for the Witch's confinement must be approaching. The prospect filled her with fear, for if the woman bore a son, she herself would be ousted from the succession—and by a bastard! The injustice and wrongness of it ate at her. She had resented Henry Fitzroy, but it was as nothing to the hatred she felt for this unborn child.

In September, Lady Salisbury sought out Mary as she was restringing a lute in the parlor, trying to distract herself from disturbing thoughts.

"It's a girl!" she announced triumphantly. "God could not have spoken more clearly."

A girl. "It is a vindication of my dear mother," Mary said, thinking of her father and how he had turned the world upside down to marry the Witch and have a son. She could almost feel sorry for him. Heaven had made a fool of him. In the eyes of Christendom, this child would never be regarded as anything other than a bastard, begotten and borne in sin by an infamous courtesan.

They had named the infant Elizabeth and she had been afforded a lavish christening, although, Henry Pole reported, the King had canceled the tournaments arranged to celebrate the birth of a prince.

"It seems he is putting a brave face on his disappointment," Lady Salisbury surmised. "My son writes that the Lady Anne is as high in favor as ever and insists on every honor being paid to her daughter as the King's heir."

"But that is my title!" Mary protested. "She has no right to it."

The Countess regarded her sadly. "Alas, dear Mary, right counts for very little these days."

Later that month, a deputation of councillors headed by the dukes of Norfolk and Suffolk returned to Hunsdon. This time, there was little deference.

Norfolk did not beat about the bush. "My Lady Mary," he said, not using her proper title, "I am to inform you that Parliament is to pass an Act declaring you illegitimate and removing you from the succession to the crown, the right to which will now devolve on the Princess Elizabeth."

"No!" Mary cried, heedless of the consequences. "I am the King's true daughter and his undoubted heir. I will accept Elizabeth as my sister, but a princess she can never be."

"Your willfulness and disobedience will bring down the King's wrath on you," Norfolk growled. "I have never seen such an ungrateful and undutiful daughter."

Mary was trembling, but she stood firm. "I will abide only by the judgment of the Pope, and I do not believe that has yet been given."

There was a pause—long enough for her to know that the shaft had gone home.

They left her then, but they were soon back, and Norfolk was in an even more bullish mood. Norfolk harrumphed. "I have spoken to the King of your obstinacy, my Lady Mary, and I am to tell you that you are forbidden to use the title of princess, and your household is to be disbanded. You are no longer of an age to have need of a tutor, so Dr. Fetherston is being dismissed."

"No!" Mary cried, reeling as from a physical blow and grasping a chair to steady herself. "They cannot do that to me! Where will I live?"

"The King's will is law, and it is his pleasure that you be sent to Hatfield to wait upon the Princess Elizabeth. Her household is to be established there in December."

Mary felt faint. She could barely speak. This was worse than anything she had anticipated, for Elizabeth's train was bound to number many of the Boleyn faction—and all of them were her enemies. "And when is my household to be disbanded?"

"Soon," Norfolk said curtly.

Lady Salisbury stepped forward, her face ashen. "My lord Duke, may I be permitted to remain with the Princess?"

"The Lady Mary!" he barked. "That title is forbidden."

Lady Salisbury looked mutinous, but bowed her head. Mary knew that as soon as Norfolk had gone, she would disobey him.

"Your task, my lady," he told her, "is to deliver up the Lady Mary's jewels. The Queen's Grace has asked for them."

Mary gasped at the sheer effrontery of it.

The Countess's eyes flashed. "If you think I will surrender the Princess's jewels to one who is the scandal of Christendom, you had best forget it!" she thundered.

Norfolk glared at her. "For that, Madam, you too are dismissed."

Mary saw her governess visibly crumple. "I beg pardon, my lord, but I was shocked at such a request. Please allow me to stay with Mary."

"No," he said, implacable. "Go home to your estates, my lady."

"I would serve her at my own expense," she persisted. Tears filled Mary's eyes. Lady Salisbury was as a second mother to her; she could not bear to lose her.

"And encourage her in her disobedience, no doubt!" the Duke retorted. "No, my lady, you will obey his Grace in this, as in all matters."

They wept that night, in each other's arms, Mary clinging to her governess as if to a raft. "I do not know how I will live without you," she sobbed.

"It will not be easy for me either," Lady Salisbury sniffed. "But know this, that I will be praying for you every day, and that you will never be far from my thoughts. And if there is any service I can do for you or the Queen your mother, you shall not find me wanting."

The weeks that followed were shadowed by misery and flew by all too fast. Before long, Mary's possessions were being packed and the house was being closed up. One by one, the servants left, many of them emotional on parting. Mary struggled to perform the courtesies without breaking down. These people had served her for years, some all her life, and it was tragic to see them go. She was so wrapped up in her inner anguish that the news of the marriage of the Duke of Orléans to Catherine de' Medici, daughter of the Duke of Urbino, conveyed by Henry Pole, barely registered.

Soon, there would be no news from Henry Pole—or from anyone else. No more cozy evenings spent by the hearth with Lady Salisbury, no stimulating intellectual discussions with Dr. Fetherston. She would be all by herself, isolated from the rest of the world, in a hostile household.

Chapter 7

1533

Christmas Day, the day she had dreaded, had arrived. Today, she would say farewell to her old life and all that was beloved and familiar. Wrapped in furs against the December wind, Mary stood in the courtyard as the litter that was to take her to Hatfield drew up. Lady Salisbury had to support her, as she would have fallen otherwise, so distressed was she. Even Dr. Fetherston's customary calm had deserted him, and Mary could see tears in his eyes as he waited to see her off.

They were holding the litter door open for her, and the Duke of Norfolk was waiting impatiently. Panic seized her.

"I will not go!" she cried.

"You will do as you are commanded!" he snapped.

"Go, Mary," Lady Salisbury murmured gently. "There is nothing to be gained by refusing."

"I will not," Mary persisted. "I will not bend the knee to that little bastard who has stolen my rightful title."

"Enough!" roared Norfolk. "I will not hear such talk." He loomed over her, exuding menace. "If my daughter offered such unnatural opposition, I would beat her and knock her head against the wall until it was as soft as a baked apple!" For a ghastly moment, Mary thought he was going to do it, and burst into floods of tears.

"Threats, my lord, will not move me," she sobbed.

"Get in!" Gripping her arm roughly, he bundled her into the litter. There was no time even to embrace Lady Salisbury and Dr. Fetherston. Landing heavily on the cushioned seat, she felt the chariot move and, with tears streaming down her face, she thrust aside the curtain.

"God keep you both!" she cried. "Pray for me!"

Dr. Fetherston raised a hand in blessing, and the Countess blew her a kiss. She was grateful that they had said their proper farewells in private earlier. She watched them, sobbing bitterly, until they were out of sight. She had never felt so alone.

It was a horrid journey, cold and uncomfortable, and throughout Mary felt a sense of menace hanging over her. She could not stop weeping, and as her small procession wended its way north of London and drew near to Hatfield, she felt sick to her stomach.

Presently, the house came into view. Her father had long since leased it from the Bishop of Ely, and she knew the redbrick palace well, for the air was clean in these parts and she had spent time here in childhood. But it seemed alien now, and as they drew to a halt in the quadrangle, she felt oppressed by the towers, buttresses, gables, and twisted chimneys that surrounded her.

There was no great company to receive her, just a sour-faced woman of about fifty, wearing rich robes and a long-lappeted, unfashionable gable hood, who stood shivering in the porch.

"My Lady Mary," she greeted her, unsmiling, as Mary stepped down on shaky legs onto the gravel. "I am Lady Shelton, the Queen's aunt. I am your new lady mistress. Come, I will show you to your chamber." Her manner was brisk, impersonal, and, Mary thought, hostile. What did she mean by chamber? Was not she, Mary, even to have her own lodgings?

It was the meanest chamber in the house. It had a small tester bed, a threadbare tapestry, an old chest, and a brazier—not even a fireplace. And although the brazier had been lit, it gave off little heat because only a mean amount of coal had been used to fill it.

"Your luggage will be brought up and you can unpack before coming down to supper in the hall," Lady Shelton said. "Tomorrow, you will begin your duties as maid-of-honor to the Princess. I will leave you now to settle in."

The door closed behind her. That was it. No kind words of welcome, no warmth. Doubtless Lady Shelton was acting on the Witch's orders.

Mary waited ages for her traveling chests, and when they were finally brought to her, she wondered where she would find space for the rich gowns and other fine clothing that Lady Salisbury had had packed for her. And where would she put her books, her musical instruments and her sewing box? There was so little room. With no maid to help her, how would she dress and lace up her gowns?

Feeling overwhelmed, she sank down on the bed and howled.

Supper was an ordeal. The great hall looked very festive with the Yule log burning on the hearth and swathes of greenery everywhere, in honor of the season, but it brought back so many poignant memories of Christmases past that Mary had to struggle to stop herself crying. As Elizabeth's entire household filed in, she saw that she had not been assigned a seat on the high table, but that a place had been set for her below the salt, and that every eye was witnessing her humiliation. Unable barely to eat a morsel, she escaped as soon as she could and hurried away to her room. But there was Lady Shelton barring her way.

"My Lady Mary, you are to attend the Princess at ten o'clock in the morning, after breakfast. Report to Lady Bryan."

Lady Bryan! Mary's heart leaped when she heard the name of her old governess, who had cared for her and run her nursery when she was very young. She had adored her and knew that Lady Bryan had returned that love. At once, her spirits lifted. Life at Hatfield might not be so awful after all. Waiting on Elizabeth, she would surely be spending more time with Lady Bryan than with Lady Shelton. All the same, she cried herself to sleep, desperately missing Lady Salisbury and Dr. Fetherston, and wishing with all her heart that she was back in her own house.

In the morning, she managed somehow to get herself dressed and arrive at the nursery in good time. Elizabeth's rooms were luxuriously appointed and staffed by an army of nursemaids, officers, and servants. And there, very much in charge, was the venerable, rosy-cheeked Lady Bryan.

"My Lady Mary!" she exclaimed, embracing her, as everyone stared. "How you have grown! But, my goodness, you look as if you need feeding up. Come and have some breakfast before you meet your half-sister. There's bread and meat and good ale." She ushered Mary to the table, signaling to a servant to bring the victuals, and Mary, who had not touched the breakfast in hall and was feeling quite faint, was suddenly hungry.

Lady Bryan sat down opposite. "I know you must be feeling very strange," she said. "But Sir John Shelton, who is governor here, runs this household well, and I'm sure you will soon settle in. And my lady Princess is a joy! You must forget about all the unpleasantness, my dear, and take pleasure in your sister. She is such a toward babe—nigh on four months old now. And this afternoon there will be revels in the hall."

Mary doubted she would enjoy them and doubted even less that she would ever take pleasure in the little bastard who had supplanted her. Never would she recognize her as princess. That title belonged to herself alone. And never would she acknowledge herself a bastard!

But the baby was adorable. Lying swaddled, not in her everyday cradle, but in the vast cradle of estate—in which, Mary guessed, she had been deliberately placed to underline her status for Mary's benefit—she lay gazing up at her half-sister with blue eyes that seemed to hold a remarkable wisdom and intelligence.

"This one's been here before." Lady Bryan smiled.

Mary leaned over the cradle, entranced, and touched the child's cheek—it was so soft, like velvet or a petal. And then Elizabeth gave her a gummy smile—and she was lost.

"May I hold her?" she asked.

"Go ahead," encouraged Lady Bryan, looking pleased.

Mary picked up the babe gingerly, fearing she might drop her. It came to her forcibly then that had things been otherwise, she herself could have been married now, with children of her own, and the pang of longing that gripped her was so fierce that she gasped. All her protective instincts came to the fore.

"She's beautiful," she breathed, loving the feel of the little head against her cheek. No, she would not call this tiny little person princess, but she would love her as a sister. After all, it was not Elizabeth's fault that her arrival had caused such devastation in Mary's life. She was an innocent, unaware of the passions that swirled around her.

1534

Mary's duties were not onerous. Her presence in Elizabeth's household was more or less decorative and, she was aware, meant to underline her newly inferior status. But it was her pleasure to spend time with her half-sister. As Elizabeth grew older and more knowing, she loved to play with her—and the child was always ready to be amused. But when Mary was not in the nursery, or could escape to the gardens that surrounded the palace, or walk off her sorrows beneath the majestic trees in the deer park, her unhappiness came surging back. She was convinced that Lady Shelton and her crony, Lady Clere—another aunt of the Witch—had been set to spy on her and make her life a misery.

Lady Shelton was no governess in the sense that Lady Salisbury had been. She evidently cared not a jot for her charge, seemed unaware of how despondent she was, and was always finding fault. And, as Mary refused to address Elizabeth as Princess, that was often. Once, she even slapped her for it, to Mary's shock, and often she threatened a beating.

Lying weeping in bed the night after the slap, Mary railed inwardly at how the Witch had alienated the King from his former humanity. It seemed she was doing her utmost to break Mary's resolve. How far she would go, Mary dared not think. There was no one here to taste her food, and in her wilder moments she feared she was in danger of being poisoned, remembering that Lady Salisbury had taken the threat seriously. She could not forget the Witch's warning that she would one day give her too much dinner, and she could well imagine Lady Shelton or Lady Clere being willing accomplices.

She was missing her mother dreadfully—coming to Hatfield had made their separation even more difficult to bear—but what was worse was fearing that her father would never let them meet now.

Hearing the clatter of horses' hooves and a commotion in the courtyard, Mary peered out of the nursery window, then drew back in dismay. The Witch was here!

She felt sick to her stomach; she couldn't breathe.

When Anne appeared at the door, everyone curtseyed, but Mary could not; she doubted she could even move.

"Your Grace!" Lady Shelton rose from her curtsey, and the Witch embraced her.

"Dear Aunt, I trust you are well." She turned to Mary. "My Lady Mary," she said, her smile forced. "I would speak with you, as a friend."

Mary bristled, jolted into retaliation. "Lady Anne"—she would not call her queen—"you can be no friend to me."

"But I would be," Anne said. "You have had a difficult time, and I appreciate that it has been hard for you having to assimilate the changes in your life. But all that can change for the better. I urge you, for the sake of your future happiness, to visit me at court and honor me as Queen."

"Never!" Mary spat.

"Hear me out," Anne insisted. "It would be a means of reconciliation with the King your father, who is as unhappy about your estrangement as you are. I myself will intercede with him for you, and then you will find yourself as well or better treated than ever."

Mary glared at her. "I know of no Queen in England save my mother, but if you would do me that favor with my father, I would be much obliged."

The Witch's smile vanished. "I exhort you to accept my offer, which was made out of kindness and in the interests of us all."

Mary's mettle was up; she could not help herself. "It would serve your cause well to have me on your side, Madam Boleyn! Don't think I'm so innocent that I don't understand the game you are playing. Thanks to you, I had to grow up very quickly!"

"Speak to me like that, and you could find yourself in a worse case than you are now," Anne hissed. "But accept my offer of friendship, and you shall find me zealous to protect your interests."

Mary flared. "You can protect them best by taking yourself and your bastard off to some distant land and leaving my father free of your bewitchment, so that he can return to my mother, the true Queen!"

"Do not speak to your Queen like that!" Lady Shelton cried.

Mary rounded on her. "My Queen is at Buckden!"

The Witch's voice was icy. "Trust me, I will bring down the pride of your unbridled Spanish blood," she warned. "As for having you at court, I will not now hear of it. You have made your bed, and now you must lie on it."

"Now see what you have done, you foolish girl!" Lady Shelton shrilled.

Mary shrugged. "It is labor wasted to press me, and you, Madam, are deceived if you think that ill-treatment, or even the threat of death, will make me change my determination."

"We shall see!" Anne retorted, and swept from the room.

Mary had thought that things could not get worse, but in March she was proved wrong. She knew something ominous was afoot when Sir John Shelton summoned the entire household to the great hall. Standing on the dais, pompous and self-important, he addressed them in a booming voice. "Be it known to you all that Parliament has passed an Act of Succession, which names the high and mighty Princess Elizabeth as heiress presumptive to the Crown. The Act also deems the Lady Mary, daughter to our dread sovereign lord, King Henry, to be a bastard."

Having been pushed toward the front by Lady Clere, Mary felt horribly exposed. Her cheeks were burning in humiliation. A bastard, without any rights! It was not to be borne. She was the King's only true daughter, and she would never say otherwise!

But Sir John had not finished. "The Act also requires all subjects, if commanded, to swear an oath to recognize the Princess Elizabeth as the undoubted heir to this realm, and the King's Majesty's title of Supreme Head of the Church of England. Under the new Treasons Act, anyone who refuses to take this oath will be subject to a charge of treason."

Mary felt faint. That meant that it would now be a capital crime for her to refuse to recognize the Witch as Queen and Elizabeth as the lawful inheritor of the crown.

Never! If she were to die for it, she would refuse to take the oath.

For all her resolve, Mary went about in fear. She knew she could not continue for long without the issue being forced, for she saw Elizabeth every day and the child was often referred to in conversation. Everyone else was making a point of calling her "my lady Princess." Mary gave her no title at all. They could not prosecute her for what she had not said.

But then—oh, happy day!—came the news she had been longing for all these long years.

It was Lady Bryan who broke it to her. "I have heard from my son Francis," she told Mary, as they were stowing away the nursery linen in a great oak chest. She lowered her voice. "He has sent a message from Messire Chapuys, who urges you—as he has urged your lady mother—to take the oath required by the King, under protest that you are taking it out of fear."

Chapuys had meant well. If they both did that, it could not prejudice their rights. But an oath was an oath; it had to be sincerely sworn. She did not think she could take it, even under protest, and she was sure her mother would not either.

"Why is my father doing this?" she muttered, tears filling her eyes.

"It is beyond comprehension," Lady Bryan whispered, then bent to Mary's ear. "The Pope has just ruled that his marriage to your mother is valid." She drew back. "Forget I told you, but I thought you should know."

Mary could not speak for pure joy. Her mother was vindicated at last. The Pope had declared her the King's true wife, and no one could now call Mary a bastard; it was Elizabeth, poor little thing, who was the bastard, although she was too young for it to affect her. Their father's new Act would have to be repealed!

Mary went about on wings that day. Soon would come the summons to court, the return to all that was dear, loved, and familiar. The Witch would be sent away, pensioned off, no doubt, to live out her life in wealthy obscurity as Lady Marquess of Pembroke. And Mother would resume her rightful place as Queen and be reconciled to Father. Exulting, Mary took herself off to the chapel and thanked God for guiding the Pope to the right decision.

Her euphoria did not last long. It was soon clear that no one else was expecting any changes to be made. Elizabeth was still deferred to as a princess, while Mary was treated as her servant. No one addressed her by her rightful title. And as the days went by and her spirits sank ever lower, she realized that there would be no summons to court and that nothing would change.

In fact, the passing of the Act of Succession had made her situation much worse. When she made it plain that even the implicit threat in it would not move her to recognize the Witch as Queen and Elizabeth as the heir, Lady Shelton's treatment of her became harsher, and she seemed to take pleasure in being unkind.

"The King your father thinks you are his worst enemy," she spat, after Mary had again referred to the Witch as the Lady Anne.

"What else should I call her?" Mary retorted, and was shocked when Lady Shelton angrily took her by the shoulders and shook her.

"The Queen's Grace!" she hissed, and pushed her away.

When Lady Bryan found Mary weeping in the nursery afterward, and Mary blurted out what had happened, the old woman patted her shoulder. "She fears for her own neck, which is why she appears so cruel. She told me that the King sent to command her to say that you are his worst enemy. He thinks to bring you to submission that way."

"Well, he won't!" Mary cried.

"Dear child, you are far too headstrong for your own good. Your defiance puts you in a dangerous position. Do attempt to moderate your behavior. You would do well to try to get on with Lady Shelton. She is in the most difficult position. I have seen her reduced to tears just thinking of the consequences of any lack of vigilance on her part."

"Yes, but those tears were for herself, not for me," Mary retorted.

The strain under which she was living and the hostility surrounding her were too much for her. That spring, she fell seriously ill.

"I feel really unwell," she muttered, when Lady Shelton came to find out why she was late for her duties and found her languishing in bed.

"What ails you?" she rapped, betraying no hint of sympathy.

"I am aching all over and I can't stop shaking—and I've been sick." Tears came to Mary's eyes.

"Then you'd better stay here. We can't have the Princess catching it. And I hope, for everyone's sake, that you will die."

It was as if she had slapped Mary, who was so shocked that she fell into a paroxysm of weeping. What had she ever done to deserve such suffering and such enmity? It was all down to the pernicious influence of the vile Boleyns.

And yet, someone must have informed her father of her illness, because Dr. Butts, one of his best physicians, arrived from court soon afterward to see her, and—to her amazement, her mother's doctor, Dr. de la Saa, was with him. He was never left alone with her, however, and had obviously been given orders not to mention the Queen.

"How is my mother?" she asked weakly, as he examined her urine.

"Rest now," he said, but he smiled at her reassuringly, which she took to mean that Mother was well and in good spirits.

The doctors conferred together. Surely they must know what ailed her, she thought. Even she knew it was nothing that could not be cured by being restored to the company of those she loved. But they diagnosed an imbalance of the humors—meaning, she concluded bitterly, that they preferred not to say what really ailed her.

Nevertheless, she rallied. From their sour demeanor, she guessed that Lady Shelton and Lady Clere were disappointed that she had not died. And when they returned from the market one day, sought her out in the still room, and pressed into her hand some pills they said they had bought from an apothecary, Mary was convinced that they were trying to poison her, and stared at them fearfully.

"Don't look like that!" Lady Shelton snapped. "They're supposed to build you up. Really, Alice, my kindness is wasted on this girl. Such ingratitude!" She turned from Lady Clere to Mary. "If I were in the King's place, I would kick you out of my house for your disobedience! Of course, *he* might go much further than that. Only yesterday, I hear, he threatened to have you beheaded for disobeying the laws of the realm."

"You lie!" cried Mary, remembering what Lady Bryan had said, and understanding where this had come from. "My father would never do that. He loves me, but he has been led astray by a she-devil!"

"Well!" breathed Lady Clere. "Now we see plainly her malice!"

A flush of pure rage suffused Lady Shelton's face, and she opened her mouth to protest, but Mary was stiff in her resolve to stand up for her rights. "I care not for your cruelties. Whatever you do, I will not be overcome. Remember that!" And she stalked away, leaving them gaping.

She sought refuge in the nursery. Alone in the household, Lady Bryan had been kind to her, but her priority was to care for Elizabeth, and she had clearly had her orders.

Elizabeth had to take precedence over Mary in everything. When Mary again referred to the baby as her sister, Lady Bryan laid a hand on her arm. "You must call her my lady Princess," she admonished.

"That I will never do," Mary declared.

The old woman's face showed concern. "Dear child, it would be unwise to disobey the King's commands. You could find yourself in the worst kind of trouble—worse than you are now. And you should not, for the world, set yourself up in opposition to Queen Anne. Be warned: everything you do and say is reported back."

"I care not!" Mary was defiant, but inwardly she trembled with fear. How far would the Witch go? If only her father would remember that she, Mary, was his daughter and be in remembrance of the love he had had for her, which she was convinced was still in him, if stifled by his passion for that evil woman. But would that love be proof against the Witch's menace?

"Take care, Mary," Lady Bryan urged, shaking her head, and walked off to find the wet nurse, for Elizabeth was grizzling in her cradle.

That afternoon, Lady Shelton found Mary in the garden, where she had retreated with a book. "Aren't you on duty?" she asked.

"Lady Bryan doesn't need me until later," Mary told her, expecting a scolding. But, to her surprise, Lady Shelton sat down beside her and her manner seemed somewhat different.

"Mary," she said, "I need to talk to you, and I am glad to find you here where we cannot be overheard. You have to listen to what I'm about to say, because I can only do so much for you."

Mary stared at her. It amazed her to find that the cold and carping Lady Shelton had a heart after all.

"I know you think me unkind," the older woman said, "but I am in a difficult position and I have my orders. The Queen is determined that you will do as the King requires of you and acknowledge Elizabeth as Princess. Today—and I will be honest with you—I have received a letter from her Grace, commanding that if you resist, I am to give you a good beating."

Such venom! Mary's heart thudded alarmingly.

Lady Shelton regarded her, tight-faced. "I am reluctant to obey such orders. My niece was ever prone to extremes, and she can be unkind when crossed. But I do not wish to be thought cruel. You are a good girl, Mary, and have had much to contend with. I want you to know that, if it is in my power, I will do my best to protect you from the malice of others, even if it seems to you that I am doing the opposite. And to show that I am in earnest, I want you to have this." She handed Mary an unmarked packet. "Open it."

Mary did so and saw, to her joy, her mother's familiar handwriting. "But how?" she asked.

Lady Shelton was actually smiling. "It was sent by Messire

Chapuys under cover of a letter to Lady Bryan from her son, Sir Francis Bryan, who is no friend to the Queen. I am risking my position to give it to you, remember that."

"I cannot thank you enough," Mary faltered. "I never thought . . ."

"No, and others must not suspect. Now I will leave you to read your letter. Keep it well hidden. Better still, burn it."

Alone again, Mary hungrily devoured her mother's words. She was well, she had written, and she remained stout in her determination to stand up for their rights. It was a heartening letter, intended to reassure Mary and let her know that she was constantly in the Queen's thoughts and prayers. *Whatever tribulations you suffer, Daughter, offer them up as sacrifices to God, and stay staunch in your convictions. He fits the back to the burden, and He will never test you beyond what you can endure.*

Mary wept at that, but when she had dried her tears, she felt better than she had in ages. Her mother loved her, God was watching over her, and Lady Shelton was really her friend. She walked back to the palace with a spring in her step.

It occurred to her that escape might be her best means of helping her mother. If she could get away from Hatfield and reach a port, she could take ship to the Emperor's dominions, where she would be in a strong position to fight for her rights. Charles would support her, she had no doubt of that. She did not want him to make war on her father—Heaven forbid!—but the threat of it might make him see sense and accept the Pope's judgment.

It seemed a daunting prospect. She could think of various ways to escape from Hatfield but had no idea how to travel to the coast, which was a long way off. She had no money, and a woman taking to the road alone was putting herself in danger. Perhaps Messire Chapuys would help her?

First, though, she must find out what her mother thought of the plan. She wrote a short letter, sealed it, and asked Lady Bryan if she would send it to her son to give to Chapuys. He had the means of sending it on to the Queen.

* * *

The palace of Hatfield was thrown into a flurry of activity when word came that the King was coming to visit the Princess. Mary's heart leaped. She was convinced that, given the chance to meet face-to-face, she could make him understand how unhappy she was, and all would be well again between them. No matter that Lady Shelton had ordered her to keep to her room during his visit. Disobedience had become a habit with her, and nothing was going to prevent her from seeing her father.

But he did not arrive. All morning, dressed up in their finery, the household waited, until Elizabeth, swathed in cloth of gold, was bawling her head off in her cradle of estate.

Her cries were making Mary's head ache. Tense at the thought of confrontations to come when she emerged defiantly from her room, and in dread at the prospect of the meeting with her father, she was trembling.

"He won't come now. We'll have to feed her." Lady Bryan sighed, lifting the baby.

"He could still arrive," Mary said wistfully.

Lady Bryan gave her a sharp look. "No. He's left it too late to get back to court afterward." Soon Mary realized, with a sinking heart, that she was right.

Later that week, with Elizabeth down for her afternoon nap and the nursery quiet, Mary sat with Lady Bryan, embroidering caps for their charge. "I wonder why my father did not come," she said.

"I know why. I've heard again from Francis. It seems the Queen does not wish his Grace to see you, and becomes very angry when he says he will do so. Francis says her rages are terrible, and because she is with child again, the King does his best to placate her."

With child? Mary had not known that, and her blood turned to ice. What if the Witch bore a son this time?

"Francis told me that when his Grace left court to come here this week, her Grace sent Master Cromwell after him, to dissuade him from seeing you."

Mary smiled. So the Witch too knew that if Father but met with her, his love for her would overcome all the unpleasantness that had lain between them. No wonder she was worried! And when, a few days later, it was announced once more that he was coming to Hatfield, Mary was convinced that he was determined to see her.

But Lady Shelton had had her orders, and Mary, protesting loudly, was locked in an attic room beneath the eaves of the palace, long before the King's arrival. It was hot, and dust and cobwebs coated the few items of old furniture that were piled up in a corner. But there was a little balcony outside the window, which overlooked the courtyard. The double doors were locked, but the lock was rusty, and Mary reckoned that if she could break it, she might be able to stand on the balcony and call down to greet her father when he arrived. And then he would surely demand to see her!

Rattling the lock, she was dismayed to find that it was seemingly stuck fast. She needed a file or a knife to work away at it, but she had nothing with her except the book Lady Shelton had permitted her. She began searching the attic for anything that might prove serviceable, even a loose nail on a floorboard. There was nothing. Then she spied an old chest in a corner, half concealed under the rafters. She pulled it out and opened it.

The first thing she saw made her pause in her search. It was a small framed portrait of her mother, which obviously no one had wanted to keep on display. At the sight of those beloved features, painted in happier times, a lump came to her throat, and she kissed the dear, familiar face, wishing it was the real thing.

But she could not go on gazing at it forever. Her father might arrive at any time. She would come back for the portrait later and hide it in her room, so she could look at it whenever she wanted. She set it aside carefully and began rummaging farther in the chest, but then heard the sound of trumpets and dashed to the window, catching her breath as she saw her father dismount and enter the house, his face hidden by his plumed bonnet. She was too late! Her only chance now of attracting his attention would be when he left. She must prise that door open!

She threw herself on her knees by the chest, flinging out old papers, musty garments and broken toys, and there—God be praised— lying at the bottom was an old hunting knife, its bone handle cracked. It was blunt, but it would serve.

She worked away at the lock for what seemed like ages, until it finally gave way. She left the window open a little, so that she would hear any activity below, and tried in vain to read.

It must have been late afternoon when the sound of men's voices and horses' hooves broke the silence. In an instant, she was out on the balcony—and there, below, was Father, mounting his horse and, by a miracle, looking up at her, his handsome face flushed with an emotion she could not decipher. She fell to her knees, raising her hands in supplication, with tears streaming down her cheeks. Visibly moved, he bowed in the saddle and touched his bonnet, at which all the members of his retinue followed suit; then he rode away without looking back.

Mary tried to swallow her bitter disappointment that he had not tarried to speak to her. Of course, he would not dare to upset the Witch, not when she was soon to bear him a child. She comforted herself with the knowledge that when Anne heard about the incident, as she surely would, she would be enraged.

When Lady Shelton came to let her out, she was in a foul mood. "Well, that was a pretty little charade!" she said caustically. "Pity it was all for nothing."

Mary ignored her, because Lady Clere was just behind her, and when they were together, they were particularly vicious in their taunts. But later that evening, Lady Shelton came alone to Mary's chamber.

"I am sorry about earlier," she said, keeping her voice low. "I had my orders. You know that it's more than my life's worth to disobey them. Already, I've gone too far." She hesitated, then leaned to Mary's ear. "There are spies in this household. Everything that happens here is known at court. Someone discovered, or guessed, that I tried to mitigate the unkindness directed at you, and before I knew it, I was being reprimanded by the Duke of Norfolk and Lord Rochford, the Queen's brother, for treating you with too much respect and kindness, instead of heaping on you the abuse deserved by a bastard."

"Oh, no," Mary faltered. "But how did they know?"

"I think they guessed, when I refused to beat you that time. But I stood up for myself, and you. I told them that, whatever your status, you deserved honor and good treatment for your goodness and virtues."

"I thank you for that," Mary said, touched again at such unexpected kindness from this outwardly hard woman. It proved that one should never take people at face value.

"It made no difference, mind," Lady Shelton sighed, "and I shall have to be more diligent, and perhaps more strict, in future. But you know my true mind. Now I must go. No one must know I was here."

Heartened by her support, Mary continued to stand by her rights as a princess and as the heir. When next there were visitors from court, Lady Shelton locked her into a room from which there was no escape, for she had nailed the windows shut with her own hands.

"It's to protect you from yourself!" she barked. "You're far too outspoken for your own good, and there are those who would report you without a second thought."

Mary endured her confinement with poor grace. She wanted to tell the world how badly she had been treated! When she escaped, they would all know! But how was it to be achieved? She longed to receive word from her mother.

When the visitors had gone and Lady Shelton unlocked the door, she pressed a letter into Mary's hand.

"Say nothing," she murmured.

Back in her room, Mary saw that it was from her mother, and her heart soared. But the Queen's tone was stern. She utterly forbade Mary even to contemplate escaping from England. She was to obey her father in all things save those that touched her conscience.

Mary sank dejectedly to the floor and wept. Now even this last resort was closed to her. And she had invested all her hopes in it. At times like these, she wished that her mother was not quite so saintly.

Chapter 8

1534

In July, Mary carried Elizabeth into the flower garden and sat her down on a quilt on the lawn. The child was ten months old and her inquisitive hands were everywhere. Now she was stuffing daisies into her mouth. Mary knelt and pulled them out, preempting her outrage by making her a daisy chain. Then Lady Bryan appeared.

"My Lady Mary, the Earl of Wiltshire is here and waiting to see you in the hall. I'll take over here."

Mary bristled. What did the Witch's father want with her? Was it to be more bullying? Smoothing her skirts, she walked at a stately pace into the palace, head high and every inch the Princess.

In the hall, she found the Earl and several other lords, with Lady Shelton present, too.

"My lord of Wiltshire," Mary said, and fixed her gaze on him until he made a sketchy bow.

"My Lady Mary," he said, "I have been sent to administer the oath to the Act of Succession, which you are to swear as required by law."

Mary's heart missed a beat as she realized she had made her decision. She was going to defy her father. There was no other course she could take. She felt sick, but she would not let any of them see it. She took a deep breath.

"I am the King's true daughter and his lawful heir," she declared, "and the Pope was appointed by Christ Himself as head of the Church. It is impossible for me to take this oath."

Before anyone could speak, Lady Shelton began shaking her violently. "If I were the King," she cried, "I would make you lose your head for your defiance!"

Mary struggled free. "It is not defiance—I am standing up for what is right—"

"Enough of your sedition!" Wiltshire interrupted. "Leave her be, good Sister. She is beyond reasoning. Let her go to perdition in her own way. Now I must take his Grace and the Queen her answer, and I can tell you now that they will not be pleased."

"Go to your room!" Lady Shelton hissed.

Mary ran upstairs as fast as her trembling legs could carry her. Slamming the door behind her, she took deep breaths until her heart had stilled. She had gone beyond the point of no return now and broken the law. She shuddered in terror to think of what her punishment might be. But she had stood her ground and not given way to fear. Her grandmother, Isabella, would have been proud of her.

She wondered how much more of this pressure she could take. Thinking of Isabella made her recall Queen Juana and the madness that tainted the Castilian royal house. Could madness be brought on by suffering? Was that what they were trying to do to her, drive her insane?

She waited in unbearable tension for the wrath of her father to descend on her. All that came was an order from the Witch, conveyed by Lady Shelton.

"She demands that I administer a good banging to you for the cursed bastard you are—her words, not mine," she told Mary, having drawn her into a window embrasure away from the nursery staff, on the pretense of administering a reprimand for some imagined transgression. "I shall do no such thing," she murmured. "And don't do it again!" she added loudly.

"Is that all the punishment I am to suffer?" Mary whispered.

"I can't say anything now," Lady Shelton muttered. "Later."

At suppertime, Lady Shelton mentioned that she might walk in the garden afterward. "The nights are drawing in and it may be my last chance to enjoy the dusk," she said.

"It's too cold for my old bones," said Lady Bryan, and the maids all nodded. They were full of plans for the celebration of Elizabeth's first birthday and were eager to decorate the nursery.

Mary said nothing. She had got the message. After the cloth had been lifted, she donned her cloak, made her way down the privy stair to the flower garden, now sadly denuded of its blooms, and strolled along the gravel paths. Lady Shelton was waiting for her in a shaded arbor.

"We must be brief," she warned. "I just wanted you to know that her Grace is not to have a child after all."

"She has lost it?"

"It was a son, born dead. Everyone has been sworn to secrecy. As you can imagine, the King is not pleased."

Mary had the feeling that Lady Shelton could have said more, but had thought it better to stay silent. After all, Anne was her niece and there was clearly some loyalty there.

"Is this why he has not punished me?"

"I think he has other things on his mind. And some say he fears the Emperor."

Yes, that made sense. While Father thought there was a threat of reprisals from her cousin Charles, she was safe—Mother, too. And, Mary thought, as she walked back alone to the palace, if Anne was out of favor—which she prayed she was in the wake of losing her son—then it was less likely that Father would heed her demands that he proceed unkindly against his daughter.

Before too many days had passed, she realized that she had been correct in her assumption. The Witch's influence seemed to be diminishing. Mary was astonished when Henry Pole, Lady Exeter, and other courtiers she had known in happier times turned up at Hatfield to see her, having no doubt realized it was safe to do so. She received them warmly, understanding that they had not slighted her of their own volition. It was good to see how pleased they were to see her.

Then came a letter from the Witch herself, telling her to be of good cheer for her troubles would soon be at an end. Mary did not quite know how to take it. Was it a warning that she would soon be dead? Or a threat? She thought not. Instead, she concluded that the woman had guessed she might one day be in need of Mary's clemency, given the insecurity of her own position. Well, she could look elsewhere for support!

Mary was feeling better, buoyed up by these recent developments and almost certain that her father would soon extend an olive branch to her. But then, in November, came news of the passing of the Act of Supremacy, enshrining in law his title of Supreme Head of the Church of England. Mary was shocked to realize that the Act marked the final severance of the English Church from the Roman Catholic Church. No more would the Pope—or the Bishop of Rome, as the King's true subjects were now supposed to call him—wield authority in England. It was momentous—and it was appalling. She could not sleep at night for agonizing about it.

She saw that England now lay isolated from the rest of Christendom. Heaven knew how the princes of Europe would react. Most were devoutly loyal to the Pope and would regard her father as a schismatic. He could only hope for friendship from the Protestant princes of Germany—he, who would have no truck with heretics, as he had often declared. But now, in the eyes of many, he was one himself. Mary trembled when she thought of him endangering his immortal soul—and those of his subjects, including her.

She was glad she had refused to take the oath. Hearing that, his Holiness and the Emperor would know her for a true daughter of the rightful Church—the only Church! How she wished she could put the clock back and have things as they were when she was a child and all was good and happy in her world. Truly, God was testing her—as so many others would now be tested, too.

1535

Christmas had been miserable. Mary had felt so weighed down by the implications of the Act, so fearful for the future, and so unhappy at spending the festival far from those she loved that she could take no pleasure in it. As had happened the year before, her low spirits made her ill. What began as a cold rapidly turned into a fever with a hacking cough, and soon there was so much phlegm on her chest that she felt as if she was suffocating. The household physicians hovered around her bed looking worried, and Lady Shelton stood there wringing her hands, not bothering to hide the anxiety she felt. It dawned on Mary that they all feared she would die.

"We are sending word to the King that you are unwell," the governess told her, as soon as the doctors had departed. "I am sure he will send his own physician to you, as before."

"If only I could have my mother with me," Mary sobbed. "A little comfort and mirth with her is all I need to get better." She envisaged the Queen caring for her with her own hands, as she had done when she was little, and watching over her when she slept. "Please beseech his Grace to send her to me! I swear I will not intrigue with her against him, if that is what he fears."

Lady Shelton looked doubtful. "I will ask, but I doubt he will agree."

"I pray he will!" Mary breathed, feeling again that horrible congestion in her chest. But no word came from the court. As her nineteenth birthday passed unmarked and February gave way to March, she felt herself going downhill and feared the worst, but then, surprisingly, she rallied, and by April, was able to rejoin Elizabeth's household, which had moved to Eltham during her illness.

In the summer, Mary was appalled to hear that Bishop Fisher and Sir Thomas More had been executed for refusing to take the oath. Sir Thomas, it was whispered, had been convicted on perjured evidence. Those upright, good men . . . It did not bear thinking about. And if they, whom Father had once loved and respected, could be condemned to a brutal death, where next would the axe fall?

They were not the only ones to suffer. She felt sick when she heard of the three Carthusian monks who had been hanged, drawn and quartered for denying the royal supremacy. Not even their tonsures had saved them. And she herself had also refused the oath! On her knees, she prayed that God would give her the strength to face with courage whatever fate was in store for her.

* * *

Chapuys managed to smuggle another message to Mary that summer. He told her to be of good cheer, for the Emperor was her friend.
The Lady—as he called the Witch—was widely hated and people
were looking to Mary as the rightful heir. Elizabeth was not yet two,
and if anything should happen to the King, she, Mary, would have a
strong chance of holding the throne. Even Cromwell—who had been
the Witch's mainstay—was now showing himself secretly supportive of Mary and had discussed with Chapuys the possibility of altering the Act of Succession with a view to naming her the King's heir.
Somehow, Anne had got to hear of this and threatened Cromwell
with execution, but he had paid her little heed. *He says she cannot
harm him now,* Chapuys wrote.

It seemed that Anne's star was falling. She had not borne Father
the son he badly wanted, and she had evidently alienated many of
her supporters. Mary began to hope that the King would realize he
had made a catastrophic mistake in marrying her, and put her away.
Then, he would surely feel obliged to recall Mother, and Mary would
be the heir once more. Together, they would persuade the King that
a queen could rule successfully, as Isabella once had. A bright future
suddenly seemed within Mary's grasp.

There was more good news in the autumn. She read Chapuys's letter as she sat in the garden, enjoying the mellow sunshine of the
season. The Emperor, who had been fighting the Turks, had won a
great victory and beaten them off the eastern reaches of the Empire.
The King and the Lady Anne, the ambassador reported, had looked
like dogs falling out of a window, so dismayed were they by the
news, for Charles was now free to make war on England on behalf of
Mother and herself. Father must be very worried. He must know
that he was regarded by most of Christendom as a schismatic rebel,
and that this would justify Charles's intervention.

That month, Mary had proof of the people's love for her. She had
been staying with Elizabeth at Greenwich Palace, and when they
left, there were crowds of women outside the gatehouse. As she rode
by, they surged around her, weeping and crying out that she was the
true Princess. Stunned, she did not know whether to smile and bow,
for it might be dangerous to encourage them; and yet such loyalty
could not go unacknowledged. But the King's guards were on the

scene almost immediately and rounded them up. To her astonishment, Mary recognized the Witch's sister-in-law, Lady Rochford, being dragged away protesting. Well! That was a sign of the way the wind was blowing.

It was not surprising, she reflected, as the procession resumed its journey, that Lady Rochford had been alienated from Anne. Her father, Lord Morley, had long been a friend of Mary. He had spent some years in the household of her great-grandmother, the Lady Margaret Beaufort, and become friends with Bishop Fisher, who had been her chaplain. Fisher's execution might well have sparked this change of heart in Lady Rochford.

In November, Mary learned that she had more influential friends when there arrived a letter from Sir Francis Bryan, assuring her that he and others were working secretly on her behalf. She was not sure what he meant by that, but she was hoping against hope that they were putting pressure on Father to restore her to the succession. It was heartening to know she had good friends, yet what she read next chilled her to the marrow. She must take the greatest care, Bryan warned. *The King your father has told his Council that he will no longer remain in fear and suspicion of your Highness and your lady mother inciting the Emperor to invade. He has insisted that proceedings be taken against you both in the next session of Parliament, or he will not wait any longer to provide for a resolution himself. When he saw his councillors looking shocked, he said that even if he were to lose his crown for it, he would do what he had set out to do. Be assured that Messire Chapuys has reported this to the Emperor and informed him that the Lady has for some time been conspiring the deaths of your mother and yourself. But his Imperial Majesty thinks that these threats are designed only to frighten you. If you find yourself in real danger, he says that you must yield to the King's will and take the oath. Yet he cannot credit that the King would be so unnatural as to put to death his own wife and daughter, even if he has treated you horribly. I am inclined to agree. I do not think his Grace would go so far, but the Lady would, for she manages and orders and governs everything, and the King does not dare to oppose her. So I urge your Highness to be on your guard.*

Tears blurred the rest of the letter. Mary could not believe that her father would be so cruel as even to contemplate executing her and Mother. Sinking down by the bed, she wept for hours until Lady

Shelton came to find her, and she was so distressed that she blurted out everything.

Lady Shelton frowned, and Mary realized that she had put her in a very difficult position. At length, she laid a hand on Mary's shoulder. "I agree with Sir Francis. I think these are idle threats. Anne is vulnerable, and she knows it. She has many enemies, and it may be that the King is tiring of her. She is inclined to lash out when she feels under threat. I do not think you should worry. But I warn you: you must cease all communication with Sir Francis Bryan. This is not the time to risk angering the King. And I would be in terrible trouble if you were discovered."

"I will not reply to him," Mary promised, grateful that Lady Shelton had not asked her not to communicate with Chapuys. She had a feeling that she was going to need his support in the weeks to come.

That feeling was reinforced when, in December, Elizabeth's household rejoiced at the news that the Witch was again with child. Mary found it hard even to smile, so worried was she about what this might portend for her. With the interests of her unborn son to protect, Anne would be like a lioness, bent on removing all threats to his safety and his right to the succession. And Mary would be seen as the greatest theat. She prayed that her father would be strong enough to withstand the Witch's demands. But what if she did bear a son?

Daily, Mary went in fear that she would be asked again to take the oath. Whatever the consequences, she must refuse. Never would she acknowledge, for any kingdom on earth, that her parents had lived for so long in adultery, nor would she contravene the Pope's judgment and declare herself a bastard. Her chief fear was not for herself, though, but for her mother. What was the strain of all this fear and misery doing to her? How was she facing a lonely Christmas isolated at Kimbolton Castle in the Fens, where she had been sent recently? Had her jailers been ordered to ill-treat her? Not knowing was agony for Mary. She longed to be with the Queen, to lay her head on that dear bosom and be comforted.

Chapter 9

1536

T he new year was just over a week old when Lady Shelton came into the nursery.

"My Lady Mary, a word, please."

Mary followed her into the gallery. Lady Clere was chatting to some of the maids a few feet away. Lady Shelton glanced at her and turned back to Mary. "Your mother is dead," she said.

Mary reeled at her words. There was a rushing in her ears and she felt faint. "No," she said. "No! She cannot be." She gripped the door handle to steady herself.

"I'm afraid it's true. She died three days ago."

"But she wasn't ill!"

"She had been ailing for some time, apparently." Lady Shelton kept looking in the direction of Alice Clere. "You may go to your room and stay there until you have recovered yourself."

Mary stumbled away, tears blinding her. She could not believe it. Her beloved mother—dead! Gone from this world. All her sufferings had been for this. It was beyond tragic. It was as if the sun had fallen out of the sky and she was adrift in a black void of grief. How would she bear it?

She did not go to her room, but made her way to the chapel, her head teeming with questions as she struggled to make sense of the news. Why had no one told her that the Queen was sick? She would have been better prepared, had she known. Or was it another of the Witch's cruelties, to keep her in the dark so that the shock would be greater?

Kneeling before the altar, trying to pray for her mother's soul—which was surely in Heaven for she had been a veritable saint on earth—Mary's suspicions deepened. Had the good Queen's end been hastened? Had she been given too much dinner, as Anne had once threatened to do to Mary? Mary longed to ask Chapuys what he knew, and if he shared her suspicions, but did not dare to write to him. It wasn't fair to Lady Bryan to keep asking her to defy the King's orders. But, oh, how she longed for a letter, for the comfort of knowing that Chapuys understood her sorrow.

Time seemed to have been suspended. How long she knelt there praying, she had no idea, and it was dark by the time she returned to the nursery. Two-year-old Elizabeth was throwing a tantrum, refusing to eat her supper; she had a temper to match her red hair. Lady Bryan just ignored her and took the food away. "There's nothing else, my lady Princess," she said. "Take it or leave it—"

She broke off when she saw Mary, and put an arm around her. "Are you all right, child?"

"I will never be all right again," Mary answered, feeling very strange, and hoping that she was not going to be as ill as she had been at this time last year, or the year before. She swayed, and would have fallen had not Lady Bryan dropped the dish of untouched food and caught her. "Bed for you, my lady," she said firmly.

Mary was glad to obey. All she wanted was the oblivion of sleep, to obliterate this terrible grief.

By evening, she was burning up and delirious. Lady Shelton sat with her, cooling her forehead with a damp cloth. Through a haze of unreality, Mary heard the doctor saying that she was in the hands of God now, but it meant little to her. Then Lady Clere's voice. "'Twere better if she died now. I don't know why you're wasting your time tending to her."

"It's my Christian duty," Lady Shelton replied. "Remember that I am answerable to the King."

"And the Queen!" Lady Clere chimed in. But Mary was drifting off again and heard no more.

It was a fortnight before she began to feel better—in body, but not in any other way. Her soul was in torment. Her mother, the lodestar of her life, was gone, and she had died alone, when she should have been surrounded and supported by those who loved her. Mary did not know how she would live without her, how she would ever come to terms with the fact that she would never see her again in this life—when that prospect had been the focus of her hopes and prayers. With her father in thrall to the Witch, the woman who had destroyed Mother's life—and her own—she might as well be an orphan.

Give her her due, Lady Shelton tried to rally her spirits, offering to play cards with her of an evening, or games of riddles. Lady Bryan made her warmly welcome in the nursery and ensured that she spent plenty of time with Elizabeth, whose imperious antics were enough to divert anyone. Mary made an effort. It was as if she was living on two planes: one where she was engulfed in grief; the other a normal life, in which she chatted and even laughed.

In the last week of January, a letter arrived for her bearing the Witch's seal. Outwardly, it was another olive branch, an invitation to court, where she would be exempt from carrying the Queen's train and would always walk by her side. But only if she submitted to her father's laws. Mary read it, seething. Never would she dishonor her mother's memory by accepting such an offer: there could now be no question of a reconciliation with Anne Boleyn. On the contrary, she was resolved to take up the cause her mother had been forced to lay down and carry on the fight to restore herself to her rightful place in the succession.

At the beginning of February, Lady Bryan slipped another letter from Messire Chapuys into Mary's hand. When she read it, her heart leaped. At last, at last, her father appeared to be coming to his senses, for on the day of Queen Katherine's funeral in Peterborough Abbey, the ambassador had seen him paying marked attention to Mistress Seymour and giving her costly presents. Jane Seymour! Of all the ladies on whom his eye could have alighted, it seemed providential that he was pursuing her. For Jane had been Mary's friend. How strong that friendship would prove had yet to be demonstrated, and this amor might go nowhere, but Mary was hoping and praying that it would flower, and that Jane would prevail on her father to be kind to her.

Then she turned the page and read on, her eyes widening. The Lady, Chapuys reported, had aborted a fetus of about fifteen weeks' growth that had all the appearance of a male. "She has miscarried of her savior," he wrote, adding that the King was deeply disappointed and angry. Mary could not but perceive the hand of God in this. Surely Father would now see that he had made a terrible mistake in marrying the Witch?

Days passed, and then weeks, and there were no more demands for Mary to acknowledge the Witch as queen and Elizabeth as the heir. Suddenly, everyone was being nicer to her, even Lady Clere. She hardly dared hope that the King had had a change of heart, but when, to her utter joy and astonishment, he sent her a goodly sum of money for her pleasures, the future suddenly began to look a lot brighter. She could see herself being recalled to court and reunited with him; Anne, of course, would be sent away to live in the kind of obscurity inflicted on poor Mother, and Elizabeth would be well provided for, just as Henry Fitzroy had been. Mary did not want to see her half-sister suffer.

The Witch, she suspected, was becoming desperate, and no wonder, for she had failed to give the King a son and had clearly alienated many who had supported her. Again, she wrote to Mary, and there was no doubt that this time she was trying to extend the hand of friendship without conditions. If Mary would come to court, she promised she would be like another mother to her at this sad time. Mary tore up the letter. How could such a woman ever take her mother's place, after she had supplanted her and hounded her to her death?

"Tell the Lady Anne," she told the waiting messenger, "that to agree to her request would conflict with my honor and my conscience."

Lady Shelton, who had been standing nearby, suddenly burst into tears. "I beg of you, my Lady Mary, to consider your position carefully."

"I have considered!" Mary retorted. "She can never be my friend. I can never forgive her for what she has done to my lady mother and me."

Lady Shelton would not desist. Repeatedly, she urged Mary to accept Anne's offer. But Mary stood firm, especially after she went to fetch some embroidery silks from the governess's room and came across a letter written by Anne to Lady Shelton, in which she admitted that what she had done had been more for charity than because she or the King cared what course Mary took.

She did not blame Lady Shelton for trying. It seemed that the woman genuinely believed that Mary would be better off at court. But Mary guessed that, in the wake of Anne's miscarriage, Lady Shelton was taking stock of her own position and thinking of the future; for if her niece fell from favor, Mary might well be restored to it.

Mary was delighted when she began to receive visits from Chapuys's servant, who brought her the latest news from court.

"I am amazed that you are allowed to come," she told the man. "It is against the King's orders."

"My master pays your governess," he told her.

So Lady Shelton was taking bribes from Chapuys, in return for allowing his servant to visit Mary. It soon became clear that the ambassador was writing to Lady Shelton herself, for she passed on to Mary the welcome news that the King was thinking of taking another wife. Mary prayed it would be Jane Seymour. Of course, some way would have to be found to get rid of the Witch—but that might not prove difficult, for she was not, in truth, Father's wife.

Despite these encouraging developments, Mary was edgy and frustrated, and plagued by her old ailments. And she was deeply disturbed by a letter in which Chapuys expressed his suspicions that her mother had been poisoned. He related how the postmortem had revealed a heart black and hideous with a growth on the outside, and said that the Queen's physician had confided that there could be no doubt as to the cause of her death. Chapuys believed that a slow and subtle poison had been mixed with a draught of Welsh beer and given to the Queen just before her final decline. He was convinced that she had been murdered through the malign efforts of that she-devil, and that Mary would be targeted next. Already, he had asked the Emperor to approve a plan to spirit her abroad to the safety of the Imperial dominions.

Mary's blood turned to ice as she read the letter. There was no doubt in her mind that the doctor was right. Hatred for the Witch welled up in her, hotter than ever before. She would not stay in England to be murdered as her mother had been. Cornered, and in fear for her future and Elizabeth's, Anne would be dangerous.

Secretly, she began to stow away her belongings, little by little, in a sack she kept under her bed. She could not take much with her, just enough for the journey, but the Emperor would provide what was lacking. It would be wonderful to be treated once more as the rightful heiress to England.

Impatiently, and not a little fearfully, she waited for news. When it came, she read Chapuys's letter in disbelief. Charles had dismissed the plan. If Mary went into voluntary exile, it might be seen as tantamount to relinquishing her rights. Despite her crushing disappointment, she knew he was right. And Chapuys was reassuring.

You must not worry about the Lady, he had written. *Your Highness has the sympathy and support of your Plantagenet relations, the Seymours, the Bryans, and all who wish to see you restored to the succession. Those who oppose the Lady are placing all their hopes in you. The King is much enamored of Mistress Seymour, who is your friend and a true Imperialist. I have no doubt that she will make an excellent Queen of England. Master Cromwell has for some time been advocating the renewal of England's friendship with the Emperor, and a new alliance can only benefit your cause. I shall do all in my power to persuade the King to acknowledge your legitimacy.*

Tears welled in Mary's eyes. She had a true and staunch friend in Chapuys; she had always known it. He had never failed her. She would have given much to be able to see and speak with him and to thank him for his kindness. If only she could one day have a husband like him! She had never met a man she liked better.

As her twentieth birthday approached, she could not help wondering if she would ever be married at all. It seemed unlikely while she was tainted with bastardy, and she could not take a husband who was of meaner rank—her pride would never allow it. So while her heart might weave fantasies about Chapuys, her head told her that it could never be, and she did not dwell on it. Besides, it was five years since she had seen him, and she had grown up a lot in that time.

In March, Mary learned from Chapuys that the Emperor had instructed him to negotiate an alliance with her father. With war breaking out between Spain and France, Charles needed a new ally. Mary rejoiced to hear this, for it meant that the Witch's days as queen were probably numbered, as her cousin would surely make Mary's restitution a condition of any treaty of friendship. *Your friends here,* the ambassador wrote, *are working for the dissolution of the King's union with the Lady, which would facilitate your restoration to the succession. The Emperor has instructed me to press for that.*

Mary could feel a burgeoning excitement in her breast. If only her sainted mother could be here to see how the world was righting itself, and how she had been vindicated. It was tragic that she had died too soon. But surely she was smiling down from Heaven in the knowledge that her tribulations had not been in vain.

If Lady Shelton was aware of what was going on, she said nothing. Privately, she showed friendship to Mary; outwardly, she was loyal to her niece. But blood, Mary learned in April, was thicker than water.

"The Imperial ambassador has finally acknowledged the Queen!" Lady Shelton announced, coming upon Mary in a gallery and waving a letter.

Mary froze. "Messire Chapuys?"

"The very same! He bowed to her in chapel. It's a sure sign that the Emperor is willing to be her friend."

Mary was speechless. For three years, Chapuys had steadfastly re-fused to recognize the Witch as queen. That he would do reverence to her now was unbelievable.

Utterly shocked, she dashed off a cold note conveying her disap-proval, and gave it to his messenger. Within a day, the man was back with a letter from Chapuys, who was clearly mortified. *The mutual reverences in church were required by politeness,* he wrote. *I was cornered; I had no choice, not with the Emperor so keen for an alliance. But I did not kiss that woman's hand or speak to her, and I am resolved never to speak to her again. I feel shame that anyone might believe I had betrayed your High-ness and our friends.*

Somewhat mollified, Mary burned the letter. It occurred to her that her father himself might have arranged or approved the encoun-ter, for Chapuys had evidently been placed in a position where he could not but have come face-to-face with the Witch. But would Father want the ambassador to acknowledge her as Queen if he was thinking of divorcing her?

The April sunset had faded, and Mary was alone in her room, set-tling down with a book, having lit candles and wrapped herself in furs because, by the King's order, no fires were lit in the royal houses after Easter. An hour later, when it was dark outside, there was a tap at the door and a maid entered.

"My Lady Mary, there is a gentleman waiting in the garden to see you. He says he is from the Imperial ambassador. He asked me not to tell anyone else that he was here."

Mary felt a shiver of fear. Was this a trap? Was she being lured to her doom?

"It's all right, my lady," the girl said. "He knows Messire Chapuys's usual messenger."

Still doubtful, Mary pulled on her cloak and made her way stealth-ily down the spiral stair to the garden door. Venturing out, she looked around her to check if anyone was waiting in the shadows, but she could see no one, so, with mounting trepidation she stepped gingerly along the path, starting at the hoot of an owl and the piercing screech of a fox. Then, from behind a hedge, she heard a voice. "My lady Princess?"

No! It could not be! But her heart knew it was, and nearly burst with joy. And there he stood, cloaked and hooded, but unmistakably Chapuys himself.

He bowed deeply. "Your Highness, I am sorry to come to you so unceremoniously, but it is essential that I speak to you alone. The matter is highly sensitive."

"There is no need to apologize, dear friend," she murmured, unable to credit that he was actually here with her, and pleased beyond measure that the years had hardly altered him. "You cannot know what a health it is to me to see you."

"It is good to see you, too, my lady, and looking so well." His eyes were kind and there was still about him that strength and assurance she had always loved. "I am glad to be able to convey in person my condolences on the passing of the Queen your mother," he continued, looking deeply sorrowful. "She was one of the bravest ladies I ever knew, the true daughter of her mother, Isabella. And you, Princess, have that same courage. You have proved it again and again. You will make a great queen one day."

Tears came to Mary's eyes. No one had spoken to her like that in years. If there had not been that formal distance between them, she would have liked to throw herself into his arms and rest her head on his breast, safe from the rest of the world. Instead, she blinked away her tears and smiled. "I thank you for those kind words. But that will not be easy. Another has usurped my place."

"And there may be a remedy for that, which is why I am here. Is there somewhere we can speak freely?"

"This way." Mary led him to a secluded corner shaded by trees and invited him to sit with her on the stone bench within it. "We can be private here."

"Good. Because I need to speak to you about the removal of the Lady, which has now become imperative."

She drew in her breath. "I agree. But how is it to be accomplished? You mentioned a divorce."

Chapuys looked grave. "It has gone beyond that. I told your Highness that your friends have united to compass her overthrow and discredit her with the King, and to encourage his interest in Mistress Seymour. I have been happy to work with them, for I am determined to see the Lady toppled, and they are doing a meritorious work that will prove a remedy for the heretical practices of the woman, who is the principal cause of the spread of Lutheranism in this country."

"Amen to that," Mary breathed. "She is the source of all the ills that have befallen this realm, and myself."

"The chief aim is to ensure your restoration to the succession. Once she is removed, the path to that will be smoother. And now, you will be glad to hear, Master Cromwell is actively working with your friends to see you restored to your rightful place in the succession. He and the Lady cordially hate each other, and he now goes in fear of his neck, for on Passion Sunday she had her almoner preach a sermon urging that wicked ministers be hanged. He has realized that joining us offers him his best chance of survival. And Fate has just played into his hands."

"What do you mean?"

"He has received certain reports from France against the Lady, which offer a pretext for her removal. He was not specific, but he said that if we were happy to leave it to him, he would see that we achieve our purpose. He's a lawyer, Highness, and a clever one. We can rely on him. What we desire is your approval."

Mary shivered and drew her cloak tighter around her, for the night air matched the chill in her spine. "But what does Master Cromwell intend? Aside from divorce, what other way is there of getting rid of her? Even if she has done something wrong, that is no pretext for dissolving the marriage!"

"She could be sent to a nunnery. That way, the King could be released from his marriage vows. Or he could divorce her by Act of Parliament. That might be what Cromwell is aiming at, and he may use these reports to persuade the King to agree to it. So you will give your approval for our plans to go forward?" Chapuys was gazing at her earnestly.

"I will. She has brought this on herself. God will never smile on her unlawful marriage." She could not feel any sympathy for Anne.

"Thank you," he said gently. "Now, regretfully, I must go. God be with you, Princess." He raised her hand and kissed it, then stood, leaving her tingling at the touch of his lips. "Farewell," he said, bowing, and vanished into the night.

She stood there feeling strangely bereft. He had always been one of her truest and most devoted friends—and she was almost certain now that he wished he could be more. She knew he would never go beyond the bounds of what was proper, and yet, whenever she tried to imagine the husband she might one day have, he had all the qualities of Messire Chapuys and looked just like him.

Chapter 10

1536

A week or so later, Mary was about to retire to bed when she heard running footsteps and a chorus of voices downstairs. Wondering what the commotion was, she descended to the great hall to find many of the household gathered around a messenger in the King's livery, all of them speaking at once. Lady Shelton and Lady Clere were standing at the back, weeping almost hysterically, and Lady Bryan stood a little apart, looking perplexed.

"What has happened?" Mary asked her.

"The Queen has been arrested and taken to the Tower," the old woman said.

Mary was stunned. She had not been anticipating that this was what her friends had intended. "What has she done?"

"No one seems to know exactly. That messenger certainly doesn't. And goodness knows what is to happen to my little lady. I can only pray for a happy outcome, for her sake. She is not yet three, far too young to lose her mother."

"Maybe it will not come to that," Mary said, but they both knew that those who were committed to the Tower rarely came out.

She turned to Lady Shelton. "Do try to calm down. There is no point in getting so upset when you know nothing of what is happening."

"You think that?" the governess cried. "The writing has been on the wall for some time. There has been a plot to bring the Queen down, mark me! And when she's gone, it will be remembered that I was her aunt and that I was cruel to you."

"But I will make sure that the truth is known," Mary reassured her. "I will repay your kindness. I know that things have been very difficult for you."

There was nothing more to be gained from staying up, so she returned to her room, wondering what charges had been leveled against Anne. What was it that Cromwell had discovered in those French reports?

She should be feeling glad that her great enemy had been arrested. There could be no clearer manifestation of divine vengeance for all the wrongs Anne had inflicted upon her mother and herself—and on the kingdom. But it seemed a hollow victory, and all she could think of, as she lay wakeful, was a little child who might soon lose her mother.

Two days later, Mary was strumming her lute in the garden when she was brought a letter from Chapuys. Her eyes widened as she read it. The Witch had been charged with treason. She was accused of betraying the King with five men, and of plotting his death. The men were even now in the Tower. One was her own brother, Lord Rochford. Another was a lowly musician, Mark Smeaton.

Mary was incredulous. The Witch was no fool. Why would she risk all by betraying the King? And why plot his death when he was the bulwark that stood between her and her enemies? Yet it was all too believable when one considered her other wickednesses and her poor reputation. Maybe she had been so desperate for a son that she had looked to other men to give her one. Mary thought immediately of Elizabeth, who was away on one of her rare visits to the court, which was now at Greenwich. How much had she seen of these dreadful events? Was she even the King's child?

Whether she was or not, what had just befallen her mother was going to have a terrible impact on her. Mary's heart sank to think of it.

Chapuys believed that Anne was guilty. He made it clear that he had been instrumental in bringing about her arrest and said he hoped to bring the matter to a successful conclusion. *The Lady Elizabeth will almost certainly now be excluded from the succession, and your Highness restored, albeit after any children that Mistress Seymour might bear the King, for it seems certain that he will marry her.*

That was the best news he could have sent. Her night thoughts forgotten, Mary resolved to waste no sympathy on this woman who had for so long cast a malign shadow over her life. She replied to Chapuys that it was her desire that he should help, and not hinder, any divorce proceedings. *I wish you to promote the matter, with Master Cromwell and our other friends, especially for the discharge of the conscience of the King my father and the advancement of Mistress Seymour. I do not care a straw whether he has lawful heirs or not, nor for all the injuries done to me or the Queen my mother, which, for the honor of God, and in charity, I pardon everyone most heartily.*

All she cared about now was that the Witch be got rid of.

She wondered how her father was taking this. Chapuys reported that the King had withdrawn into seclusion and seen no one. But before that, on the very day of Anne's arrest, he had made it plain that he believed her capable of murder. When Henry Fitzroy had come to bid him good night, he'd embraced him and wept, saying that he and his sister Mary ought to thank God for escaping that cursed and venomous whore, who had tried to poison them both.

Mary devoured the letter in the privacy of her chamber. She had taken to spending as much time there as she could, aware that the rest of the household were now wary of offending her. Even Lady Bryan, who had just returned from court with Elizabeth, had become less confiding. It was obvious that they all feared the consequences for them should Mary be restored to favor. And that seemed likely. *Mistress Seymour,* Chapuys had written, *is your true friend. When the King visited her in the lodging of her brother, Sir Edward Seymour, she*

*told him that when she is Queen, she hopes to see your Highness reinstated as
heir apparent. And when he said that she ought rather to solicit the advancement of the children they would have together, she replied that she did think
of them, but also of his Majesty's peace of mind, for unless he showed justice
to you, Englishmen would never be content.*

Mary's heart leaped when she read that. She could not help exulting too when she learned that the Witch was to be tried. It could not
be long now before the future became clearer.

Elizabeth seemed blithely unaware of the shadow looming over her
young life. She shrieked with laughter when she beat Mary at skit-
tles, then squealed as Mary chased her around the garden. They were
interrupted by Chapuys's man, who bowed and gave Mary a letter as
the child watched, her pointed face full of curiosity. "What's that?"

"A letter from a friend," Mary told her. She put it in her pocket
and resumed the game, fearing that its arrival did not portend well
for her little sister. Not that Elizabeth would miss Anne very much.
She had hardly ever seen her, the Witch's visits being infrequent, and
Elizabeth had rarely been summoned to court. Mary prayed that
Lady Bryan would be spared to her; she was more of a mother than
her own had ever been.

Burned or beheaded, at the King's pleasure.

Mary drew in her breath sharply. She had not doubted that Anne
would be found guilty, but the news still shocked her. She had
thought that divorce would be her fate—that and banishment.
Never, in England, had a queen been put to death. Of course, Anne
was not rightfully Queen, but Parliament had declared her such. And
now she had been judged a traitor. Death was no more than she deserved, and not just for adultery, incest, and plotting the King's
death, of which she had been convicted. She had plotted Mary's end,
and poor Mother's, too; had she had her way, they would have been
condemned to the same death she was to suffer. She had been a heretic, too, infecting the King and the whole realm with her subversive ideas. Well, perhaps it was fitting that she be burned. It was the

punishment the law demanded for heresy. Mary could feel no pity for her. She had brought it on herself.

She had denied the charges, of course. She had stood up to her accusers, braver than a lion. Even Chapuys seemed impressed by her courage.

Three days later, the household removed to Hunsdon. Elizabeth traveled in state, no orders having been received to the contrary, while Mary shared a chariot with Lady Shelton and Lady Clere. When they arrived, however, Mary found that she had been allocated a fine bedchamber and several maids to attend her, which was a good sign.

On the Friday following their arrival, she was walking along a gallery when she heard sobs emitting from a closet that led off it. Peering around the door, she saw Lady Shelton weeping into her kerchief.

"I'm sorry," she said, drawing back.

"She's gone!" the governess blurted out. "She was beheaded this morning, Lord save us!"

Understanding dawned. "I didn't know," Mary faltered.

"Master Cromwell's messenger is downstairs. I couldn't bear to listen to any more."

"Where's Elizabeth?"

"In the nursery. We've been ordered to keep the news from her."

"Of course." Mary felt a deep pang at the thought of that bereft innocent. "She's far too young to be told the truth. Time enough for that when she is older."

Leaving Lady Shelton to her grief, she hastened to the nursery, where she found Sir John Shelton, looking pale, talking to the chamberlain. They fell silent when they saw her, and both made a hurried reverence. Then Elizabeth toddled in from the bedchamber, followed by an anxious nursery maid.

"Why, Governor," the child asked Sir John, "why yesterday was I called my lady Princess, and today just Lady Elizabeth?"

Sir John was clearly caught off guard. He pulled at his beard,

frowned and hesitated, while Elizabeth stood before him, her imperious gaze demanding a response.

"The King your father has ordered it," he said at last.

Mary stared at him. So they were equals now, herself and
Elizabeth—but not for long, if God was just.

"Why?" asked the child, her dark eyes narrowing.

"The King's orders must always be obeyed," he declared.

The little face clouded. Elizabeth was not letting him off so easily.
At that moment, Lady Bryan entered the room, carrying a pile of
fresh laundry. The child tugged at her skirts and repeated her question.

Tears welled up in the old woman's eyes. "You have a new title,
my Lady Elizabeth," she said, in her most reassuring voice. "The
King's Highness has decreed it."

"But why?" persisted the child.

"I'm sure the King has very good reasons," answered Lady Bryan,
in a tone that forbade further discussion. "Now, where are those dolls
you were playing with earlier?"

"I put them to bed," Elizabeth pouted.

"In the morning? The very idea!" exclaimed her governess. "Look,
I've got some pretty silks in my basket, and some Holland cloth. Go
and fetch your best doll, and I'll help you to make a gown for her."

Elizabeth looked mutinous, as if she would have liked to press the
matter further, but knew that answers would not be forthcoming.
Mary could barely stop herself from crushing the child to her breast,
desperate to protect her from the dreadful consequences of her mother's crimes.

Another letter from Chapuys arrived that evening. Lying on her bed,
Mary read that the Witch had thought her execution a divine judgment upon her for having treated her stepdaughter so badly, and for
having conspired her death. *No person ever showed greater willingness to
die,* Chapuys had observed. Yet still Mary could feel no pity for
Anne—and doubted she ever would. In fact, the news of her great
enemy's death had revived her spirits considerably, for the way was

now clear toward a reconciliation with her father. And it seemed that many had reached the same conclusion. *I cannot well describe the great joy the people of London have manifested at the fall and ruin of the Lady,* Chapuys had written. *Many are elated at the prospect of your Highness being restored to your rightful place, for they still regard you as the King's lawful heiress. You can count upon the support of Mistress Seymour and the Imperialist party.*

It was time, Mary resolved, to forget the unhappy past and look to the future. She wrote to her father, begging to be taken back into his favor, humbly beseeching him to remember that she was but a woman, and his child. She prayed he would respond.

The next day, Mary was chopping herbs in the still room when Lady Shelton came to tell her that Lady Kingston had arrived and was waiting to see her in the parlor off the hall. Mary was astonished. What could the wife of the Constable of the Tower want with her? But she had not forgotten that Mary Kingston had served her mother and had always been friendly to her.

She was dismayed to see the lady looking so unwell; she had aged much since Mary was last at court. And she was shocked when her visitor clumsily fell to her knees before her.

"My dear Lady Kingston, please rise!" she cried.

"Nay, your Highness, not until I have said what I came to say. I bring a message from the late Queen." Mary stiffened at this, but Lady Kingston went on unheeding. "The day before her death, she took me into her presence chamber in the Tower and willed me to sit in her chair of estate. I said it was my duty to stand, and not to sit in her presence, much less upon the seat of state of the Queen. But she answered me, 'Ah, Madam, that title is gone. I am a condemned person, and by law have no estate left me in this life, but for clearing of my conscience.' And she prayed me to sit down. Well, I told her I had often played the fool in my youth, and to fulfill her command I would do it once more in my old age. And I sat on the throne."

The old woman paused. "I must say this to you just as she did. I must get it right, for she most humbly fell on her knees before me and held up her hands, and with tears in her eyes beseeched me, as if in the presence of God and His angels, and as she would answer before them at her judgment, that I would fall down likewise before your Highness and, on her behalf, ask your forgiveness for the wrongs she had done you. Until that was accomplished, she said, her conscience could not be quiet."

Mary stood there, speechless, not knowing what to say. Good Christians were supposed to forgive—it had been drummed into her all her life. Vengeance was the Lord's; He would repay all ill-doing, and it could be said that He had done so in Anne's case. But she struggled with herself. Her conscience was telling her that she must forgive, yet her heart and her head could not obey.

Hastily, she bade Lady Kingston rise and be seated, and helped her to a chair.

"You think she was genuine in her contrition?" she asked.

"There's no doubt of it. She was full of remorse for her cruel treatment of your Highness, and for plotting your death. Her guilt clearly weighed heavily upon her conscience."

"It is not easy to forgive," Mary murmured. A headache was threatening.

"You will feel better if you do," Lady Kingston counseled. "I am not long for this world, and I understand the importance of being at peace with my fellow humans, and with myself. It does us no good to harbor hatred and resentment. What's past is past."

Her words echoed Mary's own resolution.

"I forgive her," she said, even though it felt as if the words were being torn out of her.

"It is a beginning," Lady Kingston soothed.

It was true: Mary did feel better. She called for wine, and they sat together for an hour, during which her guest told her about Anne's final days in the Tower.

"You know that the musician Smeaton confessed?" she said. "He was the only one."

"Do you think he spoke truth?" Mary asked. Or had it been forced out of him?

"I honestly do not know. The Queen protested her innocence all along, even when she made her final confession."

"But the evidence against her was strong."

"I was at the trial," Lady Kingston said. "It seemed to me they were making an occasion to get rid of her."

Mary stared at her. "You think she was wrongly condemned?"

"I cannot say. I'm sure the judges found the evidence convincing. But did you ever see Mark Smeaton?"

Mary thought back. "If I did, I can't place him."

Lady Kingston leaned forward. "Well, I saw him many times. He often frequented the Queen's chamber and acted lovestruck around her, as foolish young men do. She took little notice of him. But it has struck me lately how much a certain child resembles him in looks. The same coloring, the same narrow face—and those hands with their long fingers: lute player's fingers."

Mary was incredulous. "You think he was her father?"

"I dare not say so. Only the resemblance struck me."

She did not believe it. She would not believe it. "But she is so like the King. She has his red hair and Roman nose. The rest, regrettably for her, is all her mother."

"My Lady, please forget I said anything." Lady Kingston looked worried. "It was just idle speculation. I should have held my tongue."

"It is forgotten," Mary assured her. But the seed planted by the old woman had taken root in her mind.

There was a short, uncomfortable pause until her visitor spoke again. "And now what will your Highness do?"

"I am still awaiting a reply from my father. I wrote to him. I am hoping that a messenger will arrive soon. I had thought to hear from his Grace by now."

"I imagine he is much occupied. There are great preparations in train for his wedding to Mistress Seymour," Lady Kingston replied.

"So soon?" Mary was a little shocked, for all that the news was welcome.

"My dear Lady Mary, he was betrothed to her on the morning after the Queen's death."

Mary forbore to comment, stunned as she was. It was indecently soon. But her father wanted a son, and he wasn't getting any younger. She wondered how she would feel about being supplanted as the heir if Jane Seymour fulfilled his hopes. No one could say that the child was not legitimately born, and princes always took precedence over princesses. So long as she was restored to her former status, she decided, she would not mind. After the turbulence of the past few years, she would appreciate a quiet life with a husband and children.

But how to achieve that?

"I do wish to be reconciled with my father," she told Lady Kingston.

Her visitor smiled. "Your Grace might try to approach him through Master Secretary Cromwell. My husband says he is secretly sympathetic toward you and might use his very considerable influence on your behalf."

It was wise advice, and after giving the matter much thought, Mary wrote to Master Secretary, begging him to intercede for her with the King.

The messenger had just departed with her letter when a deputation from the Privy Council arrived to see her. She was with Elizabeth in the nursery, teaching her simple stitches and studying her face, for the umpteenth time, to find resemblances to Father. As usual, they seemed obvious. But then she had never seen Mark Smeaton.

When Lady Bryan told her that the lords were waiting for her in the hall, she was filled with excitement, anticipating that they had come to escort her back to court. But her heart sank when she saw their solemn faces. What now?

"Good day, my lords," she bade them, trembling slightly.

They bowed, which was something, and then the Duke of Norfolk stepped forward, his face glacial. "My Lady Mary, we are come from the King with instructions to order you to acknowledge that his marriage to your mother, the Princess Dowager, was incestuous and unlawful. You are also to take the Oath of Supremacy."

"Never!" She was seized with such fury that she thought she might faint. Why was her father insisting on this now, when the past was done with and all was set fair for the future? It was unnecessary— and it was cruel. "I will never acknowledge either!"

"On your obedience to your father and your sovereign, you will submit," the Duke growled.

"No, I will not. And nothing you say will make me."

"There is no point in us making any further effort here," the Duke of Suffolk said.

"No," Norfolk agreed. "I'm not wasting any more time on this willful, unnatural girl. I warn you, my Lady Mary, that when the King learns of your defiance, he will find other ways to break your will, for he is determined to have your submission."

"I wish my father a quiet conscience," Mary said, calmer now, but still trembling as she watched them depart.

She had rarely felt so alone. All her hopes seemed to have come to nothing. Against her father's implacability, Jane Seymour would not stand a chance. When he was determined on a thing, he would not back down. But she, Mary, was not his child for nothing. She would never give in.

She thought of appealing to the Emperor for support, but she knew this was not the right time. England and the Empire were forging a new friendship, and Charles might not be inclined to interfere between father and daughter; Mary was not his subject, and he would not wish to undermine the new alliance, which was so important for trade. She was on her own now, and she could only pray that Cromwell would help her.

Chapter 11

1536

The King had married Jane Seymour! The news flew through the household at Hunsdon and Mary hastened to the chapel to give thanks. Then she fetched her writing desk and wrote to her father, congratulating him and begging leave to wait upon Queen Jane, or do her any service it pleased her to command.

I trust, by your Grace's mercy, to come soon into your presence, she continued, *which shall be the greatest comfort I can have in this world, having great hope in your Grace's natural pity. I fervently hope and pray that God will send your Grace shortly a prince, in which no creature living would more rejoice than I.* She was praying too that her words would ignite some spark of paternal affection and understanding.

She waited, but there was no reply, so she wrote to Chapuys asking what she should do. Her letter crossed with one from him telling her that Jane was begging the King to bring her back to court and be reconciled with her, but he would not agree unless Mary acknowledged her mother's marriage to be incestuous and unlawful. He had warned that unless she acknowledged his laws and statutes, he would proceed against her. It was horrifying to realize that just when she thought her perils were behind her, she was still in grave danger. She felt sick and had to rest on her bed for a time, but that did no good because all she did was lie there fretting. Even prayer could not calm her. Nothing could lift her spirits, especially after Chapuys sent to warn her that the King had been so incensed on listening to the report of the councillors who had visited her that he had threatened to have her tried for treason; and when Jane had begged him not to proceed, he had told her she must be out of her senses. Mary feared that Jane might never dare speak in her favor again.

But Chapuys wrote warmly of her. He rejoiced that such a virtuous and amiable Queen now sat upon the throne, and reported that it was impossible to comprehend the joy and pleasure that Englishmen in general had expressed on hearing of the marriage, especially as it was said that Jane was continually trying to persuade the King to restore Mary to favor. Jane was no heretic, but a good and devout woman, and a friend to the Emperor. She had herself promised Chapuys that she would continue to show favor to Mary. *I told her that, without the pain of childbirth, she had gained in your Highness a treasured daughter who would please her more than her own children by the King, and she replied that she would do all she could to make peace between his Majesty and yourself.*

But that, Mary thought, folding the letter, and locking it away in her chest, might only be achieved if she did as her father wished, which she could never bring herself to do. It went against every moral instinct.

Chapuys was of another opinion, as was the Emperor. *It is in everyone's interests for you to placate the King,* he advised.

She resisted—how she resisted. She could not sleep, for her conscience was torturing her. She longed to have her father's love again—but how could she do that without betraying and dishonoring her mother's memory?

In the morning, hating herself, she took up her pen and wrote to the King. *I beg your Highness to pardon my offenses. I will never be happy until you have forgiven me. Permit me to prostrate myself humbly before your Grace's feet to repent of my faults.* She felt sick, having to abase herself so abjectly when she had done nothing wrong, and she could write no more in that vein. But she must end on the right note. *I pray,* she concluded, *that Almighty God will preserve your Grace and the Queen, and shortly send you a prince, which I declare shall be gladder tidings to me than I can ever express.*

With a heavy heart, she sent for the messenger.

It was plain that the staff at Hunsdon were unsure how to treat her, until the day when Sir John Shelton announced the passing of a new Act of Succession. Everyone had been summoned to the hall, and Mary waited tensely to hear what the Act said.

"It has been decreed," Sir John read, "that the crown of England shall, on the King's death, pass to the children of Queen Jane. The Act speaks of the great and intolerable perils his Grace has suffered as a result of two unlawful marriages, notwithstanding which his ardent love and fervent affection for his realm and people has impelled him, of his most excellent goodness, to venture upon this third marriage, which is so pure and without impediment that the issue of it, when it shall please Almighty God to send it, will have the undisputed right of succession. It has further been enacted"— and now Sir John's gaze rested on Mary, and on Elizabeth, who was holding her hand and looking perplexed—"that the King's first two marriages were unlawful, and that the ladies Mary and Elizabeth are illegitimate and unfit to inherit the throne. Failing any issue by Queen Jane, the Act grants the King the power to appoint anyone he chooses to be his successor."

All eyes were on Mary, who was struggling to conceal her anger at the mention of her father's suffering on account of those great and intolerable perils. But what of hers? What of her mother's? And who was in peril now, thanks to him? Her cheeks burned.

She had not been expecting to be declared legitimate, but she spared a thought for Elizabeth, who had been reduced to the same bastard status as herself.

"What did he mean?" the child piped up.

"Nothing to worry yourself about, Bess," Mary said, hurrying her away to the nursery.

To everyone's credit, very few changes were made. In recognition of their royal blood, both Mary and Elizabeth were treated with def-

erence and well served. For Elizabeth, only her title had changed—
and the fact that she was growing out of her clothes and Lady Bryan
was having to pester Cromwell for new ones, the King now being
away on his honeymoon. For Mary, it was a change for the better.
Many people wanted to see her restored, while no one was speaking
up for Elizabeth. And yet, with her future so frighteningly uncertain, her position was still anomalous.

At last, a letter came from Master Cromwell. It was terse and to the
point, but although she read it with increasing dismay, she could
detect a certain sympathy. The royal justices, the secretary had written, were reluctant to proceed against her, and had suggested that,
instead of being tried for treason, she sign a paper of submission,
recognizing her father as head of the Church and her mother's marriage as incestuous and unlawful. *I urge you to comply, for I have gone to
no small trouble to persuade the King to agree, and have so incurred his
displeasure that I already regret lending you my support.*

She had placed so much hope in Cromwell that the disappointment was crushing. Screwing up the letter, and feeling entirely
abandoned, she scrawled a reply, declaring that her conscience would
never permit her to do as he asked.

Back came the response, as if borne on wings. Master Secretary
was scathing, telling her in no uncertain terms that he deplored her
unfilial stand against her father. He had enclosed a list of articles she
was to sign and warned that he would not vouch for her safety if she
refused.

She stared at them, feeling overwhelmed. She would not, *could*
not, risk her immortal soul for the favor of an earthly king, however
much she craved his love and approval. She would ignore Cromwell's
letter and wait for a reply from her father, although as the days went
by, she began to doubt he would send one. And then hope died. It
was clear that he did not intend to respond, and that any reconciliation would be dependent on her signing that hateful document. But
she could not! Dear God, it would go against everything she believed in! But even Chapuys was urging her to sign. The Emperor, he
said, strongly advised it.

She sat in her room late into the evening, with the list of articles before her, trying to bring herself to append her name. She felt ill; her head was aching, her stomach cramping from her monthly course. The words blurred as she wept.

"Dearest Mother, forgive me!" she whispered, dipping the quill in the inkwell yet again and bracing herself to do the deed. "Almighty God, forgive me!" Assuredly they would; but would she ever forgive herself?

The Devil was tempting her, enticing her to think of the benefits that would surely come to her if she did this terrible thing. He showed her herself being received back into her father's loving arms, being warmly welcomed by Queen Jane and enveloped once more in the glittering life of the court. No more humiliations, no more living under a cloud, no more fear of the future. But what was that, she countered, against living the rest of her life with an unquiet conscience, knowing she had betrayed everything her mother had fought and suffered for, failed in her courage and capitulated for worldly reasons, where others had stood firm and suffered even unto death for their principles?

Yet Cromwell—whom she still believed to be her friend—Chapuys, and the Emperor had all urged her to sign. And both Charles and Chapuys had assured her that the Pope would absolve her from all responsibility for what she was made to do under duress.

It was late. The June twilight had almost faded and left her sitting in the dark. Lighting a candle, she took up her quill once more and, trying not to think about what she was doing, signed her name.

She had done it. She had finally acknowledged her father to be Supreme Head of the Church of England, and her mother's marriage, by God's law and man's law, incestuous and unlawful. With a few strokes of the pen, she had repudiated everything she held sacred.

Hurrying to the close stool, she bent over it and retched.

The next morning, shaky and nauseous, and feeling like Judas, she sent the document to Cromwell, enclosing a letter to the King written in the most groveling terms she could summon, as Master Secretary had advised: *I beg you, of your inestimable goodness, to pardon my having so offended you that my heavy and fearful heart dare not presume to call you father. I will never be happy until you have forgiven me.* In truth, she would never be happy again. What did it matter now if she was reduced to begging to prostrate herself humbly before the King's feet to crave the favor of an audience?

Your Highness has never done a better day's work! Chapuys wrote jubilantly. *I am pleased to have relieved you of every doubt of conscience.*

But you haven't! Mary cried inwardly. *I have to live with it, and it is well-nigh unbearable!* Yet the ambassador's tone was exultant. There now remained, he said, no bar to her reconciliation to her father. She only hoped he was right and that the King was not angry that he had been made to wait so long for her submission.

Two days later, she was told that a gentleman called Sir Thomas Wriothesley had come from the court and wished to speak to her. She hurried to the hall, hoping that he brought word from her father.

"His Grace has sent me to you, my lady," he said, bowing. He was a dapper man with heavy-lidded eyes, a long nose and a luxuriant red beard, and there was about him that air of restless ambition that clung to many young men at court. "He has received the paper you signed, but requires me to obtain from you a fuller declaration of your faults in writing, to be taken to Master Cromwell."

She regarded him with dismay, twisting her hands. "But I know not what else to write."

"I will instruct you."

Mary tried to look grateful, but inwardly she was distraught. Why was Father prolonging her misery? But there was nothing for it. With Sir Thomas Wriothesley prompting her, and sometimes dictating, she wrote a long and abject letter to Cromwell, acknowledging her faults in detail and thanking him for his kindness in furthering her cause with the King.

When she had signed and sealed it, Wriothesley smiled at her. "And now I am to ask your Highness to name those ladies you would like appointed to your service, should his Majesty decide to increase your household pending a return to favor."

Sudden joy filled her. Such instructions could only have come from Father himself! Immediately, she began to feel better, remind-ing herself that his Holiness would absolve her for what she had done.

"I am content to leave the choice to the King's pleasure," she said, knowing it was now politic to show herself compliant in all things.

After that, although she still felt poorly, she went about lighter in heart and in step. Evidently, the household had had instructions, for she was treated with enhanced deference. She noticed too that there were often people crowding at the gates, trying—the guards told her—to catch a glimpse of her. And then, at the end of June, the King's officers arrived at Hunsdon, sent by him to see that she had all she required and to advise her that it would not be long before he brought the Queen to visit her.

Soon afterward, Queen Jane's brother, Edward Seymour, now Lord Beauchamp, came to visit Mary. He was a serious-faced, richly garbed young man with a stiff manner, but he was cordial enough when Mary invited him to join her for a glass of wine in the parlor.

"The Queen my sister has sent me to obtain a list of the clothing your Highness will need when you return to court," he told her. "She wishes you to be garbed as befits the King's daughter. She asked me to tell you that his gracious clemency and merciful pity have over-come his anger at your unkind and unnatural behavior, and that he is looking forward to being reunited with you."

This was all very heartening, although Mary did wonder irritably when people would cease to remind her of how deeply she had of-fended her father. Could they not put the past behind them, as she was resolved to do?

Her irritation dissipated as Lord Beauchamp gave her news of the court. She would have liked to ask if Lady Salisbury was to be re-stored to her, but decided that could wait.

She noticed that her guest was looking at her intensely.

"Is your Grace in health?" he asked.

"I have not been well," she confided. "I have been under a lot of strain lately, but I am better now."

They passed a pleasant hour, and then Lord Beauchamp stood up to leave. "I have something for your Highness," he said, as they crossed the hall and stepped into the porch. Outside, in the court-yard, a groom was holding the reins of a fine white horse.

"You have a beautiful mount, my lord." Mary smiled, patting the animal's nose.

"She is not mine, your Highness. She is my gift to you."

Mary could hardly believe it. That such a prominent courtier would give her such a gift was a sure sign indeed that she was back in favor.

When Beauchamp had gone, Mary wrote again to her father, declaring that she would never vary from her submission, and praying that God would soon send him and the Queen children.

It was not long before other influential courtiers began hurrying to Hunsdon to seek her friendship and patronage. But when, she kept wondering, would her father come?

One evening in July, Sir Thomas Wriothesley returned. "I am to escort your Highness to Hackney, where the King's Grace will receive you," he informed Mary. "He had intended for you to come to the court, but he wishes to wait until you are fully recovered from your recent illness."

She wondered if it had ever occurred to Father that he had been the cause of her illness. She doubted it! Nevertheless, he was clearly concerned about her.

"We must depart tonight," Wriothesley instructed. "I will have your litter made ready."

"Give me time to prepare!" Mary cried, her heart racing, and flew upstairs, summoning her maids to help her change into her best gown—although all were showing signs of wear. Her mind was in turmoil at the prospect of seeing her father after so long—it was five years since she had set eyes on him. She had been fifteen, a pretty, diminutive girl with beautiful red hair and the freshness of youth. But, looking in her mirror, she saw that she looked ill and haunted, and that she was much too thin. What would he think of her now?

Setting aside such thoughts, she straightened her hood, threw on a cloak and ran downstairs, where her escort was waiting. Riding through the night was an adventure such as she had not experienced in a long while, and she found the secrecy exhilarating, despite her trepidation at the meeting that was to come.

She arrived at the royal manor house at Hackney before the King and Queen, but did not have long to wait. When their arrival was announced, she stood in the great hall and made a deep obeisance, hardly able to stop trembling.

"My most dear and well-beloved daughter!" her father said warmly, and she felt his strong arms raising her, clasping her to him, saw the tears in his eyes as he gazed at her. He looked older, sterner, and he had put on weight. His fair cheeks were flushed with emotion.

He was gentle with her, kindly and affectionate.

"I have brought your good mother, Queen Jane, to meet you," he said, and Mary went to kneel, but Jane would not let her, taking her hands and embracing her instead, her broad, pale face radiant with the kind expression Mary remembered so well.

"You cannot know how good a friend you have in the Queen," Father said.

Mary ventured a smile. "I know I am much beholden to your Grace," she told Jane.

The King led them into the great chamber and bade Mary be seated between him and Jane. She was conscious of his intense blue gaze, and the emotion he did not try to hide. "I deeply regret having kept you so long away from me," he said, and at that her composure broke and tears streamed down her face.

"Oh, my dearest father, how I have missed you," she wept.

Father looked as if he might weep, too. "I will not let it happen again," he promised, taking her hand. "We must forget the past and look to the future. There is nothing I would not do for you, my child, now that we are in perfect accord again."

Jane took from her purse a little velvet bag and pressed it into Mary's hands. "And I would be your Highness's friend," she smiled.

"There is nothing I would like better, Madam. You were always kind to me." When Mary opened the bag, she could not speak, for inside was a beautiful diamond ring.

"In token of our new friendship," Jane told her.

"And this is from me," Father said, handing Mary a tasseled purse. "A thousand crowns for your little pleasures. From now on, you need have no anxiety about money, for you shall have as much as you wish."

The afternoon passed pleasantly after that, as Mary began to relax in her father's company, and Jane assured her that she had many friends at court who welcomed her return to favor.

"I look forward to receiving you there," she said, laying her hand on Mary's sleeve. "There are no ladies in my household with whom I can associate on equal terms, and, in truth, I am feeling rather lonely. I can think of none better than your Highness to be a friend and companion to me." Her words warmed Mary's heart.

"But you are not to return to court just yet," Father said. "You are looking peaky after your illness and need time to rest and recover."

Mary was grateful for that. Appearing in public with all eyes on her would be an ordeal, and she was not ready to face it.

After Vespers, as the King and Queen made ready to leave, Mary was in much happier spirits.

"I promise you shall be well treated from now on," Father called down from the saddle. "You will enjoy more freedom than you ever had, and I will see to it that you are served with honor, as the second lady in the land after the Queen. You will want for nothing! And we will see you very soon." He blew her a kiss, and then they were riding away through the gatehouse and heading for the London road.

The reunion had been everything Mary could have desired. No father could have behaved better toward his daughter. She now lacked nothing but the name of Princess of Wales and her rightful status—and was that really of much consequence now that she was henceforth to rank as second lady at court after Queen Jane and would have everything more abundantly than before?

True to his word, the King sent her gifts of money, while from Jane there were rich court gowns. Master Cromwell made a present of another fine horse and, at the King's instigation, started to reinstate Mary's household. She began to believe there was a good chance that her father would soon be thinking of restoring her to the succession.

She was thrilled when he sent her with her new household—*sans* Lady Shelton—to Richmond Palace and arrived unannounced with Jane soon afterward to visit her. Over dinner, for which her cook had miraculously and speedily produced a veritable feast, he presented Mary with a ring inset with portrait miniatures of her, himself, and Jane. "It is a gift from Master Secretary," he said, beaming. "He had it made specially for you, and I was so impressed with it that I insisted on giving it to you myself!"

Mary was touched. She slipped it on her finger and held out her hand to admire it. "I will write to Master Cromwell. I owe him much gratitude for his kindness and his wise advice. I take him for one of my chief friends after your Graces."

Conscious of her good fortune, Mary found time to spare a thought for her half-sister. On a hot day in July, she set off for Hunsdon, where Elizabeth was staying. The child was waiting for her with Lady Bryan in the courtyard, and as soon as Mary had dismounted, she ran forward and sketched a wobbly curtsey. Mary stooped to kiss her.

"My, you have grown, sweeting!" she exclaimed, stroking Elizabeth's hair. "You're nearly three now, aren't you?"

Elizabeth nodded.

"I have brought you a gift." Mary smiled, beckoning to one of her ladies, who carried over a wooden box covered in embroidered silver. Inside, wrapped in velvet, was a rosary of amber beads and a jeweled crucifix. "For your chapel," Mary said, pointing to the latter.

"Pretty," said Elizabeth, gently fingering the beads.

"How does my sister, Lady Bryan?" Mary rose to her feet and greeted the governess with a kiss. "And you yourself? It is good to see you again."

"We are well enough, both of us, I thank you," the old woman answered. "But I am glad your Highness is here." As Elizabeth skipped ahead to the porch, she lowered her voice. "Questions, questions, all the time. She knows something has happened, and she keeps asking for her mother. She has to be told something."

"I will speak with her presently," Mary offered, wondering what on earth she was going to say.

Lady Bryan nodded. "I am so grateful. But I pray you eat first, for it is nigh to eleven o'clock and dinner is almost ready."

"I have brought my fool, and she can afford a diversion later, if need be," Mary said, as they entered the hall.

Elizabeth looked up. "I like fools," she chirped. "They are funny. They make me laugh."

Roast goose and hot salad were served with appropriate ceremony. Elizabeth had been sent to the nursery to have her dinner, being too young to eat with the grown-ups.

Mary could not face food. She was dreading the coming conversation. She laid down her knife and shook her head sadly. "I hardly know how I am going to tell her, Lady Bryan," she said miserably.

Lady Bryan rested a comforting hand on hers. "I wouldn't be too explicit if I were you, Madam."

"Oh, no," agreed Mary fervently. "Do you think she will be very upset? After all, she did not see much of her mother. Will she understand?"

"There is much she understands," Lady Bryan replied. "My lady is more than ordinarily precocious. As sharp as nails, that child, and clever with it."

"But a child for all that," Mary said, "so I will break it to her as gently as I can, and may our Holy Mother and all the saints help me."

Lady Bryan steered the conversation away from the subject, but while she and Sir John Shelton chatted about household matters and the state of the weather, Mary, her heart swelling with love and compassion for her little sister, could only think of the heavy task that lay ahead of her.

Why should she feel this way? she asked herself. Elizabeth's very existence had caused her untold pain and suffering, and it was because of Elizabeth's mother that Mary had lost her own mother, her rank, her prospects of a throne and marriage, and—so nearly—the love of her father. Yet she could find nothing to resent in an innocent child, especially now that the perilous twists of cruel fate had reversed Elizabeth's fortunes too; she could only grieve for the little girl.

As soon as the meal was finished, Elizabeth was brought back and Mary took her for a walk in the sun-browned park, their attendants following a short distance behind. It was blazing hot, there was barely the stir of a breeze, and they were all sweltering in their long-sleeved silk gowns. Mary was glad that Elizabeth was wearing a wide-brimmed straw hat, for her own hood was damp with sweat.

"You have been much in my thoughts, Sister," she said. "I had to come and see you, to satisfy myself that all was well with you, and . . ." She could not go on.

"Thank you," Elizabeth replied. "What's wrong? Why are you unhappy?"

"Oh, my dear sister," Mary cried, sinking to her knees on the grass and hugging the child tightly.

Elizabeth struggled free.

"Come," Mary said, dabbing her eyes with her kerchief. "Let us sit here." She drew the child to a stone seat in the shade of an oak tree and lifted her onto it. "I have to tell you something that will make you very sad. You must be a brave girl."

"I am brave," Elizabeth assured her, swinging her legs restlessly.

Mary laid a hand on hers. She had no idea of what she was going to say. She thought of beginning by saying that Anne had gone to live with God in Paradise, but she did not believe this herself—the Witch was surely in Hell—and her inborn honesty demanded that she speak the truth.

She took a deep breath. "Elizabeth, sweeting, do you know what treason is?"

"No," said Elizabeth, her innocent eyes wide and puzzled.

"It is when someone does something bad against the King. Hurts him in some way, or plots wickedness. Do you understand?"

Elizabeth nodded. "Yes. Like the wicked fox in the story of Chanticleer?"

"Yes, in a way. But people who commit treason are punished. It is the worst crime of all, worse than murder or stealing, because it is against the King's Majesty, who is God's anointed on earth. People who commit treason are put to death. You know what that is?"

"Yes. The chaplain said you go to sleep forever and ever, and if you are good, your soul goes to Heaven to live with God and all the saints and angels. If you're bad, you are sent to Hell. It's a terrible place, and devils are horrid to you all the time and hurt you with their pitchforks."

"That's true."

Elizabeth nodded solemnly.

"Sweetheart, there is no easy way to say this"—Mary's words were coming in a rush now—"but your mother committed treason against the King our father, and she has suffered the punishment. She has been put to death."

Elizabeth looked as if she hadn't heard. She was staring at the palace basking in the sunshine, her face blank.

"Do you understand?" Mary repeated, squeezing the little hand beneath hers. Elizabeth drew it away.

Lady Bryan was walking toward them. "My lady, have you told her?" she inquired gently. Suddenly, Elizabeth slid off the bench and ran to her governess, burying her face in her skirts and bursting into violent tears.

"Mother! I want my mother! Where is she? I want her!" she wailed piteously, her small body trembling. "I want her! Get her!"

Lady Bryan and Mary knelt down, doing their best to comfort the stricken child, but she would not be consoled. "Where is my mother?" she wailed.

"She is with God, my lamb," wept Lady Bryan.

Elizabeth began to scream. "I want her! I want her!"

"You must pray for her," faltered Mary.

But Elizabeth was beyond speech, howling her heart out.

They made special efforts to be kind to her in the days that followed. Lady Bryan found her little tasks to do in the house, the cook served her favorite foods, and Mary's fool Janie made merry jests and capered before her at mealtimes, brandishing her jingling bells; but it was Mary she wanted. Mary diverted her with the presents she had brought her: yellow satin for a gown, a pearl necklace, a brooch, a gold ball with a clock in it, made to contain perfume. She spent hours playing with her, rescuing her from the tedium of the well-meaning Sir John's dull stories.

"What shall it be tonight, my lady? Patient Griselda or Theseus and the Minotaur?" he had asked.

"I had Theseus yesterday, again," sighed Elizabeth. "Read Patient Griselda."

"Listen carefully," he said, opening the book. "This is a fitting tale for a little girl such as yourself, who might profit by its example of an obedient wife. He tested her and tested her, subjecting her to many trials and tribulations, yet still she loved him."

"The Lady Mary reads stories much better than you do," his audience pronounced, fidgeting, before he had completed the first page.

"Allow me," smiled Mary, taking the book. Sir John withdrew gratefully.

Later that evening, Mary joined him and Lady Bryan for a goblet of wine before bedtime.

"Did the Lady Elizabeth enjoy her story?" he asked.

"No," smiled Mary. "She was very definite on the subject of how she would have treated Griselda's husband."

"Oh, dear," frowned Sir John. "I hope it took her mind off things."

"I think so," said Mary.

There were no more storms of tears. With the resilience of childhood, Elizabeth allowed herself to be further diverted, and responded to the comfort afforded her by others.

"Praised be God," Lady Bryan murmured, sitting in the shade next to Mary in the flower garden. "The worst moment is surely over."

Elizabeth danced over and demanded that Mary play ball with her.

"I have something to tell you," Mary said, fanning herself with her kerchief. It was still hot, and the scent of roses and honeysuckle hung heavy on the air.

Elizabeth looked at her suspiciously.

"Nothing bad. Good news, in fact. We have a new stepmother."

"I don't want a stepmother," said Elizabeth. "They're wicked. I want you!"

Mary smiled, touched by this, and patted the child's cheek. "Sister, you should rejoice. Queen Jane is a kind lady. She has been good to me, and she is ready to be a mother to you, too."

Elizabeth thought about this.

"The Queen has made me most welcome at court, and she wants you to visit her there also," Mary continued, then paused. Of the price of her return to court, and being received back into her father's favor, she still could not bear to think.

Chapter 12

1536

In August, the King came to Hunsdon and embraced his daughters warmly. It did Mary's heart good to see him so affectionate toward Elizabeth. It was clear that he loved her very much, whatever her mother had done.

Yet she could see that grief hung heavily upon him. Shortly before his visit, she had learned that Henry Fitzroy had died after a short illness that had begun with a cold and quickly escalated into something far more deadly. He had been just seventeen. Although he was her half-brother, he'd been a stranger to her, once a rival. She wondered if, had she got to know him, she would have felt the same affection for him as she felt for Elizabeth. Alas, it was too late now.

She had written to her father to express her condolences, but words had somehow seemed so inadequate. He had lost his only son. There were tears in his eyes when he spoke of him, and he changed the subject when she tried again to convey her sympathy. But he was warm to her, and clearly appreciated her attempts to cheer him.

After a good dinner, he and Mary went riding in the park. She was easier with him now, encouraged by his new kindness toward her. Belatedly, they had come to know each other as adults, although she was still deeply in awe of him, and there was a gap of years she thought they might never breach. It was like learning her father all over again.

"She took the news well?" he asked abruptly when Elizabeth had been returned to the nursery. It was the closest he had come to mentioning Anne Boleyn's fate to Mary.

"She was upset at first, naturally, but she is very young, and children are resilient."

"Aye, she seems happy enough. Forward, too!" He grinned.

"I doubt not that your Grace will cause to rejoice in her in the time to come."

"I think I shall!"

"Will you have her at court?"

"Not yet." He sighed. "The court is still lively with gossip and speculation about that woman's abominable and detestable crimes. I intend to protect her from that, because I don't want her hearing rumors that cast doubt on her paternity."

Mary was startled to hear him mention that.

"There can be no doubt that she is my child," the King went on. "She has the very look of me, and my temper, so I'm told!" He smiled ruefully.

Mary envied him his certainty. Had he ever speculated that Elizabeth might not be his? As they spurred their horses to a canter, she realized that Elizabeth looked more like him than she herself did, but she could not quell her secret doubts. She wished, how she wished, that she could call to mind Mark Smeaton.

"Your own return to court will not be long delayed," the King said, as they neared the woods and slowed to a trot. "You seem so much better—and I would like to mark our reconciliation with a public reunion. Moreover, the Queen is nagging me to bring you to court; she wants to make merry with you."

"I long to see her," Mary said. "She has always been my friend."

"More than you know," he murmured.

Early in September, he wrote to Mary commanding her to prepare for a move to court in the near future. *Apartments are being made ready for you, fitting for your rank.*

"We should start packing," she told her ladies, more than ever grateful for the sumptuous gowns Jane had sent her.

They were in the midst of sorting through her clothing when Sir John was announced. He bowed deeply.

"My Lady Mary, I'm sorry to intrude, but you will want to hear the news that has just been proclaimed in Ware—the King has named you his heir, in default of his having any issue by Queen Jane."

Mary was dizzy with elation. She had not expected this. And later that week, to crown her joy, a letter came from Lady Salisbury, who had been invited back to court in readiness for Mary's arrival and was counting the days until they could be reunited. As news of the proclamation had spread, she wrote, the people had been in a celebratory mood, and crowds had gathered around the palace when she arrived, in the hope of seeing Mary. They had even cheered the governess herself!

But when the plague returned to London later that month, Mary feared that God was displeased at her submission. It seemed wrong that so much good should come to her through such a shameful betrayal. And yet why would He send all the other blessings if she had offended him? Her confessor told her not to worry; God knew the secrets of her heart and that she had signed that document under pressure.

It was more likely, she reasoned, that He was angry with her father, who had begun to close down the monasteries and appropriate their treasures to fill his empty coffers. He had written that he was only dissolving small houses that were no longer financially viable and those that were hotbeds of Popery or fornication. Mary had blushed when she read that; she had only the vaguest concept of what fornication was, but it was clearly shameful. What mattered more to her was what her father's true intentions were. Some said he meant to close all the monasteries and that their closure was an attack on the Church. Others said good riddance, that monks and friars were parasites, and nuns no better than they should be! But Mary felt for those vowed to God, who were now to be cast out with small pensions into a secular world that must seem bewildering to them.

What would happen to all the sick, the widows, the orphans, and the beggars they had succored? She too was living in a world she barely recognized. All the old, comfortable certainties were gone.

She had been wondering if the plague would prevent her from going to Windsor, where her father had moved the court for safety. Fortunately, there had been no reports of any cases nearby, yet she would have to take a long route skirting London to get there, and who knew which places were safe? But she had now learned that the plague was not the only threat to contend with. A rebellion had broken out in Lincolnshire and spread to the north. They were calling it the Pilgrimage of Grace, because the rebels had risen in protest against the King's religious reforms and the closure of the monasteries. They wanted the old ways restored, which was what Mary longed for, too. Given the chance, she would have joined them!

But Queen Jane wrote that it was safe to come, and that the dukes of Norfolk and Suffolk had been sent north to deal with the rebels. When Mary arrived at Windsor Castle in October, she was heartened to see large crowds waiting outside the gates to cheer her, and her eyes welled up when they called down blessings on her. Nodding and smiling, she rode into the castle precincts and was overjoyed to see dear Lady Salisbury waiting to greet her with Sir William Sandys, the Lord Chamberlain and head of the King's household, both of them making deep obeisances. She dismounted and embraced her old governess, both being quite overcome with emotion, and then the Lord Chamberlain escorted her to the lodging that had been prepared for her.

When she saw the palatial apartment, she drew in her breath. It was sumptuously furnished with a great carved tester bed, brilliant tapestries showing allegorical scenes, Turkey rugs on the floor, and an array of gold and silver plate on a sideboard.

The phrase "thirty pieces of silver" came to mind. For this, she had betrayed her mother's memory. But she must not dwell on that. She could not face her conscience today. It was time to prepare for her public reception at court. Her maids were waiting to change her into the clothes the King had provided: a becoming gown of black damask bordered with pearls and a matching English gable hood. No

French hood for her—she had been pleased to hear that Queen Jane had banned them at court. No one wanted any reminders of the Witch.

Mary was trembling by the time she was announced at the entrance to the presence chamber, her new train of gorgeously attired ladies following behind her. She had been building up to this moment and knew it would be one of both triumph and humiliation, for the last time she was at court she had been the King's trueborn, but now she was returning as his bastard. Her cheeks burned at the thought. She shrank from the prospect of all eyes being upon her.

Beyond the ranks of courtiers, she could see her father and Queen Jane standing in front of a roaring fire. She curtseyed in the doorway, and again in the middle of the chamber, then fell to her knees before him.

"Sir," she said, trying to still her nerves, "I do crave your fatherly blessing."

"And I readily give it, my well-beloved daughter," the King replied, taking her hands, raising her and kissing her heartily.

Jane stepped forward; she too embraced and kissed her. "You are most welcome here!" Mary smiled at her gratefully.

Then Father turned to the Privy Councillors standing nearby and glowered. "Some of you were desirous that I should put this jewel to death!" he challenged, and there was a ghastly silence.

Mercifully, Jane stepped in. "That would have been a great pity, to have lost your chief jewel in England," she said quickly.

Father smiled. "No, no!" he replied, patting her belly. "Edward! Edward!"

Mary stared at them. The Queen was with child? The King caught her eye and nodded, beaming, as Jane blushed.

There was a sudden jolting in Mary's head that left her light-headed and shaking. The room swung around her and then she felt herself falling.

She came around to an uproar. Her father was on his knees. "Mary, wake up! Mary!" He patted her cheeks anxiously. "Send for the physicians!"

"And for a cool, damp cloth and some wine!" Jane called.

Mary stared around her, bewildered. What had happened? Had she fainted?

"Be of good cheer, Daughter," Father said. "All is well, and nothing will now go against you."

Jane gently dabbed Mary's forehead with the cool cloth, and soon she began to feel herself again. The King raised her to her feet, took her by the hand and walked her up and down until she felt better, then commanded her ladies to take her back to her lodgings.

After a refreshing sleep—easy now that the worst was over—Mary joined the King and Queen for a private supper, but she could eat little.

"Daughter, there is no cause now to fear," her father reassured her. "She who did you so much harm and prevented me from seeing you for so long has paid the penalty."

Mary looked at him uncertainly. Had he forgotten how he had hounded her into submission after Anne's death?

"To please you, I want you to have these," he said, and handed over a small gold casket that had been sitting beside his plate. Mary opened it.

"These were my mother's," she said in wonder. She held up a thick strand of pearls, then frowned. "But this cross—this was *hers.*" She could not hide the hatred she felt.

"So it is fitting that you should have it," Father said. "I am giving half her jewels to you and the rest to Elizabeth."

"Thank you, Sir," Mary replied doubtfully. "I am overjoyed to have my mother's pearls, but you will forgive me if I do not wear the cross or anything else that belonged to that woman."

"We understand," Jane said quickly.

"Sell them if you wish, or give them away," Father replied. "But you will need a goodly collection of jewels now that you are back at court. By the way, your lodgings at Hampton Court and Greenwich and my other great houses are nearly ready."

Jane reached across to Mary. "And now it will be easier to be friends, for we shall see each other daily. You shall have precedence over all other ladies, being first after myself."

Mary smiled back, fingering the pearls and fighting down tears.

* * *

As she moved around the presence chamber, many courtiers greeted her warmly, congratulating her on her restoration to favor and showing themselves eager to win her friendship—those self-same courtiers, she imagined, who had not batted an eyelid at the cruelties meted out to her. But the past was behind her now. She smiled, thanked them, and moved along, then found herself being introduced to Cromwell, who bowed low.

"I am indebted to you, my lord," she said, smiling at him. "Without your help and wise counsel, I do not know where I would be."

His shrewd eyes were warm. "Your Grace is now where you should be, or almost."

"I thank you. And I must congratulate you on your elevation to the peerage. It is well deserved."

"I do what I can, your Grace." There was no false modesty about him.

"I am proud to account you my friend," she said, and walked on.

And there, waiting next in line, was one who had never wavered. He looked older than when last they met, and there was gray at his temples, but the sight of him made her heart leap.

"Your Highness," Chapuys said, bowing. "This is a most happy day!"

"It is," she agreed, longing to tell him that she felt a traitor to her mother, but holding back because she knew how hard he had worked to broker her restoration—and knew also what he would say to make her feel better. But as they talked, and she told him how vastly her life had improved, she felt better anyway, for he was so obviously pleased for her.

"I will continue to support you all I can," he said. "And I know that this Queen is truly your friend—and a good Catholic. You can rely on her."

She dared not linger too long with him, although she wanted to, so she smiled again and moved on, her heart singing. It was enough to know that he cared for her. It was all she could ever have of him.

Jane had asked the King if Elizabeth might be brought to court, and he had agreed. The child had arrived in some state, accompanied by

Lady Bryan and a new gentlewoman, Kate Champernowne, who was kind, well educated, and good with Elizabeth.

Father had arranged for his daughters to dine with him and Jane in his privy chamber. Elizabeth was to be allowed to stay up as a special treat. As they approached his apartments, Jane had Mary walk alongside her as an equal, but at the door to the presence chamber, Mary stood back to let the Queen go first.

Jane shook her head. "No," she said, "we will go in together."

Touched by her kindness, Mary waited behind Jane's chair as they stood for the fanfare announcing the arrival of the King and waited until he was seated. Basins were brought so that he and Jane could wash their hands, and Mary performed the duty of presenting napkins to them. Then she took her place at the high table, a little lower down than Jane, as three-year-old Elizabeth arrived with her governess and was placed at a small table set at right angles to the dais. She behaved perfectly all through the meal, showing off from time to time, as Father looked on indulgently.

Every day, Jane and Lady Salisbury visited Elizabeth in the nursery apartments and played with her.

"It does my heart good to see your Highness rejoicing at the reversal in your fortunes," Lady Salisbury told Mary, as they watched Elizabeth practicing her dance steps.

"Ah, but what would my dear mother have said?" Mary murmured.

"She would have rejoiced with me," the old lady said firmly. "She would have understood. She loved you so much—you were the light of her life."

Mary could feel tears threatening. "I miss her so. I did not see her for so long, but I always knew she was there. And now, there is a great void."

Lady Salisbury squeezed her hand. "She is in bliss now, where you will surely be reunited with her in Christ one day. You must not mourn for her."

"No, I must not." Mary sniffed, and turned to watch the antics of the shaven-headed Janie the Fool. Soon, she was laughing with the rest of them.

* * *

Father enjoyed Janie's jests, too. One evening, she had him nearly crying with mirth.

"By God, that woman's jokes are priceless!" he chuckled.

"What do you get when you cross an owl and a rooster?" Janie asked, reveling in her sovereign's admiration.

"Tell us!" he commanded.

"A cock that stays up all night long!" She grinned archly.

That set them all bellowing with laughter, but Mary was puzzled. What was so funny about it?

When Janie had finished, and everything was being made ready for the masque that was to follow, the King beckoned Lady Bryan's son Francis over. Bryan was dressed up as Theseus, bracing himself to slay the Minotaur. He looked like a satyr, with his rugged dark looks and the eyepatch he never removed, for he had lost an eye in a tournament years ago. Father murmured something in his ear, and Bryan went away grinning.

The masque was beautifully done. When the dancing began, Bryan jumped off the stage and bowed to Mary, and she allowed him to lead her out to the floor. They exchanged pleasantries, and then he asked her if she would like to see his yard. "It's very impressive!"

It seemed a strange thing to ask. "I did not know that courtiers' lodgings had yards," she said. "I would like to see it, but it would be more proper if I brought my ladies with me." Bryan seemed to have trouble stifling his mirth.

Afterward, Mary heard her father remark, "By God, she *is* innocent!" She had no idea what he meant.

She still suffered torments with her courses and the headaches that plagued her. Her ailments always seemed worse in the autumn and winter, which she supposed was due to the cold weather.

"These women's troubles you have will settle down when you marry," Jane comforted her, as they sat by the fire sewing on a cold November evening.

"It is what I long for," Mary said, blushing furiously, and not quite comprehending what her stepmother meant. "That, and children. I love children. But it will not be easy for the King to arrange a marriage for me. I am a bastard, Madam! No prince will want me, and there is little likelihood that my father will allow me to marry a commoner. I must face the fact that while he lives, I will only be the Lady Mary, the unhappiest lady in Christendom."

"You are his declared heir," Jane countered. "Of course men will want you! Would you like me to press the King to find you a suitable match?"

"That would be most kind, and I should be very grateful," Mary said, vistas of a happy future opening out before her.

But then Jane miscarried her baby, much to everyone's sorrow, and no more mention was made of Mary's marriage.

Soon afterward, she went home to Hunsdon and invited Elizabeth to stay. It was a happy time, for Mary was able to indulge her maternal instincts and lavish love on her little sister. And Lady Salisbury was with them, which was a great pleasure and solace.

That winter was severe. The roads were icy and treacherous. In London, so Mary heard, the Thames had frozen over. But she and Elizabeth had been invited to court for Christmas, and nothing was going to stop her from getting there. After the year they had both had, it would be a health to them.

It proved a cold and arduous journey, but the warmth of the welcome at the various places they stayed, where nothing was too much trouble for the heir to England, was compensation for that. Mary was glad, though, to see the towers of York Place in the distance, and to be enveloped in her father's embrace and kissed by Jane.

Three days before the festival, they wrapped themselves warmly in furs and mounted their horses, Elizabeth tucked within the King's arms, and rode along the frozen river to the City, the child shrieking in delight. Jane was nervous in case her palfrey slipped on the ice, but Mary found it exhilarating to be out in that vast expanse between the two shores, with the cold wind whipping at her cheeks and crowds lining the banks to see them pass.

The City of London looked wonderful with its gay decorations. It seemed that every window was hung with tapestries or cloth of gold, while holly wreaths adorned many doors. At every street corner, priests in rich copes stood waiting to bless the royal party, and hundreds had braved the bitter chill to watch the procession, cheering loudly.

"Merry Christmas!" Father called again and again from his saddle. In his arms, Elizabeth was lisping the words in imitation and waving to the people. Mary was touched to hear so many people calling her own name as she rode behind with Jane to St. Paul's Cathedral for the service that would mark the beginning of the Yuletide celebrations.

When it was over, they emerged to a thunderous ovation, remounted and spurred their horses across the frozen river, cantering toward the Surrey shore, much to the delight of the crowds on the banks. Soon they were approaching Greenwich Palace.

She had known that this first Christmas following her mother's death would be difficult, but being part of the royal family again after so long helped to mitigate the sadness. At table, the King and Queen sat together, with Mary opposite Jane a little farther along the board. Elizabeth was too young to sit through the long feasts with the adults, but as Mary watched their father playing with her during the festivities, she could see how much he loved her. On New Year's Day, he gave her and Mary costly presents, while Mary gave some money to Elizabeth's chaplain, asking him to ensure that her little sister received a sound grounding in the true faith. The last thing she wanted was for her to come under the influence of the reformers her mother had favored.

She was touched when Chapuys presented her with a gift. It was entirely appropriate, a small missal with a leather binding, and she knew she would treasure it. She wished she had given him something in return, but it was too late now. Anyway, she knew that her delighted thanks, and her evident pleasure in the gift, had been enough for him. He had looked so pleased.

Chapter 13

1537

Preparing for bed after a merry New Year's Day, and thinking about Chapuys, Mary peered into her glass. She wondered how long it would be before her father finally found a husband for her. Would she be married this year? She was nearly twenty-one and, people told her, at the peak of her beauty. But was that mere flattery? Did she have what it took to be pleasing to men? Those pink cheeks and pale complexion might be attractive, but she was too thin. Her eyes were large and pale, with a piercing stare that made her look haughty, yet that wasn't her intention. Her eyesight was so poor that, to read, she had to hold the page close. The tragedies that had marred her life were reflected in her face. Tightly buttoning her mouth had become a habit since the years when she had had to smother her emotions. Yet did any of this matter? She was the heir to England, effectively a royal princess, even if that title was no longer hers; her marriage could seal an advantageous political alliance. That would be her chief attraction for prospective suitors.

But Chapuys, she knew, saw more in her than that. If only she could have a husband like him.

After Twelfth Night, she resumed the life of a country gentle-woman, moving between Hunsdon and Beaulieu, sometimes having

Elizabeth to stay, at other times Lady Salisbury, for she was too old now to need a resident governess. The outside world seemed a long way away, as did the Pilgrimage of Grace, which was suppressed with great brutality that spring. Mary felt sorry for the rebels, simple, honest people who—like her—cared about the old ways, but there was nothing she could do for them. At Christmas, Jane had confided that she'd tried to intercede on their behalf, but the King had retaliated with harsh words such as he'd never before used to her, and she had been so frightened that she had not dared to speak out again.

Mary was contented in her domestic existence. She visited the poor in their homes or dispensed charity to them at her gate. She loved nothing better than to hear about the children of her ladies, for her love of children was boundless. How she longed to have her own! Her friends were constantly inviting her to be godmother to their offspring, and she was always delighted to accept. In the meantime, there were many pleasures to divert her: hunting, hawking, embroidery, music, and bowls. Her chief indulgence was gambling at cards, even if she was not very skillful at it; she sometimes lost large sums to her ladies.

She had grown close to Susan Clarencieux, who had been one of her maids since Ludlow days, but had been dismissed along with other servants when Mary had been made to serve Elizabeth. Mary had recently welcomed her back as one of her ladies-in-waiting, for Susan had married a royal herald, Clarencieux King of Arms, and then been swiftly widowed, too soon for her to miss her husband too much, for they had been strangers when they wed. Although he had left her well off, she had been grateful to join Mary's household. No one was as adept at looking after the magnificent gowns and jewels Mary so delighted in wearing.

It was Susan who rejoiced with Mary when, in the spring, the King wrote to say that Queen Jane had again quickened with child and was in perfect health. Mary was glad of it and genuinely hoped that her stepmother would bear a son. Any child of Jane, brought up under her gentle influence, would surely be a kind and compassionate monarch.

It was a golden summer. Mary was aware of the weeks passing by.

She could imagine how eager her father would be for the child to be born. She liked to envisage his reaction when they told him he had a son. God, let it be so!

Hearing that Jane had a strange craving for quails, Mary sent her some in season, for which the Queen was fulsomely grateful.

"She sounds nervous," Mary said to Susan as they packed baskets of bread for the poor.

"And no wonder," Susan replied, her apple cheeks dimpling in a smile. "There's a lot riding on this pregnancy."

"Yes," Mary said. "My father is desperate for a son and heir."

"No pressure there!" Susan grimaced. "Not to mention the fears all women have when facing childbirth."

Mary tucked a clean cloth over her basket. "I think I should go to her. She will be taking to her chamber soon."

"She'll be right glad of your company!" Susan pronounced.

"Then I'll make ready to ride to Hampton Court," Mary decided.

Jane was clearly thrilled to see her. "No sight could be more welcome to me," she said, rising from the window seat and kissing her.

"Your Grace looks so well," Mary said, observing the great mound of Jane's stomach beneath the unlaced gown.

"I am well. The doctors say so. But . . ." A shadow passed over the Queen's face. "I'm just so terrified in case something goes wrong, or I catch the plague. There have been a lot of cases since the summer."

"But not nearby," Mary assured her. "All will be well. And I am here to divert you. As an unmarried lady, I can't be a gossip at your Grace's confinement, but I can be one of the first to welcome my new brother." It was true. She *would* welcome him, even if he displaced her in the succession. It was enough that the King had named her his heir. She loved her life, and what she wanted far more than a crown and scepter was a husband and children. It was not all that her dear mother had wanted for her, but she would be content with what God had given her.

* * *

Reginald Pole had been made a cardinal. Mary was sitting with Jane in the Queen's privy garden, diverting her with her lute, when Lady Salisbury brought the news.

"That is some achievement," Jane said warmly, if a little cautiously.

"To think we have a prince of the Church in our family," Lady Salisbury said. "But I fear the King will not be pleased."

No, he would not, Mary knew. He regarded Reginald's defection to Rome as treason. "I will not mention it to him," she said.

"Nor I," Jane chimed in.

"He will find out soon enough," the older woman said nervously. "And I am dreading his reaction to the tract Reginald is composing on the Great Matter. The King asked him to write it, you remember. I gather it is not complimentary toward the late Queen."

"That cannot matter now," Jane said, arching her back and rubbing it. "His Grace himself speaks no good word of her."

But it did matter, evidently. Not long afterward, late one night, there was a tap on Mary's chamber door. Mary was still up, writing letters, and sent one of her ladies to see who it was.

It was Lady Salisbury, her thin face ravaged with weeping. "Oh, my dear," she said, falling into Mary's arms. "Something terrible has happened."

"Sit down," Mary bade her. "Tell me."

"The King has read Reginald's tract. He is in a fearful rage. I was summoned before the Privy Council. They told me that my son had spoken against his Grace's marriage to the Lady Anne in such insulting terms that it was as well for him that he was out of reach in Rome. Oh, Mary, they were horrible to me. They treated me as if I was guilty, as if I should apologize for having birthed such a son. And I have no doubt that were Reginald here, he would surely lose his head. The King is no respecter of cardinals, as we saw when he executed Cardinal Fisher." She broke down, crying piteously.

Mary bent down and hugged her. "My father's anger will pass, you'll see."

Lady Salisbury shook her head. "No, I think not. My son can never come home. I shall never see him again. And I—I have been forced to abandon him. They made me write him a stern letter castigating him for his treacherous disloyalty. God forgive me, I obeyed—when in fact I ought to have been congratulating him on his plain speaking."

Mary could have wept for her. "Shall I ask the Queen to intercede for him?"

"No!" Lady Salisbury was emphatic. "The King was brutal with her when she pleaded to save the monasteries, and she has enough to cope with just now. I will not trouble her with the birth so imminent. And I know it would do no good anyway. I shall just have to live with my sorrow."

The news went winging through the palace. A prince! A prince for England!

Roused from slumber, Mary heard the shouts in the courtyard below her lodging and the excited commotion. Poor Jane had been in labor for so long that she had given up on her long vigil in the Queen's privy chamber, where she had spent the past three days praying for a happy outcome, trying to close her ears to the groans and cries coming from beyond the closed door of the bedchamber. She had been so tired that she had had to snatch an hour or so of sleep, and, of course, Fate had stolen a march on her.

Straightening her clothes, for she had lain down fully dressed, she pulled a comb through her hair, clapped on her hood, and hurried back to the Queen's apartments. And there, beside Jane's bed, she saw her father holding his son in his arms, tears of joy pouring down his face.

She looked into the tiny elfin face of her half-brother. "He's gorgeous!" she cried, weeping, too.

Father turned to Jane. "Darling, how can I ever thank you! You have given me the most precious jewel in all the world—a healthy boy. Twenty-seven years I have waited for this moment! At last, England has its heir, and my dynasty is assured. We need no longer fear the kingdom being rent by civil war."

He was bursting with pride, beside himself with elation.

"He shall be called Edward," he said, gazing down adoringly at the child, "because he was born on the eve of the feast of St. Edward the Confessor, our royal saint. He shall be titled duke of Cornwall and prince of Wales. God bless you, Edward, my precious boy." He laid his son gently in the cradle as Mary looked on, misty-eyed; then he bent over the bed and kissed Jane with profound tenderness. "A thousand thanks to you, my darling, for bringing me such joy." She smiled up at him, tired but happy.

He turned to her ladies. "Send for Cromwell!" he commanded. "I would speak with him now. Darling, I will be back presently. This cannot wait."

Mary sat down next to Jane and took her hand. "I am so pleased for you," she said.

"Even though this child takes precedence over you in the succession?" Jane asked.

"Even so!" Mary declared, peering dewy-eyed into the cradle. "Perhaps now that he has a son, my father will feel happier about arranging a marriage for me."

"I will press him on that, never fear. He will be eager to please the mother of his heir."

When the King returned, he was still jubilant. "I've had heralds dispatched to every part of my kingdom to proclaim the Prince's birth. The *Te Deum* will be sung in St. Paul's Cathedral and in every parish church in London. But for now, darling, you must have a well-earned rest, and I will try to sleep, too, although I doubt I will. I must just look once more upon my son, to assure myself that he is real!"

As he gazed into the cradle at the slumbering infant, Jane stretched out her hand and took his.

"Stay with me?" she asked. Mary blushed to witness such intimacy, and the midwife was clearly outraged, but Jane persisted. "I just want you here, close to me, on this night of all nights," she told him.

"Leave us," Father said. "I will call if the child wakes."

Mary returned to her lodging, elated and thanking God that Jane had come safely through her ordeal. The following morning, she found her sitting up in bed and signing letters.

"I feel very well," she said. She looked well, despite her late sufferings.

Father, seated beside her, beamed. "She'll be up and about in no time. And the Prince is taking suck greedily. He's a lusty child." He was bursting with pride.

The next day, when Mary returned to see how Jane was doing, the King was there again. "I've arranged for the christening to take place on Monday night," he told her. "Because of the plague, I've restricted the number of guests, but all will be done with the proper pomp and ceremony. Archbishop Cranmer and the dukes of Norfolk and Suffolk are to be the godfathers. Mary, will you be godmother?"

Mary was touched and honored. "Of course, Sir! It will be a privilege."

She dissembled her feelings about Cranmer. Given the chance, she feared, he would infect young Edward with Protestant heresies, if her suspicions of him were correct. At the very least, he would lead the child down the reformist path, away from everything she herself believed in. Well, he would meet his match in her, for she would never allow it. She intended to love and protect her new brother and see him brought up in the right ways.

For all that the King had restricted numbers, there were still about four hundred people present at the Prince's christening. Late on Monday evening, shortly before midnight, Mary skirted the procession that was forming in the courtyard. The flickering light of numerous torches illuminated the darkness, casting a warm glow on silks and satins and cloth of gold, as she made her way to the Queen's apartments, where she joined Cranmer, Norfolk, and Suffolk in the antechamber.

None of them spoke as they waited, and she could feel the tension mounting. Cranmer must know what she thought of him, and Norfolk surely remembered threatening to bang her head against a wall until it was as soft as a baked apple—one did not easily forget such things. As for Suffolk, he had been one of those sent to hound her mother into submission. She was relieved when the door opened and they were admitted to the chamber where Jane lay on an ornate bed wearing a crimson mantle edged with ermine, with her hair loose over her shoulders. Mary was the first godparent to offer her congratulations, as the King, seated by the bed in a richly upholstered chair, proudly showed off his son, who was lying in his vast state cradle.

Mary was delighted to see Lady Exeter afforded a prominent role; she had been such a friend to her and her mother. As the good woman lifted the Prince and held him aloft, the King placed a velvet mantle with a long train about his shoulders. Edward was wide awake and behaving very well, as if aware of the solemnity of the occasion. Lying on a cushion, he was carried away by Lady Exeter, with the Duke of Norfolk supporting his head, the Duke of Suffolk his feet and the Earl of Arundel carrying his train. Mary followed with Cranmer.

Downstairs in the courtyard, four gentlemen of the Privy Chamber held a canopy of cloth of gold above the Prince as he went in procession to his christening in the Chapel Royal. Mary glimpsed Chapuys with the other ambassadors, but then he was gone, swept away with the glittering throng of guests. Elizabeth was there, too, carried in the arms of Edward Seymour, Lord Beauchamp, the Queen's brother. Mary walked behind, attended by a great train of ladies.

In the Chapel Royal, Archbishop Cranmer baptized the Prince in the silver-gilt font that had been set up on a dais draped with cloth of gold. The *Te Deum* was sung and the trumpets sounded, then Garter King of Arms cried out: "God, of His almighty and infinite grace, give and grant good life and long to the right high, right excellent, and noble Prince Edward, most dear and entirely beloved son to our most dread and gracious lord, King Henry VIII!"

The ceremony over, the Prince was borne in state back to the Queen's bedchamber, with Mary following, holding Elizabeth's hand, and the guests of honor crowding in behind them.

Lady Exeter laid young Edward in his mother's arms, and Jane gave him her blessing. Mary watched as her father took him, weeping for joy, and blessed him in the name of God, the Virgin Mary, and St. George. The tiny Prince was becoming a little fretful, so he was carried back to his nursery, and refreshments were served. It was nearly morning before the last guests kissed the hands of the King and Queen and departed.

"Mary, you must come!" It was her father, standing wild-eyed at the door. "Jane is failing."

He was gone before she could reply, but she fled after him along the torchlit galleries to the Queen's lodgings. There, she found her stepmother lying breathless in bed.

"Mother of God!" The King's tone was agonized. "Jane! Jane!" The doctors standing around the bed looked distraught.

Jane could barely speak. Her breath was coming in terrible gasps. "Edward," she whispered.

"Should I fetch the Prince?" Mary asked.

"No, Madam, we dare not take the risk," Dr. Chamber said.

"There is no risk!" Father countered. "I would not be here if there was any fear of infection. Bring the child." His voice caught on a sob.

"I will fetch him." Cromwell had arrived, and just as soon disappeared.

Jane opened her eyes, then raised a weak hand and pointed at the wall opposite, looking fearful.

"What is she doing?" the King asked.

"She is delirious, I think," Mary said, trying not to cry.

They knelt as the Bishop of Carlisle gave Jane the last sacrament, anointing her with sacred oil and giving her absolution for her sins. Father was clutching her hand, weeping inconsolably.

Cromwell returned with a sleepy Edward in his arms. "They are crowding into the Chapel Royal. If prayer can save her Grace, she is not like to die."

"There has rarely been a lady more popular with everyone," Mary observed.

"Sir, I have sent for the Duke of Norfolk to help take charge while your Grace is occupied here," Cromwell said. "I warned him that as for our good mistress, there is no likelihood of her life, the more pity." His voice broke. Mary had never dreamed he was so fond of Jane.

"God, I would I could do something for her!" Father cried. "All my power is for nothing. My most precious jewel is slipping away, and I am helpless. Oh, darling, do not leave me!" He collapsed, weeping, his arm stretched out, gripping Jane's fingers.

Cromwell laid the child beside her. Gasping for breath, Jane tried to raise her hand in blessing, but had not the strength. Mary watched helplessly as her dear friend slipped away, then saw her father break down in noisy sobs.

Great lamentation was made for the death of the Queen. Mary had felt stricken by the heart-rending sight of her body lying lifeless on the bed, but no one took it more heavily than the King. She could not remember ever having seen him so affected by anything. He had withdrawn to his apartments, refusing to see anyone.

He could not bear anything to do with death, so she was not surprised to hear the next day that he had departed early for Windsor. She imagined he could not bear to stay in the same house as the cold corpse of the woman he had so loved.

Norfolk was in charge of the funeral arrangements. Mary was to be chief mourner, which she thought fitting, for Jane had done more for her than for anyone. She could never have filled the shoes of Mary's sainted mother—no one could—but she had done her very best to restore her stepdaughter to her rightful place in her father's affections, and the succession, and for that Mary would be eternally grateful.

She and the Queen's ladies were issued with mourning habits of black with white headdresses to signify that Jane had died in childbed. They took turns to keep watch over her body for a day and night. Jane looked peaceful, as if she were sleeping, but when Mary touched her hand, it was cold, and after a while her face took on a gray hue. One morning, the wax chandlers came and did their work on her. When Mary and the others returned, she was lying on a bier covered with a rich pall of cloth of gold and dressed in a robe of gold tissue and some of her jewels, with the Queen's crown on her head. Her fair hair lay loose like a cape of pale gold, her face was painted in an attempt to give a semblance of life, and there was a strong smell of herbs and spices in the bedchamber.

The women followed in procession as the bier was reverently carried to the presence chamber, where the body would lie in state for a week. Tapers were lit around it, and a black-draped altar was set to one side and furnished with a jeweled crucifix, holy images, and censers of gold.

As Masses were sung night and day for Queen Jane's soul, they kept vigil, ensuring that there were always some of them watching over her. They knelt interminably through all the services, lamenting and weeping, while Mary tried to ignore a raging toothache and the stiffness in her knees.

They took it in turns to rest. One night, as Mary emerged from the presence chamber, swaying with weariness, she saw Cromwell waiting for her. He looked anxious.

"Madam," he said, his voice low. "I am worried about the King. He is keeping himself too close and secret. The Bishop of Durham has tried to rally him, but in vain. He has taken his loss very hard."

"And no wonder," Mary said, tears welling again. "We all miss the Queen terribly. It is a great tragedy."

"Almighty God has taken to Himself a most blessed and virtuous lady," chimed in Archbishop Cranmer, joining them. "But consider what He has given to us, to the comfort of us all—our most noble Prince, to whom God hath ordained your Highness to be a mother. God gave us that noble lady, and God has taken her away, as pleased Him."

Mary did not want his comfort. How could she? He had broken her mother's marriage, and for that she could never like or approve of him.

She addressed Cromwell. "Maybe it is best to leave the King's Grace in peace for now."

He regarded her sadly. "And maybe we should not. Some of his councillors think he should be urged to marry again for the sake of his realm. He has his son at last, after waiting all these long years, but the Prince is but an infant and might at any time succumb to some childhood ailment."

Mary was shocked. "But the Queen is not yet buried! For decency's sake, my lord, let it alone for now."

"Some feel that the matter is pressing, my lady."

They left it there, and Mary went to bed, shaking her head.

A few days later, Cromwell was waiting again as she emerged from the presence chamber to seek a clove for her worsening toothache. "I have word from Windsor," he said. "The King is now taking his loss reasonably. A deputation of councillors has visited him and laid their concerns before him. He is, of course, little disposed to marry again, but he has framed his mind to be indifferent to whatever they think best. His tender zeal toward his subjects has overcome his sad disposition."

"I pray he will not be maneuvered into a fourth marriage too soon," Mary said.

"Has your ladyship ever known his Grace to do anything he does not want to do?" Cromwell asked with a wry smile.

"Of your charity, pray for the soul of the Queen!" Lancaster Herald cried, as the court assembled in silence to pay its respects. After a week, Mary and her companions were relieved when the funeral obsequies began, for all the spices in the world could not mask the stink from the body, and they were glad to see it coffined and moved to a catafalque set up in the Chapel Royal, where they were to keep vigil beside it for a further seven days.

Mary had done what she could. She had paid for Masses to be sung for Jane's soul, and taken charge of her household, which would shortly be disbanded. She had distributed her personal jewels, as Jane had directed, to those favored with bequests, and delivered the rest—the Queen's jewels, those same ones her dear mother had once been forced to surrender to that witch Boleyn—to the Master of the Jewel House.

It was as well that etiquette precluded kings from attending the funerals of their consorts, for Mary did not think her father could have borne it, although Cromwell told her that he was in good health and as merry as a widower might be, which probably wasn't saying much. At least he was attending to state business again.

There was a great public outpouring of grief in November, when, by order of the Lord Mayor, twelve hundred Masses were sung in the City of London for the Queen's soul, and a solemn service was held in St. Paul's. That day, Jane's coffin was carried with great solemnity to Windsor for burial. Riding on a palfrey caparisoned in black velvet, Mary followed the hearse. On the coffin lay a wooden effigy of the Queen in her robes of state, with false hair loose under a rich crown of gold, a scepter of gold in the right hand, rings set with precious stones on the fingers, and a jeweled necklace around the neck. Behind Mary rode twenty-nine mourning ladies, one for every year of Jane's life, and in their wake two hundred poor men, all wearing her badge and bearing aloft lighted torches. At Colnbrook, Eton, and Windsor, the poor men went ahead and lined the streets. Behind them stood the sorrowing crowds, hats in hands, watching silently as the procession passed.

At the steps of St. George's Chapel within the precincts of Windsor Castle, Mary watched bleakly as the coffin was received by the Dean and College, and followed as it was carried inside by six pallbearers. At the chancel, Archbishop Cranmer received it and led the congregation in prayer, after which the body lay in state before the high altar. Mary stayed there all night, keeping watch over it, her grief a heavy burden. Without her stepmother, the world seemed an empty place.

Outside the chapel, the congregation dispersed. As Mary made to depart for her lodgings, she saw Chapuys approaching her.

"Your Highness, allow me to offer my condolences," he said, his face filled with concern. "The world has lost a very great lady."

Mary could not speak; her heart was too full. She would have given anything to be enfolded in Chapuys's arms and comforted.

She pulled herself together. "Thank you, my lord ambassador. Yes, we are all reeling from the shock. And how tragic to be taken at the height of her triumph."

"Indeed. The Prince is thriving?"

"Oh, yes. He has an army of nurses and attendants to see to his every need."

"The King and your Highness will have cause to rejoice in him in time to come. I know you will be a mother to him." His eyes held hers. They were saying far more than words ever could.

"Thank you," she faltered, thrown into confusion by her feelings. "And now I must go. These long vigils have made me very tired."

Chapuys bowed again. "God go with you, my Princess," he murmured, so low that she wondered if she had misheard him.

The next day, the Queen was finally laid to rest with all the pomp and majesty that could be. There were many pensive hearts in that concourse of mourners. Her brothers looked especially stricken, and no wonder, for she had been the source of their advancement and prosperity. Yet there was no doubt that they would now enjoy enormous influence as uncles to the Prince. The prospect perturbed Mary not a little, for while Jane had been a devout Catholic, Edward and Thomas Seymour were known to hold radical views about religion.

She stood weeping as the coffin was lowered into a vault in the middle of the choir, before the high altar, and the officers of the Queen's household broke their staves of office over it, symbolizing the termination of their allegiance and service. It was all so final.

Wearing deepest black, Father came out of seclusion and took up the reins of everyday life once more, but the joy had gone out of him and he had put on an alarming amount of weight, for grief and a bad leg had prevented him from taking his usual exercise. It was as if a pall lay over the court.

"I must marry again," he sighed. "I have one son, and I must ensure the succession by siring others."

He and Mary were at supper in his chamber. He had sent for her to join him, saying he needed some female company to lighten his spirits. Cromwell had been invited, too, and looked alert when the King raised the matter of his marriage.

"There are great advantages to be gained by a foreign alliance, Sir," he said.

"I'm not so old," Father said thoughtfully. "I'm only forty-six, and I must still be the most eligible catch in Christendom."

Mary smiled, but she was wondering if, with three dead wives and two divorces behind him, the princesses of Europe would agree with him.

"Indeed, Sir. Many ladies would be delighted to be honored by your hand, but I have been looking into the matter, and the problem is that, just now, there are very few suitable brides available. Some are of the Protestant persuasion, and others not politically desirable."

Father waved a dismissive hand. "Well, keep looking around. I'll rely on your judgment, Crum."

Chapter 14

1538

Mary was back at Hunsdon, glad to return to her quiet, peaceful life that now seemed strangely empty. She had brought her half-sister with her, for Lady Bryan had been transferred to the Prince's household and there was a new governess, Lady Troy, to look after Elizabeth. Mary liked her, but it was a big change in a four-year-old's life and Elizabeth was unhappy about it. She seemed to feel the loss of Lady Bryan far more painfully than that of her mother, for the old woman had cared for her daily in the most loving yet firm way. But she remained a resilient child, sharp-witted, intelligent, and self-contained. Mary lavished on her all the affection she had in her. Even if she was Mark Smeaton's child, she loved her as a sister.

They spent their days enjoying simple pleasures and good food. Their table was replete with partridges, larks, pheasants, fine cheeses, cherries, apples, quinces, and pears, all washed down with wine and—once—a good bottle of sack. But Mary's tooth was bothering her again, so much so that, in the end, her father sent a surgeon to draw it out. It was a painful procedure, yet the relief was blissful.

She busied herself ordering new clothes—embroidered partlets, caps of silver and gilt, gloves of Spanish leather, and a kirtle of cloth of silver, among other fripperies. Then, of course, Elizabeth must have new clothes, too, so Mary set the tailors and seamstresses to work again, making pretty things for her. In the afternoons, she played the virginals while Elizabeth danced, and in the evenings, she gambled at cards with her ladies. She did not forget her devotions or her charities, but sent money to poor beggars and to prisoners. She acquired two more godchildren, standing sponsor at the font for each.

Chapuys wrote regularly. He told her that her father was looking for a bride in France. It hurt her to hear that he had said he did not want another Spanish bride, and she deplored the idea of a French match. But King Francis had marriageable daughters, and it was said that there were other beautiful ladies of high rank available in France.

But her father liked to keep his intentions hidden, and it was in character that even as he considered a French alliance, his ambassadors abroad were told to report on other likely brides. Rumors were rife, even at Hunsdon, but soon Mary learned that he was interested in one of her cousins, the young Duchess of Milan, niece to the Emperor.

Chapuys wrote that the Duchess Christina was sixteen years old, tall and of excellent beauty. Young as she was, she was already a widow, her elderly husband having died, and she was still in mourning. Apparently, the King was entranced by reports of her loveliness. No doubt he saw her youth as an advantage, anticipating that her character could be the more easily molded to suit him.

But then, mercurial as ever, he changed his mind. Chapuys informed Mary that he was now seeking a big wife, since he himself was big in person. She inferred from this that he had put on even more weight, which rather concerned her, as it could not be doing his health any good.

The big wife he had in mind was another widow, a French noblewoman called Marie de Guise. She was mature and sensible and— more importantly—had borne two sons. But, given advance warning of his imminent proposal, she hastily married her other suitor, the King of Scots.

Father shrugged off his disappointment and sent his painter, Master Holbein, to Brussels to paint the portrait of the Duchess of Milan. With thoughts of marriage in mind, he discarded his mourning garments. By then, Queen Jane had been dead for five months. When he summoned his daughters to join him in celebrating Easter at court,

Mary asked his permission to wear a new gown of white taffeta edged with velvet, which seemed appropriate now that she had discarded her black weeds, and was suitable for the joyful feast of the Lord's resurrection. Elizabeth had a new gown, too, and twirled about vainly in it. She was pretty and confident—far more so than Mary had been at that age. Mary kept a vigilant watch on her, lest she turn out to be too like her mother. That could not be tolerated!

Mary was dismayed to find that their father had aged since she had last seen him, and that he was suffering constant pain from a new abscess in his leg. Eventually, he was forced to submit to the barber surgeons and have it lanced, which relieved the pain, but did not cure him. It galled him to have the sporting activities he loved curtailed: no longer could he ride in the lists, but was obliged to sit and watch younger, fitter men doing what he had once done better. Increasing immobility was making him fat, and his once splendid red-gold hair was thinning. Yet he still dressed sumptuously, setting a new fashion for short gowns with built-up shoulders and bulky sleeves. Soon every man at court was wearing one, which meant that his increasing girth no longer looked conspicuous.

Pain and advancing infirmity had made his temper highly unpredictable. Mary was not the only one to suffer the fearful lash of his tongue, and poor Cromwell got bawled at every week. Sometimes, Father even hit him on the head, pounding him soundly. After one of these outbursts, Mary saw Cromwell emerge from the chamber shaking with fright and with rumpled hair, but smiling bravely. They were all learning to tiptoe around the King's sensibilities, for in certain moods he could be dangerous.

He was in such a mood when he heard that Mary's mother's old chaplain, Father Forrest, was still speaking out in her favor. Immediately, he gave orders that the old man be put on trial, and when he was condemned, he was taken to Smithfield and there roasted in chains over a fire. Forrest had been a dear, kind soul, upright and devout, and he had loved the late Queen devotedly. Mary was devastated to hear of his unimaginable sufferings. Sometimes she thought her father the most cruel man in the world.

* * *

Summer came, and with it the King's spirits seemed to revive. He
ordered that Prince Edward be brought to Hampton Court, so that
all his children could be together. Attended by his vast retinue, Edward arrived gorgeously dressed in cloth of gold, looking solemn in
the arms of Lady Bryan. He was eight months old and thriving. His
heart-shaped face, steady blue eyes, and pointed chin gave him an
elfin look. He was the goodliest babe Mary had ever set eyes on. She
never wearied of looking at him. She would sit watching him take
suck from his wet nurse, Mother Jack, and took pleasure in seeing
their father proudly carrying him around in his arms, showing him
off to the courtiers, and holding him up at a window so that the
crowds below could see their future King.

She loved to cuddle Edward and feel his sturdy little body on her
lap. He had an affectionate nature and always came joyfully to her.
When she asked her minstrels to play for him, he could not sit still,
and leaped in her arms as if he would dance. She could feel no resentment toward this child who now took precedence over her.

In June, Mary was present at a river pageant staged on the Thames
at Whitehall. She stood with the King on the roof above the privy
stairs, surrounded by courtiers, looking down on the riverbank,
which was crowded with people; she could see dozens of small craft
filled with ladies and gentlemen on the water. She watched as a mock
battle took place between two barges, one manned by actors playing
the Pope and his cardinals, the other by the King's champions. Father roared with laughter as the Papal company were tipped into the
Thames, but Mary wished she were anywhere else. For the break
with Rome, devastating on so many levels, was having frightening
consequences. France and Spain had signed a truce that left England
dangerously isolated, since Father had left himself vulnerable to the
hostility of Catholic princes. Yet still he hoped to marry the Duchess
of Milan. Mary was at court when her portrait arrived, a magnificent
full-length study that showed a demure young woman with an enig-
matic smile and inviting eyes—rather bold, she thought.

But Father was captivated, and immediately dispatched an embassy to Brussels with his proposal of marriage. Back came the young
Duchess's answer: she was perturbed that the King had so speedily
been rid of his previous three queens, the first by poison, the second

innocently put to death, and the third lost for lack of keeping in childbed. If she had two heads, she said, one would be at his Grace's service!

In short, she turned the King down. Mary believed that for all his spluttering at her impudence, he felt secretly relieved, having seen with his own disbelieving eyes the evidence of her pertness and disrespect.

"His Grace is now inclined to heed my advice and seek a bride among the Protestant princes of Germany," Cromwell told Mary as they strolled together in a garden filled with the scent of late roses. "I think he would be willing to set aside his religious scruples if it meant making an alliance that could tip the balance of power in Europe in England's favor once more."

"But—a Protestant queen?" She had long deplored the fact that some states in Germany had embraced the Lutheran faith. They were permanent thorns in the Emperor's side—and threats to the unity of Christendom.

"The princesses I have in mind have been brought up by their mother as strict Catholics," Cromwell replied, smiling. "It is their brother who has turned Lutheran. I speak of the children of John, Duke of Cleves, who has a liberal, enlightened approach to religion. He has two unmarried daughters, Anna and Amalia. He has offered the hand of Anna, the elder, to the King. He is sensible of the fact that it will be a brilliant match for her."

"I trust she is no giddy sixteen-year-old like the Duchess of Milan," Mary said, unhappy at the prospect of seeing her father married to the princess of a small German duchy. Heavens, she had no idea where it even was!

"She is twenty-three," Cromwell supplied.

"It will seem strange having a stepmother only a year my senior."

Cromwell picked a rose and handed it to her, an unusually chivalrous gesture in a man who was normally so hard-headed. "You may never have her for a stepmother. These negotiations take time—and I fear that the King's Highness is lukewarm in the matter."

One evening that month, Mary ventured up the stairs to the Queen's apartments to retrieve a book she had lent Jane. These rooms had been left untouched since her death, and when Mary pushed open the door, they smelled musty and abandoned. She found the book and left, but as she turned on the staircase, she saw a glimmer above her in the dusky twilight—and there was her late stepmother, carrying a lighted candle in her hand and wearing a trailing white night robe. It was her to the life, except that her face appeared luminous. As Mary stared, too startled to feel frightened, the figure glided past her down the stairs and out to the Inner Court. When Mary chased after her, she had disappeared.

She pondered much upon what she had seen, and if indeed she had seen the ghost of her beloved stepmother. Was it a warning against her father's proposed marriage? Jane had been a devout Catholic; she would not have wanted to see a queen with Protestant connections taking her place. She had hated Anne Boleyn's reforming zeal.

Or had she come to let Mary know that she was watching over her? On reflection, Mary preferred that explanation. If only her beloved mother had manifested herself in such a way! But her blessed soul was with God and the angels—she was waiting for her in Heaven.

Later that summer, Mary took Elizabeth back to Hunsdon. Without a queen in residence, the court was a male preserve, and their father thought it best that they depart, not just on that account, but because the country air was better for them.

Lady Bryan wrote to Mary regularly and reported that the Prince was growing fast. He had stood alone and grown four teeth before his first birthday, and when Mary read that, she grieved afresh for Queen Jane, knowing how much joy and pride she would have taken in her son. When Edward was weaned, Mother Jack was dismissed, and in her stead Mrs. Sybil Penne was appointed chief nurse under Lady Bryan.

It was of little consequence to Mary. Dark deeds were afoot, and she was deeply worried for Lady Salisbury, who might be in deadly peril.

Father was never one to forgive and forget. Obsessively suspicious of his Plantagenet kinsfolk, he had evidently now convinced himself that the Poles were a pack of traitors. Mary was shocked to hear that Reginald's younger brother Geoffrey had been imprisoned in the Tower for aiding and abetting him, and even more so when the whole family, including Lady Salisbury herself, was sent there to join him, all of them under suspicion of treason—even the children! It could not be true! Lady Salisbury had not a disloyal bone in her body.

Chapuys wrote that Lady Salisbury's house had been searched by the King's officers. They had found a banner embroidered with the royal arms of England, of the heraldic kind reserved for the sovereign alone. It looked damningly as if the old woman had been plotting to seize the crown.

"It's ludicrous!" Mary cried to Susan Clarencieux. "Lady Salisbury is sixty-five, far too old to be plotting rebellion! She would never do a thing to harm the King." Yet she had been sent to the Tower all the same. Mary wept when she read that she was being kept in a cold cell without adequate food or clothing. She despaired of her father. Where was his humanity?

He was acting like a man possessed. To her horror, he sent Lady Salisbury's oldest son, Lord Montagu, and his cousin, the Marquess of Exeter, to the scaffold, condemned for having plotted to assassinate the King. It was hard to believe that either man, especially the Marquess, who had staunchly supported Mary's mother, could have committed such a horrible crime.

She could not bear to think of how dear Lady Salisbury was enduring her imprisonment and the loss of her sons—one dead, one incarcerated, and one in permanent exile. Her grief must be terrible, for they were everything to her. Mary prayed for them all, especially for Margaret, her little grandson, Henry Pole, and Exeter's son, young Edward Courtenay. It seemed that the King was determined to punish every remaining member of the House of Plantagenet.

As the Christmas of 1538 approached, she tried to set aside her fears, and helped Elizabeth to make a cambric shirt to send as a New Year gift for Edward. They did not go to court, but kept the Yuletide season as merrily as they could at Hunsdon.

1539

In the new year, Mary received unwelcome news. The Duke of Cleves had proposed a double alliance. King Henry should marry his daughter Anna, and she, Mary, should marry his son, the abominable Protestant William. Dear God, she prayed, deliver me from such a fate!

The Duke had asked for her portrait. Cromwell informed her gallantly that he had protested against that, since William's envoy could well testify to her beauty, her grace, and her excellent virtues, which were so many that it could not be doubted that any man would hesitate to hurry her to the altar.

It was her father who saved her from her unwanted suitor. He had realized that her marriage to William of Cleves would preclude any that he himself might wish to make with Anna, since it would make him brother-in-law to his daughter. Such a union would be incestuous, and he said he had had enough of those. Of course, his marriage with Mary's mother hadn't been incestuous at all, but her father never would admit that he had been wrong.

Soon afterward, there came terrible news from Rome, news that Mary had been dreading for some years now. Shocked at the executions of Montagu and Exeter, the Pope had finally excommunicated her father.

She prayed for him as she had never prayed before. What must it feel like to be cut off from God and Christian fellowship and the sacraments of the Church? How dreadful for your soul to be in mortal peril. She could understand that, for she had feared that she too might be cast out if she betrayed her mother. Even now, she fretted that she might not be forgiven. But, of course, Father was adamant that the sentence of the Bishop of Rome had no force in England. It would make no difference. Yet it was clear from Chapuys's tactfully worded letters that France and the Empire were now more hostile than ever toward him. Daily, the prospect of an alliance with Cleves grew more attractive, for its Duke could be counted upon to remain friendly in the face of the Papal anathema.

* * *

In May, Parliament passed an Act of Attainder against Lady Salisbury, depriving her of her life, title, estates, and goods.

"No!" Mary wailed when the news came. "Not dear Lady Salisbury!" Surely the King would not have her head?

Susan held her as she wept and raged at the unfairness of it all. "How can he do this?" Mary cried.

"He does it because he is afraid," Susan soothed. "And when people are afraid, they lash out."

"But Lady Salisbury is no threat to him!"

"He believes she is, and I doubt that anyone could convince him otherwise."

Mary waited, tremulous and agitated, for news. She learned that the King had seized all Lady Salisbury's property, but there was no word of his ordering her execution. As the weeks went by, she began to relax, anticipating that he would leave the old lady to languish in prison, or even release her. She prayed that day would come soon.

But it was clear that Father had been badly shaken by these recent treasons. This was evident in the new security measures he put in place to safeguard the Prince. Edward now had a greater household than before, and no effort or expense was being spared to protect this most precious jewel in England's crown.

The coldness between England and the two allies, France and the Empire, deepened, to Mary's distress. Like her mother, she had always wished to see England and the Empire bound in eternal amity. But when the Emperor and King Francis signed a new treaty pledging not to make any fresh alliances without the consent of the other, her father finally resolved to press ahead with the Cleves marriage. He sent envoys to Germany, followed by Master Holbein with instructions to paint the likeness of the Princess Anna for his inspection.

Cromwell wrote to Mary, plainly eager for the alliance. *Every man praises the beauty of the Lady Anna. She excels the Duchess of Milan as the golden sun excels the silver moon. Every man praises her virtues.*

With a touch of his wry wit, Chapuys surmised that the King already fancied himself in love with the lady. He had even said he would take her without a dowry if her portrait pleased him. And please him it did.

Mary had very mixed feelings. She wanted to see him happy and contented again, as he had been with Queen Jane, yet she feared that the Protestant cause would be greatly advanced if Anna of Cleves became queen. Brought up a Catholic she might have been, but her brother, who now ruled Cleves, was a Lutheran, and might have infected her with his heresies. God forbid, she could turn out to be another Anne Boleyn, which was what the reformers were no doubt hoping for.

Elizabeth, at six, was most curious about her future stepmother. "Do you think she will invite me to court and let me wear pretty gowns and dance?" she asked hopefully.

"I'm not sure that she likes dancing," Mary said. By all reports, Anna had had a very strict upbringing. Apparently, even music was frowned upon at the court of Cleves. Mary was praying she would not be a dragon, disapproving of frivolous pastimes, for she herself did so enjoy dancing and music and gambling. After all, what other pleasures did she have?

"I will make her like it!" Elizabeth declared, tossing back her long red hair and skipping a few dance steps. What a willful and enchanting child she was!

In October, Mary was staying at Hertford Castle when word reached her that the marriage treaty was signed. She sighed, but she was more immediately concerned about her dwindling funds. Christmas loomed ahead, and she had realized that she had not the wherewithal to buy gifts or keep the season properly. Again, Cromwell came to her rescue and reminded her father to make good the deficit. He himself sent her another beautiful horse as a gift. It set her wondering whether Cromwell, like Chapuys, had deeper feelings for her than he could ever admit to. Why else would he have been such a friend to her all these months, when he could have made life easier for himself and cast her to the wolves?

Chapuys reported that great preparations had been set in train for the reception of the Princess Anna. There had been much jostling for places in the new Queen's household. The King was planning a Christmas wedding at Greenwich, to be followed by twelve days of festivities and Anna's coronation on Candlemas Day. Mary was pleased to hear that he was in exuberant spirits, and that his leg was troubling him less. He sounded impatient to meet his bride.

Everyone was waiting expectantly. It had been two years since the death of Queen Jane. Now England was ready for its new Queen and the benefits she would bring. Setting aside her reservations, Mary resolved to welcome her warmly and make a friend of her.

Adverse winds in early December prevented Anna from sailing, and it soon became obvious that she would not be in England in time for Christmas. Mary was wondering if she was still to go to court, or if she should make preparations to spend Yuletide at Hunsdon again, when a letter came from her father. A marriage had been proposed for her, with Duke Philip of Bavaria.

Mary was appalled. A Protestant! What was the King thinking of? Impulsively, she dashed off a letter declaring that she would rather remain unmarried than enter into such an alliance.

But her father, while privately sympathetic, was immovable. He needed all the allies he could get against the Emperor and the King of France, and was determined to press on with the negotiations. Philip was coming to London and Mary was to go to Hertford Castle to greet him. Unwillingly, she obeyed.

In the middle of December, she arrived at Hertford, where her father welcomed her warmly and led her into a parlor, where the Duke was waiting. As he was presented to her, she saw an attractive man in his late thirties with fair hair and angular, Teutonic features. He was elegantly dressed in a black gown and bonnet, with a gold-embroidered collar to his white shirt and a scarlet doublet; his voice was mellow, his English good, and there was undisguised pleasure in his eyes as he took in her appearance. She was touched when he presented her with a gift, and overcome with confusion when he leaned forward and kissed her on the lips.

"I understand that is the way you English greet ladies," he smiled.

Father was beaming at them. "I will leave you both to become acquainted," he said, and signaled to their attendants to depart with him.

Mary was in turmoil. She could feel herself blushing furiously, could still feel the pressure of Philip's lips on hers. What would people be thinking? Princesses were not greeted by kisses on the lips; such familiarity betokened a wedding to come!

But she was forgetting the courtesies. "Pray sit down," she invited, and they sat opposite each other on either side of the fire. Philip was regarding her warmly, a smile playing about his mouth. He was very good-looking. She had to remind herself that he was a heretic and that she ought to be objecting to the match. But he was so pleasant and kind and admiring that she felt quite overcome.

They spoke of the bad weather—he had had a terrible voyage—of the King's imminent wedding, and of Philip's hopes of friendship with England. "It would be, for me, an alliance based on love," he declared, his eyes twinkling, "which is always the best kind of alliance, I feel."

"Indeed," Mary faltered, wondering if he thought her silly and inane, for she was struggling to talk to him naturally. "Does your Highness like to hunt?"

"It is one of my chief pleasures," he told her.

"Mine too! And do you enjoy music and dancing at your court?"

"Sometimes. But your Highness will be able to set the fashions there."

It dawned on her, as it had not before, that if she married this man, she would have to leave England and live in Bavaria. The prospect was unwelcome, yet she was drawn to him, despite herself, and it occurred to her that life with him could be very pleasant indeed. She would be Madam the Duchess of Bavaria, and he could give her the children she craved. Why, this time next year, she might even be a mother! Of course, Philip would have to agree to let her practice her religion, but she was sure her father would see to that.

She began to relax and enjoy herself. As the afternoon wore on, she became more than ever convinced that Philip would make a good husband. When her father returned and it was time for the Duke to say farewell, he kissed her again, and she found herself liking it—very much.

At supper that evening, the King leaned back in his chair and regarded Mary. "I hear that your meeting with Duke Philip went well. He wishes to proceed with the marriage. What say you?"

Mary panicked. She had had time to think. While she was attracted to her suitor, away from his presence her reservations had reasserted themselves. She knew nothing of Bavaria, and she still had deep qualms about marrying a Protestant.

She swallowed. "I am yours to command, Father."

"But you liked him?"

"I did."

"It looked as if you liked him very well!" he guffawed, and she felt her cheeks growing hot. Suddenly, the room seemed stifling.

"If you will excuse me, Father, I am not feeling well. May I retire?"

The King was all concern. "Of course. What ails you?"

"I think I am coming down with an ague . . . It is my bad time of year."

She escaped to her chamber. She was not ill; she just needed time to sort out her thoughts and feelings. She knew that if she saw Philip, she would be lost—and this might be her only chance of marriage. But how could she leave all that was familiar for a heretic? How could she face never seeing Chapuys again?

She went home to Hunsdon under the pretext of fearing she was infectious and continued to feign illness. She could not reach a decision. It made her head ache just thinking about it. It did not help when her father wrote to say that he had advised Duke Philip to stay in England until she was better and could give him an answer. She feared that day might never come.

Chapter 15

1540

Chapuys kept her informed, as always. Anna of Cleves had arrived and had been received by the King at a state reception at Shooter's Hill by Blackheath. They had married at Greenwich, but there were rumors that her father was not pleased with his bride. Mary was sad to hear that, for she had been nursing hopes that this new stepmother would be as great a friend to her as Queen Jane had been.

The King did not press her for a decision about her marriage. She assumed he had troubles of his own to contend with. As January progressed, she began to relax. Unable to bear the strain of worrying about it, she knew now what her decision must be—unless Father insisted that she accept Philip.

But no. At the end of the month, he wrote to say that the Duke had gone home. *Both the Emperor and the King of France are suing for my friendship,* he told her, *and I no longer need the German princes. Your marriage to Duke Philip could not have taken place because he is too closely related to Queen Anna, and he is your third cousin, so the union would have been incestuous.*

Shaking with relief, if a little sad and fearing that her last chance of finding a husband had slipped away, Mary wondered why this information had not come to light when the alliance with Bavaria was

being considered—and then she understood that her father's marriage to Anna of Cleves had been unnecessary. Poor Anna—how
would she fare now?

Chapuys reported that the King remained unhappy with the Queen
and was leaving her much to her own devices. Mary wondered if he
would try to divorce her, and judged it best to stay away from court.
She had seen too much of that kind of drama already. But her heart
went out to Anna, a stranger in a foreign land.

In June, Father summoned Mary and Elizabeth from Hunsdon to
Whitehall Palace—as York Place was now known—and on the way
Mary seized the opportunity to meet her stepmother, who seemed to
have taken up permanent residence at Richmond Palace.

They were rowed along the river from Hammersmith, Elizabeth
bouncing up and down excitedly. When they reached Richmond and
were ushered into the Queen's privy chamber, Anna, richly dressed
in a gown in the English style, came hastening toward them, forgetting protocol and holding out her hands warmly. She was an angular-
faced young woman with such a pleasant manner that Mary had to
wonder why her father had taken an aversion to her.

"My Lady Mary, my Lady Elizabeth, you are most welcome," she
said in a low, guttural accent. "I am overjoyed to meet you both at
last."

"Your Grace, we are on our way to Whitehall, and I thought it
would be a pleasure to make your acquaintance," Mary said.

"You have not come from the King?" Anna looked dismayed.

"No, we are about to visit him," Mary said, sorry that she had
unwittingly caused the other woman distress and wondering why
Anna looked so upset.

The Queen beckoned to the Duchess of Richmond, Norfolk's
daughter, the widow of Henry Fitzroy. The Duchess came forward
and, at Anna's bidding, took Elizabeth off to the gardens. Then Mary
greeted Anna's other ladies, most of whom she knew. Among them
was her cousin, Lady Margaret Douglas, a witty, flame-haired beauty
who was daughter to Father's sister, the Dowager Queen of Scots.
Mary kissed her affectionately.

"The Lady Margaret was my lady-of-honor at one time," she told Anna.

"Until I was obliged to go and serve Anne Boleyn." Margaret made a face.

Mary stiffened. "That woman gave my mother and me much grief."

"I have heard that Queen Katherine was a most gracious and devout lady," Anna said kindly.

"Oh, she was!" Mary declared. "She was a wonderful mother to me, and true to her principles to the last. She was even ready to face a terrible death rather than compromise them or acknowledge herself to have been no true wife. Anne Boleyn was utterly cruel to her, and to me. It was thanks to her that my father broke with Rome. I pray daily that he will one day be reconciled to the Holy Father."

Anna nodded, looking nervous again. "But I hear that Queen Jane was kind to you and saw to it that you were reconciled to the King?" she ventured.

"Indeed, yes. She was a good woman and a kindly soul, God rest her." Mary crossed herself. "And now I must call your Grace 'Mother'!"

"Nothing would give me greater pleasure," Anna said, taking Mary's hands in hers. "I can hardly be a stepmother because we are almost of an age, yet I will try to show you a mother's kindness and be your friend. Pray, sit with me and I will send for refreshments. Then we can talk."

She poured some wine for Mary and Margaret, and quickly downed a goblet herself before pouring another.

"Before Elizabeth returns, I should warn your Grace that we do not mention her mother in her presence," Mary said. "She is a winning child, and I do the best I can for her, but there is a wayward, capricious side to her, and she needs firm moral guidance to prevent her from turning out as that woman did."

Anna nodded. "I am sad for her. It is a terrible thing to lose your mother so young."

Fortunately, Elizabeth was on her best behavior that afternoon, and Anna was much taken by the six-year-old's charm and precocious wit. Mary was moved when Elizabeth impulsively took the

Queen's hand and squeezed it, then gently touched her face, as if she was hardly able to believe that this new stepmother was real. And Mary was gaining the strong impression that Anna had taken to them both. They spent the afternoon discussing Elizabeth's education, her dogs, her dolls, and their different upbringings; they swapped anecdotes about mutual acquaintances and discussed the merits of Richmond. No word was said of the King, save for Mary asking after his health.

There was an odd moment when Anna suddenly turned to Margaret Douglas and asked her where Mistress Howard was.

"I think she is with her grandmother at Lambeth," Margaret replied uncertainly.

"She is supposed to be on duty, but she seems to absent herself whenever it pleases her," Anna said. "No matter." She smiled at Mary. "I'm sorry. Katheryn Howard is a forward girl and I've just noticed that she isn't here."

"Maybe a good whipping would cure her!" Margaret smiled grimly.

Anna shrugged, but Mary saw that she was distracted. Then the conversation turned to the hot weather and the strange exchange was forgotten.

"I must confess, I thought you would be one of those dreadful German Protestants!" Mary said, much later.

"So do a lot of people," Anna replied. "They ought not to, as I go to Mass often enough."

Mary felt even greater fondness for her after that. By the time she and Elizabeth boarded their barge to Whitehall, she was very pleased with her new friend.

The news that Cromwell had been arrested hit Mary like a blow. The conservatives at court had long resented and feared him, and now, it seemed, they had moved in for the kill. Treason—and heresy! She would not believe it. They had trumped up the evidence, made an occasion to get rid of him. Her heart bled when she heard that he had walked unwittingly into the council chamber, head held high as befitted the newly created Earl of Essex, and then been assailed by his enemies, who had roughly stripped him of the insignia of his offices and had him hauled off to the Tower. And her father had authorized them to do it!

There would be no saving him. Parliament attainted him as a traitor and condemned him to death—he, who had been the King's greatest servant. The world was going mad!

She was further saddened when, in July, she heard that Anna's marriage to the King had been annulled. But, Chapuys informed her, Anna had proved not only amenable, but remarkably cooperative—and no wonder, Mary thought, because Father could not have been an easy man to live with. He had put on such a lot of weight over the past four years, and his legs were in a poor and painful state, making him prone to terrifying outbursts of temper. Anna was probably relieved to be a free woman. She was going to stay in England and enjoy her handsome divorce settlement and the great houses the King had given her.

Mary could not help thinking that her mother's life would have been happier had she too proved amenable to an annulment. But she had had her child's rights to protect—and, having been the King's devoted wife for eighteen years, she could never have it said that she, a Princess of mighty Spain, had been living in sin, however unwittingly. Besides, her marriage had been valid—the Pope had confirmed it. Anna's marriage, so Chapuys confided, had not even been consummated. Even though Mary was not sure exactly what that meant, there was no comparing the two. Still, she could not help wishing that her mother had been able to enjoy such a comfortable retirement.

She was shocked, in August, to hear that her father had married Katheryn Howard. Suddenly, Anna's distraction on that afternoon in Richmond made sense. Mary's eyebrows rose when she learned that Katheryn was thirty years younger than the King, a girl of just nineteen! She found it discomfiting to have a stepmother five years her junior. Doubtless Father thought Katheryn was likely to bear him children. But still Mary shook her head in dismay. By all reports, he was blindly besotted with the wench.

That was by no means the worst news. On the day of the King's marriage, Cromwell had faced the executioner's axe. Mary could hardly believe that her father had got rid of perhaps the best minister he had ever had. She mourned Cromwell sincerely, for he had been a good friend to her—and she still wondered if he would have liked to have been more than that.

She felt sorry for Anna, who had lasted just six months as consort, and late in August, she decided to pay her a visit.

"This is an unexpected pleasure," Anna said, smiling and beckoning for wine to be served.

"Not for me," Mary said, waving it away.

"You won't mind if I do." Anna accepted a glass. "I trust your Grace is well."

"Tolerably," Mary replied, "but it is getting to that season when I suffer all kinds of ailments. The autumn is never good for my health. But you are in fine fettle, I see."

"I ride out daily now," Anna said proudly. "I am become a reasonable horsewoman, and I go for long walks, taking the air. Tell me, is there news of the court?"

Mary sighed. "There is, but not what you might want to hear. Queen Katheryn is leading my father a merry dance, it seems, and he leaps to indulge her. I'm told she is become greedy for new gowns, jewels, and endless diversions. Anna, she will wear him out. He is besotted."

"You do not like her?"

"I do not know her. But she is so young, and every day, I hear, she discovers some new caprice."

"She comes of a good Catholic family," Anna pointed out. "She is well placed to influence the King in the way he should go."

Mary sniffed. "I doubt she has the brains for it." She found it hard to feel the same respect for Katheryn as she had for Queen Jane and even Queen Anna. And there was no comparison with her own mother! She hesitated, reluctant to repeat the gossip she had heard in her household. "You know there is still talk that the King will take you back."

Anna started. "Not again!" she exclaimed. "I keep hearing these rumors!"

"Of course, there is no basis to it, but many of us wish he would," Mary murmured.

"I appreciate the sentiment, but I am contented as I am," Anna assured her.

"That is well, for it is not likely to happen. That girl is entrenched. He's taken her away on progress so that he can show her off."

They continued to enjoy a good gossip, and Anna insisted on Mary staying to dinner before she left for New Hall. Mary much enjoyed the game pie Anna had ordered, and the custard flavored with nutmeg, and departed full of thanks for her warm hospitality.

She visited the court early in December, sumptuously attired in velvet and furs, and glistening with jewels. When she was ushered into the Queen's chamber and curtseyed, she and Katheryn regarded each other warily. Then Katheryn smiled and Mary reciprocated. The new Queen was really quite pretty, if a little plump.

"I will leave you ladies to get better acquainted," Father said, beaming, and left, limping a little. At once, the ladies-in-waiting gathered around Mary, paying as much court to her as they did to Katheryn. For the rest of that day, she was the center of attention. Katheryn sat aloof, looking rather left out and frowning at Mary's two maids, who had their backs to her. Mary noticed this gross discourtesy and realized that her young stepmother was being ignored.

When Katheryn began playing the virginals, pointedly loudly, Mary broke away from the throng of well-wishers and joined her. "May I sit with your Grace?"

"Of course," Katheryn replied stiffly.

"I hear you are a friend to the true faith," Mary said. "It needs such a champion in these difficult times."

"Indeed," Katheryn answered, still sullen.

"I was glad to hear that my father's Grace is so happily married," Mary said. "I trust your Grace is happy, too. If you ever need any advice or help, I would be happy to give it. You are very young and inexperienced in the ways of the court. My mother was Queen and a wonderful example to all."

"Thank you," Katheryn said, flushing. "But I am nearly twenty and have the King himself to guide me. You know how attentive he is."

"Indeed. I have known him a lot longer than your Grace," Mary said, bristling.

Before Katheryn could answer, Catherine Willoughby, the Duchess of Suffolk, came over and took Mary's hand. "My dear mother loved your Grace's lady mother so much," she said. "You will be sad to hear that she died last year."

"That is the most doleful news," Mary said, tears welling in her eyes. Maria de Salinas, who had married Lord Willoughby, had come from Spain with her mother and served her devotedly. "I loved her; she was always kind to me. And my sainted mother adored her."

As they continued reminiscing and others joined in, Katheryn was again excluded. Mary realized she had little in common with her new stepmother except their faith and their love of finery. She tried to extricate herself from her friends so that she could speak to the Queen again, but could not, as they were all clamoring to talk to her.

She had been planning to stay at court for three days, so she was surprised when, the next morning, her father said she should join her brother Edward at Ashridge in Hertfordshire, because the court was moving to Oatlands Palace. Feeling somewhat disconcerted, she returned to her lodgings, where she found her two maids in tears, packing their belongings.

"What is wrong?" she asked.

"The King has dismissed us," they told her.

Everything made sense now. This was Katheryn's doing. It was the price she was exacting for being ignored.

Mary hurried back to the King's apartments and almost collided with Chapuys on the way.

"Your Highness!" he cried, sketching a hurried bow. "Why the haste?"

She told him what had happened.

"Ah," he said, regarding her with that wise smile she loved so much. "I see. Luckily, I have business to conduct with his Majesty this morning. I will raise this matter."

"You will? Oh, thank you!" If anyone could put things right, it was Chapuys.

"The King has rescinded the order," the ambassador reported just before dinner. "He believes he was overharsh. Your maids may leave with you tomorrow."

"I am indebted to you, yet again," Mary told him. "But I still have to go?"

"I fear so. But . . ." he lowered his voice. "Highness, you should be glad to get away to the pure atmosphere of your own household, which is in marvelous contrast to the tainted air of the court."

Mary blushed at the compliment. She willed Chapuys to stay and talk to her for longer, but he had a meeting with the French ambassador and had to hurry away.

When she bade a formal farewell to Katheryn the following morning, she was surprised when the little Queen presented her with a jeweled pomander. "It is a token of my esteem," she said.

Mary was nonplussed. "This is most kind of your Grace. It is a beautiful gift and I shall treasure it."

Her father was smiling broadly.

"You have a generous heart, darling," he told Katheryn, and kissed her.

Mary was back at court for Yuletide. As she neared Hampton Court, all the King's gentlemen rode out to receive her, and her father was waiting to welcome her as she entered the park, and embraced her most lovingly. The palace was festooned with evergreens, while the seasonal scent of candles set amid festive arrangements of pine cones, spiced dried oranges, and juniper berries took her back to her childhood, when this had been the most magical time of the year. But their perfume also reminded her of how many of those who had celebrated Christmas with her then were no more.

1541

She was surprised when Anna of Cleves arrived bearing gifts early in January, and even more stunned to see her father greet his former wife so warmly, and how well they were getting on together. It was touching that something good had come out of their divorce. When the King came into his crowded presence chamber to take supper, he had Katheryn on his right hand and Anna on his left. Anna exchanged warm greetings with Mary and was then shown to a seat near the bottom of the high table. Everyone was watching her closely, but she appeared in high good spirits.

During and after the meal, the conversation was lively. Katheryn put herself out to be pleasant. Mary responded in kind and joined in the laughter, but she caught her father wincing with pain once or twice. His bad leg must be giving him trouble. But Katheryn seemed oblivious.

"Are we going to dance?" she asked. "Oh, Henry, please say we can dance. I love it when you lead me out before the court!"

He smiled at her indulgently. Mary and Anna exchanged glances. Mary's mother would never have dared to call Father by his Christian name in public, but he did not seem to mind.

"I think I am rather tired and should go to bed," he said. "But you ladies can dance together." He signaled to the musicians in the gallery, and they struck up a lively tune.

"Oh, thank you, Henry!" Katheryn cried.

When he had gone, Katheryn held out her hand. "My Lady Anna, please dance with me!"

Anna glanced pleadingly at Mary, but Mary merely nodded encouragement.

Anna giggled. "It will be my pleasure," she said, taking the Queen's hand, and they stepped down to the floor, all eyes upon them.

"The pavane!" Katheryn cried, and the music began, slow and stately. By the time the Queen called for a lively branle, Anna was giving a good account of herself, and the courtiers were hastening to join them. Mary glanced over to where Chapuys was standing. How wonderful it would be if he could dance with her. But that could never happen.

Mary was always painfully aware that her beloved Lady Salisbury still languished in the Tower. Several times she had tried to intercede for her with the King, but he had made it very clear that the subject was closed, and she feared to provoke him further. She heard that, not long after she had returned to Hunsdon, Katheryn had sent some warm clothing to Lady Salisbury, and was touched, for she had not thought her stepmother had it in her to be so brave and compassionate. But if anyone could wheedle what she wanted out of Father, it was she.

Even at Hunsdon, there were rumbles, like thunder, of some rising in the north, although thankfully it was not on the scale of the Pilgrimage of Grace. But the King had ordered it to be suppressed with similar ruthlessness, and soon they heard no more of it.

One day in May, Mary was rising from the dinner table when a messenger was announced. She smoothed her skirt and went alone into her great chamber. And there, booted and spurred, stood Chapuys. She could have danced for joy to see him, but as he rose from his bow, she saw that his face was grave, and knew that he brought bad news. Only something momentous would bring him here in person.

"Your Highness," he said, and made the extraordinary gesture of reaching for her hand. She stared as his fingers closed on hers.

"My father?" She could barely get the words out.

"No." His eyes held hers, full of sympathy. "I came to break the news that Lady Salisbury suffered death this morning. I wanted to tell you myself before you hear it from anyone else."

Mary swayed, but he caught her in his strong arms and sat her down in her chair by the hearth. Then he knelt before her and took her hand again. This time, she barely noticed. It was all she could do to take in the dreadful news. That dear lady, who had been as a mother to her . . . she had *suffered death*? What did that mean?

"Are you ready to hear what happened? Or shall we talk later?" Chapuys's voice was gentle.

"No, my dear friend. Tell me now. I must hear it."

He swallowed. "She was executed within the Tower." Mary gasped and began to cry, but he continued speaking. "I was there and spoke to one who had guarded her. When the sentence of death was announced to her, she said she found the thing very strange, not knowing of what crime she was accused; but at last, perceiving that there was no remedy, and that die she must, she calmly left the dungeon where she was detained, and walked toward the green in front of the Tower. There was no scaffold, just a small block on the ground."

Mary clapped a hand to her mouth, envisaging the scene. "No," she whispered. "No . . ."

"Should I go on?"

She nodded, and Chapuys resumed his tale.

"After commending her soul to God, she asked those present to pray for the King, the Queen, the Prince, and your Highness, saying she wished to be particularly commended to you all, and more especially to yourself, her goddaughter. She sent you her blessing, and begged also for yours."

"Oh, I give it, I give it!" Mary cried, deeply moved that Lady Salisbury had thought of her at the last.

"After that, she was told to make haste and place her neck on the block, which she did. But the ordinary executioner was absent doing his work in the north, and a wretched and blundering youth had been chosen to do his office instead. He . . ." Tears filled Chapuys's eyes.

"Tell me!" Mary cried.

"He was inept. He . . . he hacked her head and shoulders to pieces in the most pitiful manner."

"No!" Mary's scream brought her ladies running. She was shaking with horror. To come to such a cruel end after leading a good and exemplary life . . .

"Fetch wine for your mistress!" Chapuys sent the women scattering. Once they had gone, he pulled Mary to him and held her in his arms, gently, reverently. "May God in His high grace pardon her soul, for certainly she was a most virtuous and honorable lady, and there was no need or haste to bring so ignominious a death upon her, considering that she was so old and could not, in the ordinary course of nature, live long."

Mary took strength from his closeness and his tenderness, yet she could not stop playing over and over in her head the image of poor Lady Salisbury being butchered to death. In any other circumstances, she would have responded differently to him. She had long dreamed of how blissful it would be to be embraced by him, but all she wanted now was the comfort he could give her. And she had it for all too short a time, for he quickly stood up at the sound of approaching footsteps. It was her ladies with the wine.

Shock and grief gave way to illness and then to a depression that lasted for months. Mary could not stop thinking about that dreadful scene in the Tower, or of the unbearable grief the Poles must be experiencing. Reginald, far away in Italy, was often in her thoughts. It was his treatise that had turned the King against his family. He must be racked with guilt.

Even the news that the Emperor and the King of France were on the brink of war with each other and each seeking her father's support did not cheer her. The King, worried about her health—of course she had not told him the reason for her melancholy—insisted that she accompany him and Katheryn on a great progress to the north, and she had no choice but to agree.

Not since the fabled Field of Cloth of Gold, more than twenty years earlier, had the King amassed such a retinue. When they departed at the end of June, Mary found herself in a train comprising five thousand horses, one thousand soldiers, the entire court, and two hundred tents and pavilions. Despite the atrocious weather, it was a relief to be away, and everyone was in a holiday mood. She soon realized it was doing her a power of good.

In August, when they were in Yorkshire, Father beckoned her to ride beside him. "King Francis has again proposed a marriage between you and your former suitor, the Duke of Orléans, who is now heir to the French throne in place of the late Dauphin."

She had almost given up hope of his finding her a husband, but the last thing she wanted was to marry into France, even to be its queen one day.

The King chuckled. "Don't look so miserable, Daughter! It's a

good match, but I am reluctant to commit myself lest I offend the
Emperor. No doubt Francis will be offended if I decline. If so, I will
just have to strengthen England's defenses and court Charles's friendship."

  Mary smiled at him, greatly relieved.

It had been a long way north to York. Mary had enjoyed seeing distant parts of the realm, yet she was saddle-sore and weary by the time
Hampton Court came into view at the end of October. She longed to
be back at Hunsdon or Beaulieu, away from the rivalries and jealou-
sies of the courtiers. She had concerns about Queen Katheryn, whose
behavior during the progress had been decidedly odd. She had
seemed edgy and watchful, unable to concentrate when spoken to.
And she was always in the company of Lady Rochford; those two
were as thick as thieves, like conspirators. Mary had had great sympathy for Lady Rochford, who had been married to the awful George
Boleyn yet managed to distance herself from his family and stand up
for Mary's mother; she could not see what the woman saw in the
giddy little Queen, or what the two of them were up to. Yet the
King seemed as enamored of Katheryn as ever, so Mary began to
think she had imagined there was something amiss.

  Back at Hampton Court, she craved leave to depart for her own
house, but Father wanted her to stay to attend a service in the Chapel
Royal on All Saints' Day, during which he intended to give thanks
for the good life he led with the Queen. Reluctantly, she agreed, but
she set off as soon as it had finished, glad to see him so happy. She
could forgive Katheryn a lot for that.

She had to read Chapuys's letter twice before she could take it in.

  "What is it, your Highness?" Susan Clarencieux asked, coming
into the closet with fresh writing paper. "You look alarmed."

  "The Queen has been arrested," Mary said, looking up from her
writing desk. "I cannot credit it. My father was so happy with her
not a week ago. He gave thanks for his life with her."

  "Why?" Susan cried, dropping the paper on the floor.

"For misconduct before marriage. Messire Chapuys doesn't say more than that." The awful thing was, Mary could believe it. That silly, flighty girl . . . "Surely they can't punish her for what happened in her youth?"

She had not liked Katheryn much, but she was sorry for her, imagining how frightened she must be. And she was worried about the impact this news would have on Elizabeth, who was at Hatfield. Elizabeth was eight now, her wits as sharp as a knife. She did not need any reminders of the fate of her mother.

Mary tried not to dwell on the matter, but Chapuys wrote that the King was devastated by the news and had left Katheryn under house arrest at Hampton Court, which suggested that there was more to this than they knew. And then it was December, and the word "treason" was in the air. This was not just misconduct—it was adultery, and that, in a queen, was a capital crime, as Anne Boleyn had found to her cost.

Mary's sympathies lay with her father, whose life must be in ruins. She longed to go to him, but her requests were ignored. She spared many a thought for Katheryn, who was now banished to the dissolved abbey of Syon, awaiting news of her fate. Her lovers had gone to the scaffold, and Mary feared it would be only a matter of time before she met a similar end. She lit candles for Katheryn, out of charity. After all, the girl was so young, and so foolish. It seemed she had had no moral guidance, and she could hardly be guilty of sinning if she had not known what sin was.

Susan disagreed. "She's Anne Boleyn's cousin; she knew what happened to her. She must have realized she was courting danger."

"Nevertheless," Mary said, "we must pray for her."

Chapter 16

1542–3

W hen she arrived at court in November, Mary was glad to see
her father looking so much better. When she had last seen
him in the spring, just weeks after Katheryn Howard's pretty head
had fallen, he had looked so old and gray that she had believed him
not long for this world. He had been sunk in misery then, but now
his spirits were restored, and she rejoiced to see it.

She stayed at court for Christmas and to celebrate her birthday in
February. Twenty-seven! It was hard to believe. Most of her female
friends and acquaintances were long wed by her age. She feared she
was drying up, an aging spinster before her time. The bloom of
youth was fast wearing off, she thought dismally as she stared into
her mirror.

Her father, however, was feeling rejuvenated. A year ago, he had
said he would never love again, but there was now a new lady in his
life, which made Mary so very glad. The recently widowed Lady Latimer, the former Katharine Parr, was one of her occasional ladies-in-
waiting, a pleasant, learned woman whom she liked and admired. Of
course, Father had not spoken to her of his love for the lady; she had
heard of it from Chapuys, who was, as ever, incredibly well informed.

But there was something niggling at Mary. She decided that she must say something to the King. Joining him one March morning when he was playing bowls, she waited until the game was finished, then strolled back to the palace with him.

"Methinks, Sir, that you have taken a fancy to Lady Latimer," she smiled.

"Aye," he grinned. "But it is more than a fancy."

"Forgive me, but I must speak to you. Did your Grace know that Sir Thomas Seymour has been courting her since before her husband died, and that he has been bragging to my ladies that they are to wed?"

Father stopped dead on the path, clearly astonished. "Thank you for telling me," he growled at length, his color rising. "I think we will soon be seeing Sir Thomas attending to his naval duties or being posted abroad on an embassy."

In June, when Mary was staying at Beddington Park in Surrey, she rode over to Richmond to see Anna. Both had profited from the fall and forfeiture of Sir Nicholas Carew, a prominent courtier who had been enmeshed in the supposed treason of the Poles and the Exeters. Richmond and Beddington had belonged to him.

They spent an enjoyable afternoon out riding at Petersham and Ham. Back at the palace, Anna hosted a lavish supper, after which they retired to her bedchamber.

"I've got that Spanish silk your Grace sent me last year," she said. "I would appreciate your advice on what style I should follow, as I was planning to make it up into a gown while you are here."

"I'd be delighted to help," Mary said. "The stand-up collar is very popular now, so you'll need some buckram. Do you have any pearls with which you can edge it?"

Having cut out the garment, they took their sewing baskets into the privy garden and settled down on a stone bench.

"Has your Grace heard of Lady Latimer?" Anna asked, unable to restrain her curiosity.

"Yes." Mary hesitated. "I assume you've heard that my father has grown close to her."

"I heard talk of it, and that she sometimes attends on you."

"She does, and I like her. She is an intelligent woman, very warm, and attractive, to my mind. She will probably be good for my father."

"They are to marry?"

"So gossip has it, although he has not said anything to me. Why, are you disappointed, Anna? There has been much speculation that you might be Queen again."

Anna smiled. "Not at all. I've known for a long while that he will never take me back. Our marriage was dissolved for just causes, and nothing has changed there. I am happy for his Grace, that he has found someone he can love. I ask only to remain his friend. I truly value the friendship that has grown between us since our divorce. He has been very good to me, you know."

"I do know, and that he values your friendship, too. He calls you his beloved sister." Mary cast off and began rethreading her needle. "I think we need not worry that Lady Latimer will be another Katheryn Howard."

"And yet I sense that your Grace has some reservation about the King marrying her?" Anna ventured.

"I heard gossip among my ladies that she loves another—Sir Thomas Seymour, Queen Jane's brother. He's a handsome man." Mary rather fancied him herself.

"Overbold, too, I've heard, and a rogue," Anna said. "If the gossip be true, then Lady Latimer is in a difficult situation. For if the King proposes marriage, she dare not refuse him."

"I think she is very unhappy to be in this predicament but she is too discreet to say so. She gives nothing away, and she never mentions my father."

"Are you worried that Sir Thomas might make trouble for her?"

"I am," Mary confessed. "He's outspoken enough to compromise her—a liability, really."

"Well, let us hope that she puts him off kindly and firmly—if things progress," Anna said.

"If," Mary added.

* * *

Father had summoned Mary and Elizabeth to Greenwich. He greeted them jovially, then, waxing mysterious, bade them go into his privy garden and wait for him in the little banqueting house.

"What's going on?" Elizabeth wondered, her sharp features tense.

"I have no idea." Mary could feel a familiar nervous knot in her stomach. "But it can't be bad news. He's in too good a mood."

"They say he smiles at those he means to destroy." Elizabeth's black eyes flashed. They were ageless, not the eyes of a child rising ten.

Mary shivered, despite the June heat. "Where did you hear that?"

"Oh, somewhere. They say it happened with Cromwell."

"You should not listen to gossip," Mary reproved.

They rose as they heard voices approaching, and she instinctively grasped her sister by the hand. When the King appeared in the garden with Lady Latimer on his arm, they sank into billowing curtseys. He raised and kissed them both. "It does my heart good to see you," he told them. "I wish to present to you your future stepmother."

Mary smiled at the comely dark-haired lady at his side. "I am so pleased for you, Sir! Lady Latimer, I congratulate you. I know you to be a good woman, and I remember your mother with affection. She served my mother well."

"I am pleased to meet you, my lady," Elizabeth greeted her. "I hope that you and my father will be very happy."

Lady Latimer flushed with pleasure. "I will do my very best to be a good mother and friend to you both." Impulsively, she leaned forward and embraced and kissed them in turn.

Father patted her arm and bade them all be seated in the banqueting house, calling for wine to be served. It came with an assortment of sweetmeats.

"Gilded marchpane!" Elizabeth cried, helping herself to two pieces.

"She has my sweet tooth," the King smiled.

Mary turned to Katharine. "You are renowned for your learning."

"I cannot hope to match your Grace's own fame in that regard," Katharine said, "but I should very much like it if we could study together, with my Lady Elizabeth, of course."

"Alas, I am not often at court." Elizabeth pouted.

"You are too young, and the court is not a healthy place for children," the King said.

"That's why Edward hardly ever comes here," Elizabeth told Katharine.

"I cannot take any risks with his health," Father declared. "He is my only son." He rose. "I will be back soon. Sit down, ladies. No ceremony." He stumped off in the direction of the royal lodgings.

"I am so glad that we are to have another stepmother," Elizabeth said, taking Katharine's hand. "The last one was quite wicked." She frowned.

"I never had a high opinion of her," Mary said quickly, "so I was not as shocked as some by her fall."

"I liked her," Elizabeth said, "although I didn't see her very often. It was horrible, what happened to her, like . . ." Her voice tailed off. Like her own mother's fate. How terrible to have to live with the knowledge that your father, however justified, had sent your mother to a violent, bloody death. It would color all your memories of her. Not that Elizabeth could have had many.

"You must try to put her out of your mind," Katharine said. "But if you ever want to talk, I am ready to listen."

"I don't want to think about it," Elizabeth said. "And I will never marry. Bad things happen if you get married."

Mary was saddened to hear her, yet it stood to reason that her sister would feel like that, considering what had happened to her mother and stepmother.

"That's nonsense," she said. "I would love to be married. But we both have to obey our father's will in that matter." There had again been talk of Father making a new match for her, but nothing had come of it.

"Your mother was devoted to mine," she said to Katharine, eager to change the subject. "She eased the difficult times for her."

Elizabeth looked uncomfortable—understandably, for it had been her mother who had caused those difficult times. Close as she and Mary were, that would always lie between them.

"I have some mementoes that were left to me and my mother by Queen Katherine," Katharine told Mary. "I will show them to you."

Mary was delighted. "I should so like that. I have very few things that were hers. Elizabeth, stop stuffing yourself, and take your elbows off the table." Elizabeth made a face.

The King married Katharine in July, in the Queen's closet at Hampton Court. Mary and Elizabeth were present, and Margaret Douglas carried Katharine's train.

Stephen Gardiner, Bishop of Winchester, was officiating. Mary had mixed feelings about him, as the suave prelate had helped to break her mother's marriage, but he was now a force for religious orthodoxy, and she could not but admire that.

It was done. Katharine was Queen of England.

Mary and Elizabeth soon found their new stepmother a very welcome presence in their lives. For Mary, it was once more a pleasure to be at court. She and Katharine quickly became close, and the Queen was assiduous in showing her the respect due to her rank.

Scholars flocked to Katharine's chamber. Always filled with flowers, it was a hub of learned discussions and laughter. Mary blossomed in this relaxed ambience, loving to be in the midst of the courtiers and clerics who gathered there. Katharine's rare goodness made every day feel like Sunday, which was unheard of at court. Most of her ladies were educated women, and there were many stimulating, occasionally heated, debates. Sometimes the King joined them, loving nothing better than an intellectual argument.

"Speak freely!" he would exhort everyone, but Katharine took care to ensure that conversations tending toward anything controversial were steered in another direction.

There were other pleasures also to be found in the Queen's apartments. She and Mary shared a love of rich clothing, although Mary's tastes were more flamboyant—to compensate for what she perceived as her plain looks. Katharine was always giving her gowns and pieces of jewelry.

"I cannot tell you what a pleasure it is to have you as a stepdaughter," she told Mary one day as they sat sipping wine in her privy garden. "I am only four years older than you, but I hope you can think of me as a mother figure—and a true friend."

"You are certainly that, Madam," Mary smiled.

"I have written to Prince Edward and the Lady Elizabeth saying I look forward to the day when they can visit me at court." Elizabeth, protesting, had gone back to Hatfield after the wedding, for there was plague in London.

"It may be some time before my father will allow it."

Katharine nodded sadly. "Elizabeth replied to me. Her letters are very sophisticated; one would think she was a woman of forty!"

"She was ever precocious."

The Queen smiled. "When she does come, I am going to make the two of you my chief ladies-in-waiting. You have both had difficult times, and I have been touched to see how you look after Elizabeth."

"She needs someone to guide her. Kate Champernowne, her lady mistress, is too soft with her. Elizabeth is too much like her mother. She loves flattery, and her temper is changeable."

Katharine took up her embroidery. "She is young and perhaps defensive about her status. As, I imagine, are you."

Their eyes met, and Mary nodded. "It has not been easy. When you have been an adored princess with the world at your feet, and then . . . To have it all taken away and be declared a bastard was devastating. I am sure it is a barrier to finding a husband. And I do so long to marry and have children."

Katharine leaned across and took her hand. "I feel for you. It is good that you are lavishing those maternal feelings on Elizabeth. She needs you. And Mistress Champernowne is a learned woman and a fine teacher, whatever her other faults."

"Oh, yes," Mary admitted. "She has taught Elizabeth languages, at which she excels, and made her familiar with classical writers. She has also helped her to become proficient on the lute and virginals."

"I'm sure you played no small part in that," Katharine smiled. "You are a talented musician yourself."

Mary blushed with pleasure. "I love music, like my father," she said. "It is in our blood." She hesitated, wondering if she should voice what had now taken root almost as a conviction, then took the plunge. "I help Elizabeth because she is a winning child, not because we are tied by blood. In fact, I fear she is not my father's daughter."

Katharine stared at her.

"Her father was a musician called Mark Smeaton. He was one of Anne Boleyn's lovers. People say she looks like him."

Katharine shook her head. "I can't believe what you are telling me. She looks like your father—that struck me forcibly when I met her."

"But your Grace never met Mark Smeaton," Mary pointed out. "If you had, maybe you would see the resemblance. I have been told it is strong."

Katharine looked unconvinced. "I am not qualified to comment. Shall we walk a little?"

Mary rose. "As you wish."

"I am longing to meet Prince Edward," Katharine said, changing the subject as they emerged into the palace gardens and made for the bowling alley, where a game was in progress. "It would be a pleasure to have us all together as a family."

"It would be indeed," Mary replied, wishing she had not voiced her suspicions to the Queen and praying that her stepmother would not see fit to tell her father of her suspicions.

"Edward will be six soon," she said. "The King is talking of engaging his chaplain, Dr. Cox, as his tutor. That worries me. There is talk that Dr. Cox was sent down from Oxford for spouting Lutheran views. I would not want such a man to be near my brother."

"I doubt your father would have appointed him chaplain if the rumors were true," Katharine said.

Mary shuddered. "I hate these reformists; they're all Protestants underneath. It was a sorry day for England when my father broke with Rome."

"Shh! Mind what you say!" Katharine hissed. They were approaching the bowling alley and might be overheard. Already, people were bowing and curtseying to them. Mary made herself smile and nod at them. Sometimes she felt completely out of place in the world she now inhabited.

Katharine did not betray Mary's confidence, and she was as good as her word. She persuaded the King that all three of his children should join them for Christmas. It was a joy to be together under one roof, a united family, and Mary felt happier than she had done in years. Elizabeth was throwing herself with gusto into the preparations, making mistletoe boughs and wrapping New Year's gifts; and Edward, now a solemn six-year-old, looked as excited as any ordinary child.

Mary adored Edward. From a chubby babe, he had grown into a beautiful fair-haired boy, and she doted on him, as did Elizabeth. Elizabeth, of course, was closer in age, and a playmate for him, but he was fond of Mary, too, as much as a serious, self-contained child could be. Mary put this down to his lack of a mother, and—as she had done with Elizabeth—had always tried to make it up to him, showering him with gifts, many of which she made herself, and taking a warm interest in his education and progress. He now responded with gifts of his own and carefully written letters in which he told her he loved her more than anyone else. He took obvious delight in her company and assured her she would always be his special friend. As she sat cradling him on her lap, watching the courtiers dancing, with her cheek against his silky hair, she prayed that in time to come, his reformist tutors would not infect him with their subversive views, for he surely had the makings of a great king.

Chapter 17

1544

"I have some news for you, Daughter," Father said, smiling at Mary across the dinner table. "A new Act of Parliament is to restore you to the succession."

Such a great wave of happiness engulfed Mary that she was struck speechless. Her first thought was that her mother would be rejoicing in Heaven to see this day. "Sir, I cannot express the joy I feel at hearing that."

He beamed. "The Queen and I are still hoping for children, and any sons we have will come after Edward in the order of succession. Failing that, the crown will go to you and your heirs, then to Elizabeth and hers."

It was fair and it was just. Mary could not have asked for more.

She couldn't eat a morsel after that. When the King had retired to bed, she turned to Katharine with tears in her eyes. "I know I have you to thank for this. I cannot tell you how happy I am. It was what my sainted mother fought for—that I should take my rightful place in the succession. I do not look for a crown; I hope that Edward thrives and grows up to have children. I only ever wanted my right to the throne acknowledged. I cannot speak for happiness!"

* * *

The King had commissioned a special painting to mark the Act of Succession, and an artist came to make sketches of Mary. When the King took her and Katharine to see the finished masterpiece, they were both taken aback. There was Father, seated on his canopied throne in the presence chamber at Whitehall, with Edward at his knee and Mary and Elizabeth standing at either side, beyond the pillars that framed the central group—pillars, Mary sadly realized, representing legitimacy. And there, seated beside the King, was not Katharine, but Queen Jane.

Katharine looked disconcerted, but she admired the painting. "It is a fine work," she said.

"You understand why I had to include Jane," the King said. "She gave me my heir. It is fitting that she is portrayed as the founding matriarch of my dynasty."

Katharine smiled. "Of course. It is only right that she is there."

Soon afterward, the Queen asked Mary to assist her in entertaining the Spanish Duke of Najera, for Mary could speak Spanish after a fashion. They both dressed lavishly in their finest court gowns and entered the presence chamber glittering with diamonds and gems, attended by a great train of ladies headed by Margaret Douglas. Mary was delighted to see her cousin again; her presence always enlivened any occasion. While they waited for the Duke's audience with the King to be over, she had them all giggling over a joke about a pair of Caesars cutting the Roman Empire in half.

Presently, the Duke of Najera arrived, escorted by several nobles and attended by Chapuys. Mary had noticed lately that Chapuys was aging rapidly. His hair was gray, his features drawn, and his gait seemed painful and unsteady. It grieved her to see him so altered, but there was still that light in his eyes when he looked upon her; that had not dimmed. She worried that he might not be able to continue in his post for much longer and felt dread at the prospect of his leaving England, but she thrust the thought away and greeted their guest with a smile.

Katharine led the Duke and his company into her privy chamber, where, at her signal, the musicians struck up and the dancing began. She took to the floor first with her brother, the Earl of Essex, while Mary danced with the Duke. Then she and Margaret Douglas danced together, their ladies whirling around them in jeweled hoods and silks of many colors. Afterward, they all stood at the side to watch a dextrous Venetian in the King's service dancing galliards with such extraordinary agility that he seemed to have wings on his feet.

Mary was with Anna of Cleves, who had been invited to the reception. Later, when the Duke had been bidden farewell, and people were departing, she touched Anna's sleeve. "I am worried about my father," she muttered, under cover of all the chatter going on around them. "He is ill. Anyone can see it. The Queen says he spends most of his time in his secret lodgings, and seldom stirs out of his chamber, unless it is to walk in his privy gardens—when he is able. I think she is having a difficult time, for his temper is worse than ever, and his legs give him so much pain that he becomes exceedingly perverse and is inclined to lash out on the slightest provocation."

Anna took Mary's hand and squeezed it. "Anyone can see that his health is failing. It is plain how badly his legs trouble him."

"He tries to hide it, but you can see by his face that it is worse than he pretends." Mary could not hide her distress. "He cannot go up and down stairs now; he has to be hauled up and down by a pulley device, and he has had two chairs made with extended arms, so that he can be carried to and fro in his galleries and chambers."

She glanced around at the company, then bent close to Anna's ear. "Let us walk in the gallery, where we can be private. We might be overheard here."

The gallery, by good fortune, was deserted.

"In faith, Anna, I do not see how he can last much longer." Mary paused, feeling the need to voice another worry. "Then we shall have my brother, and I fear for us, and for England, because he is being tutored by Cambridge gospelers—heretics all, I do not doubt! I wince when I read his letters, poor child. And I fear, perhaps, the Queen encourages them. It seems to me she is hot for reform, as are the ladies of her household."

Anna looked alarmed.

Anna was silent, and Mary wondered if she had had her own suspicions.

"No, Anna," she continued, "the future is very uncertain for those of us who are of the true faith. We must pray that my father lives longer, but already the wolves are chafing at the muzzle for a new order. And there is nothing to be done about it!" Her voice was bitter. "Do they not fear for their immortal souls?" She sighed deeply, fingering her rosary. "We should rejoin the company, lest we are missed."

After the Duke of Najera had left the court, Mary stayed on. Katharine told her, not for the first time, that she needed a project to occupy her. She herself was writing a book of prayers and was certain that Mary's scholarship qualified her to undertake something similar. Some time ago, she had suggested that Mary translate Erasmus's paraphrases of the Gospels into English. Mary had not been sure that her Latin was good enough, or if she was the right person to do it, yet she had liked the idea. And Katharine had encouraged her. "Do you not agree that it becomes a woman of rank to undertake intellectual pursuits?" she had said. Mary had had to agree. Now, finally, she set to work, fired up by Katharine's enthusiasm.

That summer, diplomatic relations with France having foundered, the King revived his long-cherished plan to invade that kingdom. Mary and Katharine were concerned about his leading the campaign in person, for his health was so uncertain, but he would hear none of their objections. And, indeed, the thought of conquering France seemed to be breathing new life into him. Determined and ebullient, he sailed away, having appointed Katharine regent in his absence.

Mary soon saw that this was no empty title. Katharine was kept busy from dawn to dusk, meeting with the Privy Council, dealing with matters of state, malefactors, and finance, and ensuring that the army and the fleet were kept well provisioned. On top of all that, she was anxious about the King, and about a new outbreak of plague, and kept all her stepchildren with her as she moved from house to house to avoid the contagion.

"I don't know how you do it," Mary said, as the Queen started to fall asleep over supper one evening.

"It is a marvel to see a woman ruling England," Elizabeth chimed in, her eyes full of admiration. "It just goes to prove that it can be done."

"Don't let our father hear you saying that," Mary smiled. "He doesn't approve of women ruling."

"Strange, then, that he made your stepmother regent," pointed out the Duchess of Suffolk, one of the Queen's chief ladies.

"Ah, but I am to rely on the lords of the Council!" Katharine pointed out, with a wry smile.

"It seems they are relying on you!" her friend retorted, ever outspoken.

The King had taken Boulogne! The court erupted in jubilation at the triumphant news, and Mary gave fervent thanks to God for her father's victory. Now he was coming home. Katharine's workload was lighter, and the plague was abating. But Mary was suffering her usual autumnal complaints. It was time to return to Hunsdon to rest and press on with her translation of St. John's Gospel. But she would be back at court for Christmas!

1545

On a sunny January day, Mary invited Chapuys to join her for a short stroll in the palace gardens, so that he could give her the news from abroad. The walk was as much as he could manage, for his legs were stiff and painful, and soon she insisted that he sit with her awhile on a bench, for he looked drained.

"I thank your Highness. Alas, I fear I shall soon have to be carried about in a chair." He tried to smile. "Your Highness and the Queen are always most considerate to me."

"I have much for which to be grateful to you," Mary told him. "You have ever been my champion."

"And always will be," he said. "I am so pleased that you have a friend in the Queen, and so is his Imperial Majesty. I thanked her at Christmas, on his behalf, for all that she has done for you, and she replied very graciously that she did not deserve so much courtesy, for what she did for you was less than she would like to do. She also said that she would do her utmost to maintain the friendship between England and Spain."

"She has come as a blessing to us all," Mary replied.

"It is a blessing of which you will have need," he replied, his face suddenly grave. "I am growing old, and I must tell your Highness that I have applied for my recall. I am awaiting the Emperor's assent."

Mary could not speak. Her eyes met his, and in them she saw the same sadness and regret that were consuming her. She could not bear the thought of his leaving her forever. How would she live without his warm, reassuring presence, his care for her, his—yes, his love? Although they had never declared any feelings for each other—how could they?—she was in no doubt that hers were reciprocated in equal measure.

She gazed into his face, knowing that soon she would be seeing it for the last time.

How sad it was that two people who were clearly meant to be united were kept apart by rank and the dictates of society.

"I am so sorry," she said, then her voice broke and she was crying inconsolably, unable to hide her distress.

She felt his hand on hers. "I cannot tell you how many regrets I have," he murmured, then looked away. "I dare not say more." He sounded choked. "Please do not weep like that. You are young. You should be happily married with children. It is what I have long wanted for you. I promise you that when I return to Savoy, I shall keep abreast of affairs in England and will do my very best to watch over you from afar."

Mary made a huge effort to compose herself. "I cannot thank you enough for everything you have done for me. Words are so inadequate." She shivered, for it was cold. She should not have sat here so long with him or shown such emotion. But she was glad she had, for she would never forget what he had said. It had been, effectively, the declaration of love she had never thought to hear.

"We should go in," she said. "Take my arm."

In May, after Chapuys had taken formal leave of the King, he was due to come to the Queen's privy garden and bid farewell to Katharine and Mary. As they waited for him, Mary could not blink back her tears. "He has been such a friend to me," she sobbed. "He was a rock of strength to my dear mother and me during our tribulations. He went a long way beyond the call of duty." She lowered her voice, feeling the need to speak of what was in her heart. "I know little about these things, but I once thought he had feelings for me," she confided, her cheeks growing hot. "If he had been of higher rank, I would have let myself reciprocate, for I could not have found a better man. And now he is old and ill, and I shall never see him again."

Katharine held her until her tears were spent, then bade her go and wash her face and straighten her hood. "Let his last memory of you be a smiling one."

As Mary spent a few moments in Katharine's oratory trying to compose herself, she noticed that there were few statues or ornaments, which set her wondering again. Was her stepmother truly orthodox in her faith? Yes, surely. But if so, where were the images in her chapel?

She remembered a garbled rumor that Bishop Gardiner had tried to have Katharine arrested for heresy, but that she had convinced the King of her innocence and so escaped arrest. She could not quite believe it, for Katharine seemed as cheerful as ever, and the King clearly still doted on her. Nor could she believe that Katharine was a heretic. She did not want to believe it. And yet, during those gatherings in the Queen's chamber, opinions had been voiced that had led Mary to suspect that some around the Queen harbored subversive views. But Katharine? No. She would not credit it.

They waited in the garden until Chapuys arrived, wheeled in his

chair by the new ambassador, who introduced himself as Francis van
der Delft and seemed urbane and genial. Katharine gave them both
her hand to kiss.

"My lord ambassador, I am sad that you are leaving us," she told
Chapuys. "His Majesty has told me that you have always performed
your duties well, and I know he trusts you and likes you very much.
But I doubt not that your health will be better on the other side of
the sea, and that you can do more there to maintain the friendship
between England and the Empire, which you have done so much to
promote."

"You are very kind to say so, Madam," Chapuys said.

Katharine took Mary by the hand. "You must say farewell to my
Lady Mary, whose friend you have been for so many years.

The ambassadors turned to Mary and conveyed the Emperor's
greetings, and she had to extend the usual pleasantries. It was all so
formal! She had not expected the new ambassador to be present; she
had been hoping to say a more personal farewell. But it was impossible. The audience was at an end. As Chapuys bowed over her hand
and said goodbye, she wanted to throw her arms around him; and
when he looked up, his eyes were misty. She watched him being
wheeled away, out of her life, and felt sick and empty.

She sought solace in her faith. It was becoming increasingly important to her. In the familiar, loved rites of the Church, she could redis-
cover the security of her early childhood. She found herself deploring
more and more the spread of heresy. The Protestant religion was a
very serious threat indeed. It endangered the time-honored concept
of an ordered world, a united Christendom, which was rapidly being
overthrown. Such heresies should be ruthlessly stamped out and
eradicated.

One autumn day, Katharine came upon her when she was feeling
particularly sad. "You should see this, Mary." She handed her a letter
in the Prince's distinctive handwriting. Mary read it with increasing
disbelief. Edward had actually asked his stepmother to remind Mary
that the only real love was the love of God and that she was ruining
her good reputation by her famed love of dancing and what he called

frivolous entertainments. He thought she should avoid foreign dances and merriments, for they did not become a most Christian princess.

"*He* thinks to tell *me* how to conduct myself?" she cried, incredulous and hurt, for until now she had been unable to do any wrong in Edward's eyes. "He is eight years old and knows nothing of the world! I am nearly thirty! Where is he getting this from?"

Katharine shook her head. "I do not know."

But Mary did. "It is those reformist tutors he has. They are the ones putting such notions into his head. Goodness knows what else they are teaching him!" Anger burned within her.

"He is a child, aware of his great destiny, and likes to think himself superior," Katharine said.

It was true. From babyhood, Edward had been exhorted to emulate his august father. He now imitated him in every way he could, down to his majestic stance, with hand on hip and feet planted firmly apart. He even had Father's forbidding scowl to the life!

"I suppose I must not blame him," Mary said. "He is very young." Yet she felt deeply saddened, and also belittled, by his letter.

"You must not let him upset you," Katharine said. But Mary *was* upset. She felt as if she was losing the brother she loved as if he were her own child.

Chapter 18

1546

It had been a difficult year, what with Father's declining health and Mary's escalating concerns as to what Edward's tutors were teaching him. In the autumn, the King was again confined to his bed and Katharine was fraught with anxiety. She sent Edward to Ashridge, but kept Mary and Elizabeth with her at court. She did not tell them exactly how ill the King was, but Mary guessed that it was serious. She thought constantly of nine-year-old Edward, who was unaware that the heavy burden of kingship might soon fall on his slight shoulders, and could have wept for him. She wept for her father, too, knowing she would grieve terribly to lose him.

But the crisis passed, and soon he was announcing his intention of undertaking a short progress. Because of his precarious health, the court moved in slow stages through Surrey to Greenwich, where they were to keep Christmas. Looking at him, Mary wondered if he would see another Christmas.

"He is so infirm that I fear any new attack would surely carry him off," she confided to his chaplain, Dr. Ridley, who was waiting to enter the royal bedchamber as she was leaving it. "I do not want to lose him!" She was near to tears.

Unexpectedly, he patted her hand. "Do not distress yourself, my daughter." His eyes were kind. "God has his Majesty in His keeping. You do not need to worry."

His words heartened her and gave her strength.

"Bless you," he said.

They were at Greenwich when, late one evening, Katharine sent for Mary. She seemed very distressed, pacing up and down her privy chamber, wringing her hands.

"The King is leaving for Whitehall tomorrow," she said. "He wants us to stay here with the court. Whitehall is to be closed to everyone except the Privy Council and a few of his gentlemen. He says it's because he needs to give his full attention to this matter of the Howards."

Mary had been as shocked as everyone else at the recent arrests of the Duke of Norfolk and his son, the Earl of Surrey, which had been the talk of the court for days. It was said that Surrey had plotted to seize the throne, and that Norfolk had abetted him—treason of the highest order.

"I wish his Grace would stay here," Katharine was saying. "It will be so lonely and bleak for him, spending Christmas apart from the court—and us. But he says he needs solitude. He feels his strength ebbing and needs to rest and recover." She looked near to tears. "I protested, of course, but he commanded me to obey. I am to pretend that he is well and detained only by these treasons. He said he will send for me as soon as he can, and with that, I suppose, I must be content."

The next morning was Christmas Eve. Mary and Elizabeth went with the Queen to bid their father farewell. He kissed Katharine lovingly and gave his daughters his blessing. Looking upon him lying on his bed, his body wasted, his cheeks sunken, his hair graying, Mary felt her tears welling up. But she kept smiling as he assured them that he would see them soon—and then there was nothing to do but leave, which she did with a heavy heart.

She knew he had drawn up his will before he left for Boulogne. It chimed with the provisions of the Act of Succession, except that, in the event of Edward, herself, and Elizabeth all dying without issue, it expressed his desire that the crown descend to the granddaughters of his beloved sister Mary—her cousins Lady Jane, Lady Katherine, and Lady Mary Grey, all little girls still. Mary hardly knew them, and neither did most other people. But it did not matter. The likelihood of their ever coming to the throne was utterly remote.

What was more pressing was the question of who was to rule England while Edward was a child. Mary knew Katharine believed that Father wanted her to be regent; he had heavily hinted as much. But would she be a match for the lords of the Council, especially the ambitious Seymours?

1547

The New Year was in, and Mary and Katharine were becoming more and more anxious about the King. There had been no word from him since he left them on Christmas Eve. There were upsetting rumors that he was dead, and Mary feared that the silence from Whitehall might betoken that. But surely such news would not be kept secret?

Not wishing Elizabeth to hear speculation that might upset her, Katharine sent her to Ashridge to join Edward. Again and again she dispatched messengers to inquire after the King's health, but they were all turned away.

"I'm going to Whitehall myself," she decided. "They cannot deny me entry. I am the Queen."

She was soon back.

"They turned me away!" she fumed. "By order of the Privy Council! Nothing I said moved them. Something is very wrong."

Mary wondered again if her father had died already. The thought brought a lump to her throat; she could not imagine a world without him, and the future suddenly looked very bleak indeed. On reflection, she would not put it past Hertford and his cronies to cover up the King's passing until their plans to wrest power from the Queen had come to fruition.

"They might let you see him," Katharine said.

Their eyes met. Mary needed no second bidding. She sped away and took a barge along the river to Whitehall. But she too found her way barred, and arguing made no difference.

When she returned, she sank into a chair. "If he is dying, it is cruelty to keep us out," she sobbed.

"Maybe he is not so ill," Katharine wondered.

"Then why can't we go to him?"

"I don't think it is your father who is keeping us out." Katharine shivered. "I am certain that Edward Seymour, now my lord Earl of Hertford, is making sure of the regency. He is Edward's uncle, after all. But your father certainly intimated that I should have it."

Much as she liked his feisty wife, Nan Stanhope, Mary did not want that cold fish Edward Seymour ruling England. He was a rabid reformist, and she did not trust him. Katharine would be by far the better choice, and she had proved her capabilities during her previous regency.

"That would be an answer to prayer," Mary said.

The news sent shivers around the court. The Earl of Surrey had been beheaded, after being adjudged guilty of treason. Norfolk was still in the Tower, and there was speculation that he would soon follow his son to the block. Mary could not spare much pity for either of them. She had not forgotten Norfolk's unkindness to her when she was alone and friendless. Yet he was the premier Catholic peer of the realm, and she could not but regret that the true faith had lost such a stalwart champion, especially at this crucial time.

At Greenwich, she and Katharine speculated that the King must still be alive if he was signing death warrants. But the royal apartments at Whitehall remained closed to all but the Privy Council and some gentlemen of the Privy Chamber. The Imperial ambassador, van der Delft, told Mary and the Queen that his Majesty's physicians had confided to him that they were in despair, for he was in great danger and very ill. Mary resigned herself to hearing the worst.

* * *

At the end of January, the bells began tolling. Mary looked up from her prayer desk just as Katharine entered the chapel. She rose and made to curtsey, but the Queen wrapped her arms around her.

"The King is dead," she said. "Three days ago. They did not think to tell me—or anyone else!"

It was hard to believe, even though Mary had been expecting it. Her father had been a constant, massive presence all her life. For nearly thirty-eight years he had ruled England, and his fame was legendary. Now he was no more. She was utterly appalled that the news had been kept from them.

"Why did they not tell us?" she cried.

"They have been determined all along to exclude me from the regency," Katharine said bitterly. "My Lord Hertford has just made it very clear to me that I shall have no part in it. Oh, he was respectful enough, but he is determined to wield all the power."

"It was wicked of him to bar us from being with my father at the end. I should have loved to see him one more time."

"The councillors lied to everyone," Katharine said, her eyes flashing. "They told all the foreign ambassadors that the King was slightly indisposed, but attending to business in private; they even had his meals borne into his apartments to the sound of trumpets. He was already dead, but Hertford was playing for time in which to consolidate his bid to seize power, I am sure of it. Your father intended it to be shared among trusted councillors, under my auspices; he did not mean for one of them to be in charge. Yet Hertford is now to be Lord Protector."

Feeling numb and shocked, Mary made the sign of the Cross and knelt to pray for the King's soul, which must now be meeting his Maker and accounting for his sins. They were many, she feared, and he would have need of her prayers.

Katharine knelt, too, head bent, beside her. After a while, they both rose and retired into the Queen's bedchamber.

"We shall have to order mourning weeds," Katharine said dismally.

"I shall wear those I had when my mother died," Mary decided. She sank down on the bed. "What happens now?"

"We have a new king—Edward the Sixth. My lord of Hertford

had him and Elizabeth taken to Enfield, where he broke the news to them and made formal obeisance on his knees to Edward as king. He told me that both children burst into tears, which was so heart-rending that their servants were soon crying, too."

Mary almost wept herself to think of the grief of those two inno-cents, and of the heavy burden that was now laid upon young Edward's shoulders.

"Hertford has now brought your brother to London," Katharine told her. "He is to be proclaimed King this very day."

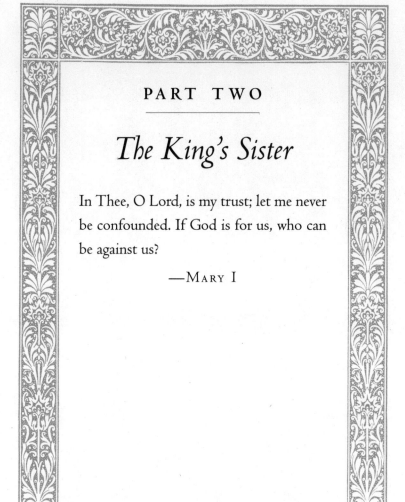

PART TWO

The King's Sister

In Thee, O Lord, is my trust; let me never be confounded. If God is for us, who can be against us?

—MARY I

Chapter 19

1547

As the woeful days passed, Mary remained secluded in her lodgings, trying to come to terms with her loss. She had anticipated that Hertford would visit her quickly, even out of courtesy, but he did not come, which she thought most rude, especially as she was now next in line to the throne.

When he finally arrived, he was full of apologies for the delay.

"Your Highness will understand that I have been very busy," he explained, standing tall and dignified before her. He had a stiff manner about him and none of the warmth of his sister, Jane. He might have been handsome, with his fair hair and magnificent beard, but he was too dry and pompous. From conversations with his wife, Nan, Mary had inferred that he always had to be right and was insensitive to the opinions and feelings of others. But while he was ambitious and high-handed, and often, it seemed, driven by greed and self-interest, he was also well intentioned and kind.

"Your Highness will have heard about the arrangements for the regency," he said, clearly expecting to be asked to sit.

Mary kept him standing. "Indeed, my lord, but they are not as I expected them to be."

"No?" He gave her a sharp look.

"I understood that the Queen was to have a leading role."

"With respect, Madam, women do not rule."

"In Spain they do," she countered. "And I am now the King's heir; my father clearly believed that a woman can rule successfully."

"But this is England," he retorted. "As the King's uncle, I am most fitted for the role of Lord Protector, and in this I have the support of the Council."

"But I believe my father intended that the Council itself should wield power during the King's minority, not one man. That is what he said to me, more than once."

Hertford was bristling. "It was felt that the Council was too large to wield power effectively without a leader." He cleared his throat. "King Edward has signified his approval of my appointment by signing the commission authorizing it."

Mary inclined her head. At least she had made her point.

"Actually, Madam, I came to inform you of the provision made for you in the late King's will. He has left an annual income of three thousand pounds each to your Highness and the Lady Elizabeth. It will be paid until you marry, when you will each receive a final payment of ten thousand pounds. However, this payment is conditional upon the Council approving the husband you choose; if you marry without obtaining that approval, you will be struck out of the succession as though you were dead. Is that clear?"

"Perfectly," Mary said, realizing that she was now a wealthy woman with the freedom to make her own choices.

Hertford bowed himself out, leaving her with the feeling that she had made an enemy. But it did not trouble her greatly. She had great advantages, notably powerful European connections, and the income and properties her father had left her; she had been made a great territorial magnate. And as heir apparent, she was a personage of importance in the kingdom, and would now enjoy a degree of independence.

She would not be staying at court. There was no place for her here anyway—or for any woman, as the King was not married, and not likely to be for a long time. She would go home to Beaulieu and enjoy the peace of the countryside, far from the political rivalries of the court. It saddened her that she would not be here to see Edward settling into kingship, but she would write to him regularly and offer him all the support she could. She guessed that she would not be a welcome influence anyway, for Hertford seemed determined to be in control of everything.

She saw Katharine and told her of her decision.

"I understand," Katharine said, looking pale in her voluminous widow's weeds. "Go, with my blessing. I am leaving court, too, and taking up residence in my palace at Chelsea. Elizabeth is coming to live with me. It was your father's wish. She is on her way here from Hertford."

"That seems a fine arrangement," Mary said.

After Elizabeth arrived at court, Mary found herself envying her. "I would far rather come with you to Chelsea than go to Beaulieu," she told Katharine. "I would enjoy the company, and I can help Elizabeth with her studies."

She had expected Katharine to jump at the suggestion, but she seemed hesitant. "Of course you can come," she said at length.

They were watching Elizabeth as she showed off her expertise in dancing to their ladies.

"She grows more like Anne Boleyn every day," Mary muttered. "Have you seen the coquettish way she looks at men?"

"She's just growing up," Katharine replied. "Life has not been kind to her, so she boosts her confidence with vanities. I am keeping an eye on her, don't worry."

"I just don't want her to be like her mother," Mary said. "I do love her, you know, even though she is not my true sister."

Katharine sighed. "Mary, anyone can see that she is," she said gently.

"Well, I can't see it," Mary retorted, looking hurt. "And I will never believe it."

Katharine just shook her head, clearly unwilling to argue further.

It had been arranged that Mary would go to Beaulieu, then join Katharine after she had moved to Chelsea.

They embraced on parting and bade each other a fond farewell.

"But it will not be for long," Mary said warmly. Again, she sensed that hesitancy in Katharine. Then her stepmother smiled.

"We shall see each other very soon," she said.

Before she left court, Mary tried to see Edward.

"It is not possible, Madam," Hertford declared. "He will be in council all day, learning the business of government."

"Then pray bid him goodbye for me. Give him my blessing."

She almost wept as she walked away. It seemed that they were determined to keep her from her brother.

Wrapped in furs against the cold, Mary traveled toward Essex, her large household of ladies, gentlemen, officers, and servants riding in her wake, as was appropriate for the heir to the throne. Her mind was filled with thoughts of the future. Who would she marry? Who *could* she marry? As the second lady in the land, she might now be a prey to ambitious fortune-hunters. If she married a foreign prince—if the Council let her—she ran the risk of embroiling the kingdom in foreign politics or wars, which would be anathema to the insular people of England. Yet if she married an English nobleman, factional rivalries might ensue, should she ever come to the throne. Suddenly, it seemed as if she had no options at all. And yet she still very much wanted to marry and—above all—have children.

Lying sleepless in the best bedchamber of a roadside inn, she felt sad that she would not be attending her father's funeral at Windsor, or Edward's coronation. But there was no place for her at either. She realized that in moving to Essex, she was cutting herself off from the court. There was no Chapuys now to keep her up to date with affairs; van der Delft did his best, but they had never established a close friendship and she doubted he would write often.

Yet she had not been settled at Beaulieu for a week when she heard from him. Hertford had knighted the King, as was proper before a monarch was crowned, and had created himself Duke of Somerset, a title in keeping with his new dignity, which brought with it a vast income. His younger brother, Thomas, had been appointed Lord High Admiral and created Baron Seymour of Sudeley. Already, the ambassador reported, there were tensions on the Council. John Dudley, Earl of Warwick, hitherto Somerset's ally, was resentful of his power and nursing hopes of depriving him of the protectorship, and Thomas Seymour was seething with resentment at having been denied a leading role in government by his brother, of whom he was deeply jealous. Mary laid down the letter, shaking her head. She was glad to be away from it all.

That afternoon, Sir William Paget was announced. Mary greeted him warmly, for he had been a loyal and diligent servant to her father and a very able minister. She was a little wary of him, though, because he was thick with the Lord Protector.

"Your Highness, I come as your father's executor," he told her, as they sat by the fire, partaking of the wine and sweetmeats she had called for. "I have been entrusted with the supervision of your household, and while I in no way wish to interfere, I know you will be pleased to hear that I have arranged for a priest to be always in attendance to say the offices of the Church. Every member of the household is to attend these services, unless they have a good excuse for not doing so, and the local people may attend, too; they can be summoned by a bell rung by your Highness's clerk of the closet."

Mary relaxed on hearing this. She had long been concerned about Edward being under the influence of reformist tutors, and latterly about the regency Council consisting of men of questionable opinions, but now she felt reassured. It seemed there was to be no more reform. She would have her own chaplains and could worship as she wished.

Enjoying her new freedoms, Mary spent the spring visiting her residences. She stayed at the great castle of Framlingham in Suffolk, one of the properties confiscated from the Howards, and then moved to Wanstead and Havering-atte-Bower in Essex. Some days later, she returned to Greenwich to help Queen Katharine prepare for the move to Chelsea.

One morning, as she was overseeing the packing of her chests, she was astonished when her usher informed her that Lord Seymour was in the antechamber, asking to see her.

What could he want with me? she wondered, as he was shown into her chamber.

"My lord," she greeted him, extending her hand. "This is an un-expected pleasure."

Thomas Seymour made an extravagant bow. He was dashingly handsome, tall and athletic, boisterous and flamboyant, in direct contrast to his brother's grave demeanor.

"I have long been meaning to call upon your Highness," he told her in his loud, penetrating voice, grinning like a satyr.

Mary was not impervious to his charm; indeed, she found him very attractive. Yet she had heard that he was a philanderer and a swaggerer. Her greeting, therefore, was guarded.

"I am pleased to see your lordship. What can I do for you?" Was he seeking her patronage? Did he know she had no power?

"Your Highness may be interested to know that I have been dis-cussing my marriage with the King." His smile was dazzling.

Suddenly, Mary saw where this was going. She felt herself grow-ing hot. "And what did he say?"

"He warmly recommended that I should marry your Highness, which is why I am here."

Mary was stunned by his boldness. "Are you aware, my lord, that my marriage is subject to the approval of the Council?"

"His Majesty did not feel that would be an obstacle."

"And you have approached them?"

"Not as yet. I wished to sound your Highness out first."

She bridled. "Sir, you should have obtained their consent before asking me."

"Very well," he said gaily, undaunted. "I will go and see them now." And he was gone.

Her head spinning, Mary returned to the parlor, where Susan Clarencieux was sewing, and told her what had happened.

"And does your Highness want to wed him?"

Mary hesitated. "I don't know. He is very handsome, but . . ."

"He's a rogue! Methinks he's looking to advance himself by way of a great marriage. But would it be to *your* advantage? People say he is shallow, irresponsible, and unstable."

"Not a good prospective husband, then?" Mary asked wryly, won-dering what it would be like to be held and kissed by such a man.

"Definitely not, Madam!"

* * *

The next day, a letter came from Seymour. He had spoken to his brother, the Lord Protector. Alas, he had been reproved and told that neither of them was born to be king, nor to marry a king's daughter. *I am to be satisfied with what I have and not presume to advance myself any higher. He said your Highness would never consent to such a marriage. I said I would win you in my own fashion, but he warned me most strongly not to pursue the matter further. I wait to know your Highness's pleasure.*

Was there no end to the man's arrogance?

"There is no reply," Mary told the messenger. She would make sure that no one but Susan knew of this strange proposal.

When they moved to Chelsea in March, the Queen was still in mourning, yet seemed much more cheerful once they had arrived. The palace was delightful, despite the rooms being shrouded in black. They walked together in the budding gardens, or listened to Katharine's musicians. When they played one of the late King's songs, Mary was overcome with a wave of grief, as the realization that she would never see him again hit her anew. Katharine held her hands and encouraged her to speak of her feelings, and they sat long into the night, remembering him.

Mary liked being at Chelsea; she enjoyed the company and helping Elizabeth with her studies. But Elizabeth, quite the young lady at thirteen, and very strong-willed, evaded all her attempts to mother her.

"How sad it is that they grow up so quickly," Mary observed to Katharine, after Elizabeth had declined her offer to help her choose fabric for a gown. "By the way, have you seen the King my brother?"

"No." Katharine looked vexed. "When I left court, he sent me a touching note bidding me farewell. But it was as if he was saying goodbye to me for good. Since then, all my requests to visit him have been ignored. I write to him every week, but have yet to receive a reply. Since his coronation, he has been closely guarded—or controlled, I should say—by the councillors. It worries me. When I visit the court, people are hailing him as a new David or Samuel, or as a young Josias."

Mary froze. Josias had been a boy king of Israel who had stamped out idolatry and established the true worship of God. Did that mean that Edward had been turned, and that he would now seek to infect England with heresy?

"He's just a child," Katharine was saying, "but some say he is so advanced for his years that he could be a father to his people already."

"His upbringing, not to mention all this flattery, has made him precocious," Mary commented, wondering if she could confide her fears to her stepmother. "I suppose we should rejoice in such a King. He is intelligent and he has had a fine education. But I am disturbed to hear that you are being kept from him. You have been a loving mother to him."

"We have Somerset to thank for that!" Katharine's tone was tart. "People praise that man for his liberal views and call him the Good Duke. How little they know him! And we have to put up with his rule until the King reaches eighteen."

It was small wonder that Katharine was hostile toward Somerset. After all, he had ousted her from the regency.

Spring was blossoming and it was good to be out in the fresh air. Mary and Katharine spent much of their time in the gardens, gloved and aproned, assisting the gardeners in their seasonal tasks, while Elizabeth pored over her books or played with her dogs. It was a peaceful existence, yet something was troubling Mary. Lying wakeful at night, grieving for her father and wondering what the future might hold, she often rose from her bed to find a book, for reading took her mind off things. But two nights ago, she had paused by the window, gazing through the diamond panes at the garden below, which looked beautiful in the silvery moonlight. And then she had seen two people running toward each other and meeting in a passionate embrace. It had moved her to see such a joyful manifestation of love, until they turned back toward the house, and she saw that it was her stepmother and—she could barely believe it—Thomas Seymour, who had only just come a-courting Mary herself. The brazen cheek of the man! As for Katharine, she could barely credit it. With the late King not two months dead, how could she even think about becoming involved with another man? It was disgraceful and dishonorable conduct!

She watched, horrified, as the couple disappeared into the palace. Could she have been mistaken? But no! She had seen their faces clearly enough, and there was no misreading the nature of their relationship. No wonder Katharine had seemed hesitant about her coming here!

She watched again the next night, just to be sure, and Seymour came again. Katharine was waiting for him, and there was a tender reunion. Mary drew back, disgusted. The following day, when they took a barge along the Thames to see Somerset's magnificent new mansion rising above the Strand, she did not know how to be civil to her stepmother.

"He acts as if he was king himself," Katharine muttered. "And that wife of his is no better. Such airs and graces she gives herself!"

Mary said nothing. She liked the Duchess and would have welcomed her at Chelsea, but she knew that Katharine would have hated it. She found herself longing to get away.

On Easter Saturday, she called on Nan at Syon Abbey, another of the Protector's houses. That too was encased in scaffolding, and the air resounded with the clatter of hammering.

Nan received her in some state, decked out in velvet and jewels and acting like a queen. Mary was dismayed to see a change in her and to sense a new distance between them. She had never been condescending to her friends, and was frankly irritated.

Wine was served in what Nan termed her presence chamber, as if she were royalty, and they talked of recent events. Mary asked after her brother the King, but Nan was not forthcoming. "I have not seen him. My husband orders all he does."

Mary gritted her teeth. "I must congratulate you on your elevation in rank."

"My lord felt that such advancement was in order, given his position," Nan said loftily.

There was a silence. "How are the children?" Mary asked.

"They are well." Nan leaned forward, and there was an unsettling air about her. "Your Highness, being of the old faith, should know that there are great changes afoot."

"What changes?" Mary asked, alarmed.

"My lord Duke, the King, and Archbishop Cranmer are committed to establishing a Protestant state in England."

"What?" Mary clenched her hands, appalled. "They cannot! The people will not stand for it, and I cannot believe that Bishop Gardiner and the conservatives on the Council will agree."

"I think you will find that their objections have been overruled."

"But it is wicked to overthrow the true faith and deprive so many souls of spiritual consolation!" Mary was beside herself.

Nan smiled. "Some might argue that it is wicked to uphold a religion rooted in superstition and a corrupt Church."

"Superstition? The faith handed down directly from Our Lord to St. Peter and to all Christendom? Pray do not tell me that the King has been corrupted by such heretical nonsense!"

"The King, Madam, is especially keen to see the Protestant faith recognized as the official religion in England. He wishes to turn the opinions of all, especially you, his sister."

"Never!" Mary stood up, outraged. "I will not abjure the true faith. I will defend it with my life, if need be! And now, my Lady Somerset, I will take my leave, as I see they have infected you too with their heresies." She swept out of the room before Nan had a chance to reply, and hurried back to her waiting barge, shaking with indignation. All the way home to Chelsea, she kept assuring herself that it could not be true, that Nan had got it wrong. She could not stop thinking of how the woman had almost baited her, and had appeared to be enjoying breaking the news.

"Whatever is wrong?" Katharine asked when she saw Mary's face.

Mary burst into tears and told her, too distressed to hold back. "I won't believe it!" she sobbed. Katharine patted her shoulder, but said nothing, and in that moment, Mary knew instinctively that she was aware of what was afoot, and feared that that she too had embraced the new religion. She felt doubly betrayed.

On Easter Sunday, Katharine joined Mary and Elizabeth for Mass. As they walked to the chapel, Elizabeth was extolling the delights of Plato, but Mary could not stop thinking about what Nan had told her—and what she should do in regard to her stepmother's shameful dalliance.

"Are you all right?" Katharine asked her.

"I have been better," Mary said.

The Queen smiled sympathetically. Doubtless she thought Mary was fretting only about religion.

The household had gathered. There was silence as Father Parker, the Queen's chaplain, mounted the pulpit.

"I have an important announcement to make," he said. "Henceforth, by order of the King's Majesty, the Protestant faith is to be the official religion of England. Church services will be in English, not Latin, and will conform to Protestant rites."

Mary was speechless. They could not inflict this evil upon the kingdom! They could not place so many souls in peril. God would not be mocked, and they would discover that to their cost. But what damage would have been done by then?

Trembling, she knew she could not stay here to be tainted by heretical practices. She stood up, made the sign of the Cross, curtseyed to the Host, then burst into tears as she walked out, aware of all eyes being upon her. Let them report her! People would see what she was made of!

Katharine hastened after her and caught up with her at the top of the stairs, just as Mary was donning her cloak.

"I'm so sorry," she said. "I know how you must be feeling."

"No, you don't!" Mary cried. "This is the final iniquity, but don't think I don't know about the rest!"

"What do you mean?" Katharine asked, clearly shocked.

"You should know!" Mary flung back. "I will not stay here to consort with heretics or see my father's memory dishonored. I am not blind to the fact that Sir Thomas Seymour has been visiting this house nightly. I've seen the two of you from my window. I cannot believe you could so far forget yourself as to entertain another man so soon after my father's death."

"It's not what you think," Katharine said. "We are married."

"Married?" Mary was horrified, almost speechless. "That's almost worse than fornication!" she hissed. "Couldn't you have waited a decent interval?"

"Mary, I want children," Katharine cried. "I can't afford to wait. I will be thirty-six in August, and I had promised myself to Sir Thomas before your father courted me. I was in love with him, but I chose a higher duty. And I did come to love your father. I miss him, believe me."

"You have no excuse for your conduct," Mary said. She swept past her stepmother and hurried down the stairs, calling for her attendants and her barge master. With tears in her eyes, she hastened to the jetty, bristling with outrage—and with another kind of grief, for she knew she had just lost one of her best friends.

At Whitehall, she asked to see the King, but was refused. Weeping with frustration, she sent Susan back to Chelsea with instructions to have all her stuff sent on to Beaulieu. Then she commandeered horses from the royal stables and set off on the long ride toward Essex. There, she would not have to encounter Katharine daily, or ever again. And she could have her Mass—whatever the law said—and observe her religion in peace and privacy.

Chapter 20

1547

In June, that peace was disturbed by a letter from the Lord Protector, who was complaining about her disobedience in hearing Mass and exhorting her to convert to the Protestant faith. She ignored it.

She then received another, this time from Thomas Seymour, in which he informed her that he had asked Queen Katharine to be his wife and prayed her to use her influence on his behalf and that of the Queen, whose close friend he knew her to be.

"How dare he!" she muttered. He obviously did not know that Katharine had told her they were married. And what did he expect her to do? Put in a good word for them with the Council, the very people she was doing her best to avoid? The bare-faced arrogance of the lying, deceiving rogue!

Furious, she sat down to pen a reply in the stiffest of tones. *My lord, I trust you have considered that it does not stand with my honor to meddle in this matter, considering whose wife Her Grace was of late. If the memory of the King's Majesty my father will not allow her to grant your suit, I cannot persuade her to forget the loss of him, who is as yet very ripe in my own remembrance.*

She wrote to Katharine as well, asking again how she could have contemplated remarrying so soon after the King's death. How, she asked, could she forget her great loss?

In May, the news of the Queen's misalliance broke, causing a great scandal, the reverberations from which were felt even at Beaulieu. The servants were openly gossiping. People were saying Katharine was a woman of easy virtue, a fool who had unthinkingly compromised the royal succession. It worried Mary that Elizabeth might be in moral danger, residing in the Queen's household. She wrote urgently to her sister, inviting her to come and live at Beaulieu, and was deeply perturbed when Elizabeth replied that she was happy at Chelsea and did not wish to leave. Mary read her words with a sinking heart, praying that Elizabeth was not becoming as easy of virtue as her mother had been.

She had to do something to protect the girl. She could not let her remain at Chelsea. She wrote back warning her sister that she would be morally at risk if she remained in the household of a woman ruled by lust. *We share common interests,* she scrawled, *and the grief we feel in seeing the scarcely cold body of the King our father so shamefully dishonored by the Queen ought to be common to us also. Dearest Sister, it is of urgent necessity that you leave there at once and come to live with me.*

She prayed that Elizabeth would now take heed. She longed to get the girl away from that household, not only because of the scandal, but also because she feared she was being infected by the heresy that was embraced there. Thirteen was an impressionable age, and at Beaulieu, Elizabeth would be free of pernicious influences and could be channeled toward the true faith.

But Elizabeth refused to budge. *I am happy where I am,* she wrote. It was like a slap in the face.

Mary spent the summer visiting her properties in East Anglia and appointing the chief officers of her household, which now numbered over a hundred servants. She chose Sir Robert Rochester, a middle-aged man who had looked after her accounts for some years, as her comptroller, and two local gentlemen, Sir Francis Englefield and Sir Edward Waldegrave, were made chamberlain and steward. She took on a new maid-of-honor, Jane Dormer, a sweet, devout, fair-haired girl not twelve years old, yet willing and capable. Mary soon came to adore her and treated her as the daughter she had never had.

In East Anglia, she was warmly received wherever she went. She made certain to hear four Masses a day, demonstrating that she remained firm in the faith in which she had been raised. But otherwise, she lived quietly, because she was still in mourning for her father. She had not dined in public since his death, but when van der Delft visited her in July, she invited him to share her table.

She asked him what he thought of Queen Katharine's marriage.

"I approve of it," he said, to her surprise, then smiled. "But rumor has it that Lord Seymour had first meant to marry your Highness."

Mary shrugged. "I have never spoken to him in my life," she lied, wishing to blot out that humiliating betrayal. "I have not given marriage much thought, since I am in mourning."

The ambassador was no longer smiling. "The Emperor is of the opinion that the Council will not allow you to wed until King Edward himself is of an age to marry and father children, in case your husband leads a rebellion on behalf of the Catholic cause, with the aim of setting you on the throne."

"That I would never allow," Mary declared, as the realization of her situation hit home. "I fear you may be right. But by the time Edward begets an heir, I might be too old for marriage and children." She struggled to hide her distress, quickly changing the subject.

In bed that night, she lay wakeful. Van der Delft's words had also reminded her forcibly that should anything happen to Edward, she would be Queen—and able to reverse this terrible swing toward heresy. Cause enough for the Council to fear her! Yet, deplore their policies as she did, she would never do anything to undermine Edward's rule. He was England's lawful King, her father's precious jewel, called by God to reign. And even though God's purpose was, in this particular instance, unfathomable, she trusted Him to reveal it in due course. In the meantime, she would stay safely in the country and live a quiet life.

But it was not easy. The world she had known was being turned upside down, and the faith she held dear was under constant attack. It was decreed that the veneration of images and relics was to cease;

chantry chapels in which priests offered Masses for the souls of the dead were to be abolished; and her father's heresy laws were being reversed. He would be turning in his grave! What was so incomprehensible was that, according to what Mary had heard, most clergy had accepted the changes without protest. Only a few, notably Gardiner and Edmund Bonner, Bishop of London, had publicly denounced the changes. It made Mary wonder just how many people had been secret Protestants in her father's reign—or were they all mere time-servers?

When she heard that the sacrament of the Mass was no longer celebrated in Somerset's household, she felt compelled to write to him; something had to be said. *My father,* she pointed out, *left this realm in godly order and quietness, but the Council now seems to be making every effort to promote heresy and disorder by introducing newfangled methods of worship. I am concerned that the King, who is still only a child and incapable of making mature judgments in religious matters, is being led astray.*

Afterward, she wished she hadn't sent such a strong reprimand. But no! she admonished herself. If others were brave enough to speak out, then she should be, too.

When a letter arrived bearing Somerset's seal, she opened it warily, her heart pounding. Yet he had replied courteously, expressing astonishment at her concerns and asserting that most subjects approved of what he termed the King's "godly proceedings," pointing out that it was people like herself who were causing disruption. *I do not wish to persecute your Highness,* he continued, *and I will leave you alone to practise your religion in peace, but you must not challenge your brother's authority nor his lawful decrees. His Majesty is committed to doing away with Popish doctrine.*

It was an ultimatum. Cease complaining, and you will not be molested. For now, she decided, it was better not to challenge Somerset further, however much she deplored the corrupting of young Edward.

From Hanworth, in September, there came an olive branch from Queen Katharine, who wrote to ask if Mary had finished translating St. John's Gospel. To tell the truth, Mary had been missing her stepmother, who had, after all, been very kind to her in the past. Now that the furor provoked by that scandalous marriage had died down, she was ready to be friendly again. She sent the Queen the finished work with a pleasant reply, saying she had completed it, but with help from various people, and therefore felt that it should be published anonymously.

You must take the credit, Katharine replied, having warmly commended the translation. *You will do us all a real injury if you refuse to let it go down to posterity under your own name!* But Mary shrank from that, as she did not want the world to judge her scholarship.

In her next letter, Katharine was firm. She did not see why Mary would reject the praise everyone would give her. Mary thought about it, then wrote that she was willing to have the work published, but only under a pseudonym. She was glad afterward that she had agreed. When her translation appeared in print, it was widely read and received high acclaim from renowned scholars. Even Gardiner, Katharine informed her, had been impressed.

To Mary's great surprise, she was invited to Hampton Court for Christmas. Elizabeth was there, too, and Katharine and Seymour. She had anticipated a happy family reunion, for she had not seen them all, or her brother, for months, and was looking forward to twelve days of merrymaking.

She was taken aback at the rigorous etiquette that now surrounded the ten-year-old King. He sat on his throne like some oriental potentate, staring out haughtily at his assembled courtiers. There was none of the seasonal levity and hilarity of the Christmases presided over by their father. Edward received her and Elizabeth with great ceremony, keeping them kneeling before him as he talked with them. He was courteous enough to Mary, but there was a coldness in his manner when he addressed her, making it obvious that she was out of favor. But he was much warmer toward Elizabeth. He kept the conversation general, constantly referring to Somerset, who was always at his side—and not kneeling, Mary noted indignantly. She found it hard to keep smiling. How she wished she could have ten minutes alone with her little brother!

Thomas Seymour tried to lift the mood with his jests, and it was hard not to respond to his roguish charm or sympathize with his barbed remarks about his brother.

"You must visit us at Hanworth, my Lady Mary," he invited. "We keep a merry household."

Mary caught Katharine looking askance at him, and wondered if all was well between them. But then she smiled.

"Do come!"

"I should like that," Mary said. "Maybe in the spring."

She was glad of the opportunity to talk with Elizabeth, who had grown up a lot in the months they had been apart, but her sister was clearly not in the mood to be confidential.

"I like it at Hanworth!" she declared, tossing back her mane of red hair. "The Queen is good to me. And Lady Jane Grey has come to live with us. We are taking lessons together."

Yes, and what are they teaching you both? Mary wondered. She sighed to herself. There was no point in persisting. Elizabeth was headstrong. She would do as she pleased, regardless of what her sister said.

1548

In the summer, Katharine wrote joyfully to say that she was with child, news that caused Mary many a pang, because the Queen was thirty-six, old to be giving birth for the first time. When she learned that Seymour had taken her to his castle at Sudeley, she assumed that her half-sister was with them, but then she learned that Elizabeth had left the Queen's household and gone to stay at Cheshunt with Sir Anthony and Lady Denny. Maybe it had not been thought appropriate that an unmarried girl be with Katharine at such a time. Yet when she heard that Jane Grey had gone to Sudeley, Mary wondered if there had been some sort of falling-out between Katharine and Elizabeth, although that seemed unlikely. After all, Lady Denny was the sister of Mrs. Ashley, Elizabeth's governess, to whom she was close; why should Elizabeth not stay with her? Then news came that Elizabeth was unwell, so it was obvious that she had been taken to Cheshunt to recover.

Mary wrote to her, kind letters expressing her concern and her good wishes for a speedy recovery. But Elizabeth's replies were brief, and she would not be drawn into discussing the nature of her malady. Mary shook her head. When had her sister become so secretive? She was turning into a mistress of dissimulation! But at least she seemed to be getting better.

Mary had other things to worry about. The government had now ordered the removal of the images of saints from churches, and forbidden the carrying of candles during services, the bearing of palms on Palm Sunday, and the custom of creeping to the Cross on one's knees on Good Friday. Gardiner, having publicly preached against these changes, was now in the Tower. That sent a shiver down Mary's spine. Who knew if, one day, she might be joining him there? But they would seize the statues in her chapel over her dead body, whatever the Council decreed!

Katharine was nearing her time now. Her brother William called unexpectedly at Beaulieu in August and, over a dinner of choice beef and quail pie, told Mary that the Queen was in good health and impatient to greet her child. Before he left, Mary hurriedly dashed off a letter to her, saying she hoped to hear good news very soon and asking to be commended to Seymour. Knowing that Katharine was soon to face a perilous ordeal, and desiring to make things right between them, she signed herself "your Highness's humble and loving daughter." It was time that they were true friends again, whatever the differences between them.

She was delighted when Seymour wrote to tell her that the Queen had given birth to a daughter, whom they had named Mary in her honor. She and her ladies had a little celebration in the garden to toast the baby's health, and she began making plans to visit Sudeley with a christening gift. It would be worth the long journey just to see her little namesake.

She had just ordered a silver-gilt porringer for Mary Seymour when another messenger arrived, clad in black. Queen Katharine was dead, of childbed fever. Tears streamed down Mary's face as she read Seymour's letter. He sounded crazed with grief. She was poised to go winging across the country to support him and his poor motherless infant, and see her stepmother laid to rest, but the messenger informed her that she would arrive too late. Lady Jane Grey was to be chief mourner at the funeral in the castle chapel.

It was a dank and dismal autumn. Mary feared she would never be out of mourning. First her father, and now her stepmother. She grieved for them both. The world was an emptier place without them.

She was dismayed in November to hear that that great heretic Archbishop Cranmer was writing a new English Book of Common Prayer, which was to be placed in all churches—and that the clergy, hitherto bound by a vow of celibacy, were now to be allowed to marry. She ground her teeth as she read that. Was there to be no end to this wickedness?

She was staying at Framlingham then, and felt so wound up by what was happening in the wider world that she suddenly needed to be on the move again. So it was back to Beaulieu. But when she arrived in December, she was horrified to hear from her friends at court that Cranmer and the bishops had publicly announced their rejection of the doctrine of transubstantiation in Parliament. She was so distressed that she burst into tears, and her ladies had all to do to calm her down.

"They cannot do this!" she cried, wringing her wet kerchief. "It is heresy of the first order, and they are forcing it on innocent people! They cannot deny the miracle of the Mass, that sacred moment when the bread and the wine become the actual body and blood of our Lord Jesus. It is not merely symbolic! If my father were alive, they would not have dared. He would have sent them to the stake!"

Young Jane Dormer, kneeling at Mary's feet, shuddered. "Why would he have done that, Madam?"

"Bless you, child," Mary replied, "because heretics must be utterly destroyed lest they infect the faithful. Burning puts people in mind of the fires of Hell to come if they stray from the path of righteousness. Fire cleanses the soul—a taste of Hell on earth gives the sinner one last chance to recant and achieve Heaven. And if he does not, the destruction of his body means that it can never be resurrected when the Lord comes again at the End of Days. It is a cruel punishment, but it may save souls for Christ."

Jane looked doubtful.

"Without such punishment, or the example of it," Mary sighed, "many will be lost."

"Heed your mistress, Jane," Susan said, handing Mary a clean kerchief. "No one has a purer heart or a greater zeal for the true faith."

Mary squeezed her hand. "We must all pray that the Lord Protector and his friends see the light and return to the fold."

She opened another letter. "God have mercy! Parliament has drawn up an Act confirming the Council's order to ban the Mass." She stood up, reminding herself that she was the granddaughter of Queen Isabella, whose courage had been legendary. "Law or no law, I will not stand for it!"

She gave the order to her chaplains. Nothing was to change.

"Render unto Caesar the things that are Caesar's, and to God the things that are God's," she quoted. "Mass will continue to be said here in the ancient manner, whatever Parliament decrees!"

She never discovered who reported her. It could have been someone in her household, or one of her few visitors; or perhaps it was an informer pretending to be one of the local people who came to Beaulieu to worship in the old manner. But later that December, a deputation of the lords of the Council turned up at her door.

She received them in the hall, bristling with indignation and apprehension.

"What brings you here, my lords?" she asked.

Sir William Paget, who had once been her friend, spoke for them all. "Madam, we are come to ask you to exercise discretion in the practice of your faith. My Lord Protector has stated that you may continue to observe it, but concerns have been expressed about the overlavish ceremonial and display that attend the celebration of Mass in your household. This cannot be tolerated."

Mary straightened her back. "I do not agree, my lords. One can never do too much honor to Our Lord."

"Remember, Madam, that the Council is being extraordinarily lenient in allowing you to break the law."

"I do no one harm living quietly here in the country. May I remind your lordships that it was you who sent me a priest, so that my household and people living nearby could have the consolation of the Mass. And I dare say that his Imperial Majesty the Emperor will be pleased to hear that we are still being allowed to do so."

Paget did not reply, and the other lords were looking at each other uneasily. They were scared of her. They feared her influence and her popularity, and she knew they dared not censure her too openly for fear of offending her powerful cousin. Maybe they were thinking that one day, she might be their Queen. Smiling, she bade them a courteous farewell.

She wasn't invited to court that Christmas, but she would not have gone anyway. It was prudent to stay away.

Chapter 21

1549

Thomas Seymour had been arrested! Mary read the letter from Nan Stanhope standing by the window in her night robe on a chilly January evening. The fire in her bedchamber had been stoked, but there was a draught rattling the casements.

She read on, incredulous. The fool had somehow broken into the King's apartments with the intention, it was believed, of kidnapping him, ousting his brother and seizing power. He had shot Edward's dog in the process and been immediately arrested. The King, Nan wrote, had been terrified. Mary could imagine it. Now Seymour was in the Tower. She shook her head. He had ever been rash and impulsive.

Little by little, the full extent of his offenses had become clear. He had even schemed to marry Elizabeth in secret, which would have been treason without the Council's consent; and it was thought that he had intended to capture the King and Mary herself and murder the councillors. Mary smiled grimly at that. But as she read on, she was no longer smiling. Elizabeth herself was being questioned, for it was feared that she had consented to a treasonous marriage.

Mary sank into a chair. Her half-sister might be only fifteen, but she was intelligent and sharp as nails. Surely she would have had the sense not to embroil herself in such a mad scheme. She knew as well as Mary that she could not wed without royal permission, and that the consequences did not bear thinking about. Why, her very life might be in danger! Mary prayed that she would clear herself. She wished she could go to her and give her good counsel.

She was relieved to hear from Nan that Elizabeth had protested her innocence, even under rigorous questioning. *Nothing can be got from her,* Nan wrote, giving Mary the impression that she believed there was something to be got. Mary did not know what to think.

Susan told her that the servants were gossiping. "Saving your presence, Madam, they are speculating that the Lady Elizabeth is already in the Tower and that she is with child."

"I will not believe it!" Mary cried, yet she could not help remembering that Elizabeth was Anne Boleyn's daughter.

Her fears intensified when Nan informed her that Mrs. Ashley had confessed that Seymour had behaved outrageously toward Elizabeth when the Queen was alive, and that she had later encouraged them to marry. Nan gave no details of what form his behavior had taken, and Mary could not quite imagine what she meant, for she still had little idea of what passed between a man and a maid. But she was very worried.

In March, Seymour went to the block, indicted on thirty-three counts of treason. Mary was terrified lest Elizabeth follow him. She felt for eleven-year-old Edward, who had had to sanction his uncle's death—and for poor little Mary Seymour, orphaned at just two years old. She even spared a thought for Somerset, who had had to sign the warrant that sent his brother to a bloody end.

But there was no more bloodshed. Elizabeth was left alone, and Mary soon heard that she was doing her best to distance herself from the scandal, even wearing sober black-and-white clothing that proclaimed her a virtuous Protestant maiden. Mary shuddered. Her half-sister ever was one for being dramatic, she thought, still unsure what to believe about Elizabeth's role in the whole sorry affair. But it appalled her that she had blithely embraced the new religion.

* * *

Later that month, when Mary was at Kenninghall, another of Norfolk's confiscated properties that had been granted to her, Parliament passed a new Act of Uniformity. In future, any priest caught celebrating Mass would be fined; if he persisted in his disobedience, he could face life imprisonment.

Mary feared for her chaplains. With the might of the Emperor behind her—on which van der Delft had assured her she could rely—the Council could not touch her, but they could well arrest her priests. If sufficiently provoked, they might even try to make her renounce her faith and conform to the new laws.

"I would rather face death than do that," she told her officers and ladies over dinner on the day they learned of the passing of the Act. "I am ready to set myself up as a champion of the Catholic religion, whatever it costs me."

That afternoon, she showed her defiance by ordering her chaplains to celebrate a particularly ceremonious Mass in her presence in the chapel. She had hitherto attended two Masses each day, but from now on she would make a point of going to three—and inviting the local people to join her, for some had fallen away for fear of making trouble for her. Next, she wrote to the Emperor, begging him to take steps to ensure that she would be able to continue to live in the ancient faith, at peace with her conscience. *In life or death, I will not forsake the Catholic religion of the Church our mother, even if compelled by threats or violence,* she declared.

She thought Charles would respond in a similar fighting spirit, and was disappointed when he replied that, whatever she did, she must avoid making an enemy of Somerset. If it came to her being forbidden to hear Mass, she could submit with a clear conscience because she was acting under compulsion.

Never! She was no longer the young girl she had been when they had browbeaten her into taking the Oath of Supremacy and he had given her similar advice. She would not be bullied. But, as she had nervously anticipated, the Council made it clear that they were not going to leave her be. A letter arrived warning her that, like all other subjects, she was expected to conform to the new laws.

"They can think again!" she fumed, seating herself at her writing desk. Shaking with indignation, she wrote to Somerset, saying it was no small grief to her to see that those in whom her father had put his trust had made laws contrary to his wishes and against the custom of all Christendom, and against the law of God and His Church. *But though some among you have forgotten the King my father, yet God's commandment and my nature will not suffer me to do so, wherefore with His help I will remain an obedient child to his laws as he left them, till such time as the King's Majesty my brother shall have discretion to wield the power God has sent him to be a judge in these matters himself; and I doubt not that he will then do what is right.*

She felt better for having vented her feelings and made her position clear. She would never swerve from it. It was better that they knew that now.

That month, she was a guest at the christening of Temperance, the child of John Dudley, Earl of Warwick, one of the Privy Councillors, which was encouraging, as the invitation showed that they still felt the need to treat her with the respect due to the heir. In the church she found herself placed next to van der Delft, and while they waited for the infant to be borne in, she told him about Somerset's letter and her response, speaking in Spanish and Latin so that the other guests should not guess what they were talking about. He looked deeply moved and promised to take up her case with the Emperor.

At the end of March, van der Delft visited her at Kenninghall. After receiving him formally in the hall, she took him into her private parlor, where they could be alone.

"I am glad to see your Excellency," she said. "I am so distressed at the changes that are being implemented in this kingdom, and so frightened for the future and for my priests, for I fear that a confrontation with the Council is now unavoidable. I should not be surprised if I end up in the Tower, but I will endure that or worse, for I would rather give up my life than my religion."

"Highness, I am sure it will not come to that," the ambassador tried to assure her.

"But what is the Emperor doing to help me?" Mary blurted out. "He does not seem to be aware of how awful things are here."

"That is why I came here, Highness, for he has instructed me to tell you that he is determined to stand by you."

Mary was so overcome on hearing this that she could not speak for a few moments. "His Imperial Majesty is my only solace. I am profoundly grateful for his support, and I will try to be worthy of him." She drew from her pocket a much-fingered, yellowing letter. "He sent this to me many years ago, when I was alone and in need of comfort. It is my most treasured possession, and I always carry it with me." She did not say that she also carried one from Chapuys, who still wrote to her from time to time, although not as often as she would have liked, for his time was taken up with acting as an adviser to Charles and founding a new college in his native Savoy.

Van der Delft handed back the letter. "I will tell my master that your Highness's life and your salvation are in his keeping," he promised.

Mary spent a few anxious weeks before van der Delft informed her that Charles had instructed him to extract from Somerset a written assurance that, notwithstanding all the new laws, she would be allowed to observe the old religion, and that neither the King nor Parliament would ever molest her, directly or indirectly, by any means. Her heart leaped when she read that. But she trembled when she learned that Somerset had flatly refused, arguing that he could not override the laws made by Parliament. *He said that if the King's sister, the heiress to the Crown, were to differ in matters of religion, dissension would certainly spring up among the people, for your Highness is much loved.*

But all was not lost. After a long discussion with the ambassador, Somerset had capitulated and given a verbal undertaking that as long as Mary was discreet, did not publicize what she was doing, and heard Mass only in her own chamber, she could do as she pleased until the King came of age. Again, she felt a tremendous sense of relief, and her racing heart was filled with gratitude toward Charles and his ambassador, who had brought about this compromise.

Soon afterward, though, she began to realize why the Protector had let himself be persuaded to back down. He had too many troubles of his own to alienate the King's heir.

"He's become very unpopular," Sir Robert Rochester, her comptroller, told her, as she sat discussing her finances and other matters with her officers one day in May. "People are appalled at what they see as an act of fratricide. They call him a murderer, a bloodsucker, and many say openly that he let his brother go to the block without lifting a finger to save him. He's a wicked man, no doubt about it, and a weak one, too." Mary was not surprised at the vitriol in Sir Robert's voice. He too loathed this new world they lived in, which was understandable, given that his brother John, a priest, had been executed after supporting the Pilgrimage of Grace. Yet he had never criticized her father.

Sir Francis Englefield, gathering up his papers, nodded. "Aye, he's weak. And the word from the court is that the wolves are circling. By wolves, I mean Warwick and his supporters." Mary called to mind the handsome, saturnine face of her recent host, the coldness in his eyes and the air of ruthless confidence that clung to him. She would not like to make an enemy of such a man.

"I would not be surprised if the fall of one brother turns out to be the overthrow of the other," opined Sir Edward Waldegrave. "Many councillors resent Somerset's power and his policies, and he has lost support because he cannot control inflation or the escalating enclosure of common land. Some think he has gone too far in his religious reforms."

"Although I'll wager there are hotheads on the Council who think he has not gone far enough," Sir Robert grimaced.

Mary nodded. "The Imperial ambassador informed me that many have objected to the new prayer book and the English liturgy. They say it makes a Christmas game of worship. And there have been risings in the West Country against the outlawing of the ancient rites. We must pray that change comes before more damage is done."

There was a knock. An usher entered and handed Mary a letter. She recognized van der Delft's seal. "Excuse me, good sirs," she said. "I must read this."

They waited while she broke the seal. Then she froze. The lords of the Council had refused to agree to Somerset's promise to leave her alone to practice her religion in private. She must conform like all the King's other subjects. A deputation from the Council was coming to see her, the ambassador warned; she should stand her ground, but take care not to antagonize them, and deny their requests pleasantly. She must remember always that the Emperor would support her, and if her own chaplains were too intimidated to say Mass, she could call upon the services of van der Delft's priests at need.

"Gentlemen, I think I must prepare to do battle," she said grimly.

On Whit Sunday, the Lord Chancellor, Sir Richard Rich, and Sir William Petre waited upon her at Kenninghall. She looked on Rich with distaste, for it was he who had perjured himself to send that saintly soul Sir Thomas More to the block. But he left that great time-server, the beetle-browed Petre, whose sails bent with the wind, to do the talking.

"Madam," Petre said, "you must accept that you and your household are subject to the new Act, like everyone else. We have come to give you instruction in the new rites."

Mary gave him a gracious smile, suppressing her anger. "Sir William, I fear I cannot agree. I will not conform to the new Act, and I will never use the Book of Common Prayer."

Petre's expression was thunderous. "Your servants will be punished for defying the law."

"My servants are my responsibility, which I will not shirk," she said firmly, but pleasantly, wondering how she was going to protect them. "And now, my lords, you will partake of some refreshment before you leave?" They did not; they departed, unable to hide their exasperation. But she was pleased at the way she had seen them off. Catholics all over the kingdom would be looking to her, the heiress to the throne, as their champion.

She anticipated that the Council would not tolerate that. In June, she was not surprised to receive a stern letter advising her to conform and obey his Majesty's laws. She was to ensure that Mass was no longer said in her house, and have the Protestant communion put in its place.

Fury rose in her. Had they not heard what she had said? Did she have to keep repeating herself? But she reined in her anger and refused to give way to the impulse to dash off an irate letter at once.

Yet this nastiness was making her ill; a vile headache had suddenly descended on her, and she felt shivery. She must look to her well-being.

She took to her bed and stayed there for six days, giving the matter much thought. Then she got up and composed her reply. *I have offended no law,* she wrote, *unless it be a late law of your own making for the altering of matters of religion, which, in my conscience, is not worthy to have the name of law. When His Majesty comes of age, he shall find me his good and obedient subject in this, as in every other matter, but until then I have no intention of changing the practices dictated by my conscience.* Using all the weapons in her arsenal, she said she was ill and probably had only a short time to live—let them think that!—but while she lived, she intended to obey her father's laws, which had been consented to without compulsion by the whole kingdom. The recent changes could only result in the displeasure of God and the unquietness of the realm.

The response did not come in the form of a letter or deputation. Instead, Sir Robert Rochester, Sir Francis Englefield, and her senior chaplain, Dr. Hopton, received a summons to appear before the Council for questioning.

Trembling with fury, Mary scribbled another letter of protest, insisting that she needed her servants.

Again there was no reply, and it was not long before Mary learned why. Around London, in Oxfordshire, and in the West Country, the people had risen in protest and riots against the Act of Uniformity, and clearly the Council had more pressing matters to deal with than harassing her.

"Maybe they will see sense now and realize that good subjects will not tolerate their heresies," she said to her ladies, as they sat in a circle, sewing.

"We can only pray that the good Lord leads them in the right direction," Susan replied fervently.

The good Lord was certainly busy, it seemed. That summer, while the government was trying to suppress the riots, a great revolt erupted in Norfolk, led by Robert Ket, a local landowner. His rebels were incensed at rising food prices and rents, and fondly believed that the good Duke of Somerset would sympathize with their grievances. At least twelve thousand men had assembled near Norwich, not twenty-five miles from where Mary was staying at Kenninghall. Glad that the Council would be further diverted, but fearful that the insurgents might try to involve her in their plans, she sent her grooms out to see what news they could garner. If it looked like Ket's army was marching her way, she would up and leave for Essex instantly.

After the grooms had departed, one of her men-at-arms reported that a shifty-looking individual had turned up at the gatehouse asking to see her. He had refused to state his business, so they had sent him away, but not before he had pressed on them a letter for her. She took it distastefully, seeing it smudged with dirty thumbprints. As she had feared, it was a plea from the rebels for her support.

"Never!" she said, returning it to the man-at-arms. "Keep that as evidence against them, if we need it. And double the guard at the gates." She felt as if she had been punched. The Council must never think for a moment that she had encouraged the rebels or been involved with them in any way.

The grooms returned and reported that an army led by Warwick was marching north to crush the insurgents. But there was talk in the taverns that Mary was encouraging them and had even sent agents to help foment the rising.

She stared at her officers, who looked as outraged as she felt. "Why would I foment treason? Even if they had risen in defense of the true faith, I would not lift a finger to help them. But as a landowner, I cannot sympathize with them."

She was not surprised to receive a letter from the Council warning her not to traffic with the rebels. Immediately, she replied that if those who were accusing her of doing so cared to look, they would find her so-called agents in her household, where they belonged, not meddling with traitors. In case they still suspected her, she sent van der Delft a full statement of her dealings in the matter, which he was to forward to the Emperor.

She was relieved to hear that the risings in Norfolk and the west had been suppressed, although not without bloodshed, for Warwick had ruthlessly crushed those of Ket's men who had not scattered. It was butchery, no less, and Ket himself had been hanged on the ramparts of Norwich Castle. Warwick was the hero of the hour, receiving praise from every quarter for his bravery and his military expertise.

Mary's sense of relief instantly dissipated when van der Delft reported that Somerset had privately complained to him that she was increasingly making a public spectacle of her Mass, and said he hoped the ambassador would persuade her to be more discreet in future, especially as he had heard that one of her chaplains was suspected of being involved with the rebels.

Was he now threatening her personally? Her anger flared, especially when a summons arrived, again ordering her to send Rochester, Englefield, and Hopton for questioning by the Council. She knew she had no choice in the matter, but, determined to go down fighting, she sent a letter berating the councillors for the inhuman treatment shown to her servants and their lack of respect for herself.

She took leave of her three faithful officers with a heavy heart, wondering if she would see them again. She was surprised, therefore, when, eight weeks later, they returned to Kenninghall apparently unharmed. She welcomed them effusively, but she could see in their eyes that all was not well. When they were seated by the fire and had been served with hot possets to warm them, she gently asked what had happened.

"Madam, we suffered a grueling interrogation by the Council," Rochester told her, "but we refused to say anything against your Highness's beliefs."

Father Hopton looked uncomfortable. "Madam, forgive me, but they compelled me to bring you a document outlining your obligations and strict instructions for implementing the new law." The chaplain was shaking.

"You are telling me that the Lord Protector has reneged on his promise to allow me my Mass?"

"That is true, I fear. The other councillors have overridden him."

"And if I do not comply?"

"Then, Madam, I face imprisonment, which I am willing to undergo for your Highness's sake."

"That will not be necessary," Mary said grimly. "By all means convey these commands to my household. But I shall be writing to the

Imperial ambassador at once. I cannot obey this new law without doing violence to my conscience."

She hastened to her closet, seething at Somerset's perfidy. She could not be without her Mass and the consolation of her faith—she could not! And she would never allow any heretic rites to be observed under her roof—ever!

Much against her will, but to be on the safe side, she ordered the temporary cessation of all religious observances at Beaulieu as she and her household held their collective breath to see what the Emperor would say. At last, van der Delft informed her that his Imperial Majesty had bidden him remind Somerset of his promise and obtain his written undertaking to allow her the freedom to worship as she wished in private. *On my master's instructions,* the ambassador had written, *I warned the Lord Protector that, unless he honored his promise, the Emperor would be obliged to take action against him rather than keep sending verbal demands. At this, the Duke agreed that your Highness might do as you please in the matter, quietly and without scandal.* Yet he had still refused to put this in writing.

Van der Delft was clearly angry about that, but Mary replied that she was satisfied with Somerset's promise. *Tell the Emperor,* she concluded, *that I will continue to pray daily that matters might be restored as they were when the King my father left us.*

Charles, however, persisted in pressing for a written undertaking. That autumn, Mary was gratified finally to receive Letters Patent signed by the King, permitting her to have Mass celebrated by her own priests and attended by up to twenty named members of her household. With it came a cold note from her brother, expressing the wish that his dearest sister would seek instruction from some godly and learned men in order to banish her doubts of conscience over embracing the reformed faith and thus enable her to retain the affection and brotherly love he bore toward her.

She bristled at this little homily. How old was Edward? Twelve? How dare he lecture her, she, who was older and wiser by far? She had no doubt that the words had been put in his mouth by others. But at least she was now to be left unmolested to practice her religion in peace.

Chapter 22

1549

Since midsummer, Elizabeth had been unwell with various vague complaints. Mary worried about her, for sixteen was a difficult age, and she remembered herself how hard it had been to cope with painful courses and other ailments, especially if you were going through a difficult time. And there had been that talk about Seymour, although Mary could barely credit that Elizabeth had been a willing partner.

One morning, as she sat in her closet writing letters, Susan came to her, looking concerned. "Madam, Jane Dormer says the servants are gossiping about a midwife who is said to have been taken blindfolded in the middle of the night to a great mansion to attend a fair young lady who was in travail. When the child was born, the man who had brought the midwife caused it to be miserably destroyed. They are saying that the young woman was the Lady Elizabeth."

"I cannot believe it!" Mary declared, shocked, although she could not help wondering if there was any grain of truth in it. Had Elizabeth really been so foolish as to have embroiled herself with a married man, one whom she perhaps knew was plotting treason? "It's just malicious gossip," she added, more to reassure herself. She wished that she and Elizabeth had not endured such a long separation. She could not help feeling that they had grown apart, and that things would go better with her sister if she was there to comfort and guide her. It hurt that Elizabeth had willingly embraced the new religion. But she was young and had been cozened by unscrupulous men—and she had been through so much. It was easy to find excuses for her. She needed only to be set back on the path to righteousness. Mary would have written to her, yet she feared to offend her or provoke the Council.

Later that autumn, at Kenninghall, Mary was astonished to receive a message from the Earl of Warwick asking her to back a move for Somerset's impeachment before Parliament.

She was aware that Somerset's popularity had continued to dwindle since he had sent his brother to the block. But it was not just on account of that. His rule had brought nothing but troubles. His attempts to follow a middle road in his religious policies had offended both Catholics and Protestants. His economic decisions had been disastrous, as the late rebellion had shown; Mary had heard Sir Robert, her comptroller, grumbling that the price of food had almost doubled since Edward's accession. It was evident that Somerset had alienated many lords who should have been his friends and allies. Law and order seemed to be breaking down—increasingly, there had been reports of local thefts, assaults, and other disturbances—and Mary feared that the Crown was nearing bankruptcy. Moreover, Somerset was deeply enmeshed in seemingly unwinnable wars with Scotland and France.

"My master can enlarge on all the ills the Duke has caused," declared the messenger, "and he can tell your Grace how deeply the King's Majesty resents the strict regime he has imposed upon him. Madam, my lord of Warwick says the country needs a new ruler with the ability to put matters right. He believes he has that ability, and he needs the help of yourself and others who adhere to the true faith. He asks that you give him your support, and he promises you will not regret it. He wishes you to know that he loathes the reformed faith."

Mary turned away and walked to the window, gazing unseeing

over the flat Norfolk landscape. This was a surprise! For Warwick
had openly embraced the Protestant faith at the King's accession and
enthusiastically endorsed the recent legislation. It seemed that for
him, faith was dictated by pragmatism!

She did not trust him. If he was a turncoat in religion, he could
not be relied on to keep his promises. This was all about seizing
power for himself. She suspected he had no intention of restoring
Catholicism, for Edward, by all reports, was a passionate convert to
the new religion and would come of age in a few short years' time.
Warwick's England would be the Protestant state Edward wished it
to be. And yet . . .

Leaving the messenger, she retired to her closet and summoned
her chief officers and ladies. She told them about Warwick's appeal
and asked for their advice. "Do you think he might be sincere?"

"No, Madam," said Rochester firmly. "You are right not to trust
him."

"But this could be the beginning of an upsurge in your fortunes,
Madam!" Susan countered.

"Indeed," added Father Hopton. "It seems significant that he has
acknowledged your importance as the heir."

"He is merely counting on the Catholics being more vehement
against Somerset!" Rochester retorted.

Mary stood up. "Thank you, all. I'm afraid I agree with Sir Robert. I will tell the messenger that I cannot become involved."

Somerset had been arrested. Sir Francis Englefield got the news
piecemeal from a friend at court. Apparently, the Duke had got wind
of a conspiracy against him and shut himself up with the King at
Hampton Court, where he tried to incite the Londoners to rise in his
favor. Mary could not bear to think of what it had been like for Edward, a helpless pawn, to be caught up in a conflict he probably did
not fully understand. Learning that Warwick had gathered a force
and was preparing to march to Hampton Court, Somerset had
dragged the King from his bed and borne him off to the greater
safety of Windsor Castle, a fortress she knew Edward hated. And
there, the Duke had quite obviously lost his nerve, promising to

agree to the Council's terms if they agreed to spare his life. But he was promptly arrested and clapped in the Tower on a charge of conspiring against his colleagues.

Reading the letters alone in her chamber, late at night, Mary could not believe that Somerset had such malice in him. Spineless as he was, she would rather have had him in power any day than the slippery Warwick, and she would pray for him, even though she feared his soul was lost. She was glad to be far from the court and not embroiled in this nastiness.

Soon afterward, a letter from the Council arrived at Kenninghall, listing Somerset's many alleged crimes and informing Mary that he was to be deposed from his office. He had hinted that she had treasonably conspired with him to set herself up as regent for her brother, but she would be pleased to hear that no one had believed him.

She gasped at that. They could have seized on it as a pretext to move against her. But when she thought about it, she concluded that someone had fabricated that calumny to bring down the Protector— and she could venture a guess at who it had been. There was, of course, no truth in it, she wrote to van der Delft, describing what had happened. *Warwick and his associates are motivated by envy and ambition only. In my opinion, the Earl is the most unstable man in England. You will see that no good will come of this move, but that it is a punishment from Heaven and may be only the beginning of our misfortunes.* She could not help seeing it that way. This was divine vengeance on a land that had inflicted heresy upon its people.

In October, she learned that Warwick had set himself up as Lord President of the Council, rather than Lord Protector. He was now the effective ruler of England, since Edward was still only twelve. Doubtless he would be exerting his famous shallow charm on the boy, believing that a grateful sovereign would keep him in power for many years to come. Mary shuddered to think of how he would be practicing on her brother, suborning the King's will to his own.

And yet, Warwick seemed to be keeping his word to her about the true faith. He restored some Catholic lords to the Council, and it was proclaimed that Mass could once more be celebrated in churches. There were great rejoicings at Kenninghall, and Mary flung open its doors and invited the hordes who had gathered outside to come in and join her in chapel. There were so many people that they spilled out into the hall, and the chaplains were still distributing bread and wine at dinnertime. Oh, that was a joyful day!

But Mary's friends at court were soon reporting that Warwick was courting radical Protestants, such as the firebrands John Knox and John Hooper, the Bishop of Gloucester. There was speculation that there would be wholesale destruction of chantries and shrines, which could be stripped of endowments and jewels, which (Mary suspected) would go to line the Earl's pocket, and those of his cronies. It was wicked—sheer wickedness!

It was becoming more obvious with each week where Warwick's sympathies really lay. Van der Delft reported that even Archbishop Cranmer had lost favor because his planned reforms were not extreme enough to satisfy the Lord President, while Bishop Latimer had offended in preaching that the rich had obligations toward the poor. Most of the clergy, doubtless fearful for their livings, were meekly complying with Warwick's policies. *He is being hailed as an intrepid soldier of Christ and the thunderbolt and terror of the Papists,* the ambassador concluded, outraged.

Mary was not surprised. She had known what Warwick's true affinities were. But she was worried about the future. If life had been difficult for her under Somerset, it might be far more so under Warwick. She could not hide her distress when—after just one week—the Mass was banned again, with no word as to whether the new government would honor Somerset's promise to her.

In great agitation, she confided to van der Delft that she was waiting apprehensively to see how Warwick would deal with her, and received a nasty jolt when he wrote back to say that the Council already suspected her of gathering a Catholic faction around her. *They say that your Highness is the conduit by which the rats of Rome might creep into their stronghold, and I do fear they might make this an excuse to proceed against you, and that Somerset's previous assurances to you are worth nothing.*

Mary let the letter fall to the floor. Her first instinct was to flee England, for there now seemed a very real possibility that she would be arrested and end up in the Tower, like Somerset.

"What ails you, Madam?" Susan asked, looking up from her embroidery, her plump face etched with concern.

"I've just realized that my lord of Warwick sees me as a threat to his power and his policies. Indeed, I am the greatest threat, because I could easily become a focus for those who wish to see heresy overthrown." She grasped Susan's hand. "My dear friend, I may have no choice but to flee abroad."

"No, surely . . ." Susan looked horrified.

"You think I want to leave England?" Mary asked, tears welling up. "This kingdom is my life. I love it like a mother. But it is not safe for me to be here. If I am to survive to help restore the old faith, then I fear I have no choice but to leave." She shivered. "I feel like a cornered animal. There is no time to waste. I must ask for the Emperor's help."

Sitting at her writing desk, she remembered how she had thought of escaping all those years before, when Anne Boleyn had been out for her blood. This time, she would go. It was imperative.

She sent van der Delft a ring to forward to Charles, a token of her distress and a plea for a refuge, then waited in trepidation for a reply. It was not what she had expected. She drew in her breath as she read that the Emperor feared that once she had left England, she might as well renounce for good any chance of ever becoming queen, and that he could never permit, for it would be quite contrary to Imperial interests.

Van der Delft had been commanded to dissuade her from following through her plan. *My master fears it will be too dangerous to smuggle you out of England,* he warned. *However, a better escape route for your Highness might be through marriage to a Catholic prince, and I am to inform you that Dom Luis of Portugal is ready to press his suit.*

Mary felt a spasm of panic. Her cousin Dom Luis was one of several suitors her father had considered and rejected. He was forty-three, older than her by ten years, and the last thing she wanted was to marry him and live in Portugal. She wanted a refuge in the Emperor's dominions. Yet what mattered most now was her safety. Suppressing her qualms, she informed van der Delft that if the Emperor approved of the match, she would accept Dom Luis's proposal, although she would really prefer some other means of escape; and if he could not arrange for the marriage to take place very soon, he must secure for her a refuge in Flanders, as she feared for her safety if she stayed in England.

She suspected that the ambassador agreed with Charles that there were too many risks involved in an escape attempt, and she understood their reasons. If it failed, the consequences could be terrible; even if it succeeded, it could lead to war, or prejudice diplomatic relations between the Empire and England. Yet her terror was such that these considerations seemed trivial beside the danger in which she stood. At any moment, they might come for her. *If the King died, she wrote to van der Delft, the Council might put me to death rather than allow a Catholic to take the throne. I would sooner escape to some country where I can practice my religion in peace than aspire to a crown.*

The ambassador made it very plain that he was reluctant to convey her concerns to the Emperor, but he did do so—and not a moment too soon, for at the end of November, Warwick excluded all Catholics from the Council, and Parliament resolved to enforce the Act of Uniformity.

Then, to her dismay, Mary received a letter from the King inviting her to court for Christmas. She could not help but read something sinister into it.

"I shall not go," she told Susan. "I shall plead illness and stay at Beaulieu with my true friends and servants. Even if there is no plot to seize me, or trick me into incriminating myself, I fear they want me at court so that I will be obliged to accompany the King to hear their sermons and attend their communion. I would rather not go there for anything in the world."

"Quite rightly, too!" Susan agreed.

Mary gripped her hand. "Do you ever fear that God will take revenge upon England? He has hardened the hearts of the Privy Councillors as He did Pharaoh's. Remember the plagues He loosed upon Egypt! I just long to escape from the wrath to come." She realized she was sounding a little hysterical, but that was what living in fear did to you.

Susan hugged her. "God is more merciful than that! It's the wicked who reap what they sow."

Mary could have wept when she thought of her brother. It broke her heart to know that the little boy who had once loved her was now hostile to the ancient faith. Those responsible had much to answer for, setting the child up as an authority on religion. But if she could be with Edward for just a little time, she was sure she could make him understand how she felt and persuade him to press his councillors to exercise tolerance.

It was worth taking a risk. She informed van der Delft that she intended to spend four or five days in London in the new year, staying in her own house. She could then visit Edward privately without arousing too much controversy. But then she wondered if she was doing the right thing. She could not shake off her anxiety. And her fears were real: there was no doubt about that. She was in imminent danger of persecution, at the mercy of ruthless men. It chilled her to hear that fanatical Protestant preachers were spouting sermons against her. In the end, she abandoned her plan to go to London.

Van der Delft was now in no doubt as to what she should do. *The most dangerous crime a man can commit in this kingdom is to be a good Catholic and lead a righteous life. Your Highness must escape. It is your only remedy.*

But the Emperor would not agree. If the Catholic faith was to be restored in England, Mary must remain. He would bring pressure to bear on the Council on her behalf, but he would not welcome her as a refugee. The news reduced Mary to floods of tears. It was all very well for Charles to take that stance, but he was not living in England under the threat of arrest—and worse.

Chapter 23

1550

Van der Delft had heard the councillors arguing over what should happen to Somerset. In February, he reported that the fallen Duke had been released from the Tower after admitting his faults and restored to the Council. But he was a chastened man who had no choice but to support Warwick's policies. Mary realized that there was no hope of his taking a liberal view now. Warwick was absolute master.

In March, she moved to Hunsdon, desperate to escape from a situation that was fast becoming intolerable. She was still hoping that the Emperor would change his mind and come to her rescue. She had heard that Elizabeth had visited the King, attended by a large retinue, and been received with great favor—the sister who had happily conformed to the new laws. Another soul lost, Mary thought sadly, once more deploring the ease with which Elizabeth had switched faiths, yet missing the closeness that had once existed between them.

Van der Delft wrote that Warwick had refused to pay for a dowry so that she could marry Dom Luis. Another escape route had closed to her.

But she would not let herself be intimidated. No one had as yet moved against her, so she was calmer now. She would continue to celebrate Mass in her own houses. Her steadfastness to her faith was no secret, and the Catholic nobility and gentry were increasingly looking to her as an inspirational figurehead and seeking places in her household for their daughters. Every week, she found some hopeful father at her door, desperate to see his girl brought up in the true religion.

The Emperor had not ceased to demand that the Council allow Mary the freedom to continue practicing her faith, but all they would concede was that she could hear Mass in her private chamber, with just two or three serving women. Warwick made it clear that they were pandering to her ignorance and imbecility and warned that she must not cause scandal by permitting her entire household to be present at the services, and that this great concession would only be permitted for a limited period. When she learned to embrace the Protestant faith, it would be withdrawn.

She was so incandescent when she read this that she thought her heart might give out, and had to grip the chair back to steady herself. Not even van der Delft's assurance that he had left the Council in no doubt that she would never offend her conscience by forsaking the ancient religion could quell the rage that filled her being.

Sir Francis Englefield took the ambassador's letter from her and read it. "He certainly riled my lord of Warwick!" he chortled. "He says Warwick was so furious he would have done his Excellency some harm had not his colleagues restrained him."

"Would they could see him for what he is!" Mary muttered, knowing that his hateful words would be echoing in her head for days to come. *Ignorance . . . imbecility . . .* How dare they!

Worse still, she could foresee a time—not far off—when they would ban her Mass altogether, placing her in a position where she would be forced to suffer the consequences of breaking the law. That was what her friends at court believed. What would it be like to be immured in the Tower? Would she be housed in the splendor of the Queen's lodgings, as Anne Boleyn had been? Or would it be a dank cell with windows open to the wind and rain?

She would not be browbeaten! Her conscience told her that it was her duty to allow faithful Catholics to come to her house to hear Mass, even if she had to defy the Council to do so.

But the situation took a more ominous turn when England signed a peace treaty with France, and it became clear that Warwick had no intention of pursuing a similar alliance with the Emperor. Mary suspected that Charles's support for her had precluded that. She also received an official complaint about her public Masses, with a hint that Warwick was considering taking firm action against her. She protested that the councillors were reneging on the assurances given by Somerset, but she doubted anyone was listening. And then the King himself began to bombard her with letters in which he urged her to convert to what he called the true religion.

She replied patiently, to begin with, reminding Edward that he was too young to judge of such matters. When he became more vehement, she sent a sharper response, invoking the memory of their father, who would never have tolerated the changes made in Edward's name. And so the arguments flew back and forth between Essex and the court, becoming increasingly fraught.

She was deeply perturbed when the Council informed her that the Protestant Margrave of Brandenburg had asked for her hand. So that was how they planned to be rid of her! Fearful lest Warwick agree to the match, she replied that she considered the Emperor to be as a father to her and would do nothing without his consent. But would that be enough to deter them?

In April, she moved to Woodham Walter Hall, a small house she owned near the Essex coast, two miles from Maldon. There, she reasoned, she could be ready to make her escape by sea, if need be. Desperate to get away by some means or other, she summoned van der Delft to visit her so that she could ask his advice.

She was saddened to see him looking unwell, and hoped she had not caused him too much stress with her repeated demands for his help. When she inquired after his health, he was dismissive, but his pallor and sunken flesh worried her. It was through illness that she had lost her dear Chapuys, who still occupied a special place in her heart.

"What shall I do?" she cried, pacing up and down the dining room, where her untouched dinner sat on the long table.

"Highness," the ambassador replied, "wait and see what happens."

"Yes, and end up married to a heretic, or in the Tower!" she flared. "Have you forgotten the godlessness of the Council? I believe they mean to make a martyr of me!"

"Madam, pray calm down!"

She rounded on him. "It is evident that they fear no God and respect no persons, but follow their own fancy. But my cause is righteous in God's sight, and if his Imperial Majesty favors me with his help, I will not delay. For I tell you, good friends have warned me that I will shortly be forced to conform to the Act of Uniformity. Naturally, I must refuse. When they forbid me my Mass, I shall expect to suffer as I suffered during my father's lifetime."

She sank down on a dining chair beside van der Delft and held his gaze. "I must escape soon because I have been warned that they will order me to withdraw thirty miles inland from any navigable river or seaport, and deprive me of my confidential servants. Then, having reduced me to the utmost destitution, they will deal with me as they please. Sir, I would rather suffer death than stain my conscience. I beg you to help me! I am like a little, ignorant girl, and I care neither for my goods nor for the world, but only for God's service and my conscience. If there is peril in going and peril in staying, I must choose the lesser of two evils."

The ambassador looked at her helplessly, and she was deeply disappointed when, clearly going against his personal inclinations, he merely repeated the Emperor's arguments and tried to dissuade her from leaving England.

"No!" she said. "No! No!"

"I can see your Highness is quite determined not to wait here until the blow falls," he said at length.

"Not for any consideration whatever," she declared.

"I wonder if the Emperor might be persuaded to reopen marriage negotiations with Portugal," he pondered.

"Not that," she said.

"Then I must agree that your Highness should be secretly evacuated from England as a matter of urgency. As soon as you are safely in the Emperor's dominions, his agents could assist the English Catholics to overthrow Warwick and his evil associates."

"I would not ask his Majesty to take things that far," Mary said, fearing that a revolt against the Council could easily become one against the King himself.

"Madam, I do sympathize deeply with your predicament," van der Delft told her. She knew she had aroused his chivalrous instincts and prayed he would prevail upon his master. "Let us discuss how your escape is to be accomplished," he smiled.

They came up with two plans before he left. But then, to Mary's consternation, he confided that he was soon to be recalled to Brussels.

"It is because of my health, Madam, as I think you will appreciate. But it will be to our advantage."

Mary was sad to be losing him, but fired up at the thought that she might be going with him. "So, to be clear: either I disguise myself and find some means of sailing out to your ship, which will be waiting in the Thames estuary; or you will send a boat into Maldon, pretending to trade there, and I board it at a convenient time. Which is the better plan?"

"That is for your Highness to decide, for you will need to make the arrangements. But I think the latter is the safest course."

"I agree, and I should like to bring at least two of my servants with me—"

"No, Madam!" Van der Delft looked alarmed. "The escape will be dangerous enough without anyone else being involved. The Emperor will provide you with new attendants."

Mary nodded, still determined to take Susan, whatever he said.

He took his leave, bidding her sleep on the matter and let him know what she decided.

"I will not waver," she declared.

"Then I shall write at once to the Emperor—and may God preserve us."

She waited patiently, hoping to receive instructions. Of course, van der Delft would be awaiting the final arrangements for his recall—and doubtless for a replacement to be found. She could not expect a letter yet.

The days dragged by. She did not know whether to pack some things, so as to be ready when the summons came, or whether it would be wiser to wait until the last minute. Only Susan and Sir Robert knew what was afoot. Mary did not want to alert anyone else in her household to what she intended. The fewer people who knew about it, the better. She trusted her servants, but who knew?

At last, a letter arrived from the ambassador, enclosed in a more innocent missive and brought by his own secretary. She took it to her closet, locked the door, and broke the seal, her heart pounding. It was good news. The Emperor had been persuaded that escaping was the best course to take, and had reluctantly given his consent. He had enlisted the aid of his sister Mary, Regent of the Netherlands, and they had agreed that the second plan should be pursued, for it carried the least risk of Charles's ambassador being incriminated, should the escape plot be foiled.

It was really happening. Mary felt a little shaky as she stared out of the open lattice window and realized what it would mean to be leaving England, this land that she loved, that was in her soul, and of which one day she might be Queen. She thought of all those dear ones she would be leaving behind, and knew that, however royally she was treated wherever she was going, she could never replace the household she had gathered around her.

Sinking to her knees at the prayer desk, she sought guidance from on high, and was strengthened by the conviction that escaping was the right thing to do, for staying could well imperil her very life— and the future of the Catholic faith in England. Abroad, she could fight for its survival unhindered, aided by its champion, the Emperor.

Van der Delft intended to sail for Flanders at the beginning of June, but Mary now realized that this was not the best time to be planning an escape. She had received a visit from the Lord Lieutenant of Essex, who had come to warn her that there had been rumblings of a local revolt.

"But fear not, Madam," he assured her as they stood looking out of her chamber window, as if seeking any sign of intruders in the gardens below. "I have arranged for all coastal villages and towns to be placed on alert, and ordered all householders to challenge anyone found on quiet back roads, especially at night."

"Very wise," Mary observed, dismayed to hear of these precautions, and still recovering from the shock of seeing him approaching the house with his men. She had thought he had come to arrest her. "It seems the country at large is still in a state of unrest."

"It's a consequence of the recent rebellions," he told her.

"Whenever I ride abroad, I see bands of soldiers and an increased number of constables guarding the roads."

"It is because there is talk that the Emperor might be planning an invasion," he said.

Mary raised her eyebrows. "Now that is news to me."

He regarded her shrewdly. "If he did, Madam, it would be on your behalf."

She was taken aback by his directness. "I should hope not! I would not have anyone thinking I would be a party to such a thing. I am my brother's loyal subject!" Be careful, she admonished herself—don't protest too much.

"Of course not, Madam, I did not mean to imply . . ."

"I know you did not." She smiled. "Should you need any reinforcements, I have men-at-arms to spare."

"I thank you, Madam, but you may need them. Make sure your house is well guarded."

Van der Delft knew all about the security measures that were being taken. *They pose a serious threat to our plans,* he wrote. *There are no roads, no crossroads, no harbors or creeks, nor any passage or outlet that is not most carefully watched all night.* Mary shared his consternation. She knew she would have no choice but to disguise herself and walk the three miles to Maldon with her luggage and her one or two companions. She might be challenged at any time. It was a terrifying prospect at best, but made even worse by the awareness that there was now every chance she might be discovered.

Van der Delft came to see her, ostensibly to say goodbye. She received him in the hall with her officers and ladies present to witness the courtesies. "The new ambassador has arrived," he informed her. "His name is Jehan Scheyfve, and he comes from Flanders. I think your Highness will find him most agreeable and helpful."

They talked of the court, the weather in Brussels, whither van der Delft was bound, and his plans for his retirement. Then Mary invited him to take a goblet of wine with her in private, and they retired to her chamber.

"Scheyfve knows nothing of the escape plan," he said. "He can truthfully plead ignorance of it if questioned by the Council."

"But can it still go ahead?" Mary was desperate to get away.

"Yes, but you cannot come with me now. The risk is too high. My master fears to provoke a war."

"But you will send a boat—any boat, even a fishing smack—to take me across the sea?"

"I will do better than that," he assured her. "I will come back for you as soon as possible. I will not fail you."

More waiting. The suspense was making her ill. May slid into June, and still she was stuck at Woodham Walter, saddened to hear of the death of little Mary Seymour, the late Queen Katharine's child. The poor mite had not even celebrated her second birthday. But she was now among God's holy innocents and reunited with her mother.

By the end of the month, Mary was beginning to fear that van der Delft had abandoned her. But there was still the Emperor. Surely he would not throw her to the wolves?

On the morning of 2 July, she was awakened by Susan. "Madam, rouse yourself! Sir Robert wants to see you urgently." He and Susan were the two she had chosen to go with her. She knew she was asking a lot, for they would both have to make sacrifices, and probably expose themselves to danger, but they had not hesitated.

Instantly awake, Mary pulled on her night robe and hurried out to her privy chamber, where her comptroller was waiting.

"Your Highness, I have received a message from Messire Dubois."

Mary's heart leaped. Jean Dubois was van der Delft's secretary. They had met several times.

"His ship docked in Maldon harbor at two o'clock this morning. He has sent to say that all is ready for your escape."

Her heart faltered. The moment had come, but she was not ready. She had still not packed anything, and was suddenly shivering in panic at the thought of what lay ahead. Was it really the right thing to do? And there was something else that had been bothering her increasingly—her fear of the sea. She could not stop thinking about the dreadful voyage from Spain her mother had endured all those years ago, of which she had spoken often to Mary. But she must not give way to cowardice. Come, come! She must make a decision!

"What is it, Madam?" Sir Robert asked. "If you are set on going, we should be making haste."

The thought of putting her servants in peril made Mary feel even more tremulous about leaving. "No, I can't. I am not ready. Oh, I don't know. I can't decide." She ran her fingers through her hair, distraught, imagining how she would feel when she stepped onto the ship and committed herself to the uncontrollable deep. No, she could not do it. "Tell my groom, Henry, to go to Maldon. He must pretend he is buying corn for us. Instruct him to inform Messire Dubois that I am not leaving after all." She burst into tears and Susan folded her in her arms, telling Sir Robert to stop just standing there and get a move on.

Mary had calmed down by the time Henry returned. She was still not sure that she had made the right decision.

She was surprised to see that the groom had brought with him a tall, broad-set gentleman, who introduced himself as Master Merchant, brother-in-law to Messire Dubois.

"Your Highness," he said, with grave courtesy, "Messire Dubois was dismayed to receive your message. He has come to England on the Emperor's orders. His Majesty has sent four great imperial warships and four smaller boats, all under the command of the Imperial Admiral and Vice Admiral. They have endured a stormy crossing and are waiting off Maldon and Harwich to convey you to safety, making a pretense of looking for Scottish pirates. Messire Dubois has disguised himself as the master of a merchant ship bringing corn from the Low Countries to Maldon and sailing under the protection of the men-of-war because of the threat of piracy. He has sold his cargo at Maldon, and now waits to smuggle your Highness on board and return to the fleet. He is then to take you to Antwerp or Brussels."

Mary was trembling. She felt guilty knowing that the Emperor had gone to so much trouble on her behalf. If she did not go, how could she ever ask him for help again? As for van der Delft, when she thought of all he had done to bring this about, and how she was letting him down, she hated herself. This was no time to be a coward, she admonished herself. It wasn't too late, surely, to change her mind?

"Is the ambassador with Messire Dubois?" she asked, knowing she would feel better if she was bolstered by van der Delft's presence on the ship.

Master Merchant's face turned somber. "Alas, Madam, his health quickly deteriorated after his return. He died not two weeks ago, God rest him."

Mary crossed herself, feeling the tears threatening again. "He was a good man," she said. "I shall miss him dreadfully. I shall pray for him and his family."

"But now, Madam, we must make haste if you are to come with us," Master Merchant urged. "There is danger in delay. Messire Dubois has no choice but to sail with the next tide. If he remains any longer, he risks discovery. Your Highness, there will be no better opportunity than now. This undertaking is passing through so many hands that it is daily becoming more difficult, and I fear it may not remain secret for much longer."

Mary was panicking again, torn first one way and then another. "Let me think about it," she pleaded. "It is a big decision. Just a few hours. Go back to your boat, and Sir Robert shall let you know my answer."

Merchant departed, shaking his head.

"I do not think your Highness should go," Sir Robert opined.

It was midnight, and they were still in Mary's chamber, anxiously debating what she should do. Susan and Sir Francis were all for her leaving, but Mary was still undecided.

"Madam, the increased watch will make escape doubly dangerous," Sir Robert argued. "There may be spies in this household, planted by the Council, and if so, they could have got wind of our plans. And do you really need to leave England? All these months you have been left alone. It may be that you are not in any imminent danger, and by leaving you might forfeit your place in the succession. I can just see Warwick gleefully writing you out."

So could Mary.

Sir Robert lowered his voice. "Moreover—and I did not wish to tell you this—I have recently consulted two astrologers, and both predicted that the King would be dead within the year." There was an audible intake of breath. "I know, it is treason to cast a royal horoscope or speak of the King's death. Madam, if I thought you were truly in danger, I would give my right arm to see you out of the country and in safety."

"It's the only way to ensure her safety!" Susan cried, throwing up her hands. "You never know what that demon Warwick will do next. It's more of a risk to stay here. Madam, please go!"

"I agree with Lady Susan," weighed in Sir Francis. "The Emperor will not see her Highness ousted from the succession. It would suit his interests to have England ruled by a Catholic queen, and I doubt not he would go to war to defend her."

Mary was thinking about what the astrologers had said, but was unsure whether to give credence to it, for by all reports Edward was in good health. It pained her to hear the others discussing her coming to the throne, for that could only happen if he died, and she could not bear the thought of that, remembering how precious he had been to her father, and how he had once loved her.

"It's no good," she said, hugging herself. "It's late and I can't think straight. Maybe Messire Dubois could help me to decide; he comes from the Emperor. Could someone go and fetch him?"

"I will go myself," said Sir Robert.

"No, it's too risky," Mary protested. "If you are caught plotting my escape, you would both face the death penalty, you as a traitor and Dubois as a spy."

"Nevertheless, I shall go in the morning," he insisted. "I shall be heavily disguised."

Mary feared for him. She half hoped he would bring Dubois around to his point of view, and that the man would just sail away.

When he had left, Susan insisted they should start to pack for the journey. Reluctantly, Mary agreed and began stuffing some clothes into hopsacks: nothing grand, nothing too heavy. She would dress like a countrywoman for the journey and carry a basket on her arm.

She spent the next day in a state of agitation, terrified lest Sir Robert be discovered. But at sunset, he returned with Dubois. Susan brought them to Mary's chamber and kept watch by the door.

"We came by a secret way," Sir Robert said. "No one saw us."

The Fleming had a weather-beaten face and sharp features, and he was visibly unhappy about the delay. "Your Highness, there is little time left for deliberation. You must make up your mind now whether to go or stay."

"I know, Master Dubois," she said. "I am most grateful for everything that you and the Admiral are doing on my behalf. But I am ill prepared." She pointed at the hopsacks. "Yet I do not know how the Emperor would take it if it turned out to be impossible to go now, after I have so often importuned him on the subject."

Dubois gave her a long look. "If you are satisfied to stay, Madam, the Emperor would be content. If you do not wish to accompany me, I will leave England discreetly, but if you are coming, then you must not delay any further."

Mary was still in an agony of indecision. "If you leave without me, will you take my jewels with you to safety?"

"Your Highness might as well accompany them," he answered.

Sir Robert spoke quietly to her. "Madam, if the astrologers' predictions come to pass and you are still in England, you will become Queen. Remember that."

Mary's head had begun to ache. "What shall I do?" she asked helplessly, horribly aware that once she said yes, she would be committed to facing that unforgiving sea. "I definitely wish to escape, but I am not ready yet. Messire Dubois, could you wait just another two days? Susan and I could be on the beach at four in the morning; that, I have learned, is when the watch goes off duty and the coast will literally be clear."

"It would be courting extreme danger to wait that long," Dubois protested. "Your Highness must leave everything and come at once. The Emperor will provide all that is needful. I've sold my corn and have no excuse for remaining in Maldon any longer. To do so would arouse the deepest suspicions. If the attempt is to take place at all, it will have to be now."

Mary considered, her head in turmoil. "It is more than time I left," she said, almost to herself, "for things are going worse than ever. A short time ago, they took the altars away from the King's palace."

At that moment, there was a loud knock at the front door and they all started. Sir Robert left the room, then returned, looking worried, with a plainly dressed man in tow.

"Everything is going wrong," he announced. "There is nothing to be done. Master Dubois, this is my trusted friend, Master Schurts, who works in Maldon and has ridden hard from there to warn me that the bailiff and other folk of the village mean to arrest your boat, for they suspect you of having some understanding with the warship now standing off the coast."

Dubois was visibly shaken, and Mary was quaking. "What shall we do?" she cried. "What is to become of me?"

"Messire Dubois, you had best depart at once, for the men of the town are not well disposed," Rochester said. "Master Schurts can escort you back through the woods. There is no question now but that the escape attempt must be abandoned for the present."

"They are going to double the watch tonight, Madam," Schurts said, "and post men on the church tower, where they can see all the country roundabouts. There are also plans to light a great beacon to warn the inhabitants of the surrounding countryside that there is danger afoot. The fools think we are about to be invaded."

"What is to become of me?" Mary cried again, beginning to think she should have escaped when she could. Queen Isabella would not have flinched at the prospect of crossing the sea, and neither should she have done.

"Oh, Madam, do not distress yourself!" Susan cried, putting a motherly arm around her. But Dubois was losing patience.

"Madam," he said testily, "I have risked my life to help you, and the best way I can serve you now will be by leaving your house immediately."

"No," she said, putting out a hand to stay him. "If I leave for Beaulieu in a few days' time, can you not come back for me? I will send a messenger with instructions to rendezvous with me at Stansgate, on the coast."

Dubois looked at her as if she was mad. "I will not abandon your Highness, I promise," was all he said, then made a hasty departure, leaving her in tears.

"I'll go after him," said Susan. "He can't just leave you like this!"

"No!" Mary cried. But Susan was already snatching up her cloak and making for the door.

"I can ride better than most men!" she called back.

She returned within the hour, her face flushed with anger. "Where's Sir Robert?" she asked.

Mary summoned him. "Lady Susan wishes to speak to you." He looked a touch disconcerted.

Susan faced him. "I followed Master Schurts and Messire Dubois to Maldon," she said. "I dared not catch them up because they were stopped by a gang of twenty watchmen, and I had to hide behind some trees while they bribed them to let them pass. But there was no sign that the watchmen were hostile or suspicious toward them; in fact, they were laughing with them. And when we got to Maldon, the town was quiet and all seemed normal. There was no one in the church tower. It seems to me, Sir Robert, that Master Schurts invented a tale to dissuade her Highness from escaping. And I wonder who told him to do that?"

"I don't know what you are implying," Sir Robert said stiffly, as Mary began to realize that the decision had been made for her. "How was I supposed to know what was going on in Maldon? I took Schurts at his word."

Susan threw him a look that said *I don't believe you,* but refrained from calling him a liar to his face.

"One day, Madam," he said, turning to Mary, "you will have cause to be grateful to Master Schurts."

Chapter 24

1550

The Emperor vetoed any further plans for Mary's escape, and the Regent Mary expressed the hope that she would be sensible enough not to suggest it again. Somehow, the Council had got wind of what had so nearly happened, and rumors were flying around the country. Scheyfve informed Mary that to calm the people, it had been given out that the Emperor, wishing to marry the heiress to the throne to his heir, Philip, and so claim England for the Habsburgs, had attempted to kidnap her, but had failed in the attempt. The official stance was one of shocked incredulity that Charles should have contemplated such a thing, and the English ambassadors in Europe were ordered to express their indignation, and the Council's justifiable anger, at such dishonorable behavior.

Bands of armed horsemen descended on Essex to prevent any further attempt to spirit Mary away. She received a letter from Lord Chancellor Rich and Sir William Petre, pressing her to come to court to discuss her recent conduct. Firmly, she declined. She had no intention of placing herself in Warwick's clutches.

On the day she left Woodham Walter for Beaulieu, she sent one of her chaplains, Dr. Mallet, ahead to prepare for the celebration of Mass on her arrival. But she was delayed on rutted roads, and when she arrived, the service was already over. It perturbed her, since the Council had decreed that Mass could only be celebrated for her and a few others.

There must be an informer in her household, she concluded, when the Sheriff of Essex had Dr. Mallet and Dr. Barclay (who had assisted at the Mass) proclaimed offenders against the law.

"Take no notice!" she exhorted them.

"I shall not!" declared Father Barclay. "I shall continue to say Mass as usual."

But that night, Father Mallet disappeared—gone to ground, Mary suspected, greatly distressed.

She waited in anguished suspense to see what the Council would do. Members of her household, going about their daily business, reported seeing an increased military presence in the vicinity of Beaulieu—and doubtless the ports were being watched, too, in case she tried to escape. The atmosphere in the house was tense.

The blow fell in August, when an order came from the sheriff, commanding her chaplains, in the King's name, to cease holding unlawful services.

Mary sank into her chair. How much longer would she have to go on battling to have her Mass? Well, she would not desist! They would see that there was more steel to her than they had bargained for.

She wrote to Scheyfve, pouring out her fears and her indignation, and he promised he would write to the Emperor. He reported that many believed there would be a war, incited by her, and that rumors to that effect were being spread by the councillors themselves to gain the people's approval for any action they planned to take against her. This brought home to Mary the fact that she was in a very perilous position indeed. She wished she had escaped while she could. What a fool she had been!

She wept with relief when, in September, the Emperor demanded that the Council give an unconditional assurance that she be allowed to worship as she pleased. She herself wrote to Warwick, reminding him that she had received official permission to do so.

But Scheyfve soon informed her that Warwick had denied that any such assurance had ever been made. *I know this will make you angry, but I counsel you to write in a less imperious tone to the Lord Presi-dent, lest you arouse his ire against you.* That sent her hurrying to her closet, where she slapped a sheet of paper on the desk and sat down determinedly.

"Whose side are you on?" she muttered to herself, irritated, as she jabbed her quill in the inkpot. *If I adopt a meeker approach,* she wrote furiously, *he might think I had capitulated. Now will you please, of your goodness, press him on the matter?*

She tried to put her troubles out of her mind, because she was looking forward to having dinner with the French Queen's daughter, her cousin Frances Brandon, Marchioness of Dorset, and her husband, Henry Grey. Frances had leased the gatehouse of the dissolved Tilty Abbey in Essex, which was less than twenty miles from Beaulieu, and Mary had been pleased to receive the invitation. She and Frances were much of an age, and she had fond memories of their playing together when they were little girls and their mothers were good friends—before Anne Boleyn came along and ruined everything. But as she rode to visit the Dorsets that October, she began to wonder if it was to be purely a social gathering.

The couple could not have been friendlier. Mary had seen her cousin Frances from time to time over the years, and while she could not warm to the bossy, strident woman she had become, she could not fault her courtesy. The Marquess was as entertaining as a man obsessed with hunting could be, a bluff, hearty fellow who could not hope to match his wife's sharp intellect, yet the dinner they served was sumptuous, and Mary was made most welcome. There was no attempt to persuade her to change her religion, as she had feared—the matter was not even raised. Instead, she was treated to a paean of praise of the accomplishments of the Dorsets' three daughters, who sat dutifully at table, looking like the well-brought-up Protestant maidens they were in their plain black-and-white garb, although Mary noticed that their parents had not adopted the same modest attire; indeed, Frances was dripping with jewels. It was sad that these young girls were not allowed pretty clothes.

Jane was the eldest, at fourteen. She was a plain, thin child with sandy hair and freckles, but she had a formidable intelligence. She spoke four languages, including Greek, and was even learning Hebrew.

"And she corresponds with scholars," Frances boasted. "They marvel at her intellect and declare she has no peer among women."

"Indeed," Mary said, then reeled off a question in Latin, which Jane answered flawlessly, looking at her as if she was stupid.

Mary nodded. "Excellent," she said. "And you, Katherine—are you a scholar, too?"

"I try my best, Madam," murmured ten-year-old Katherine.

"She has not the capacity of Jane," her mother said.

No, Mary thought, but she makes up for it in looks! Fair Katherine was certainly the beauty of the family, unlike poor Mary, the five-year-old hunchback, who sat stolidly eating, having no doubt been told to keep her mouth shut.

"We go to visit the King soon," Frances said.

"Do remember me to him and say I was asking after his health," Mary asked.

It was a long time since she had seen her brother, and she almost wished she could go to court, too, but not while Warwick and his cronies were lying in wait for her.

The rest of the meal passed pleasantly enough, although by the end of it Mary was exhausted by Frances's constant need to assert herself. Afterward, a masque was performed by strolling players and actors sent by the Earl of Oxford, which she much enjoyed, for she rarely got to see such entertainments these days. In the morning, she thanked her hosts warmly and invited them to visit her before they left Tilty. Then she hastened home to Beaulieu to prepare everything for them.

Giving orders for bedchambers to be aired and meats to be purchased from the market, it occurred to her that her guests might look askance at the lack of a chapel for them to worship in the heretic manner. But they would just have to take her as she was. Anyway, they would not be staying for longer than a week. And she was not going to cease hearing Mass for anyone.

The visit was not a success. The Dorsets remained tight-lipped when they saw that Mass was being celebrated regularly in Mary's chapel. When Mary attended one morning, she saw Jane Grey standing in the gallery, watching disapprovingly, and heard her whisper loudly to her sister Katherine, "Superstitious idolatry!" She fought the urge to scold the girl, as that would have broken all the rules of hospitality, but she fumed inwardly at the superior attitude of the child. It was wicked, how her parents had indoctrinated her.

The next day, Anne Radcliffe, one of Mary's ladies, came to her, a vexed look on her face.

"Well, I never, Madam!" she huffed. "I was passing through the chapel, and curtseying to the Host on the altar, when Lady Jane Grey walked in. She asked why I was making my obeisance; she had thought you were in the chapel. I could not believe she was so ignorant, and I told her that I made my curtsey to Him that made us all. And do you know what she said? She asked, how He could be there that made us all, when the baker made Him?"

Mary was shocked. "What blasphemy!" she murmured. "I had a good opinion of her; indeed, I have done her several kindnesses. Now I wish I hadn't!"

She strove to be civil toward the girl for the rest of the visit, but could not like her, especially when she learned that Jane had called the Catholic God a detestable idol invented by Romish popes and the abominable college of crafty cardinals. And that to one of Mary's own maids! She was glad when the visit was at an end.

"Never again!" she told Susan, watching the Dorsets and their showy entourage riding away.

Mary had long been dreading a summons to court, and when it finally came, she resolved to ignore it. But the Council persisted. This time, she pleaded ill health; it was no lie, for she was suffering from one of her autumnal spells of sickness.

Lord Chancellor Rich began plaguing her with letters, hectoring her to cooperate with the Sheriff of Essex in bringing her chaplains to justice for defying the law. She had not seen Dr. Mallet since the sheriff had issued his proclamation against them, and feared losing Dr. Barclay as well. Repeatedly, she replied that she and her priests had been given the Council's assurance that they might worship God as they pleased. Rich denied that any such assurance had ever been given and reiterated his demand that she come to court. At length, she agreed to meet with him and Sir William Petre at the former priory at Prittlewell near the Essex coast.

She could barely ride her horse, so ill did she feel, and when the two men saw her trying to dismount, they hastened out of the porch.

"My Lady Mary, we did not realize you were so unwell," Rich said, extending a hand. She ignored it, for she had seen the coldness in his eyes and knew him for a man who had turned the rack with his own hands on a woman accused of heresy.

Petre was the more affable of the two. He bowed, offered his arm to help her to her seat in the one-time refectory, and presented her with letters. "Madam, here are credences signed by the King and the Council, guaranteeing your safety if you come to court. The Council feels it is imperative to move you away from the coast, in case there is another attempt to carry you abroad."

"Look at me," Mary said. "You see how it is with me. I have no intention of letting myself be abducted overseas. I wish to remain at Beaulieu."

"A change of air might be beneficial for your health," Rich said.

Mary shook her head. "Neither my house nor the air in these parts is the cause of my illness. It is the time of year. As soon as the leaves fall, I am plagued with ailments, which I have seldom escaped these many years. Now, my lords, if you would be so kind as to let me return home, I would be much obliged to you."

They let her go, but Rich would not leave the matter alone. He sent gifts and cajoling letters. In November, he turned up at Beaulieu, bringing his sour-faced wife with him, and took Mary hunting, for she was feeling better by then. But when he invited her back to his own house, she refused to go.

"I am not strong enough to travel long distances," she told him. She could tell by his expression that he was losing patience with her.

* * *

"Your Highness!" Sir Robert burst into Mary's chamber unannounced, and out of breath. "Ill news, I fear. It's just been proclaimed in Chelmsford that the altars are to be removed from every church in the land."

"Heathens!" Susan hissed, jabbing her needle into her embroidery.

"Is there no end to their depredations?" Mary asked wearily.

"That is not all, Madam." Sir Robert's face was working in distress. "From now on, the penalty for so-called heresy will be death. One woman has already been sent to the stake."

Mary could not speak. This was aimed at her, she was sure. They were looking for an excuse to be rid of her. Her flesh crawled at the thought of what they might do. But they would be mad to attempt it. They must know that punishing her for practicing her faith would mean war with Charles—and the treasury was empty. There was no money to fight the might of the Empire. No, she must not panic. She must hold her nerve and trust in God.

She was filled with dread, though, when her priests were summoned to appear before the Council, yet she was determined to protect them and all her people from persecution. She wrote to the councillors, protesting that the promises made to her applied to her servants also. *If you do not recall such promises being made, I will know that you are liars,* she scrawled. *You, in your own consciences, know it also. There can be no question of my allowing my priests to appear before you and, anyway, neither are staying in my household at present.*

With all this weighing on her mind, Christmas was a tense time, and she had no heart for the festivities her servants had planned. Things seemed even bleaker when she received a long, lecturing letter from the councillors. They conceded, they wrote, that she had received some form of undertaking about her private worship, but they insisted that it applied only to herself, her chaplains, and a couple of servants attending Mass in her closet or private chapel. It did not extend to the rest of her household, nor to services held in her absence, and if anyone flouted the rules they would be prosecuted. It made her want to scream with frustration!

The letter ended with a summons to Greenwich Palace, and Mary knew she had no choice but to obey if she wished to protect her chaplains from persecution. Then came another letter from King Edward, urging her most forcefully to abandon her religion and conform to the reformed faith, as all his other true subjects had done. She did not believe that her brother could write such a letter; she was sure that Warwick and his cronies had written it for him, and that it was but a preamble to the pressure that would be brought to bear on her at court. She replied in her usual vein, gently chiding him for attempting to instruct her, who was so much older and wiser.

Back came a letter from the Council, who informed her that the King's Majesty had directed them to condemn her wayward misunderstanding. So that she should know that the order came from him, he had added a paragraph in his own hand. *You are our nearest sister, who should be our greatest comfort in our tender years, but you are causing us great grief. You have never been granted official sanction to continue attending Mass in your house, and because you are our sister, your offense is the more heinous, for you are setting a pernicious example to my people.*

Mary gasped. She would not be harangued by a thirteen-year-old! But there was more, for Edward was well into his stride.

We will not permit so great a subject to break our laws. We will give orders that you be taught and instructed in the true religion, and ensure you do your duty willingly. You err in many things, such as our father would not have suffered, whatever you say about things needing to remain as he left them. Truly, Sister, I will not say more because my duty would compel me to use harsher and angrier words. But this I will say, that I will see my laws strictly obeyed, and those who break them shall be watched and denounced.

Mary was devastated to read this stinging rebuke, for it put paid to her hopes that Edward would set matters right when he attained his majority. His cold and imperious tone made her feel bereft and sick, and she sat weeping for a long time and would not be consoled. Only after Jane Dormer had persuaded her to drink a large goblet of sweet sack did she begin to rally, and then she was suddenly consumed with anger.

While the mood was on her, she sat down and composed a reply, in which she did not trouble to hide her desolation. *Your letter,* she wrote to Edward, *has caused me more suffering than any illness; I am now sick, even unto death. I have never done you any harm and would never bring injury upon you or your kingdom. However, my first duty is to God: rather than offend Him or my conscience, I would lose all I have left in the world,*

and my life, too. Death seems a likely end to my troubles anyway, for my
health is unstable and I feel so ill that I can barely lift the pen. Your Maj-
esty has been misled by wicked and vindictive advisers. Although you have
far more knowledge and greater gifts than others of your years, it is not pos-
sible that, at your age, you can be a judge in matters of religion. You will
know better when you reach ripe and fuller years. In the meantime, I do not
intend to rule my conscience according to the dictates of the Council.

When the letter had been dispatched, she appealed to the Emperor and the Regent Mary for help, and prayed that any intervention on their part would not come too late. For at any moment, she
might be carried off forcibly to court, or to the Tower, or worse . . .

Chapter 25

1551

Mary smiled as she read Scheyfve's report. The Emperor had not let her down. He had bidden the ambassador go before the Council and demand that they cease molesting her and that they permit her to celebrate Mass with her household. But the smile slipped as she read on. The lords had argued and refused to give way, insisting that the concession extended only to her and her personal servants—and Scheyfve had withdrawn, defeated. He feared, he wrote, that Warwick intended to bring even greater pressure to bear on her.

As if that was not bad enough, Mary was greatly disturbed by news that Elizabeth had visited the court and been made much of by Warwick, with whom she had apparently got on very well. It was not beyond the bounds of probability that Mary might be ousted from the succession in favor of Elizabeth. It was time, she decided, to go to court.

On a blustery March day, she arrived at her lodging in the Hospital of St. John at Clerkenwell; she came in state, with fifty knights and gentlemen in velvet coats and chains of gold marching before her, and eighty gentlemen and ladies following, each carrying black rosary beads. She was determined to show herself to the people as the heir to the throne, a great magnate worthy of their love and respect, and a defiantly Catholic one. As she neared London, crowds of cheering citizens ran joyfully to greet her. They were plainly thrilled to see her, and showed clearly how much they loved her.

"God bless your Highness!" they cried. "God bless Great Harry's daughter!" By the time she rode through the gates of the City, four hundred people were following in her wake. Reaching her lodging, she wept, but this time it was for joy.

Two days later, she went in procession to Whitehall to see the King, and caused such a stir among the people that she could hardly make any progress through the dense crowds. Her reception at the palace was modest by comparison, doubtless reflecting official disapproval, and as the acclaim of the crowds faded into the distance, and she was escorted through the state apartments, her ladies following, her heart began to falter. She felt like Daniel, walking into the lion's den.

Edward was waiting for her in a gallery, surrounded by his entire Council. Aware of the cold stare of Warwick and a low buzz of murmuring, she fell to her knees.

"Your Majesty, I am sorry I did not come before," she said. "I was not well."

Edward kept her there for long moments, then bade her rise and kissed her, without warmth. He had grown tall and very like his mother: he had Jane Seymour's pointed chin and full cheeks. But he was his father in his aggressive stance and imperious mien. The child who had loved her was no more.

"Does it not seem significant to you, my Lady Mary, that God has sent you illness while granting me health?" he said, his voice still high-pitched. It was like a slap in the face. He indicated that she should follow him into an adjoining chamber, and her heart sank when the councillors followed and the door was closed in the face of her ladies. She was alone.

Edward took his time seating himself beneath his canopy of estate, regarding her with steely eyes. He did not invite her to sit. "I have heard," he said, "that you habitually hear Mass." Mary could not answer. His coldness to her was so painful that she could not hold back the tears.

When she looked up, she was astounded to see that he was weeping, too, although he quickly regained command of himself. "I think no ill of you, Sister," he said.

Warwick stepped forward. "His Majesty means to say that he cannot condone your Highness living in error." After that, one by one, the other councillors weighed in, accusing Mary of breaking the King's laws by maintaining the old faith.

"In defying your brother, you are disobeying the will of your father," Rich said, with impenetrable logic.

"I do not know how that can be," she retorted. "You have swept away all my father's laws! But if you mean that I have failed in my duty to my sovereign, then you are wrong. I love and honor him, and as Scripture enjoins, I will render unto Caesar the things that are Caesar's—and unto God those things that are His." She saw Edward bridle at that.

Sir William Petre addressed him. "To avoid offending the Emperor, your Majesty might tolerate your sister's disobedience and make a single exception for her." Warwick glared at him, but it was Edward who answered.

"Is it lawful by Scripture to sanction idolatry?" he asked.

Mary rounded on him. "There have been good kings, Sir, who built altars and lived lives ruled by faith."

"We must follow the example of good men when they have done well," the boy declared loftily. "We do not follow them in evil. I fear the danger that will come to my realm if I allow you to have your Mass. This evil I will not allow."

Mary could feel frustration welling up. "Brother, I must remind you that Protector Somerset assured both me and the Emperor's ambassador that I might follow my religion within the privacy of my household."

"That is not true," Warwick flared, as the other councillors nodded in support.

"My lord," Mary retorted, "there is no subject more humble or obedient than I am, but you must surely realize that the King cannot expect me to change my religion at my age." She turned to her brother. "Does your Majesty know nothing of Somerset's promise?"

Edward shook his head. "I do not, since I have only taken an active share in affairs during the last year."

"In that case, it was not your Majesty who drew up the ordinances for the new religion," she retorted, "and therefore I am not bound to obey them. Nor have I infringed the terms of our father's will, which merely obliges me to consult the Council before marrying. It is his executors, your councillors, who have betrayed him, for they were enjoined to order two daily Masses and four annual obsequies for his soul, and have so far failed to do so. I appeal to you, Brother, allow the matter to rest until you are of an age to reach a mature judgment in matters of religion." She held out her hands in supplication.

Edward's cheeks flushed. "You too, Sister, might have something to learn—no one is too old for that. I am as concerned about your conduct as I am about your religion. You are my subject and must obey me, lest your example breed disrespect. I would have you know that my Master of Horse, Sir Anthony Browne, has just been incarcerated in the Fleet prison for twice attending Mass recently at your house."

Mary struggled to hide her shock. They must not think they could scare her into compliance. "Brother, I will not change my faith. And these new laws are not of your making. Our father cared more for the good of the kingdom than all the members of your Council put together." Her gaze swept around the lords standing by. She could see the anger in their faces.

"It seems that your Grace is trying to show us in a hateful light to the King our master without any cause whatsoever," Warwick growled.

"That was not my intention, but since you are pressing me, I have no choice but to tell the truth. There are two things only, body and soul. Although my soul belongs to God, I offer my body to the King's service; may it please him to take away my life rather than the old religion."

"Mary, I have no desire for such a sacrifice," Edward said, more kindly. "You look weary. You should go back to Clerkenwell while I discuss your case with the Council."

And let them cozen and overrule you! But they had been wrangling for the past two hours and Edward was right: she was exhausted.

"Give no credit to any person who might desire to make your Majesty believe evil of me," she begged. "Remember that I will always remain your humble, obedient, and unworthy sister."

Sitting in her lodging at Clerkenwell, Mary fretted about what was being discussed at Whitehall. The open hostility of Warwick and other councillors had unnerved her, and she knew they would try to suborn the King. Why, tonight, she might even be in the Tower! The thought made her moan involuntarily. But some, she prayed, might feel it politic to turn a blind eye to her disobedience.

She heard nothing that day, and so suffered a sleepless night with all the terrors darkness brought. The silence continued until after dinner, and then it was Scheyfve who appeared, looking triumphant.

"I have been with the Council, your Highness," he announced. "This morning, I received a letter from the Emperor ordering me to inform the lords that if you are forbidden to attend Mass, he will declare war on England."

Mary's hand flew to her mouth; her eyes stung with tears of gratitude. She had not expected so swift, so uncompromising, a response.

"I went to the Council immediately," Scheyfve continued. "It is clear that the English are in no position to involve themselves in war. There was a distinct change in their attitude. They will not put any further pressure on your Highness for the moment—and they are sending an envoy to pacify the Emperor."

It was a better outcome than Mary could ever have hoped for. She was safe. Her servants were safe. Praise be to God!

The ambassador smiled, well satisfied with his day's work. "His Imperial Majesty privately counsels you to be content with hearing Mass in your own house without admitting any strangers. Obey that command, and all will be well."

Mary sighed. She would have preferred to follow her conscience rather than resort to pragmatism, but she saw the wisdom in this advice. If it meant that they left her alone, it was worth compromising her principles a little. At least she could have her Mass.

The following morning, she felt quite ill—doubtless a reaction to the strain she had been under—and when Mr. Secretary Petre waited upon her at Clerkenwell, she was obliged to receive him sitting up in bed, propped against the bolster.

"Madam," he said, bowing, "I am sorry to see you indisposed. I am come to inform you that you may leave court without hindrance, and to assure your Highness of the most cordial affection of his Majesty and his Council. The King will without doubt be distressed to learn of your condition and would not wish me to trouble you further. Nevertheless, he asks again if you will give up the old faith."

If Mary had not felt so weak, she would have roared with frustration. "Pray excuse the brevity of my reply," she groaned, "but my soul is God's. My body is the King's to command."

Petre did not press her further, but respectfully withdrew.

A few days later, feeling much better, Mary left London for Beaulieu. She had been granted a respite from persecution, but she felt very bitter toward those who had subjected her to such an ordeal. And she felt even worse when it was brought home to her forcefully that while she herself might now be exempt from persecution, her priests would not be if they celebrated Mass for anyone other than herself and the two servants permitted to attend her at services. Late in March, Sir Robert Rochester was summoned to appear before the Council to answer questions concerning the activities of her chaplains. Clearly, it had not been forgotten that Dr. Mallet had celebrated Mass in Mary's absence.

"I said nothing that might compromise your Grace," he reported afterward, visibly shaken by his ordeal. "It seemed to me that the councillors fear your house might become a focus for disaffected Catholics. That is why they do not want outsiders to be admitted to Mass."

Late in April, for all Mary's protests, Dr. Mallet was arrested and imprisoned in the Tower. Then things went from bad to worse. England made a new defensive alliance with France, which was at war with the Emperor. Mary's heart plummeted when it dawned on her that there could be no question now of Charles declaring war on her behalf. It sank further when Scheyfve informed her that his Imperial Majesty was urging her not to provoke the Council too far. Even if she was forced to conform to the new laws, she would be committing no sin, because she would be doing so under duress. Then the Regent Mary weighed in, assuring Mary that a victim of force would be blameless in God's sight. Mary, however, was trying to brace herself for martyrdom.

In August, Sir Robert, Sir Francis, and Sir Edward Waldegrave were summoned before the Council at Hampton Court. When they returned to Copt Hall, near Epping, where Mary was staying, she guessed from their heavy demeanor that they brought ill news.

"Do not repeat to me anything that the Council said to you," she said, before they could speak. "If you do, I will not listen." She left them and shut herself in her closet, where she wrote a letter to the King, complaining about her servants being harassed, and sent Sir Robert and the others back to Hampton Court with it. Then she waited for news. The time seemed endless. If only her officers would return. If Sir Robert wasn't back soon, she would have to perform his duties for him.

At the end of August, hearing the sound of horses' hooves, she flew to the window and saw Lord Chancellor Rich, Sir William Petre, and Sir Anthony Wingfield riding into the courtyard of Copt Hall. Smoothing her skirts and taking a deep breath, she went out to meet them, reminding herself to keep defiant and cool, so as not to betray any womanly weakness. She greeted them courteously, and when they said they had come to deliver a letter from the King, she fell on her knees to receive it.

"I kiss this letter because his Majesty has signed it," she said, "and not for the matter contained in it, which I believe to be merely the doing of the Council." Rising, she broke the seal and read the letter there and then in the courtyard.

It was another hectoring missive, intended to intimidate her into converting to the new religion. She must realize, Edward wrote, that Somerset's promise had applied only for a short time while she came to see the error of her ways. That time had now expired, and he required her to obey his laws like all other true subjects. From now on, if she and her chaplains broke the law, the same penalties would apply to them as to everyone else.

She did not believe that Edward had composed the letter himself;

it had surely been written by one of the secretaries of state—Warwick's creature, William Cecil. As she read on, she murmured, "Ah, good Mr. Cecil took much pains here!"

She looked up at the lords. "I am the King's most humble, most obedient subject and poor sister, and I will obey him in everything that accords with my conscience; but rather than adopt the reformed faith, I will lay my head on the block and suffer death. When his Majesty is old enough to judge these things, I will obey him in religion, but now, in his youth, although he is a good, sweet king and has more knowledge than any other of his years, it is not possible that he can be a judge in these matters."

Rich's temper flared. "Madam, his Majesty's patience with you is exhausted. Henceforth, no services may be held in your house except those authorized by law. You should know that your officers have been committed to the Tower for having refused to comply with his Majesty's order that they stop Mass being said here." The threat was implicit.

Horrified, Mary groped for words, trying to maintain her composure. "Their refusal shows them to be more honest men than I believed them to be. Let me tell you, my lords, that I have in my possession a letter from the Emperor that makes the terms of the Duke of Somerset's promise very clear, and I give it more credence than any of your words." She registered the scorn on their faces, but was undeterred. "Though you have little esteem for the Emperor, you should show more favor to me for my father's sake, who made most of you out of nothing. And believe me, the Emperor's ambassador shall know how I am used at your hands—"

"Madam," Rich interrupted, "I have brought with me a trusty, skillful man for you to appoint as your new comptroller."

"You may take him away with you," she said. "I will appoint my own officers, and if you leave your new comptroller within my gates, I will go straight out of them, for I will not abide the two of us in the same house." She paused, sighing. "My Lord Chancellor, I am sickly, yet I will do the best I can to preserve my life. But if I should die, I will protest openly, on my deathbed, that you and the Council are the cause. You give me fair words, but you are always ill-disposed toward me." She turned round and swept past him, back into the house.

Standing in the shadows behind a curtain, she watched as the lords vented their wrath. When the front door opened, she hurried up the spiral stair to the gallery above the hall, where she heard Wingfield summoning her household. After everyone had gone into the courtyard, she returned to the window and heard Rich announcing that Mass was no longer to be celebrated in her houses, on pain of imprisonment. Then he turned to her chaplains. She counted only three of them, and wondered where the fourth, Father Hall, could be. Had he fled, too? But there was no time to wonder, for Rich was warning them that if they used any prayer book but the Book of Common Prayer, they would be deemed guilty of treason.

Mary watched in agony as they fearfully promised to comply. She was alarmed when she heard Rich order his men to search the house for any priest who might be hiding. At that, fearful for Father Hall, she showed herself at the window and beckoned him over, even as the guards raced into the hall.

"My Lord Chancellor, you will not find my priest Father Hall here, for he has left my service," she said. "Call your men off." But he would not, and she could only pray that the chaplain was well hidden or had got away.

"My lord," she continued, keeping her tone even, "I pray you, ask the councillors to permit my comptroller to return, for since his departure, I have had to attend to the accounts, and learn how many loaves of bread can be made from a bushel of wheat, and you will understand that my father and mother never brought me up to do baking and brewing. To be plain with you, I am weary of my office, and if my lords would send Sir Robert home, they shall do me a pleasure."

With a courteous farewell, she withdrew from the window and went upstairs to her bedchamber, just as the soldiers were descending to the hall—empty-handed, she noticed, to her satisfaction. When the councillors had gone, she was utterly relieved to see Father Hall emerge from a panel in the wall, so cunningly designed that even she had not known it was actually a door. He showed her his hiding place—a tiny cupboard not three feet square—and asked what the lords had come for.

"You mean you did not hear what they said?" she asked hopefully.

"No, my daughter." He looked bewildered.

"Then you can say with truth that you did not hear any order forbidding my priests to say Mass," she said joyfully.

"Indeed, I did not," he said, smiling.

The next day, although it grieved her to do it, Mary dismissed her other chaplains from her service.

"I do this unwillingly, to spare you all the misery of having to compromise your principles," she told them, and wept when they came to bless her and bid her adieu.

She continued to attend Mass, in the greatest secrecy.

"I would rather live in fear of betrayal and punishment than be deprived of the consolations of my faith," she told Father Hall. The services had to be held in her private chamber with only her closest confidantes present, for she feared there were almost certainly spies in her household.

Early in September, Nicholas Ridley, the Protestant Bishop of London, rode over from his house at Hadham to visit Mary, who had just returned to Hunsdon. Despite their widely differing opinions on religion, Mary knew him to be a sincere man, if somewhat overzealous in his views, and welcomed him in a friendly and courteous manner, recalling how kind he had been to her when her father was dying.

As they sat on either side of the hearth, their conversation centered upon general matters, but then Ridley offered to come to Hunsdon the following Sunday and preach to Mary's household. "I can also lend your Highness some books and tracts."

She knew then that he had been sent to turn her, and felt deeply disappointed.

"I will not listen to a Protestant sermon," she told him firmly.

"Madam, I trust you will not refuse God's word," he countered.

She bridled at that. "I cannot tell what you call God's word. God's word now is not what it was in my father's day."

"God's word is one in all times, but has been better understood and practiced in some ages than in others," returned the Bishop smoothly.

"You would not have dared to say that in my father's day!" retorted Mary. "As for your books, I thank God I never read any of them. I never did, nor ever will." She rose, indicating that the visit was at an end.

"My lord," she said as they parted, "for your gentleness to come and see me, I thank you; but for your offering to preach before me, I thank you not at all."

Scheyfve had formally protested against the Council's latest move against Mary, but they replied that the King was adamant that his laws be obeyed; no one, least of all his sister and heir, could be exempted.

As the weeks went by, Mary found it increasingly miraculous that the Council had not learned of what was going on in her household. Or if they had, they had made no move to stop it. It was her private belief that they knew very well that she was continuing to attend Mass, and she wondered if they still feared reprisals from the Emperor. Whatever the extent of Charles's military commitments, he still had far greater resources than England, and might choose to divert them from France if sufficiently provoked. She hoped there was a tacit official assumption that she was conforming to the law.

In the autumn, she learned that Edward had created Warwick duke of Northumberland, and sniffed at that, for the man was utterly unworthy. At the same time, the Marquess of Dorset was elevated to the dukedom of Suffolk, making her cousin Frances a duchess, while several other lords received peerages. Northumberland, she suspected, was extending his affinity and consolidating his hold upon the King.

In October, she learned that Somerset was in the Tower again, accused of treason and conspiracy, and wondered if he had been intriguing to overthrow the new Duke of Northumberland. Her old friend, his Duchess—not so puffed up with pride now—had been permitted to join him there. Mary did not hold out much hope for a happy outcome to the matter. She could almost feel sorry for the fallen Duke.

The court was then preparing for a state visit by the Queen Regent of Scotland. Mary was invited to attend the official reception, but felt it prudent to decline, using her health as an excuse. Out of sight, out of mind! It was better that she avoid any occasion for being subjected to further questioning on matters of religion.

Then she heard that her young cousin, Lady Jane Grey, was to attend the reception with her parents. Remembering that thin, plain little girl in her drab clothes, she gave way to a generous impulse and sent her a gorgeous gown of cloth of gold and velvet, overlaid with parchment lace of gold, to wear for the occasion. Later, she heard from her friends at court that Jane had worn it, and looked very becoming, although Elizabeth had turned up in severely cut black attire. Mary could imagine the effect, with her sister's red hair. She must have looked striking, which was surely what she had intended. God forbid, she was turning out just like her mother!

In December, Somerset was tried in Westminster Hall and sentenced to death. There were outraged public protests and demonstrations, for he had been popular with the commons, and Northumberland held a great muster of men-of-arms in Hyde Park, a show of strength calculated to warn the people not to provoke their betters. Mary was glad to be tucked away in the country. She felt sorry for Somerset; she had never had a good opinion of him, but he was infinitely preferable to his successor.

She had received a letter from the Emperor, reproving her for not attending the Queen of Scots's reception at court. As heiress to the throne, he'd pointed out, it would be wise if she showed herself there at every opportunity. She told him that she had been planning to visit her brother in the new year—until she had heard a rumor that she was to be forced to attend Protestant services. He must understand that it was best for her to stay away from the court for the foreseeable future.

She kept Christmas as a guest of the newly created Duke and Duchess of Suffolk at Tilty. When Jane Grey thanked her for the gown, Mary gained the strong impression that she had not liked it and had been pressed into being courteous. Nor did she seem much taken with the beautiful necklace of pearls and rubies that Mary gave her on Twelfth Night. She was a funny child—well, hardly a child at sixteen, although her diminutive stature made her seem younger. She was bookish and intelligent, but too solemn by far, and Mary always had the feeling that she was watching her critically, scrutinizing, disapproving . . . It seemed that the world was plagued by opinionated children!

Her cousin Frances was welcoming in her forthright way, and Suffolk was his usual bluff self, interested only in hunting. They made Mary welcome, but always there was that undercurrent of tension, and it stemmed from their religious differences. She had not brought Father Hall with her, and she repeatedly absented herself from Protestant services in the family chapel. She soon sensed that her hosts were longing to be rid of her. She was glad to get home in January.

Chapter 26

1552–3

Somerset had been beheaded. Mary's heart went out to his widow and children—and to the young King, who had had to sign a death warrant for yet another uncle. What would Queen Jane have said if she had known that her own son would send her brothers to their deaths? Mary was glad that she was not here to see it, God rest her.

In March, Mary's three officers were quietly released from the Tower and allowed to return to her service, for which she gave profound thanks. It had been a hard winter for them, and they rejoiced in their freedom, but she knew she must not burden them with any more secrets, so she did not tell them that she was still secretly attending Mass. Life had resumed its usual quiet course, and she was determined to keep it that way.

In the winter, she was astonished to receive not one, but several respectful, friendly letters from Northumberland, informing her of affairs of state and news of the court, and suggesting she resume the coat of arms she had borne in childhood as her father's sole heiress. Then he granted her £500 for repairs to ruinous dikes on her Essex estates. It was all rather perplexing, such a sudden about-turn that it made her suspicious. What did Northumberland want of her?

She wrote to friends at court, asking if all was well there. The King was looking tired, they replied. He had been a long time recovering from a bout of smallpox in the spring, but he was definitely better now.

She wondered how true this was. Could it be—God forfend!—that Edward was more sick than most people realized and that Northumberland was currying favor with the heiress to the throne? Well, if that was the case—and she prayed it wasn't—he would have to think again!

In January, Scheyfve wrote to say that he had concerns about the King's health. Edward had a nasty cough and had lost weight. *I fear, Madam, that a crisis is approaching. My lord of Northumberland has placed himself in control of the treasury and is hoarding huge sums of money.*

Mary was alarmed to read this letter, which arrived just after an invitation from Northumberland to attend a Candlemas masque at court, which was to be performed by a troupe of children. She did not hesitate. She must go to court and see for herself what was happening.

In February, she rode to London, accompanied again by a great train of her household knights and ladies and several lords who had joined her on the way. An hour's ride from the City, she was astonished to see Northumberland himself waiting to receive her, attended by a hundred mounted gentlemen.

"Your Highness is most welcome," he said warmly, making an elaborate bow. She could not have faulted him on his courtesy as he escorted her to the priory of St. John at Clerkenwell.

"His Majesty," he said apologetically, as they rode side by side, "is too ill to receive your Highness, being in bed with a fever, but I hope he will be better tomorrow."

Mary wasn't sure what to think. Scheyfve's letter had alarmed her, and she wondered at the change in Northumberland's treatment of her. Was Edward really ill? And how bad was he?

The next day, she rode to Whitehall, where she was welcomed at the palace gate by Northumberland and the entire Council, with as much respect as if she were a reigning queen. Her heart clenched. She was sure now that Edward was very ill indeed and that her accession was expected. But she did not trust Northumberland; for all she knew, he might be plotting some new villainy.

She waited at court for three days, while Edward remained too unwell to see her. She became aware of wild rumors circulating. People were openly speculating that the King had been given a slow-working poison, or even that he was dead. It was with some relief, therefore, that she was finally admitted to his bedchamber.

She caught her breath, profoundly shocked, for he looked so ill that he surely could not live long with whatever disease was ravaging his poor body.

"Do not look so worried, dearest Sister," he croaked. "I look worse than I feel. I am on the mend, and very pleased to see you." For all his brave words, he looked awful, bloated and wan.

They talked of pleasant things, both avoiding the thorny topic of religion. Then Edward was seized by a harsh, racking cough that robbed him of speech and left spots of blood on his pillow. Mary stared at them in horror, dreading to think what they betokened.

"Can I get you anything?" she asked, seeking refuge in practicality.

"No," he replied hoarsely, when the spasms had subsided. But he was clearly exhausted, and Mary left him to sleep.

She was not surprised to learn, later that day, that the masque had been canceled and the children sent home. She too went home, troubled in her mind, not only about Edward—for surely that blood was symptomatic of some mortal illness—but also about Northumberland's intentions. Did he really mean to welcome her as Queen when the time came, as come it surely would? Or was he dissembling, trying to lull her into a false sense of security?

When she had been back at Beaulieu for a week, Scheyfve reported that the King had sufficiently recovered to open a new Parliament, but that people had been shocked to see how weak he was. He had now gone to Greenwich, insisting that his illness was not serious and that he would soon be restored to health. A few peaceful weeks enjoying the fresh air would effect a cure.

Mary prayed that was true, but she could not help thinking of what might happen if he died. The throne would be hers, her right

sanctioned by law and her father's will. But neither Northumberland
nor Edward had shown much respect for the late King's laws. Northumberland must know that if Mary succeeded, it would mean a
Catholic revival, the outlawing of the reformed religion, and the end
of his own power. She shivered. How could she be safe when he had
so much at stake? And yet, she knew herself to be loved by the people. Surely they would not tolerate any subversion of her rights? Yes,
but what if she were done away with in secret? She would not put it
past the Duke to commit murder, if there was profit in it for him.

She went about her daily life in a state of high anxiety. Attending
Mass was the only thing that gave her comfort. She was all too aware
that others beside Northumberland might be appalled at the prospect of her becoming Queen. She was strongly identified with the
Catholic cause and Imperial interests. Several influential people had
much to lose if she came to the throne; others perhaps feared the
Emperor's interference in English affairs.

She was frustrated at the lack of information about the King, who
seemed to have retreated within the confines of Greenwich Palace
and had not been seen in public for some time. Everyone was speculating about the state of his health, and she knew, from her servants'
increased deference, that they believed she would soon be Queen.
That only brought her sadness, since Edward would have to die for
it to happen, and she could not bear the thought.

The weeks dragged by. In May, she heard from Scheyfve that Lady
Jane Grey had been married to Guildford Dudley, one of Northumberland's younger sons, amid great splendor at Durham House in the
Strand. It had been a double wedding, for Jane's sister Katherine had
also been wed, her bridegroom being William, Lord Herbert, son of
the Earl of Pembroke, an ally and friend of Northumberland.

But the King had not been present. Mary fretted about that, for it
was well known that he loved a lavish celebration, and the brides
were his cousins. It galled her that Northumberland had presumed
to ally his blood with that of the royal house, but doubtless it was
apiece with his desire to bind himself irrevocably to the King. Somehow, she suspected that it boded ill for herself.

She was surprised when Northumberland began sending her optimistic bulletins about the King's health. Edward was doing well. He would soon be better. She did not believe it. Scheyfve kept telling her otherwise.

In June, unable to bear the anxiety any longer, she confided to him her fears that she might be ousted from the succession or even done away with. *Please ask the Emperor what I should do,* she begged. But no reply came, and she wondered if her correspondence was being intercepted.

At the end of June, Scheyfve sent her the alarming news that Northumberland had altered the succession, although he knew no details. *The Duke's designs to deprive your Highness of the crown are now only too plain. He will dissemble with you until the King dies, then kidnap you, on the grounds that your accession may bring ruin and establish the Catholic faith in England. But when it comes to it, his party may desert him. He is hated and loathed for a tyrant, while your Highness is loved throughout the land. With your help, Northumberland may be worsted.*

That was a vain hope, Mary thought, trembling with anger and fear. Could the ambassador have got it wrong? She could not share his optimism, and when she learned that she and Elizabeth were no longer being prayed for in church services, she knew she must fear the worst.

She was heartened to hear from Scheyfve that the Emperor, concerned about the situation in England and worried about her safety, had dispatched three special envoys to assist him, under the guise of offering his commiserations to King Edward over his illness. Their real mission was to persuade Northumberland to alter his mysterious plans for the succession and protect Mary's interests, allaying the fears of the English by saying that the Emperor believed she should marry an Englishman and not a foreigner. *They will ask your Highness to issue a declaration that you do not intend to make any sweeping changes with regard to foreign policy or religion, and that you will pardon all those councillors who have given you cause for offense. If you agree to take this advice, there will be no cause for opposition.*

Mary laid down his letter and walked over to the window, staring down unseeing at the garden below. It seemed she would have to dissemble her principles once again, which went against all her instincts. She knew she must do it to survive, but one day, one fine day, she would bring the true faith back into this Godforsaken country. For now, she would hold herself in readiness to take up the great task that God was about to lay upon her, whatever the cost to herself. She would do her mother and her grandmother proud.

Mary was at Hunsdon in early July when she received a summons from the Council to attend on the King at Greenwich. It was accompanied by a letter from Northumberland, telling her that her presence would be a great comfort to her brother.

She thanked the messenger and sent him away, then hastened to her closet to confer with her officers and ladies.

"I am sure that my brother's condition is critical," she said, fighting down panic, "but I distrust the Duke's intentions. I am a lone woman, in a precarious state of health, with little influence and few powerful friends. I am in great perplexity. How should I respond to the summons?"

"It might be a ruse to lure your Highness to court," Sir Robert said heavily. "They may wish to put you out of the way. At best, you could be imprisoned; at worst . . ."

His words chilled Mary's heart. "You have just confirmed my worst fears. And yet I have a duty to my brother, especially if he is dying. I must go to Greenwich."

"No, Madam!" cried Susan.

"I must," Mary declared. "I would never forgive myself if I failed him."

"Then God help your Highness," said Sir Robert. "You might be walking into danger. As soon as the King is dead, they may attempt to seize you."

"God will protect me," she said. She left them and went to kneel in her chapel, raising her eyes to the bejeweled crucifix on the altar. "In Thee, O Lord, is my trust," she said fervently. "Let me never be confounded. If God is for us, who can be against us?"

She left Hunsdon with a stout escort and reached Hoddesdon on the evening of 6 July. There, she was alarmed to find Sir Nicholas

Throckmorton, one of Northumberland's associates, waiting for her. So they had been watching her! But as she made to rein her horse around in the other direction, he fell to his knees on the dusty road.

"Your Highness, do not leave!" he cried. "I am come in friendship, and at some risk to myself, to warn you."

Mary paused. "How do I know that Northumberland has not sent you?"

"I swear it, by all the saints," he declared. "I too hold to the true faith, and I do not want to see your Highness disparaged for a usurper. They mean to make the Lady Jane Grey queen."

Mary could not believe her ears. "But I and my sister Elizabeth go before her!"

"Not according to this new device for the succession that his Majesty has drawn up. He is determined to ensure a Protestant succession. You are both to be disinherited."

"What is this device?" Mary flared. "It can be of no force against the Act of Succession!"

"Indeed, it cannot," Sir Nicholas agreed, "but they have no respect for legal niceties. It is a document the King himself drew up."

So Edward had betrayed her, and Elizabeth, the sister he had professed to love.

"He still lives?" she asked.

"I know not, but he was in a very poor case when I left. I warn you, Madam, this summons to Greenwich is a trap; you should stay away from the court and ride north without delay to one of your strongholds in the eastern counties, where you will be surrounded and protected by men of your affinity."

Mary's instinct told her that he was speaking truth. She made a quick decision.

Gathering her train around her, she told them what Throckmorton had said, and was reassured to hear them agreeing that she should follow his advice.

She thanked him and promised to reward him one day. Sitting in the saddle, she scribbled a hasty note to Scheyfve, informing him of her intention to proclaim herself Queen as soon as she heard that the King was dead, and another to Northumberland, telling him that she was ill and unable to travel.

Summoning Susan, Jane Dormer, and six armed gentlemen of her household to attend her, she sent the rest home.

"And now to Kenninghall!" she cried.

They rode through the night, as fast as they could go in the darkness, for the roads were uneven and there was only a crescent moon. They spoke in low voices, saving their strength for the long journey ahead.

"Pray God we get there safely," Mary said to Susan. "If my bid for the crown fails, then at least I will be well placed to escape across the sea to Flanders. Lowestoft is not that far off."

"They may have anticipated that, Madam," Susan said, spurring her horse on. "There could be warships waiting off the coast, in case you try to flee the kingdom."

"There might indeed," Mary said grimly. "But we shall outwit them." It was strange, but against so many odds, she felt calm and confident. She would win through because she had right on her side. She was under God's protection. It was for this that He had preserved her through the difficult years.

"Madam, remember that all the forces of the country are at Northumberland's disposal; you have little hope of raising enough men to face him."

"We shall see!" Mary said. "I am not giving up yet. I have a kingdom to win."

By the evening of the next day, exhausted, sweating, and bedraggled, they arrived at Sawston Hall near Cambridge, the manor house of John Huddlestone, a prominent Catholic gentleman. He welcomed Mary warmly and even defied the law to have Mass celebrated in her presence, refusing to heed her protests that he was putting himself in danger. But then it dawned on her that he did not believe there *was* any danger—not anymore. She prayed, nevertheless, that God would preserve her brother. She could not forget the little boy she had loved, her father's precious jewel. Edward must live, for his sake.

Refreshed after a wash and a good night's rest, and clad in clean clothes provided by Mistress Huddlestone, she left in the morning with her small party and rode on to Bury St. Edmunds, where she was heartened by the enthusiastic reception extended to her by the people, who came running to see her.

That night Mary slept at Euston Hall near Thetford, the home of a friend, Lady Burgh. While they were at supper, there was a loud banging on the door, and she leaped to her feet, ready to flee, for she thought Northumberland's men had found her. But it was her goldsmith, Master Raynes, who was announced.

"Your Majesty," he said, kneeling before her, his clothes spattered with mud, "the King is dead. Long live the Queen!"

She felt no sorrow, no exultation. "Who sent you?" she asked suspiciously, fearing a trap to entice her to London.

"Sir Nicholas Throckmorton, Madam."

"Thank you, Master Rayne." She dismissed him, then turned to her hostess. "I am not sure that I should trust Sir Nicholas Throckmorton. He did warn me to flee to my estates, but why should he help me? He works for Northumberland."

"Your Highness may be right," Lady Burgh said, her face pale beneath her widow's hood. "It may be a bait to trap you."

"Or it might be that Northumberland is provoking me to declare myself Queen while my brother still lives, in which case I would be guilty of high treason and could be legally disposed of. It might be better to keep Master Rayne's news to myself and continue on my way—and hope for confirmation from another source."

"Yes, Madam, that would be the best course. And I will never tell anyone that you were here."

Mary was alarmed when she approached Norwich and the citizens shut its gates against her. But as she retreated, one loyal man rode after her and warned her that Lord Robert Dudley, Northumberland's son, was closing in on her with an armed force. That impelled her to change clothes with one of her maids and make all speed to Kenninghall. They were nearly there when they heard the sound of hoofbeats behind them. It struck fear into Mary, and she was utterly relieved when she saw that the rider wore the Emperor's livery.

Scheyfve had sent his secretary, a man she knew she could trust.

"Your Highness," he panted, falling to his knees in the road, "the King is dead."

Mary crossed herself, feeling unutterably sad. So it was true. That poor, misguided boy . . . But she must save her mourning for later, for the man was speaking.

"My master bade me warn you that you cannot hope to prevail against Northumberland; nor is it possible for you to escape from England because the way is barred by ships stationed all along the eastern coast. The Duke has sent his son after you, and it would be wiser to negotiate terms while there is still time." He glanced behind him, as if to reassure himself that Lord Robert Dudley's force was not hard on his heels.

"I thank you, good sir," Mary said. "I will send the ambassador a reply when I have had time to think about what I should do."

She was suddenly aware that her ladies and gentlemen had dismounted and were now falling to their knees around her. It brought home to her the fact that she was now Queen—by right, if not yet in fact. She extended her hand to be kissed, and it was seized fervently by each and every one of her people, bringing tears to her eyes.

"I thank you all, my dear friends," she said. "Now we must press on. The time for celebrating is not yet."

When she reached Kenninghall, she had been joined by thirty loyal gentlemen and their men. It was a profound relief to see ahead of her the magnificent brick manor house beyond the moat of the ancient castle. As she walked into the great chamber, which was hung with fourteen tapestries depicting the labors of Hercules, she was enveloped by a sense of security. The armory here was well stocked with weapons. Best of all, her chief officers were awaiting her, having ridden up from Hunsdon at her summons. They had heard the news of the King's death, although not from the Council, who had sent no communication to Hunsdon; they too now made their obeisances to her as Queen.

Mary summoned every member of her household into the great chamber. When they had crowded into the room, she rose from her chair on the dais. "My lords and ladies, it is my heavy duty to tell you that our sovereign lord King Edward is departed to God. In accordance with the Act of Succession and King Henry's will, I proclaim myself the rightful Queen of England by divine and human law."

The cheers were heartfelt and deafening, and Mary was deeply moved. But there were almost insurmountable obstacles to be overcome before she was Queen in deed as well as title. First, she must inform Northumberland of her intentions. In the privacy of her closet, she wrote to the Council in the unmistakable tone of royal command. She said she was grieved by the death of her brother, but submitted to the will and pleasure of God. She reminded them of the terms of her father's will. *We trust that there is no good, true subject who will pretend to be ignorant of it. And, as God shall aid and strengthen us, we have ourselves caused our right and title to be proclaimed.*

But it seemed strange to her, she continued, that her brother had died some days ago and they had not thought to inform her. Nevertheless, she trusted in their loyalty and service, and that they would, as noble men, do everything for the best. She made it plain that she was not ignorant of their plans, although she tactfully suggested that some political consideration had impelled them toward disloyalty. *Yet doubt not, my lords, that we take your doings in gracious part, being ready fully and freely to pardon you, to avoid bloodshed and vengeance. We trust you will take and accept this grace in such good part that we shall not be forced to use the services of our true subjects and friends in our just and rightful cause. Wherefore, my lords, we require and charge you, for the allegiance you owe to God and to us, that, for your honor and the surety of your persons, you cause our right and title to the crown and government of this realm to be proclaimed in our city of London and other places.*

Having signed herself as Queen, Mary dispatched her messenger. She also had copies of her letter sent to cities and towns throughout the kingdom, and to many who held public office, and summoned all loyal men to swear fealty to her as their sovereign. She then announced that she would maintain the religion of England as established by her brother and make no drastic changes. Clearly, this was a popular move, for local gentlemen now came hastening with their tenantry to Kenninghall, offering her their swords.

She was gratified by the speed with which the great men of En-

gland responded to her summons; it was almost as if they had been
waiting for it.

The first to arrive was Sir Henry Bedingfield of Oxburgh Hall in
Norfolk, whose father had been jailer to Mary's mother in the dark
days of the 1530s. She welcomed him warmly, for it seemed like a
kind of reparation. Then came the wealthy Sir Richard Southwell,
who brought with him men, arms, money, and provisions, and after
him the Earl of Bath and the Earl of Sussex, each with men of their
affinity. And now they came in their droves, from the eastern counties and presently from farther afield. Soon, Kenninghall was surrounded by an armed camp, which grew larger by the hour. All over
the country, Mary was told, the people were proclaiming her Queen.
It astonished her to see, as she walked around the camp, greeting and
thanking her supporters, that not only Catholics had turned out for
her, but also Protestants, anxious to see the lawful heir ascend the
throne.

It quickly became clear that she should move to a larger stronghold with better fortifications. She marched south with her forces to
Framlingham Castle in Suffolk, which stood only fifteen miles from
the coast. It was a mighty fortress, with walls forty feet long and
eight feet thick, and as Mary looked up at its thirteen great towers,
she knew she would be safe here. Let Lord Robert Dudley do his
worst!

She almost wept at the sight that greeted her in the deer park
below the castle, for it was packed with local people come to offer
their allegiance. She raised her standard on the battlements to resounding cheers.

"There must be more than fifteen thousand men," Bedingfield
said, standing at Mary's elbow with her other captains, looking down
on the sea of faces.

"They come because of the rightness of your Majesty's claim,"
Southwell said.

"And because of the love they bear you," Sir Robert Rochester
chimed in.

Their numbers increased daily, boosted by innumerable small
companies of the common people, armed with scythes and staves and
whatever else had come to hand.

There was good news. Lord Robert Dudley had been routed at King's Lynn and forced to retreat to Bury St. Edmunds to await re-inforcements. And Norwich, which had closed its gates against Mary just days before, had now recognized her as Queen and sent men and supplies. She was thrilled to see how many men of the eastern counties had risen in her favor and astonished to hear that Robert Dudley had now had her proclaimed Queen in King's Lynn. Presently, many councillors, having heard of her triumphs, came to offer her their support, having slipped quietly away from the Tower, where Jane Grey was in residence. Sir Edmund Peckham, the royal cofferer, had even brought some of the royal treasure. But he and others warned that Northumberland had gathered an army and was planning to march toward Newmarket, where he intended to intercept Mary as she marched south to London. As if she would be so foolish, knowing him to be out for her blood!

There was a pervading sense that the tide was turning in her favor. The lords told her that their fellow councillors had been waiting upon events, but really wanted to declare for her. Her captains said they were confident that her forces now outnumbered any Northumberland could raise. Jubilantly, she reviewed her troops, riding between the massed ranks drawn up below the castle. So many had come that their commanders had lost count of their number. As she passed, she was greeted by shouts and acclamation. Men cried out, "Long live our good Queen Mary!" and "Death to traitors!" and fired their arquebuses into the air with such deafening reports that her palfrey reared in fright. Calming the beast, she dismounted and continued her review on foot, walking the mile from one end of the camp to the other, thanking the soldiers for their goodwill, her eyes brimming with tears at their demonstrations of love and loyalty. Not even the news that Lady Jane had been proclaimed Queen in London could dampen her spirits. That chit of a girl could be dealt with. It was Northumberland who was the greatest threat, but she was certain now that she was a match for him.

Riders kept galloping up to the castle, bringing more news by the hour. Mary had been proclaimed in four more counties. Sir William

Paget, one of the leading councillors, had changed sides and was planning to march on Westminster. The treasurer of the Mint had slipped away, laden with all the gold in Lady Jane's privy purse. Broadsheets in support of Mary were circulating in London. The crews of the warships anchored off Yarmouth had mutinied in her favor and threatened to throw their officers into the sea if they did not join them; soon afterward, two thousand sailors with a hundred great cannon arrived at Framlingham. Even Bishop Hooper, a fervent Protestant, had urged his flock to support Mary. Reports claimed that Northumberland was having difficulty in enlisting men, for the common people had no love for him. Even so, he was definitely marching north, accompanied by an army and all his sons except Robert and Guildford, and was even now on the Cambridge road.

"If Northumberland thinks he cannot overcome your Majesty, he will declare for you," Sir Francis Englefield said, bringing Mary the latest reports from the City. "It seems he can no longer command the loyalty of the Council."

"They are all straws that bend with the wind," she said. "They care not for any principle, only for their own prosperity."

"Your Majesty should not disparage their support," ventured Sir Robert. "You will need them when you come into your own. And you will, very soon. Your army numbers over thirty thousand men and is still growing. More towns have proclaimed you. The authorities are now bold to voice their loyalty."

"You are right, of course." Mary attempted a smile, although in truth her emotions were in turmoil. This was all happening because a young boy had tragically died, and it might yet end in death and misfortune for many more. "I never realized that the people loved me so much."

A messenger was admitted. "Your Majesty, the Duke of Northumberland has arrived in Cambridge. His men are deserting in large numbers, but he is to march on Bury St. Edmunds with those that remain."

"It is only a matter of time," said Bedingfield.

Morale in Mary's camp was high, especially after Lord Wentworth changed sides and rode in with his men, resplendent in a fine suit of shining armor. Mary now appointed the Earl of Sussex her commander-

in-chief and made Wentworth his deputy. Then she left them vigor-
ously drilling the ranks and making battle plans.

Northumberland had reached Bury, not thirty miles away! The word
went around the camp like wildfire, and Mary, standing on the battlements, braced herself for the battle to come.

She was not unduly worried. The powerful Earl of Oxford had just
joined her with twenty thousand men. Northumberland could not
hope to prevail against such a host. Doubtless he realized this, for
they soon learned that he had retreated to Cambridge, where he was
desperately trying to raise men to fight for him. But the people were
turning their backs and rioting. In reprisal, his men were looting
and burning villages. Mary was sickened when she read the reports,
for the Duke seemed to be lifting no finger to stop them. His men
were now deserting him in their hundreds.

Presently, she was told that all but three members of the Council
had abandoned Northumberland and fled the Tower, leaving Lady
Jane alone there. They had gone to Baynard's Castle, the London
residence of the Earl of Pembroke, where the Earl of Arundel, having
hastily abandoned Jane, had declared for Mary and persuaded his
colleagues to do the same. A reward had been offered to anyone
apprehending Northumberland. The councillors had then gone to
St. Paul's Cathedral to give thanks for the kingdom's deliverance
from treachery, and had ordered that Mass be celebrated there. That
pleased Mary more than anything. It brought tears of joy to her eyes.

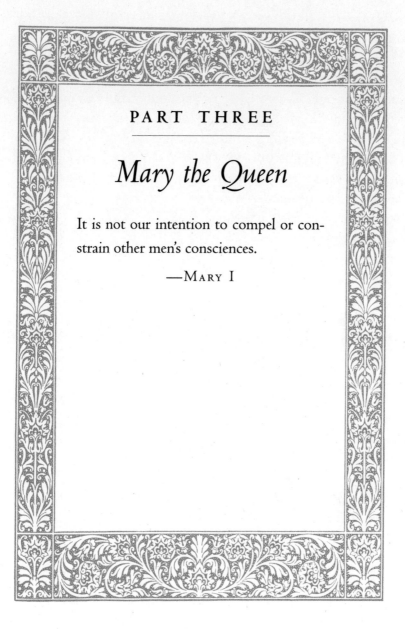

PART THREE

Mary the Queen

It is not our intention to compel or constrain other men's consciences.

—MARY I

Chapter 27

1553

Seated on the chair of estate on the dais in the great hall of Framlingham, with her small court around her, Mary inclined her head as the Earl of Arundel and Sir William Paget were ushered in and fell to their knees before her.

"Your Majesty," Arundel said, "we come to offer our allegiance and to tell you that you have been proclaimed Queen in London. We bring you the Great Seal of England."

An usher came forward to take the embroidered velvet bag containing the seal and place it in Mary's hands. She waited, looking down on the kneeling councillors severely.

Paget's voice was hoarse, he who was always so urbane and confident. "Your Majesty should know that we and our colleagues on the Council have always remained loyal to you in our hearts. It was because of the Duke of Northumberland's pernicious influence that we did not dare to declare our fealty, for fear of provoking destruction and bloodshed. We hope that your Majesty will accept our deepest apologies."

Mary had already decided that she could hardly consign the entire Privy Council to the Tower.

"Madam," Arundel weighed in, before she could answer, "we crave your pardon for the offense we committed in taking the Lady Jane for our Queen." Then he and Paget made the dramatic gesture of drawing their daggers and pointing them toward their stomachs, looking up at her pleadingly.

"There is no need to fall on your swords," she said, smiling, for she could afford to be magnanimous in victory. It was a heady, joyous moment, and nothing should mar it; all should share her elation. "I forgive you readily," she said. "I am only grateful that an armed conflict has been avoided and that I am Queen by the will of the people. God has worked a miracle."

Her heart full of thankfulness, she rose and led the councillors and her household to the chapel, where she commanded that the crucifix be openly placed on the altar. She had a *Te Deum* sung, and everyone present gave praise to God for this miraculous, bloodless victory. In granting her such an astonishing triumph over her enemies, He had set the seal of divine approval upon her accession. She was Queen not only by her own rightful title, but by God's will.

"To prove our loyalty," Arundel said afterward, "we will go now, with your Majesty's leave, to Cambridge to arrest the Duke."

Mary watched them ride away, certain that they would not fail her.

Arundel and Paget had been so eager to get to Framlingham that they had not waited to hear her proclaimed in London, but news from the capital soon came pouring in. When the Lord Mayor and aldermen of London had made the proclamation in Cheapside, the crowds had been so great that they had had to fight their way to the Eleanor Cross, where the heralds were waiting. There was such a shout from the people that the words could not be heard.

London had gone wild. People had run in all directions, throwing their bonnets in the air and crying, "The Lady Mary is proclaimed queen!" The citizens had lit bonfires in many streets and the bells had rung out in every parish church as the crowds feasted and celebrated. Scheyfve wrote that he was unable to describe the exultation he witnessed. *No one can remember there ever having been public rejoicing such as this. I never saw the like.*

It had seemed that nearly every citizen was on the streets, and the city fathers had hastily arranged for the fountains and conduits to run with wine. Even dignified aldermen and wealthy merchants had cast off their stately gowns and leaped and danced with the rest, joyfully joining in the common people's songs. The celebrations had continued throughout the night and into the next morning, with everybody inviting everybody else to dinner afterward. The *Te Deum* had been sung in every parish church that day, and the church bells had not ceased pealing until evening. *It seemed,* wrote Scheyfve, *as if everyone had gone to Heaven.*

Mary's eyes misted over. How she wished she had been there to see it. She had spent long hours in chapel, thanking God for all these blessings and telling herself that the rejoicing and jubilation could not possibly be for her personally—it must be for joy that right had prevailed; she was merely the vessel in which that right was invested. She must not give way to the sin of pride.

As great preparations were made for the coming move to London, she went about as if on wings. It was exalting to be able to worship freely again, to hear Mass without fear of reprisals, to see the anxiety gone from the faces of her beloved servants.

In the midst of her happiness, she spared a thought for Lady Jane, who had been a pawn in Northumberland's deadly game. She was still in the Tower, in the palace that had now become her prison, for the Council had posted guards outside the doors. Her parents had abandoned her and fled, Mary heard, her lips curling with disapproval. How could they do that to their child when she stood in such peril? And, by all reports, Jane had not even wanted the crown, had been forced to accept it.

She said as much to Sir Robert and Susan one evening.

"Yes, Madam, but in accepting it, she committed treason," Sir Robert reminded her.

"But she is very young," Susan put in.

"Old enough to know right from wrong," Sir Robert said severely.

"But not perhaps to withstand the combined will of Northumberland and the Council," Mary pointed out, remembering how terrified she herself had been, standing her ground against them. "I will deal leniently with her." She pretended she had not noticed Sir Robert shaking his head.

"How the coward does turn his coat," Mary murmured, as she read Paget's letter describing the arrest of Northumberland, along with that of his son, Lord Robert Dudley. The Duke had already declared for Mary and had one of his heralds proclaim her Queen in the market square at Cambridge. He had tossed his bonnet into the air, shouting, "God save Queen Mary! God save Queen Mary! God save Queen Mary!" He had even ordered that Mass be celebrated. Then he had been about to make his escape, when Arundel burst into his lodging and apprehended him in the Queen's name.

By then, Mary was riding southward at the head of a large company, having dismissed most of the vast host that had rallied to her at Framlingham. She had been delighted by her welcome at Ipswich, where the city fathers met her outside the town and presented her with a large purse of gold. She had ridden through streets packed with cheering crowds and been touched when a group of angelic-looking little boys gave her a solid-gold heart inscribed "The heart of the people." She had lodged in Wingfield House, where she received yet more turncoats come to pay homage and ask forgiveness. As she proceeded with her journey, scores of men of rank and importance had come riding to meet her, some to crave her pardon for their disloyalty. She warmly welcomed and forgave most of them, but she refused to receive Northumberland's staunchest supporters or his sons. She was already finding it hard to trust those who had so recently changed sides. For all her fair welcome, she would never trust some of them again.

"I am aware," she said one night at her crowded supper table at Beaulieu, "that people are speculating as to whom I might marry. The Emperor himself has instructed his envoys not only to congratulate me on my accession, but also to say that it will be necessary for me to marry, and soon, in order to be supported in the labor of governing and assisted in matters for which ladies do not have the capacity. He advises that I choose a person who appears to me the best befitted for the honor." She did not add that Charles had offered to assist in that choice. She did not want people thinking that she was ruled by Spain and the Empire. Naturally, he would want her to make a marriage that would benefit Habsburg interests, but it might be more politic for her to wed one of her own subjects.

The lords around the table seemed to agree.

"Your Majesty might like to consider Edward Courtenay," Wentworth suggested, offering Mary some bread to mop up her sauce. "He has been a prisoner in the Tower since King Harry's time, but he is of the old royal blood of this realm."

"He is very young," Mary said doubtfully.

"He is twenty-six," Oxford replied.

Eleven years younger than she was, Mary thought sadly. Somehow, the years had flown by and now here she was, thirty-seven years old—and looking it. Her mirror did not lie. People praised her fairness, but she knew they flattered her. She might dress gorgeously, as a queen should, in the rich gowns that had been ready for her when she'd arrived at Beaulieu, but it did not disguise her thin body or her aging face. Her red-gold hair was as fine as ever, but her brows knitted above her wary eyes, and her mouth had a pinched look. What man would find her desirable, especially one of young and virile years? Besides, she felt dried up inside; she shrank inwardly from what marriage would mean. She had never understood exactly what passed between a man and a woman in a bed; she knew only that it was essential for the bearing of children—and that it was exceedingly immodest and somehow shameful.

"I cannot think about marriage now," she said. "I have so many other matters on my mind—and my councillors will have a view." She had reappointed all those lords who had come to beg her pardon; they would serve alongside the faithful members of her household. The chief councillors, and the most experienced, would be Arundel and Paget.

She had to make a decision about her brother's funeral. She wanted to hold a requiem Mass, even though Scheyfve and the Imperial en-

voys had written to urge that King Edward be buried in the faith in
which he had lived and died. Disappointed, for she had hoped for
their support, she decided to follow her instincts.

"My priority," she said to the assembled lords, "is religion. Now
that God has seen fit to place me on the throne, I believe it is my
sacred duty to restore the true faith. But I intend to make no sweeping changes." Not at first; she had to go carefully. She had not told a
soul that she had written secretly to the Pope, asking him to lift the
interdict placed upon the English Church during her father's reign
and receive her kingdom back into obedience to the Apostolic See.
She feared there might be violent opposition to a return to Rome.
People must be persuaded to it gently and diplomatically. She did
not want to lose the popularity that had won her the crown.

Nonetheless, she had been astonished at the speed with which
men had reverted to the old faith. The markets must be doing a roaring trade in rosaries and crucifixes. Still, if it brought souls back to
Christ, that was all to the good.

Everyone was looking at her approvingly. "Is your Grace determined to press on to London?" Bedingfield asked. "It will be hot and
stinking, and there is plague about."

"That did not worry those who were celebrating my accession,"
she smiled, "and I will not let it bother me. Yes, I am going to London."

"A wise decision, Madam," Oxford beamed. "It is best to return
while public feeling is riding so high in your favor."

She had given orders that Northumberland, his sons, and his treacherous associates be imprisoned in the Tower. She had also commanded
that Lady Jane surrender the crown jewels and other property that
belonged rightfully to herself, and that she formally relinquish the
crown. Jane was then to be moved from the royal apartments to the
house of the Gentleman Gaoler and treated as an honored guest, although under no circumstances was she to be allowed to communicate with the Dudleys, who were being held nearby.

One day, Mary was told that the Duchess of Northumberland was
at the door, begging to see her.

"No," she said. "I will not receive her. Send her away." From her window, she watched as the dejected Duchess rode sorrowfully home.

But she did receive Frances Suffolk, for the sake of their kinship. It was not Frances's fault that her craven husband had gone into hiding; indeed, she was in a state of panic. Throwing herself on her knees at Mary's feet, she burst into floods of tears. "Your Majesty, I beg of you, spare my lord and my innocent child!"

"Calm down, cousin," Mary soothed, taking her hands and raising her—reminding herself that this woman had put pressure on her daughter to accept the crown. "Jane is quite safe and well. She is housed comfortably in the Tower and has books and writing materials."

"Yes, but what will happen to her?"

Mary frowned. "I mean to be merciful."

"You should know," Frances went on, wild-eyed, "that Northumberland tried to poison the late King, and my lord."

Mary stiffened. "You have proof of this?"

"Madam, an apothecary employed by Northumberland has just killed himself. Is that not proof enough?"

Mary was not sure whether to believe it. It was horrible to think that Edward had been poisoned, but Jane Dormer had heard a rumor that Northumberland had brought in a woman who claimed to be able to prolong the young King's life, and it was said she had attempted to do so by administering arsenic to him. That might be true, given what Frances had alleged.

"Frances," Mary said, "I know that Northumberland is a wicked man. I suspect that Jane was more sinned against than sinning. Let me assure you that I will not harm her or her father. Now, go home to Sheen."

Frances went meekly, almost sobbing with relief. Soon afterward, Mary heard that Suffolk had joined her at Sheen and been arrested there and committed to the Tower. When he pleaded for clemency, she immediately gave the order for his release. Never let it be said that she was not merciful!

London, she heard, was still celebrating, and a constant procession of lords, councillors, household officials, and other dignitaries, bent on declaring their loyalty to her, was making its way to Essex. She received most in a spirit of reconciliation, reserving her wrath only for her most hardened opponents.

She was delighted to receive from Elizabeth a warm letter of congratulation, informing her that she was leaving Hatfield at once for London in order to make her obeisance to her Queen. Mary had been uneasy about her sister's loyalty—at one stage she had even feared that she might make a bid for the crown—yet it seemed that the old affection between them was still lively.

Before she left Beaulieu, Scheyfve and the Emperor's envoys waited on her. As they congratulated her on her accession, her eyes were drawn to the tall, arresting figure of Simon Renard, a strikingly handsome man with sensual lips and inviting eyes. He was about forty and, he told her, a lawyer and a native of Franche-Comté. That brought to mind poignant memories of Chapuys, and she warmed to the man at once. As they all exchanged pleasantries and caught up on Mary's news, she saw that Renard was charming, wise, and perspicacious, with a wealth of diplomatic experience behind him. He was by far the most accomplished and able of the three men before her; beside him, Scheyfve appeared insignificant.

But it was Scheyfve who acted as chief spokesman. "His Imperial Majesty is delighted that God has been pleased to dispose all things in so excellent a manner, but he advises your Majesty to take very great care not to be led by your admirable zeal for religious reform, but to show yourself to be accommodating. It is best to dissemble for the present and not seek to change things too much, but wait until you are able to summon Parliament and take necessary measures with its participation. Be in all things what you ought to be—a good Englishwoman, wholly bent on the kingdom's welfare."

Mary nodded graciously and thanked the Emperor for his kind advice. Later, she asked if one of the ambassadors might visit her in her private oratory to discuss more confidential matters, and was thrilled when Simon Renard entered by the back door, as directed. It was not just that she felt she could place her confidence in him, but also—and this she hardly dared admit to herself—that she felt drawn to him in the way she had long ago felt drawn to Chapuys. She could not help it, or suppress the racing of her heart. It was exhilarating to be in the presence of such a good-looking, confident man. And the way he was looking at her . . . Suddenly, she felt young again, even desirable.

Desist! she admonished herself. *He is just showing you the deference due to the Queen.* He was here purely to advise her, and she guessed that Charles had sent him because he knew she would find him trustworthy, which was as well, as she trusted none of her councillors.

"I have to tell your Majesty," he said, "that my colleagues and I feel somewhat embarrassed, since we did virtually nothing to support your cause until we were convinced of the success of it. In fact, we were making plans to spirit you away. But now, here you are, Queen of this land!"

She readily forgave him. As they talked, she saw that he was sympathetic, well informed, and such a good listener that she found herself confiding to him her concerns about the momentous decisions that lay ahead of her. It was, of course, most unusual for a monarch to ask for confidential advice from a foreigner. It would greatly have displeased her lords, had they known about it, but Mary had no faith in the counsel of heretics and turncoats. All her life she had relied on the Emperor's support, and the personable Renard could now provide a direct and useful link between herself and her beloved mother's country.

"I can only reiterate my master's advice to go carefully in the first weeks of your reign and marry as soon as possible," he urged.

"I do so much appreciate his guidance," Mary said, blushing, not wanting him to think her immodestly eager to secure a husband. "I must confess that, although as a private individual I have no desire to marry, I recognize that it is my duty to do so. And after God, I desire to obey no one but the Emperor, whom I have always looked upon as a father. So I am determined to follow his Majesty's advice and choose whoever he might recommend." She hesitated, for it was not easy to talk about these matters, although she felt that Renard would understand. "I hope the Emperor will remember that I am now thirty-seven and do not wish to marry a man I have never met."

"I am sure his Majesty appreciates that." Renard's sudden smile was devastating, and Mary found herself wishfully wondering again if a queen could marry an ambassador . . .

"As for religion," he was saying, "one can only applaud your Majesty for wishing to lead your people back into the fold of the true Church. I have noticed you looking constantly upon the Sacrament on the altar here. No one could doubt your passionate sincerity for the faith."

She smiled at that. "It gives me great joy to see it there, after all these years of having to hide it. Messire Renard, I am determined to have a Mass celebrated for my brother, to discharge my own conscience and out of respect for the will of the late King Henry, my father. I will force no one to go to Mass, but I mean to see that those who wish to go should be free to do so."

Renard frowned. "Madam, you might alienate the people by having your brother buried with Catholic rites."

"No," she cried, "I feel so strongly on the matter that I will not be moved."

"It might be more politic to have the late King buried as a Protestant and absent yourself as custom demands of a monarch's successor. Then you could hold a private requiem Mass for him later."

Mary sighed. "Very well. I heed what you say. But there is another matter which troubles me. I am not happy with my councillors; I cannot trust them. I am amazed at the divisions in the Council over the matter of the Lady Jane's usurpation. They are always accusing one another, or chopping and changing their stories in such a manner that I am unable to get at the truth of what actually happened. How am I to bind them together in amity?"

Renard stroked his short, neat beard, looking uncomfortable. "Your Majesty, again, I urge caution. I do not think your councillors would be happy if they learned that you have secretly consulted me. It could rebound on good relations between England and Spain. I urge you to reassure them that although you are half Spanish by birth, and a friend to Spain, you intend to rule with their advice, especially in regard to religion."

Mary sniffed. "My councillors know my mind on that. They know I have been celebrating Mass in secret for years; they expect me to restore the old forms of worship. I can do no less, for I must not be thankless for the favor shown me by God in choosing me, His unworthy servant, for this high office. But I cannot easily confide in those I do not trust."

Renard nodded. "I am always happy to advise your Majesty, but you must not let your councillors think I have usurped their place."

The next morning, Mary left Beaulieu for London. As her retinue gathered in the courtyard, there was a tangible sense of expectancy and excitement. She felt it herself, and no wonder. She was going to her capital to claim her throne—a life-changing moment that only a few short weeks ago she had never thought to see. Her heart was full; she could not cease rendering thanks to God, who had preserved her from her enemies and vouchsafed her this triumph.

Along the way, the people came running, cheering and calling blessings upon her. When she reached Wanstead at the beginning of August, by a happy chance she encountered Elizabeth, a vision in black and white, riding toward her at the head of a great train of nobles. They both dismounted, and Elizabeth, disregarding her beautiful silk skirts, knelt in the road, but Mary raised and embraced her, taking her hand and kissing her warmly.

"Sister, I am heartily pleased to see you," she said, as they smiled at each other, and she was reassured to detect no guile in Elizabeth's hooded eyes. How graceful she was—and how young, not yet twenty! Again, Mary felt old. But she did not let it spoil the moment and gladly turned to greet and kiss all the noble ladies in Elizabeth's train. Then the two great processions formed into one for the Queen's state entry into London, with Elizabeth riding at Mary's side, cutting a fine figure on her horse. With her hooked nose and thin, clever face, she was not conventionally beautiful, yet she exuded a powerful charm and had a regal air. Mary soon realized that the people were cheering for her sister almost as much as for herself; they seemed drawn to her, and no wonder.

She could not fault Elizabeth, who, while acknowledging the acclaim of the people, continually deferred to her. Yet what message was she giving out by wearing her sober attire? Was she telling the crowds that she was the Protestant heir? It gave Mary pause for thought amid the celebrations.

It had been arranged that, so that she should look her best for her state entry into London, Mary should change in the house of a prosperous merchant in Whitechapel. There, in the best bedchamber, after her eager hosts had plied her with fine wines and delicacies, her ladies dressed her in a gown of purple velvet and satin in the French style, laden with goldsmiths' work and jewels. Around her neck they hung a thick chain of gold, pearls, and precious stones, and on her head they placed a French hood trimmed with gems and pearls.

When she emerged, a little breathless with apprehension, her horse was waiting, caparisoned in cloth of gold with intricate embroideries. And there was Sir Anthony Browne, who was to ride behind her and bear her long train over his arm. She mounted her steed and sat straight in the saddle. Today, she was to enter her capital city.

It was late afternoon when the Queen's procession passed into London through Aldgate, where the Lord Mayor was waiting to surrender the City's mace in token of his loyalty and homage. Smiling, Mary promptly returned it to him with a gracious speech of thanks, at which those standing by wept for joy. Trumpets were sounding and there was the loud report of guns being fired in salute from Tower Wharf, while the church bells rang out and triumphal music was played. With the Earl of Arundel going ahead, bearing the sword of state and preceded by an army of gentlemen in velvet coats and numerous ladies and gentlewomen, the great procession began its slow way through the City. Throngs of citizens cheered themselves hoarse as Mary passed by, crying "Jesus save Her Grace!" Every street was gaily bedecked with flowers, banners and streamers, while tapestries and painted cloths hung from many windows. There were placards on display everywhere, bearing the legend "The voice of the people is the voice of God."

Mary felt quite overwhelmed by it all. Her cheeks ached with smiling, her hand from waving, but she could not have been happier.

Riding beside her, at her insistence, was Elizabeth, dressed in white and smiling and nodding at the people; and behind them rode Anna of Cleves, who had congratulated Mary so warmly when they were reunited at Whitechapel. It was fitting that Anna, a princess of Cleves, should have the honor of a prominent place in the procession. After her came the Duchess of Norfolk and the Marchioness of Exeter, she who had so stoutly championed Mary's mother and was therefore worthy of the highest favor. Then marched the foreign ambassadors; somewhere among them was Renard. Mary wished that Chapuys could have been here to see this day, but he was long into retirement now and, she suspected, not in good health. She had been gratified to hear that the French envoy, Antoine de Noailles, was staying away, having rather overtly supported Northumberland.

Outside the Tower of London, where Mary was to lodge for the next two weeks, a hundred children made an oration to her. She listened intently, smiling again, then passed on over the drawbridge of the fortress as the cannon sounded continually like great claps of thunder. She could not help remembering how often she had expected to be brought here in very different circumstances.

Inside the Tower precincts, more crowds awaited her, but her gaze was drawn to the four prisoners kneeling on the grass by the chapel, who were present by her command. There was Stephen Gardiner, Bishop of Winchester, who had been imprisoned at the beginning of Edward's reign for resisting Somerset's religious reforms. Then the Duke of Norfolk, who must now be eighty, and whose neck had been spared only because her father had died before he could sign the death warrant. There was her erstwhile friend Nan Stanhope, Duchess of Somerset, widow of the Lord Protector; and Lady Exeter's son, Edward Courtenay, a debonair young man who had suffered imprisonment since 1539, when most of his family had been executed. He had been a child then, and had grown up in captivity.

In unison, they craved Mary's pardon. She looked upon them with compassion, even old Norfolk, who had once spoken brutally to her, and Gardiner, who had done his best to have her mother's marriage annulled. For all their faults, they were good Catholics, and she had need of them.

"These are my prisoners!" she announced. "I command that they be immediately set at liberty." Then she dismounted and bent to raise, embrace, and kiss them, her eyes brimming with tears.

"My lord Bishop," she said to Gardiner, "I here and now restore you to your see and appoint you one of my councillors. You will all receive written pardons tomorrow and, my lord of Norfolk, I will have the Act of Attainder against you reversed in my first Parliament. In the meantime, your titles and lands will be returned to you." The two men were vociferous with their thanks, and Mary's eyes glistened as she watched Courtenay being clasped in his weeping mother's embrace. Then she led them all, with her retinue, into the White Tower.

Chapter 28

1553

The next day, the Privy Council made its formal submission to Mary. She refused to issue immediate pardons to those who had declared for Jane, and rebuked them gently for their disloyalty. But she had no choice but to be conciliatory, and at length invited them to kiss her hand. Some wept at her magnanimity.

The following morning, Renard sought an audience. "Your Majesty," he said, rising from his bow, "no one can fault your compassionate nature, but it is important that you are not seen to be over-merciful. The Emperor urges that you be ruthless in punishing traitors, especially those who are a threat to your security, such as Lady Jane, Northumberland, Suffolk, and Guildford Dudley. They should be put to death."

"No," Mary said. "Not all. Jane was the innocent tool of treacherous men."

Renard betrayed his exasperation. "Madam, if you spare her, it will be seen as weakness and might have fatal results."

Mary rounded on him, grieved that they were so soon at odds. "I said no, Messire Renard! I will consider putting the men to death, but not Jane. You must accept that, in most respects, I have no choice but to be merciful. If I executed all those involved in Northumberland's plot, I would have very few councillors left!"

He had to smile at that.

"I need to keep them loyal," she went on. "I must confess, I am finding them hard to control. I seem to spend my days shouting at them, and it makes no difference at all. But I must be grateful that many have changed their religion, if only to placate me and retain my favor. To others I owe a debt of gratitude for their assistance in helping me to overcome my enemies, even if it was belated in many cases. But they are men of the world, and I have far less experience, so I need to rely on them."

"No doubt they are finding it an adjustment to answer to a Queen," Renard said.

"Yes." Mary sighed. "And there, I am at a disadvantage. They treat me as if I know nothing! Of course, England has never been ruled by a queen."

"But Spain has," Renard pointed out, smiling, "and I doubt not you will show them that you are the true granddaughter of Isabella."

She smiled back. "That is my dearest wish, to be worthy of her. But there are those here at court who think me a lightweight. They believe that, as a woman, I am incapable of governing."

"That," said Renard, "will be remedied when your Majesty finds a husband to shoulder the burdens of government with you. You have made an excellent start, but you are inexpert in worldly affairs. And a woman is never feared or respected as a man is, whatever her rank. In time of war, it is impossible for a woman to govern alone satisfactorily. But all will be remedied when you marry."

It was not what Mary had wanted to hear, especially from this man with whom she had established so good a rapport. Yet, she reminded herself, Isabella had not ruled alone. She had shared the burdens of state with King Ferdinand, her husband. And it was inescapable that Renard had spoken the truth. Her sex was going to be an impediment. But she would do her best to rise above it.

She chose Gardiner—the best statesman of them all—as Lord Chancellor and her chief councillor. He was vastly experienced in politics, even if, regrettably, like so many bishops, he was an ambitious, worldly man. If he was strident in voicing his opinions, he was moderate in his views, having mellowed during his years in the Tower, and full of wisdom. There was no doubting his love for England, or that he would work tirelessly all his life for its benefit. At heart, Mary did not like him, because he had once supported Anne Boleyn. Yet he shared with her a common desire to restore the old faith, and therefore she was prepared to work with him.

She was determined to rule well, to work hard and conscientiously. She now rose early, spending several hours of each day at prayer or conferring with her Council, which met each morning with Gardiner presiding. The rest of her time was devoted to giving audiences or attending to state business, doing her best to promote trade and improve the kingdom's finances. It made sense to do so, for if her merchants prospered, they would pay more tax into her depleted treasury.

She wrote many official letters in her own hand. Often, she did not lay down her pen or cease reading official papers until late at night. She was bountiful to those who came to her with petitions or grievances, and rarely turned anyone away; when she could afford it, she intended to found hospitals and provide for her clergy to be better educated. She was particularly anxious to ensure that justice was administered fairly in her name.

She was determined to rule only by the advice and consent of Parliament and the dictates of her conscience; she did not flinch at carrying out what she believed to be her duty. If her conscience did not point the way, she suffered agonies of indecision; if it did, she found she did not lack the courage of her convictions. In public, she took care to be regal and dignified. She prided herself on conversing with foreign ambassadors in Latin, French, Spanish, and Italian. People praised her for her goodness; she remembered that when her councillors lost patience at her inability to dissemble.

The constant hard work was already taking its toll. She suffered miseries from headaches and palpitations. Her doctors prescribed tonics and regular bleeding, although these had little effect. Susan kept nagging her to take out time for rest, but she would not; there was no time to take out.

Yet there were many compensations. On the day she was shown the first coins minted with her image, she was deeply moved. She had chosen the motto that appeared on them: "Truth, the daughter of time," which commemorated her miraculous triumph over her enemies.

It was gratifying to preside over her own court. Of course, there was no money—Edward had left an empty treasury—so it lacked the splendor and extravagance of her father's. Yet still she indulged her fondness for music, dancing, and plays, even though such entertainments were rare luxuries. She saw to it that her court was ceremonious, dignified, and free from scandal and licentiousness. What was most important was that it was famed for its Catholic piety. She set the example, having six or seven Masses sung each day in her chapel, which her councillors were zealous in attending, she was pleased to note.

The one extravagance in which she did indulge herself was her queenly attire. She had always delighted in gorgeous clothes, and now she had inherited the great jewelry collection of the Kings and Queens of England. If she had had the money, she would have bought more! But it was essential that she looked like a queen, for magnificent display gave the impression of wealth. So she changed her outfits several times each day, and wore cloth of silver or gold even when attending to routine duties.

Lack of money did not prevent her from being generous to her friends and servants, and to the poor she was compassionate and bountiful. Three days after her entry into London, she dressed as a private gentlewoman and took Jane Dormer with her to visit humble homes, bearing baskets of bread and cheese and chatting to the citizens and their wives. Few guessed who she was; some assumed she was a servant of the Queen. If there was a child in the house, Mary always gave the parents money.

"Live thriftily and in the fear of God," she always said, as she bade them farewell.

Jane loved these expeditions, and Mary cherished her company; she asked her to share her bed at night, alternating with Lady Exeter.

"I hope you never marry, dear Jane," she told the girl, as Jane served her meat at table. "I should hate to lose you. Anyway, no man is good enough for you." Many had asked for Jane's hand, but Mary had sent them all away.

When Mary appeared in public, she ensured that Elizabeth was in the place of honor at her side and held her hand affectionately. The young woman was witty and good company, very popular and much admired at court and by the people. Sometimes Mary felt a little eclipsed by her, but it did not matter. They were reunited after all the long years of struggle, and she was sure that her sister felt as happy about that as she did.

Neither referred to Elizabeth having embraced the reformed faith during Edward's reign. But Mary liked to think that, like so many other people, she had conformed in order to enjoy an easier life, especially after the scandal that had engulfed her. She still wondered about that, but Elizabeth appeared virtuous; it was hard to believe that she had ever succumbed to the advances of that wretch Thomas Seymour. No, she had surely been more sinned against than sinning, and she had been very young. Mary was convinced that she would return to the Catholic fold. She must, for it was unthinkable that her heir should be a Protestant.

On her fourth evening in London, as they sat at supper, she smiled at Elizabeth. "It would make me so happy if you would attend Mass with me."

To her dismay, Elizabeth did not answer immediately. In fact, she looked uncomfortable. "You know I wish to please your Majesty, but I should be grateful for a little time to accustom myself to the changes in religion."

Mary felt crushed. She had been so sure that her sister would agree instantly.

"If you come to Mass, it will bring you much joy," she said.

"I will think about it, I promise," Elizabeth said, her eyes downcast.

"Very well," Mary agreed, but she could not let the matter rest there.

The next morning, she told Renard about their conversation.

"Madam, I distrust the enchantments of the Lady Elizabeth," he said. "She might not wish to offend your Majesty, but nor does she desire to alienate the heretics who support her."

"But she must comply."

"Indeed. Might I suggest that your Majesty put pressure on her?"

Her Majesty did, only to become increasingly exasperated when Elizabeth again refused to go to Mass.

It had an immediate, corrosive effect on Mary's affection for her. She had been noticing more and more about Elizabeth that reminded her of Anne Boleyn. And every time she looked at her, she recalled the injuries, insults, and ignominy that she and her mother had suffered as a result of that woman's bewitchment of her father. Elizabeth was vain, like her mother. She thrived on the attention and compliments of courtiers—her mother all over again. She was also temperamental, like Anne, and could be sharp and caustic when provoked—although never to Mary.

Mary had truly loved the child Elizabeth, had tried to be a second mother to her. Yet now, she could not help seeing her as a rival—and a dangerous one. At night, she found herself lying awake, wondering yet again if Elizabeth really was their father's child. Had not Lady Kingston said long ago that the girl had the face and countenance of Mark Smeaton? If it was true, Elizabeth was not royal in any way and ought to be removed from the succession. Mary wished there was some way of proving her paternity. And yet, as Susan had often said when Mary expressed her doubts, their father had never questioned Elizabeth's legitimacy, even in the face of all the evidence against Anne Boleyn; and he had not been a man to tolerate the impugning of the royal line—as many had found to their cost.

The sad thing was, thought Mary, tossing under the bedclothes, her sympathy for Elizabeth had definitely soured, leaving only suspicion and resentment. But whose fault was that?

She was resolved to take the Emperor's advice to go cautiously in religious matters—at first. In time, she would bring her subjects back to the true faith. Their rapturous reception of her as Queen had been proof enough that they would welcome a return to the Roman Catholic fold. It was her dearest wish. She was certain that those who had turned Protestant had done so under pressure from the government in her brother's time and would happily revert to the true faith.

Sitting at the head of the council table, she addressed the men seated along it. "My lords, it is my intention to restore the Mass and the religious settlement that existed at my father's death, with myself as Supreme Head of the Church. I intend to surrender that title when the time is ripe for a return to Rome, but in the meantime, I will make use of it to reverse the changes that were made under King Edward. But it is not my intention to compel or constrain other people's consciences. All I intend is for my subjects to be brought to God's truth by the offices of godly, virtuous, and learned preachers."

They were nodding their approval, a little too eagerly, for they were zealous to a man in demonstrating their love for the old faith.

"Your Majesty's moderation is to be praised," Gardiner intoned. "I think I may speak for us all in saying that we support your aims wholeheartedly. It is fitting that Almighty God take pity on His people and the Church in England through the instrument of a virgin called Mary, whom He has raised to the throne."

There were murmurs of "Hear! Hear!"

Arundel spoke. "I hesitate to report that there has been a riot in London, incited by extreme Protestants. One even hurled a dagger at a priest who was celebrating Mass in St. Paul's."

"We will not let a few hotheads deter us," Mary declared. "Have them arrested and punished."

Mary had decided that King Edward should be buried in Westminster Abbey, and conceded that Archbishop Cranmer could conduct a Protestant funeral service. But while it was taking place, she had Gardiner celebrate a requiem Mass in her private chapel in the Tower. She had also ordered that Masses be sung perpetually for her brother's soul, in the fervent hope of saving it.

Soon afterward, she received a letter from her cousin, Cardinal Pole, in Rome. It was good to hear from him, for it had been too dangerous to write to him while her father and brother reigned. It now felt strange to think that she and Reginald might once have married, if their mothers had had their way. But now he was wedded to the Church, and even though no one would be more suitable as a husband, it could not be.

His Holiness, Reginald wrote, had been surprised and greatly delighted that her Majesty should seek to reconcile the Church of England to the Church of Rome, and he had appointed himself, Cardinal Pole, as his legate to England. *There is no time to lose,* he continued, *for souls are daily perishing, cast out from the communion of the Church. I exhort you, Madam, as a true daughter of the Church, to undo the evil your father did.*

Mary replied that although she was zealous to do his bidding, there were political obstacles that must first be overcome.

Back came the stinging reply. *Would that other Mary have refused St. Peter admission to her house?*

Distressed, Mary answered that her task would be considerably easier if Pole could persuade the Pope to allow all those who had profited from the dissolution of the monasteries to keep their lands, as this was the issue likeliest to make Parliament hesitate. Many of her councillors had converted former abbeys into grand stately homes. It would not help matters if the Church demanded them back.

Pole expressed himself horrified that such temporal concerns should be allowed to stand in the way of the unity of the Church, and refused even to think of passing on her request to his Holiness. *Madam, I know thoroughly the sentiments of the English people with regard to the Holy See, and they will understand that the Church must claim its own.*

Mary was not so sure about that. She was beginning to think that Pole had little real understanding of the changes that had taken place in England during the twenty years of his exile.

She was astonished when Renard told her that her councillors were conjecturing that she meant to marry Pole, cardinal though he was.

"That I could never do," she declared. "How could they think it?"

The matter of her marriage had been raised more than once by the Council. As a maiden who had lived a quiet and virtuous life, Mary was overcome by modesty whenever the subject came under discussion. She found it difficult to speak to men of such a delicate matter.

"I will choose a husband as God inspires me, without having regard to fleshly considerations," she told her councillors when they brought up the subject again. Her choice, she knew, must naturally be dictated by political and religious factors. She was well aware that she must marry soon. She had no time to waste if she was to present her subjects with an heir who would maintain the Catholic faith in England.

"Cardinal Pole, being of the old royal blood, might make your Majesty an excellent husband," Paget said slyly. "He has never been ordained a priest and could easily be released by the Pope from his deacon's vows."

She felt the heat in her cheeks. "I know he has no intention of leaving the Church or taking a wife." When she had written to him about the gossip, he had firmly repudiated the idea. In fact, he had advised her that her best course was to stay single. But how then would she get an heir? No, her cousin was too unworldly.

Gardiner looked up. "Why not marry Edward Courtenay? He is of the ancient blood royal."

"Your protégé," Arundel said dismissively.

"I do not deny that I took him under my wing when we were prisoners," the Bishop countered. "His father was executed when Courtenay was twelve, and the boy was shut up here in the Tower for fifteen years, for King Henry and King Edward both thought that his royal blood posed a threat to the crown. However, he was given a tutor and devoted himself to study. He now knows several languages and is a competent musician. But he was living in isolation, and I took it upon myself to befriend him." He smiled at the recollection. "We came to know each other well, for we were allowed to exercise together in the Lieutenant's garden. He even came to refer to me as his father, and I suppose I looked upon him as the son I never had."

"I am sure we all feel for him," said Arundel, "but he has neither the spirit nor the experience to be a king. By God, he is unable even to ride a horse."

"That is not his fault," Gardiner pointed out. "He can be taught."

"He has too many things to learn," Arundel countered.

Mary listened wearily to their wrangling. She was in two minds about Courtenay. He was extraordinarily handsome, fair-haired, tall and elegant, with a natural courtesy. He came from one of the greatest Catholic families in the country and had remained true to the faith. But Renard had been continually dismissive of him, arguing that he was proud, obstinate, vindictive, and self-indulgent—although, thought Mary, you could hardly blame him for the latter after all those years of deprivation. As for his other vices, on the few occasions their paths had crossed, she had seen no evidence of them, and concluded that Renard had just been trying to put her off. But she was aware that people at court were poking fun at Courtenay's naïvety and ignorance of polite society.

"Most of your Majesty's subjects want you to marry an Englishman," Gardiner said, "and by taking Courtenay, you would be bowing to public opinion. I think most of my lords here agree he is the best choice."

"Maybe we should have a show of hands," Mary suggested, and was surprised to see about two thirds of those present voting in favor.

"I marvel that you have not asked for my view," she said wryly, "since the matter touches me so nearly." Two rows of sheepish eyes turned toward her questioningly. "I should tell you that Courtenay is not to my liking; he is too lowly in rank, too young and untried."

"As your Majesty pleases," Gardiner muttered, looking exasperated.

"Perhaps, my lords, you will give further thought to the matter of my marriage, and to whether that young man really would be a suitable consort," Mary said, rising, and left them.

In the middle of August, she moved her court from the Tower to Richmond Palace. Soon afterward, Northumberland was tried by his peers for high treason and found guilty, and the Duke of Norfolk, as Earl Marshal of England, sentenced him to be hanged, drawn and quartered as a traitor. Mary hastily commuted this to beheading, as was the customary privilege of peers of the realm.

Gardiner went to see Northumberland in the Tower and came back grave-faced. "Madam, he is adamant in his desire to convert to the Catholic faith," he reported.

Mary gaped at him. "What?"

"Clearly, he hopes that will save him. He said he would do penance all the days of his life for the injuries he did you, and asked me if there was no hope of mercy. I told him I thought he must die, and he wept to hear it. He protested that he was always a Catholic at heart and that he complied in King Edward's day only out of ambition, for which he is now praying God to forgive him. Madam, his distress was so great that I too found myself weeping. Will you not spare him?"

"I will think about it," Mary said, trying to reconcile the man who had terrorized her over religion with this abject penitent in the Tower.

She summoned Renard, whose advice she now heeded more than any other.

"Madam, you must let the law take its course," he said firmly.

When she conveyed her decision to Gardiner, she could tell that he was disappointed, but he said nothing. And so Northumberland went to the public scaffold on Tower Hill and had his head chopped off in front of ten thousand onlookers, protesting at the end that his conversion had been unfeigned and that he had deserved a thousand deaths.

Mary had decided that the time had come for her to make a statement of her intentions in regard to religion, and issued a proclamation affirming her devotion to the Catholic faith and her hope that her subjects would embrace it as fervently. There would be no reclamation of lands formerly belonging to the Church—a needful concession, she had finally decided. She declared that she did not intend to compel anyone to change their religion until a new settlement was made with the consent of Parliament. In the meantime, the clergy were forbidden to preach, which—observed Gardiner—effectively removed the most powerful weapon of the reformers.

But there was one person who must be compelled to change her faith: her heir. By the end of August, however, it was clear to Mary that Elizabeth was determined to resist her attempts to persuade her to go to Mass. Antagonism was festering; the matter lay as an unsheathed sword between them, and Mary was beginning to suspect

that the French ambassador, the odious Messire de Noailles, was
courting Elizabeth's favor. It irritated her to see the young woman
smiling at his compliments and the two of them chatting familiarly
as if they were great friends.

De Noailles was wily, and Mary had no love for him because he
had openly supported Northumberland. It would not be surprising
if he was still working against her, for she was the friend of the Emperor, France's enemy. Was he setting Elizabeth up as a rival for the
crown? Surely not! Mary was running away with herself. King Henri
would not want a Protestant queen on England's throne. But Renard
took a strident view.

"Madam, the Lady Elizabeth is intriguing with the French," he
declared, as they strolled in the privy garden in the early September
sunshine. "Her popularity is a threat to your Majesty's security. She
is clever, ambitious, and sly."

Mary sighed. "I fear you are right. I have made sincere efforts to
preserve the affection between us, but she has changed, and I can no
longer be sure of her loyalty. I am finding it impossible to hide my
dislike for her."

"Madam, she is the cause of that dislike. You have bent over back-
ward to be good to her. I urge you to keep her under your eye."

She nodded. "I will take your advice."

Renard turned his handsome gaze on her, and for a moment Mary
found it difficult to remember that she was the Queen. It was marvelous to have this strong, confident man to support her, to be able
to summon him to give her counsel she could rely on—and to spend
time in his company. She was just thinking that she would invite
him to sit awhile with her in the shade of an old tree—her ladies
being only a little way distant, for propriety's sake—when he spoke
and recalled her to reality.

"Madam, about the Lady Jane Grey . . . It is the Emperor's opinion, and mine, that you should have her executed as a traitor."

"No, Messire, I will not hear of it," she told him firmly. "Lady
Jane and her husband are to remain in the Tower in honorable confinement until such time as it is safe to grant them pardons and release them. They will be tried and condemned, as a matter of form,

The Passionate Tudor 341

but my conscience will not permit me to put them to death, even though they have, strictly speaking, committed treason."

Again, Renard showed himself exasperated with her. "Your Majesty, that is unwise. While Jane lives, she will be a focus for Protestant plots against you. I urge you to reconsider."

"I'm sorry, but my mind is made up," she insisted. "But I will be watchful in case Lady Jane does become the focus of any new conspiracy, and I will ensure that the realm is quiet before I set her free."

"Well, Madam," he said, unsmiling, "I hope you will not regret such extraordinary clemency. For myself, I will not rest easy until you have agreed to the obliteration of the whole House of Suffolk."

"You ask too much, Messire," Mary said. Then she made herself turn and lead the way back to the palace, sorrowing inwardly that she had displeased him.

She asked Gardiner for his opinion, and he categorically agreed with Renard.

"To show mercy in this case would be foolhardy," he opined.

She refused to listen. In fact, she had been most impressed by a lengthy letter sent her by Jane, giving a full and honest account of her nine days' reign without making too many excuses for herself. What came across very clearly was that Jane had had no choice in the matter, even though she'd admitted that she had done wrong in accepting the crown and was ashamed to ask pardon for such a crime. *No one can ever say that I sought it or that I was pleased with it,* she had written. *I wished to say this to your Majesty to demonstrate my innocence and disburden my conscience.*

How could I hurt such an honest soul? Mary asked herself. It was evident now that Jane really had been an unwilling pawn in a dangerous game of chess and did not deserve to lose her life. No. It was right to show clemency. But the trial would go ahead after she was crowned.

Chapter 29

1553

"Your Majesty," said Renard, rising tall and debonair from his bow, "I have asked for an audience because I am concerned that the Lady Elizabeth is showing a more than friendly interest in Edward Courtenay."

His words sounded an alarm in Mary's head. What game was Elizabeth playing? Was she looking to steal a potential husband from under her sister's very nose?

"I fear that Messire de Noailles is behind it," Renard fumed. "He has ingratiated himself with your sister and is now carefully cultivating Courtenay. He invites him to supper and is probably trying to persuade him that if your Majesty will not wed him, the Lady Elizabeth might. And Courtenay is gullible. I warn you, those two could pose a danger. With their Plantagenet and Tudor blood intermingled, they would stand as youthful and charismatic figureheads. Backed by the King of France, they could raise a powerful opposition and overthrow your Majesty."

Mary felt a little sick. Elizabeth would not do that to her, surely? "I fear you are making a catastrophe of a flirtation," she said.

"Never underestimate that young woman—or the French!" Renard warned.

She dismissed him, feeling very disturbed. There seemed to be trouble threatening from several directions. Now she understood why her father had been so obsessed with hunting out treason.

But she would nip this trouble in the bud by securing Courtenay's loyalty. She restored him to his ancestral earldom of Devon and endowed him with lands worth £3,000 per annum. She also gave him sumptuous clothes and a diamond ring of her father's, worth 16,000 crowns. She realized, of course, that many thought this largesse betokened that she would marry the young man. Her courtiers were flocking to pay court to him, even kneeling as they addressed him. The Earl of Pembroke had presented him with a fine sword and costly horses. Lady Exeter had shown Mary a flattering letter sent to her son by King Henri, which he had asked her to take to the Queen. And Courtenay had made it known that he would employ only Catholics in his household.

"He's now trying to ingratiate himself with your ladies," Susan told Mary one evening, as they sat up late compiling a guest list for the coming coronation. "He's even taken to calling me 'Mother.'"

"He gives himself airs," sniffed Jane. "He throws his weight about and has become insufferable. I heard him boasting to Anne Bassett that at the coronation, he would be wearing a splendid suit of blue velvet with gold embroidery."

"Oh no he won't," retorted Mary, and immediately dashed off a note ordering him to wear another color, as she herself was planning to wear blue velvet for her coronation.

When she returned to her seat, Susan was eyeing her speculatively. "I don't know if I should tell you this, Madam, but Catherine Brydges heard gossip that my lord of Devon is making up for lost time in the stews of Bankside."

Mary had no idea what a stew was, but it sounded rather unsavory. "What do you mean?"

"He frequents brothels, saving your presence, Madam."

She did not know what a brothel was either, but did not like to ask.

Susan came to her aid. "It is where men go to pay for what should pass in the marriage bed."

Mary was utterly shocked. Whatever people did in the marriage bed, it was surely not something one would pay for?

"I am glad I know no more," she said, and quickly changed the subject.

Lying wakeful that night, Susan's words reverberating in her head, Mary came to a firm decision. She would not marry Courtenay. She would set aside the matter of her marriage for now. The prime issue to be dealt with was religion. And it came to her that turning the clock back to how things had stood at her father's death would not be enough. She must be wholehearted in her mission to restore the Catholic faith in England; half measures were an insult to God.

The next day, she summoned the Imperial ambassadors and formally informed them that it was her intention to restore the Church of England to the obedience of the Holy See of Rome.

She had expected them to be overjoyed, but all she saw in their faces was dismay. They glanced at each other, frowning, and then nodded.

"Madam," said Scheyfve, "it would not be wise to go beyond the restitution of the Mass. We urge you to keep to your plan of reverting to things as they were at the time of the late King Henry's death."

"But my duty is to bring England back to Christ," she protested, exasperated that they were putting pragmatic considerations before the sacred obligation that had been laid on her. "That is what God put me on this throne for. I have been in constant contact with the Pope, and his legate, Cardinal Pole, will be coming here soon."

"Madam," Renard said sharply, "I beg you to consult Parliament before you allow him into the kingdom. Your subjects will need reassurance on the subject of church property, and the Cardinal's views on that are well known."

"Has your Majesty consulted your Council on this matter?" Scheyfve asked.

Mary hesitated. Why were they browbeating her like this? The matter was a simple one. She was Queen and her will must prevail. "Not yet," she said.

"Then, Madam," he replied, "tell no one but Bishop Gardiner what you have in mind, to avoid malicious persons seizing the occasion for plotting against you."

"The last thing the Emperor wants is a religious war in England," Renard added. "And you cannot afford one. Just wait a while, I urge you. God will show you the right moment for a return to Rome."

Mary allowed herself to be persuaded. It was frustrating having to defer the matter, but with Elizabeth and Courtenay under suspicion, and Jane and Guildford Dudley in the Tower—living reminders of how close she had come to being ousted from the throne—she had to concede that she should go cautiously for now. Reluctantly, she wrote to the Pope, instructing that Pole should not be sent until the time was more propitious.

Later that day, she was writing letters in her closet when Gardiner was announced. He bustled in, all beetling brows and consternation, an ecclesiastical whirlwind.

"Your Majesty, Messire de Noailles has rather pointedly informed me of a rumor going about the court that the Emperor has offered his son, Prince Philip, as a husband for you. Naturally, the French are in an uproar. They will do all they can to prevent such an alliance. I fear that de Noailles is busy enlisting the support of the Protestants and those Englishmen who oppose the idea of a foreign king."

Mary was astounded, but the news made her heart skip a beat. It should have been obvious from the first—Philip of Spain would be the perfect husband for her.

"Madam?" barked Gardiner.

She gathered her wits. "What did you say to Messire de Noailles?"

"I said we had received no such offer from the Emperor. But I fear he did not believe me. He warned me that once the Spanish have a foothold in England, they will make it a client state of the Empire and introduce the Inquisition, bringing ruthless religious persecution, as has happened in Spain. He said that if your Majesty marries Prince Philip, the Prince will not stay in England long because he has too many commitments abroad. You would be fortunate if he spent as much as a fortnight with you, and what good would that be to a Queen who needs heirs?"

"How dare he!" Mary hissed, outraged.

"He knows no self-restraint! He said that England would be forced to participate in the Emperor's war with France, which she is in no position to afford. Madam, many are heeding his warnings, and I fear that an anti-Imperialist faction is forming around him. We cannot trust him. I urge you to call Parliament as soon as possible, in order to obtain support for an English marriage."

"I would send de Noailles packing if I could," Mary fumed, "but I cannot risk provoking the French any more than I am doing already."

She felt beset on all sides—by the Imperial ambassadors, by Gardiner, and now, when she next met with them, by her councillors, who were aware that rumors of a Spanish marriage were spreading.

"It is being discussed in public taverns!" Paget said disgustedly. "Madam, do you know something that we do not?"

Mary flared. "No, I don't!"

"We are aware," said Arundel, "that you confide in the Imperial ambassadors. It would be better if your audiences with them took place in public, to avoid people concluding that you are secretly intriguing with them. Or maybe you should send at least two of them home."

Mary was about to protest loudly, but then she remembered all those secret discussions about her plans for the English Church, of which her Council knew nothing.

"There will be no need for that," she said. "I wonder that you doubt my honesty. Nothing has been said to me about a Spanish marriage."

They sat watching her, some pulling their beards. She feared they still did not believe her.

Clearly, she could not go on giving private audiences to the Imperial ambassadors. And yet she could not be without Renard's advice, for she had come to rely on him and, truth to tell, his presence lit up her days. She asked him if he would don a disguise and meet her, as if by chance, outdoors, and he agreed, turning up in a dark cloak and a wide-brimmed hat pulled down over his eyes. But when he tried to raise the matter of her marriage, she refused to discuss it.

"Not with you, or with my Council. There are too many rumors, and I would give the lie to them."

But he persisted. "Madam, I too have heard rumors, that you are to marry my lord of Devon. Is it true?"

"No," she said firmly, rising from the bench and indicating that he should walk with her along by the river. "I have barely seen him since the day I liberated him from the Tower. There is not one of my subjects whom I wish to marry." She hesitated for a moment, then took the plunge. "Has the Emperor made any suggestions?"

Renard was suddenly animated. "Yes, Madam, he has. He would like to offer you his son, Prince Philip. I am to sound you out on the matter."

Mary felt a little lightheaded when she heard that. It was what she had been waiting and hoping for.

"I should be honored," she said.

"No, Madam, it is Prince Philip who will be honored, if you accept him."

"Do you know him?" she asked, eager to learn more about this prospective bridegroom.

"I have met him many times," Renard said, as they stood gazing out at the busy Thames. "He is a most gracious prince, a man of many accomplishments. He knows Latin and Greek, and is learned in mathematics, geography, and history, and superbly proficient in all martial arts. He loves architecture, music, and painting."

Mary smiled. It was so obviously a rehearsed speech. "Messire, I am not considering him for an office at court! What is he like as a man?"

Renard flushed slightly, taking his time to answer. "He is fair-haired and blue-eyed, more like his Flemish forebears than his Spanish ones. Women find him attractive, although you must not let that concern you, as he is a virtuous man. But you have to remember that his mother died when he was twelve. It had an effect on him. He is somewhat reserved, and may appear a little stiff, but he is courteous and once he warms to you, he is good company."

"I know he is a widower," she said, thinking that she would prefer a reserved man to a flamboyant one; Thomas Seymour came suddenly to mind. What a disaster marriage to him would have been!

"The Prince was married at sixteen to Maria of Portugal, but she died two years later, bearing his only child, Don Carlos. He was so grief-stricken that it was not until recently that he contemplated marrying again."

"So he has been unattached for seven years?"

Was it Mary's imagination, or did Renard hesitate?

"Indeed, he has, Madam. He was sent to serve his father in the Low Countries. Two years ago, he returned to Spain, where he has been ruling in his father's stead—wisely and well, I might add."

It was a diplomat's assessment, meant to impress her. Mary wondered, however, if Renard was telling her everything she needed to know. Philip was the finest match in Europe, heir to a huge empire—Spain, the Low Countries, Austria, Sicily, Naples, parts of Germany, and the Americas. Yet, over the years, she had heard the odd rumor about him, mainly about his harsh treatment of heretics. Well, she could not quibble with that. She needed a champion of the faith to assist her in the great task that lay before her.

Standing in the autumn breeze, listening to Renard extolling Philip's good qualities to the skies, Mary thought it all very well and good that he had wise judgment, moderation, and common sense, and sound experience in government, but what of the age gap between them?

"I fear," she said at length, "that his Highness is too young for me. He is twenty-six and I am thirty-seven."

"Madam," said Renard, smiling broadly, "do not fret about that. Prince Philip is an old married man with a son aged eight."

Mary laughed nervously. "Maybe it won't matter, then. Well, Messire, I will give the matter much thought."

She walked around court and performed her daily tasks in a daze. She liked the idea of marrying Philip, but she remained nervous at the prospect of marriage, reluctant to commit herself and fearful of her Council's reaction to the proposal.

"I have never felt that which is called love," she confessed later to Renard, feeling herself blushing furiously. "But now that God has raised me to the throne, I must think seriously of marriage. It is not easy for me to discuss such a delicate matter with gentlemen. I would prefer to leave all negotiations to the Emperor, whom I regard as a father. He must approach the Council."

"My master will do as your Majesty wishes, I assure you," Renard promised.

It was September. The court was still at Richmond, and Mary was becoming increasingly angered by her sister's failure to attend Mass. She had asked her countless times, and the Council had been moved to censure Elizabeth to her face for ignoring the Queen's wishes—and received what Gardiner called a very rude response. Elizabeth had also failed to take Mary's heavy hints that she abandon the plain clothes she wore to please the Protestants in favor of magnificent gowns like the Queen's own.

Now, out of the blue, Elizabeth had requested an audience. Mary kept her waiting for two days before agreeing to see her. First, she consulted Renard, summoning him to the chapel late at night.

"Do not trust her," he repeated, looking alarmed. "She is in league with the French ambassador, and with heretics and dissidents. In the taverns, it is being said that the Papists are having their turn, but the Lady Elizabeth will remedy all in time."

Mary did not want to hear any more. It was as if the certainties that had sustained her were crumbling under her feet. Would Elizabeth go so far as to undermine her throne? Or was it all wishful thinking on the part of others?

But Renard was relentless. "I suspect she is clinging to the new religion out of policy to retain the support of the Protestants. I may be mistaken, but at this early stage it is safer to forestall than be forestalled. The lady is clever and sly, and possessed of a spirit full of enchantment. She should be sent to the Tower, or, at the very least, away from court, for her presence here is a threat to your Majesty's security, and she might, out of ambition or persuasion, conceive some dangerous design with Courtenay and put it to execution."

Mary began pacing up and down the chancel, wringing her hands in distress. "I have to confess that I share your suspicions, and that the same considerations had occurred to me. But I will not agree to sending my sister to the Tower. What I earnestly desire, which will remedy all, is her conversion to the Catholic faith."

"You are asking for the moon," Renard said, and again there was that barely suppressed exasperation in his voice.

"Well, I am meeting her tomorrow, and we shall see what comes of it. I shall pray that God moves her to see the light."

She waited for Elizabeth in her private gallery at Richmond, dreading the confrontation ahead. But when Elizabeth appeared, a vision in virginal white, she was visibly trembling. Approaching Mary timidly, she fell to her knees and burst into tears.

"I see only too clearly that your Majesty is not well disposed toward me," she faltered, "and I can think of no other cause except religion. But I beg to be excused on this issue, as I was brought up a Protestant and never taught the doctrines of the ancient religion." Mary bit her tongue, thinking that all her past efforts to ensure that her sister was raised in the true faith had been in vain. "I entreat your Majesty to arrange for me to take instruction from a learned man and be given books, so that I can decide if my conscience will allow me to be persuaded."

It was—almost—everything Mary wanted to hear, and while it was not an undertaking to convert, she told herself that an uninformed decision might look a little suspect. She had to allow time for Elizabeth to reconcile her conscience. Smiling, she raised and kissed her.

"I willingly grant your requests, Sister. In the meantime, be assured that if you go to Mass, belief will surely follow. And it is my pleasure that you attend the Mass in celebration of the Nativity of the Blessed Virgin Mary next week, after we move to Whitehall."

Elizabeth looked alarmed. "I hope I will be well enough, Madam. I have been suffering the most dreadful stomach pains."

Mary stiffened. "Have you seen a doctor?"

"No, but I shall have to, as the pains are not getting any better." The hooded eyes regarded her innocently.

"Make sure you do," Mary said. "I would like you to be at Mass next week."

* * *

She was inordinately gratified when Elizabeth joined her for the procession to the Chapel Royal, and greeted her warmly, bestowing a triumphant smile on de Noailles, who was standing by, looking decidedly put out. But as they walked along the gallery, Elizabeth began complaining loudly.

"Oh, my belly aches," she groaned, clutching it and looking the image of a suffering martyr. She turned to the Queen's ladies. "Will you rub it for me?"

They looked astonished, but Mary nodded at them, certain that Elizabeth was contriving to avoid attending Mass.

They were at the chapel doors now, and Mary swept ahead, leaving her sister with no choice but to follow her. All through the service, she watched her, but she could not fault Elizabeth's demeanor. And then she saw the miniature gold book containing their brother's deathbed prayer at her girdle. Had the girl worn it deliberately to convey a message to her Protestant supporters? Mary could not credit it; there were no Protestants here.

She was so overjoyed by Elizabeth's apparent conversion that after the Mass, she led her to her privy chamber and lavished gifts upon her: a diamond, a ruby brooch, and a coral rosary. Elizabeth thanked her sweetly.

Mary's joy was short-lived, however. When Elizabeth failed to attend Mass the following Sunday, all her distrust and doubts were revived, fueled by Gardiner and Renard, who separately voiced the belief that Elizabeth was merely dissembling.

"She is acting rather from fear of danger and peril than from real devotion," Gardiner growled.

Mary had to face the truth. "I fear her request for books and instruction was prompted by mere hypocrisy."

Fuming inwardly, she summoned Elizabeth. "Speak freely," she said, "and say if you firmly believe what Catholics have always believed, that the Holy Sacrament becomes the actual body and blood of Christ at the miracle of the Mass."

Elizabeth was shaking. "Madam, I have seen the error of my former ways. I will make a public declaration that I go to Mass because my conscience moves me to it, and of my own free will and without fear, hypocrisy, or dissimulation."

Mary did not know whether to believe her. "I am pleased to hear it," she said. "I will look to see you in chapel next Sunday."

She dismissed her, then sent for Renard.

"And she was shaking?" he asked, after she had related what Elizabeth had said. Mary nodded. "It was because you demanded a straight answer," he said. "Of course, you did not get one. I am convinced she is deceiving us all and lying about her conversion."

"That is what I fear. Messire Renard, I cannot bear to think that if I die before I can bear an heir, my throne will pass to one whose religious views are suspect. It would burden my conscience too heavily to allow Elizabeth to succeed. It would be a disgrace to the kingdom." Anger and grief welled up in Mary at the thought. "Moreover, she is the offspring of one of whose good fame you might have heard, who received her just punishment."

"Your Majesty can easily eliminate all possibility of her ever becoming queen if you marry soon and get an heir."

"That rather depends on the Emperor," she replied.

"I will tell him that the time is right to make an approach," Renard promised.

Gardiner sought an audience, and arrived with a deputation of councillors, which included Mary's former devoted servants, Sir Robert Rochester, Sir Francis Englefield, and Sir Edward Waldegrave.

"Madam," the Bishop began, "we beg your Majesty to come to a decision soon about your marriage, and we again urge you seriously to consider my lord of Devon as a husband."

Trust Gardiner to flog that horse! He loved Courtenay as a son. He could not know that she had heard disquieting reports of the young man's behavior, or that he had become friendly with the French ambassador and had probably been intriguing to marry Elizabeth.

"He is too young," she said dismissively.

The councillors tried to argue, but she refused to listen.

"I will not marry him!" she declared.

Trying to put marriage and all her other cares out of her mind, she immersed herself in preparations for her coronation. She was sorry to hear that Scheyfve was being recalled by the Emperor, but rejoiced when she learned that Renard would from now on be the sole Imperial ambassador in England. Yet she was too busy to see him to congratulate him, for she had a thousand matters to settle for her crowning.

Late in September, fanfares sounded and cannon fired deafening salutes when Mary, with Elizabeth beside her, was conveyed in the royal barge from Whitehall to the Tower, where monarchs traditionally stayed before their crowning. Tradition also demanded that the sovereign create new Knights of the Bath at the Tower, but it had been agreed that this ceremony would be performed by Arundel, as Great Master of the Household, for it was unthinkable that the Queen should participate in a ritual that required the knights to bathe naked with their monarch and kiss their bare shoulder on the day before their vigil. Mary had blushed furiously at the very thought!

Three days later, her ladies dressed her in cloth of gold, blue velvet, and ermine, and placed on her head a glittering trellised tinsel-and-pearl caul, so weighty that she had to keep supporting it with her hands. To gasps of admiration, she climbed into a chariot upholstered in cloth of gold and rode in procession through streets hung with tapestries and adorned with ceremonial arches and flowers. There were pageants with painted backdrops at every corner. Children sang and made pretty speeches, the crowds cheered, and the conduits and fountains ran with free wine.

It should have been a wonderful, triumphant experience, but Mary could not enjoy it. She was nervous. A Protestant plot to assassinate Gardiner had been discovered, and the Council had fears for her safety. The City of London had been searched for hidden weapons, yet nothing had been found. Nevertheless, she was on edge.

Ahead of her rode the new Knights of the Bath, with Courtenay foremost among them; then came Gardiner, Norfolk, Oxford, bearing the sword of state, and the Lord Mayor and aldermen of London. Behind Mary's chariot trundled one hung with cloth of silver, in which sat Elizabeth and Anna of Cleves, wearing identical gowns of crimson velvet. Did Mary imagine it, or were the cheers slightly

louder when her sister came into view? Elizabeth had been notice-
ably absent that morning when Anna joined Mary for Mass in the
Chapel of St. John, high in the White Tower. Mary had been kneeling devoutly, adoring the Sacrament, when she noticed that her sister's chair was empty. Yet Elizabeth was her heir! Mary felt she could
have made some compromise with her conscience to please her on
this day of all days.

Thankfully, the procession passed without incident, and Mary was
calmer when she herself kept vigil that night in her oratory at Whitehall, praying that God would grant her the grace and wisdom to rule
her people mercifully and bring about the reforms she so desired.

As she entered Westminster Abbey the following morning, the
bells pealed out and the trumpets sounded. The church floor was laid
with blue cloth. Supported on either side by a bishop, Mary walked
slowly up the nave, dressed in a regal purple robe, with her train
borne by Elizabeth, who was a vision in a white-and-silver gown
beneath a scarlet-and-ermine mantle. When it was time to take the
sovereign's oath, Mary swore to keep the just laws of England, neatly
avoiding swearing to uphold the Protestant settlement that was still
law.

Seated in St. Edward's chair for the climax of the long ceremony,
she was filled with a holy exultation as Gardiner placed the crown on
her head. God had brought her to this day; He had shown her the
way clear.

At the homage that followed, Elizabeth was the first to take the
oath of allegiance. There followed a long line of peers, all come to
swear loyalty. After seven hours, the solemnities ended at five in the
afternoon, when a magnificent coronation banquet was served in
Westminster Hall. Seated beneath a canopy of estate at the high
table, with Elizabeth and Anna of Cleves sitting next to each other
at the end, Mary feasted on wild boar sent by the Regent Mary, just
one of the three hundred dishes offered to her. While the august
company ate, Norfolk, Arundel, and the Earl of Derby rode around
the hall on horses trapped with cloth of gold, ensuring that everything ran smoothly. After the second course had been served, Sir
Edward Dymoke, the Queen's Champion, rode in and challenged

any man to dispute her title, throwing down his gauntlet as he did so. No one did.

But there was one jarring note. Late in the evening, when spiced wine and wafers had been served and everyone was mingling, Mary saw Renard watching Elizabeth, who was deep in conversation with Messire de Noailles. She edged her way toward him, smiling graciously at those she passed.

"Is all well, Messire Renard?" she asked.

"Your Majesty!" He bowed. "Your sister was complaining about the weight of her coronet. Messire de Noailles advised her to have patience; I distinctly heard him say that that small crown would soon bring her a better one. Madam, I fear they are hatching some conspiracy."

Mary drew in her breath. "I will have them watched."

It was not an auspicious end to what should have been the greatest day of her life, and she lay wakeful that night, her heart burning with resentment against Elizabeth, who had spoiled it—and might well be plotting against her.

Chapter 30

1553

M ary sat at the head of the council board, with the lords assembled on the benches on either side. There were blue damask hangings on the walls and a desk in the corner, where the clerk was recording the proceedings. He had closed the windows at her request, to shut out the autumnal chill.

"There are signs that the true faith is gaining ground," Gardiner reported. "Altars are being set up again; crucifixes are being replaced."

"But Protestants are still resisting any attempt to enforce uniformity of worship upon them; some are even disrupting the celebration of Mass," Norfolk said, frowning.

"Aye," chimed in Paget, "a number of Protestant priests are defying the Queen's edict banning preaching, not to mention some bishops."

"They should be deprived of their sees," Mary insisted. "See to it."

Her order was obeyed. Several bishops were deposed and imprisoned. Archbishop Cranmer, the worst heretic of all—he who had unlawfully broken the marriage of Mary's parents and done more than anyone else to sweep away the true faith—was heard to criticize the Mass, which gave Mary the pretext she needed to have him arrested and taken to the Tower.

She was saddened to hear that some Protestants were choosing to leave England rather than conform. She had fervently hoped that all her subjects would joyfully embrace the old religion.

"They should be refused safe-conducts," Gardiner growled.

"Let them go," Mary said. "We do not want dissidents here. I would have saved their souls if I could, but they would rather persist in their heresy."

Five days after Mary's coronation, her first Parliament met and, under Gardiner's leadership, began cautiously to repeal her brother's laws, restoring the religious settlement that had existed at the end of King Henry's reign. The Catholic faith was now the official religion of England, but the English Church still had the Queen, not the Pope, as its Supreme Head. Mary was disappointed to hear that Parliament was refusing to consider a reconciliation with Rome until his Holiness agreed not to demand the restitution of church property. She disliked bearing the title Supreme Head, which she felt did not become a woman, and could never bring herself to write it.

But she was gratified that so much had been achieved so soon. It was now forbidden to criticize the Mass, and Cranmer's Book of Common Prayer had been suppressed.

Protestants everywhere were in an uproar. Reports were coming in of disturbances and affrays. Churches were being vandalized, priests attacked, and propaganda tracts circulated.

"The offenders," Mary told her Council, "must be dealt with severely."

Shortly afterward, however, there was good news. When Gardiner came hurrying to her closet to tell her that Parliament had passed an Act of Restitution declaring her parents' marriage valid and she herself legitimate, she burst into tears of happiness. At long last, her mother had been vindicated and her father's error acknowledged. For the first time in twenty years, she was free of the taint of bastardy.

Elizabeth, still officially baseborn, remained heiress to the throne under the terms of their father's will.

"Would it be possible to disinherit her?" Mary asked Paget, having summoned him to her closet.

"Alas, Madam, Parliament would never agree to it." He hesitated. "Might I suggest that you marry her off to Courtenay? If the Emperor does offer his son as a consort for you, it might make your subjects more amenable to the idea of a Spanish marriage for yourself."

"No!" Mary said sharply. "I will not consider it. I fear that Courtenay has pretensions to a crown."

She made a point of drawing Elizabeth's attention to the restored legality of her parents' union. When next they met, she presented her with a miniature gold diptych containing portraits of them, to wear at her girdle. Elizabeth glanced at it, smiled, and put it in her pocket. Mary wondered if she would ever see it again.

Late one evening in October, an usher brought Renard to Mary's private chamber at Whitehall.

"You wished to see me, Messire?" she said, when they were alone.

"I do indeed, your Majesty." Again, there was that devastating smile. "The Emperor wishes you to know that he would gladly have offered himself as a husband for you, but it would be a poor match because of his age and ill health." Mary had a sudden memory of a tall, solemn, royally garbed young man with a large jaw bending down and greeting a little girl; it had been more than thirty years since her betrothal to Charles, and yet it seemed like yesterday.

"His Majesty intends formally to offer as a most fitting substitute his son, Prince Philip," Renard said.

Mary could not speak; she was fighting down panic. Making an effort, she smiled. "I thank the Emperor for suggesting a greater match than I deserve. I am honored. But I am unsure how well my subjects will take to a foreign consort, and I do not know if my Council would consent."

She rose from her chair and began pacing the room. "I have been giving this marriage much thought. Prince Philip has many responsibilities abroad. He might be too busy to spend much time with me in England. He might involve my kingdom in his wars. And, however mature he may be, he is young, only twenty-six."

"A man of twenty-six," replied Renard, "can hardly be called young, but rather middle-aged, because nowadays a man of nearly thirty is considered as old as men formerly were at forty, and few men survive to more than fifty or sixty."

"A man of twenty-six," Mary retorted, "is likely to be disposed to be amorous, and it is not my desire, at my time of life, to have such a husband."

Renard grinned. "Madam, be a husband twenty-six or sixty-six, he might be disposed to be amorous. It is the way of men, and it is necessary for the getting of heirs."

Mary could feel the hot flush infusing her cheeks. The conversation was taking an unfortunate turn. "Nevertheless, I cannot possibly make up my mind quickly."

"The Emperor is not looking for a speedy decision," Renard replied soothingly. "I have perhaps not sufficiently extolled Prince Philip's excellent qualities. Far from being young and amorous, his Highness is a man of stable and settled character. He is so admirable, so virtuous, prudent, and modest as to appear too wonderful to be human. If your Majesty accepts this proposal, you would be relieved of the pains and travails that are men's work rather than suitable for ladies."

Mary tried to conceal her irritation. She had been raised to be Queen and was sure she was capable of enduring such pains and travails; she did not want to be relieved of them.

"His Highness is a mighty prince to whom this kingdom could turn for protection and succor," Renard was saying, unheeding. "Your Majesty and your Council would do well to remember that you have several enemies: the heretics, your late rebels, the French, the Scots, and the Lady Elizabeth. They will never cease to trouble you and may even rise against you."

Mary drew in her breath, feeling cornered. Did she really want to cede some of her sovereign power to a foreign prince? She could already hear Gardiner's vociferous protests, not to mention those of her insular subjects.

"I will consider the matter carefully," she said. "And now, Messire, it is late and I should like to retire." She gave him her hand to kiss, refusing to acknowledge the crestfallen look on his face.

She did not sleep well that night. She was torn asunder by doubts. The idea of the Spanish marriage appealed to her, but the imminent reality was a nerve-racking prospect. How would she cope with a man in her bed? What would happen to her kingdom if she died in childbirth? How could she even face childbirth? By all accounts, it was a horrendous ordeal.

And yet . . .

Two days later, she summoned Renard again and begged him to confirm that what he had said about Philip was the truth. "Is he indeed of even temper and balanced judgment?"

"His Highness," he declared, "has qualities as virtuous as any prince in this world."

"I rejoice to hear it," Mary replied, "but are you sure you are not speaking out of affection for him?"

Renard patted her hand. "Madam, I beg you to take my honor and my life as hostages for the honesty of my words."

Still Mary was not reassured. "Would it be at all possible for the Prince to visit me, so that I can see him before making up my mind?"

The normally urbane Renard looked shocked. "No, Madam," he said. "No prince would condescend to be exhibited like goods in a market." Mary cringed in shame for having suggested it, but then he smiled at her. "But I am certain that he will hasten here as soon as you accept his proposal, for he has heard much about your great virtues."

With that, she had to rest content.

Thinking over the proposal again, she could see that there were great advantages to it. Philip already had considerable experience in statecraft. He was wealthy and backed by the vast resources of the Habsburgs, making him more than a match for the unruly factions on her Council. Above all, he was her beloved mother's kinsman, and a champion of Catholicism.

She just wished she knew more about the man, rather than the Prince. She still suspected that Renard's extravagant praise owed much to diplomacy. She also wished she had not heard disquieting rumors about Philip. It seemed that such rumors had proliferated recently, and she had an idea that Courtenay was responsible, and that Gardiner had encouraged him. Maybe Courtenay had not abandoned his hopes of marrying her himself; she had been relieved when he told her recently, categorically, that he did not wish to wed her sister. His mother, Lady Exeter, had only this afternoon begged Mary not to wed a foreigner. Of course, she had ambitions for her son, but Mary had been so furious at her interference that she had had her former friend evicted from her lodging at court. When the Marchioness had flung herself to her knees before her, distraught at having given offense, Mary forgave her and rescinded the order. She could not bear a grudge for long.

But she was worried about Gardiner. He was very persuasive, and might be trying to convince her councillors that a Spanish marriage would not be in England's interests. Yet many clearly believed that a marriage between herself and Courtenay would not be in England's interests either, although some felt that Courtenay should marry Elizabeth.

Renard was prickling with concern. "Never underestimate those two, Madam," he urged, as they walked in the gardens, shuffling through autumn leaves. "The Lady Elizabeth shows Courtenay marked favor and she is often in his company. Their friendship is a threat to your Majesty!"

Mary stopped suddenly. "The ideal solution has just come to me. I will find a good Catholic prince to marry my sister as soon as possible."

Renard nodded. "But even a good Catholic prince might entertain ambitions for a crown," he warned.

"Then what am I to do?" Mary asked.

"Keep close watch on the lady."

* * *

A few days later, Elizabeth came to Mary, looking agitated. "Madam, I must tell you that my lord of Devon has spoken to me of love and marriage. I told him he had overreached himself, my marriage being in your gift, but he will not take no for an answer. Sister, please give me leave to withdraw from court." She held up her long, elegant hands in supplication.

Mary eyed her suspiciously, wondering if this was a ruse to cover up some intrigue with Courtenay.

"No," she said. She wanted Elizabeth to be where she could keep watch on her. "I need you here. I intend to give my mind to the matter of your marriage. You may tell Courtenay that, if he persists in his unwanted attentions."

Elizabeth bowed her head in acquiescence, but not before Mary had spied the flash of anger in her eyes.

Mary confided in Gardiner, who looked thunderous when she told him of her fears, and then in Renard. Both were of the same opinion, that Elizabeth was plotting with Courtenay and de Noailles against her. Both begged her to send Elizabeth to the Tower, but she shrank from that.

"If she is intriguing with Courtenay, I would hear of it more easily if they are at court, because he would doubtless tell his mother, and she would tell me."

This was not the only matter that was depriving Mary of sleep. She was still agonizing over whether or not to accept Philip. Susan, Jane, and her other ladies-in-waiting were urging her to do so.

"All women should be married," said Susan, who had made no secret of the fact that she would have liked another husband, yet would never leave Mary's service.

"I think a woman can only be complete when she weds," Jane opined.

"Aye, that's true, and even more complete, they say, when she has children." Susan's eyes were wistful.

"I hear what you are saying," Mary said slowly.

"Is there something about marriage that troubles your Grace?" her friend asked, with her usual perception.

Mary shrank from saying that she balked at the prospect of the mysterious physical aspect of marriage. She could not confide that even to her women. Too embarrassed to consult her physicians, she had even searched the royal library for a treatise on childbirth and found in one a warning that to run the risk of pregnancy at her age, having had a history of monthly problems, was to court disaster. Yet she knew it was her duty to present the kingdom with an heir. She spent hours praying for guidance, and night after night wept into her pillow. Her inner turmoil affected her so badly that it made her ill with all her old autumnal complaints, obliging her to keep to her apartments.

But she was not allowed to rest for long. One morning late in October, she had to drag herself out of bed because Renard and a deputation of councillors were asking to see her on an urgent matter. Pulling on a black velvet nightgown that buttoned to the neck, and leaving her long red hair loose about her shoulders, she entered the presence chamber to find them all waiting for her. Renard stepped forward and handed her a document. It was the Emperor's formal written proposal of marriage to his son.

Mary could hardly speak for emotion. Moving unsteadily out of earshot of the lords, she murmured to Renard that she had wept for two hours that morning and prayed God to give her guidance in her decision. "I am almost resolved to agree to the Emperor's proposal," she told him.

"My lords," she said aloud, "I will speak more of this matter anon."

As she turned to leave the room, she whispered in Renard's ear, "Believe!"

The following evening, feeling a little better, she granted a private audience to him in her oratory, with only Susan present.

"I cannot describe the agony my indecision has caused me," she said. Then she knelt before the altar, where the Holy Sacrament stood, and began praying aloud for guidance. Renard and Susan knelt also, joining her in prayer.

Suddenly, Mary knew what her decision must be. "*Veni, Creator Spiritus!*" she breathed in gratitude, then stood up. "God, who has performed so many miracles in my favor, has now performed one more," she said. "He has inspired me to give a solemn promise before the Holy Sacrament to marry Prince Philip." Overcome, she broke down in tears, and Susan drew her into a motherly embrace.

"It is done," Mary said, looking over her shoulder at a smiling Renard. "My mind is made up and I can never change it. I will love his Highness perfectly and never give him any cause to feel jealous."

Renard could not hide his jubilation, though his face still showed concern. "Madam, that is the best news you could have given me, but you must know that we have a difficult task ahead of us in persuading your Council and your subjects to accept the Prince as king consort."

Mary nodded, disentangling herself from Susan's arms. "I know, and I think that the announcement of my betrothal should await an opportune moment."

"That is very wise," Renard agreed. "In the meantime, I will do my best to convince your councillors of the advantages of the match."

The strain of the past weeks had taken its toll. Early in November, Mary suffered such bad palpitations that she was obliged to keep to her chamber again, this time for a week. When she had recovered, she summoned her Privy Council to hear her answer to the Emperor's proposal. She trembled as she took her seat at the head of the table, but maintained a regal dignity. "My lords, I am most grateful to the Emperor for proposing his son as a husband for me, and I am delighted to announce that I intend to marry Prince Philip."

There was a silence. All she could see in the faces of her councillors was shocked surprise. But they quickly recovered themselves and congratulated her on having secured such a mighty prince as her consort. Even Gardiner, who had wanted her to wed Courtenay, joined in.

It was a huge relief, and Mary now realized that she had become quite enamored of the idea of marrying Philip. She was to be married to one of the greatest princes in the world! Besides that, her fears seemed of little account.

"You have made me fall in love with his Highness," she told Renard, "although he might not be obliged to you for that! Yet I will do my best to please him in every way."

"I think your Majesty is beginning to understand what love is," he smiled.

It was true. Every time he mentioned Philip, her heart fluttered. Of course, one could not be in love with a man one had never seen, but she was in love with the idea of him, and she prayed she would love him in the flesh, as was her duty—and her desire. In the flesh . . . She shivered at the thought of it. Soon, married love would no longer be a mystery to her.

But when the news of her forthcoming marriage became public knowledge, her subjects were anything but overjoyed.

"There seems to be widespread dismay and alarm," Paget said, sifting through a pile of reports in the council chamber. "The people fear that England might be dragged into ruinous foreign wars. They simply will not stand for it." Of course, Paget had wanted to see Mary marry Courtenay.

It seemed that everyone was raising objections to the match. Other councillors now began to express doubts.

"The English," Sir William Petre pointed out, "have long been an insular people, suspicious of foreigners."

"It seems that they resent Spain monopolizing trade with the Americas," Oxford chimed in.

"Most of all," said Gardiner, "they fear that the Spanish Inquisition will be established here. Until now, your Majesty's religious reforms have been accepted by many, but from now on, your subjects may see them as the fruit of Spanish influence, and it will be regarded as patriotic to be Protestant."

"That's nonsense!" Mary retorted. "I launched my reforms before ever the Emperor offered his son to me."

"Even so, the people will not believe it," Arundel declared. "In London, they are saying they will not welcome the Prince to England because he is a proud villain notorious for his vices, his thieving and his lechery. Some say they would rather die than suffer Spaniards to rule this country."

Gardiner weighed in. "They fear that your Majesty will give England to the Prince as your dowry, and that it will become his property on marriage, as is the usual custom. They foresee him ruling harshly, as the Spanish are known for. Above all, they fear that England will become an outpost of the vast Habsburg Empire."

Mary held up her hand for silence. "My lords, I am as sensitive to these concerns as you are, and I will do my utmost to allay them. I will wholly love and obey him to whom I have chosen to give myself and will do nothing against his will; but if he wishes to encroach upon the government of my kingdom, I will not permit it."

That quelled them a little. But there was still the question of Philip's title to be settled. Determined that she should retain the sovereignty of her kingdom, Mary's councillors insisted that he should be merely her consort. Renard agreed.

"It is the Emperor's wish that nothing must be allowed to stand in the way of the alliance. And it is even more crucial now for your Majesty to keep an eye on the Lady Elizabeth."

Mary agreed. She was losing patience with her sister and took great satisfaction in treating her as subordinate in rank to their cousins, the Duchess of Suffolk and Margaret Douglas, who had married the Earl of Lennox, and for whom Mary still cherished great affection. She also gave orders that no one was to visit Elizabeth without her permission. A miserable Elizabeth again asked for leave to retire to her estates, but Mary refused.

While Mary had been preoccupied with so many dilemmas and cares, she had not forgotten Lady Jane. Now it was November, and Jane was to be tried with her husband, Lord Guildford Dudley, his brothers, and Archbishop Cranmer at the Guildhall in London on charges of high treason. Mary insisted that their trials be fair, ensured that witnesses could speak freely, and directed the Lord Chief Justice to administer the law impartially. "It is my pleasure that whatever can be produced in favor of the accused shall be heard," she told him.

All pleaded guilty and all were condemned to death. Jane was sentenced to be beheaded or burned alive on Tower Hill, at the Queen's pleasure. The men were sentenced to be hanged, drawn and quartered.

Mary had no intention of having the sentences on Jane and Guildford carried out. She was resolved to be merciful and resist those who warned her that it was foolishness. They would remain in the Tower for now, and when the time was right, she would consider releasing them.

Soon afterward, Gardiner arrived at the head of a deputation of members of both houses of Parliament and, kneeling in the presence chamber at Whitehall, presented a petition to Mary, begging her to abandon the idea of a foreign match and marry an Englishman. When the speaker began ponderously to read it out, she angrily rounded on him.

"Parliament is not accustomed to use such language to the Kings of England!" she cried. "Monarchs marry where they choose. You can trust me to remember my coronation oath and always put my country first!" Glaring at the kneeling petitioners, she burst out, "If you try to force me to take a husband not to my liking, you would cause my death, for if I were to be married against my will, I would not live three months, and would consequently have no children, and then you would be sorry! Is it appropriate to expect me to marry someone just because my Lord Chancellor has made friends with him in prison?"

Gardiner colored. "The people will never stomach a foreigner," he barked.

"My mind is made up," Mary answered, "and if you, my Lord Chancellor, prefer the will of the people to my wishes, then you are forgetting your oath of allegiance to me."

Gardiner subsided, defeated. "I assure your Majesty that I will obey the man you have chosen as your consort." As he withdrew, she heard him mutter to his fellows, "It is too dangerous to meddle in the marriages of princes."

Arundel, hearing him, laughed. "Truly, he lost his post as Chancellor today, for the Queen usurped it!" which drew wry laughter from some of the deputation.

* * *

De Noailles was doing his best to whip up anti-Spanish feeling in England—no difficult task—and busily spreading rumors. A Spanish army would shortly arrive to subjugate the people; Philip would make England a mere province of the Empire; the Pope's authority would be forced on the English court. Public feeling was now running so high, especially in London, that Mary felt the need to issue a proclamation forbidding unlawful assemblies and the spreading of sedition.

Renard could not conceal his anxiety, plainly fearing that she would bow to pressure and abandon the Spanish match. One day, he arrived for his audience accompanied by two men, who were carrying a large gilt-framed painting. As they stood it upright, supporting it on either side, Mary saw that it was a portrait. Philip! She stared at the dignified young man clad in armor, his dark, luxuriant hair, neat beard, firm jaw, full lips, and fine eyes—averting her gaze from the muscular legs and prominent codpiece—and felt quite weak. Here was a very proper man indeed!

"I feel half in love with the Prince already," she declared.

The protests against her marriage would die down as soon as her subjects saw the advantages—she was certain of it. Her councillors were not so sure, and kept muttering about conspiracies brewing and the need to be watchful. But Mary was optimistic, so much so that, when Elizabeth again begged for permission to leave court and go to Ashridge, she agreed, though she sent Paget and Arundel to warn her that if she refused to follow the path of duty and persisted in associating herself with French and heretical conspiracies, she would bitterly repent it.

Paget reported back to Mary afterward. "Her Highness protested that she would never conspire against your Majesty. She says she is a devout Catholic and will be taking priests with her so that Mass can be celebrated at Ashridge. She promises to do all in her power to please you."

"Hmm," murmured Mary, wanting to believe it, but still fearful that her sister would cause trouble. "Have men placed in her household. I want her every move watched."

* * *

The marriage treaty between England and Spain was drawn up. Thanks to Gardiner's efforts to safeguard England's sovereignty, it provided for Philip to enjoy the title of King and aid Mary in the administration of her realm, but real power was to remain with her. If she died without heirs to her body, he would have no claim upon her kingdom, although their eldest son would inherit England, Burgundy, and the Low Countries, while Don Carlos would have Spain and all Philip's other continental territories. The treaty also bound Philip to obey the laws and customs of England. He would not be allowed to appoint his servants to English offices or involve England in his father's war with France. No Spaniard was to interfere in English politics, and Philip and Mary were to be counseled only by English ministers. These terms were accepted by Renard, on behalf of the Emperor, early in December.

Soon afterward, Mary received a letter from Philip, the first he had ever sent her. It was brief and formal. He was pleased she had accepted his suit, and he would be coming to England whenever she was ready to receive him. Mary kissed it and placed it in a casket by her bed. He had touched it and made it precious, and she wanted to keep it near her.

Because the Church would not allow marriages to be solemnized during Lent, she agreed that her wedding should take place in the spring. When Parliament was dissolved in December, the Council seemed to be reconciled to the marriage—but others were clearly not. On that day, Mary was sitting with her ladies in her privy chamber, happily discussing wedding plans, when the door was pushed open and a dead dog with clipped ears, a rope around its neck, and its head tonsured like a priest's was hurled into the room. The women jumped up, screaming, bringing the guards running, and Mary felt sick to think that whoever did this had so easily evaded them and breached the security of her apartments.

"Take it away," she commanded, averting her eyes from the horrible sight and scrutinizing the faces of the guards to see if she could read any guilt in them. But they were as impassive as they had been trained to be.

She summoned her councillors, who were shocked when she related what had happened. "Let it be known," she commanded, still shaking, "that I will retaliate with severity if anything of this sort happens again."

But her warning did not stop the flow of seditious pamphlets or the intermittent acts of vandalism perpetrated by disloyal and irresponsible Protestants.

Elizabeth left court on the day after the dead dog incident. When Mary bade her farewell, she embraced and kissed her warmly, as Renard had advised.

"Madam," Elizabeth said, the hooded eyes earnest and pleading, "I pray you, do not believe anyone who spreads evil reports of me without doing me the honor of giving me a chance to prove the false and malicious nature of such slanders."

"I will not," Mary assured her, then gave her two ropes of pearls and a warm sable hood. They embraced again, and Elizabeth curtseyed and withdrew.

Soon afterward, there came a letter from Ashridge, asking if copes, chasubles, chalices, and other ornaments for her chapel might be sent on. Mary again suspected hypocrisy, but did as her sister asked, since it was for God's service.

The Council soon learned that even with Elizabeth gone, de Noailles was still plotting for her to wed Courtenay and claim the crown.

"Madam," they told Mary, their faces grave, "we cannot have the people looking to the Lady Elizabeth as a focus of opposition to the Spanish marriage."

"Indeed," she agreed. "And I will not have her exploiting that, as I fear she might."

In fact, there was no evidence that Elizabeth was involved in anything underhand. The watchers in her household repeatedly reported that nothing was amiss; she was giving every appearance of being utterly loyal. Or maybe, Mary thought, in those long reaches of the night when sleep eluded her, she was far too canny to involve herself directly in any conspiracy.

Renard's spies soon heard rumors that trouble was brewing, yet could uncover no hard evidence.

"But, Madam," he said, as he and Mary took their usual daily stroll in the gardens, "I fear that before Easter there will be some new turmoil in England. The whisper is that some disaffected Englishmen are now trying to induce Courtenay or the Lady Elizabeth to act as their leader."

Mary shivered, and not just from the cold. "Elizabeth has summoned her tenants to come armed to Ashridge, to protect her from her enemies. I hope it is not a cover for something more sinister."

"I am convinced she is plotting something," Renard said.

"But there is no proof! I receive daily reports of her doings."

"Ah, but she is clever! The Emperor would rest happier in his bed if he knew that your Majesty would never allow her to marry Courtenay."

"I never would!" Mary smiled grimly. "He can rest easily."

Meanwhile, Gardiner, give him his due, was doing his best to reconcile the people to the Spanish marriage, preaching at Westminster that it would lead to the enriching of the realm. But his words merely provoked an outcry of disgust and increased tension in London, and when the Emperor's commissioners arrived after Christmas to conclude the marriage treaty, they were met with sullen hostility, demonstrations, and protests. Their servants were pelted with snowballs by a crowd of jeering boys, while a rash of seditious placards mysteriously appeared in the capital. Mary's ladies were in a jittery state, fearful that a rebellion was about to break out. She herself was so furious that the envoys had been treated to such an unfriendly reception that she suffered a vile headache and had to retire to bed. From there, she let it be known that anyone insulting the Emperor's representatives would incur severe penalties.

Chapter 31

1554

Susan was bending over Mary's bed, gently shaking her by the shoulder.

"Your Majesty, wake up! The Council require your presence."

Mary struggled awake. "What hour is it?"

"Just past midnight."

She clambered out of bed, fearful of what this urgent summons portended, and Susan brought her velvet night robe and slippers, and combed her hair. Then Mary hurried to the presence chamber, where the entire Council was waiting for her.

"Your Majesty, forgive the intrusion, but we have a serious and widespread rebellion on our hands," Gardiner informed her. "Letters written by the conspirators have just come into our possession. One is the French ambassador."

"Another," said Norfolk, "is Sir Thomas Wyatt."

Mary stood there trembling, trying to take in the news. She was not surprised that de Noailles was fomenting rebellion, but why would Sir Thomas Wyatt do so? His father had been a poet and diplomat, and he himself had led the life of a country gentleman in Kent until he took up soldiering. "But he is a staunch Catholic; he rose on my behalf back in July."

"Even so, he has been in Spain and has apparently come to detest all Spaniards," Paget told her. "We have learned that he has gathered around himself men committed to preventing your Majesty from marrying Prince Philip, by force, if need be. And we have intercepted a letter from Messire de Noailles agreeing to ask the French King for aid."

"So Wyatt intends merely to prevent my marriage," Mary said, feeling more in command of herself now. "There is no proof that he means to depose me and make Elizabeth and Courtenay King and Queen in my place?"

"Not as yet," Gardiner said, frowning, "but that does not mean that is not his aim."

"We have the names of some of the other conspirators, and several are men of standing," Arundel told Mary. "They include the late King's clerk to the Council, Sir Peter Carew, who owns lands in the West Country, and Sir Nicholas Throckmorton."

"Throckmorton?" Mary echoed. "He too helped me to gain my throne."

"Nevertheless, he and the others are committed to keeping the Spaniards out of England," Petre said.

"We know that Courtenay has joined the plotters," Gardiner continued, "and we know something of their plans. Before the Prince arrives in England, there will be four simultaneous risings orchestrated to take place on Palm Sunday. Wyatt is to raise the men of Kent, Sir James Crofts those of Herefordshire and the Welsh Marches, and Courtenay will join forces with Peter Carew to orchestrate a rising in the west."

Mary was listening with mounting horror. It seemed that Renard's fears were justified. "And who will lead the fourth uprising?"

Gardiner regarded her gravely. "The Duke of Suffolk. He will raise the commons of Leicestershire. Doubtless he has some madcap scheme of his own to restore his daughter to the throne—he's stupid enough. The four rebel armies will then march on London and, with the aid of the French, prevent your Majesty from marrying the Prince of Spain. You will no doubt then be forced to wed Courtenay."

"How dare they!" Mary exploded. "I will never marry that wretch."

"I am sorry that I ever advocated it," Gardiner confessed. Paget looked uncomfortable, too.

Norfolk spoke. "Your Majesty should know that the French ambassador implied in his letter that the Lady Elizabeth is involved in this conspiracy and has full knowledge of what is intended."

Mary faltered at that, remembering that Elizabeth had summoned her tenantry. She had known all along that she could not trust her sister.

"What is to be done?" she asked.

"We have already summoned Sir Peter Carew to London to account for his behavior, and we have dispatched captains and lieutenants to recruit men to keep the peace."

"Are we in immediate danger?" Mary wanted to know.

"No, Madam," Gardiner assured her. "We will thwart these traitors before they become a real threat."

Mary was determined not to let the malcontents deter her from her chosen course. On 9 January, her marriage treaty was concluded at Winchester House, Gardiner's London residence; three days later, she signed it. Soon afterward, she heard that the Pope had issued the necessary dispensation, which was followed by the gift of a great diamond from the Emperor, accompanied by a note telling the Queen that he now considered her as his own daughter.

The signing of the treaty was proclaimed throughout England, but the news was received frostily. Mary nevertheless believed that the people would soon come around to the idea.

She was eagerly anticipating Philip's arrival. The spring could not come soon enough. With the Prince beside her, she knew she would feel invincible. If only he was here now. But the Council seemed to have everything under control. They had sent troops to occupy Exeter and put paid to the revolt in the west. Crofts had fled for the Welsh border and Suffolk was apparently behaving himself at Sheen, a long way from Leicestershire. But Wyatt was at Allington Castle, his seat in Kent, and no one knew what he was up to.

Gardiner had summoned Courtenay to Winchester House. Afterward, he hastened to Whitehall to see Mary, who received him in her closet.

"He has confessed everything," he told her, a gleam of triumph in his eyes. "He fears for his own skin and has betrayed the traitors who tried to lure him into their conspiracy. He revealed that many local gentlemen have joined Wyatt at Allington, and that Suffolk is riding north."

Mary's eyes narrowed. "Was Courtenay actually involved in the plot?"

Gardiner looked shifty. "No, but he knew about it."

"And did not reveal it. That's misprision of treason, my Lord Chancellor."

"He realizes that now, Madam, and craves your forgiveness. He said he would rather go back to the Tower than marry the Lady Elizabeth."

"That's as may be, but he's either a traitor or a fool," Mary snapped.

"A fool, undoubtedly," Gardiner said firmly. "Madam, we must raise men and send them in pursuit of the rebels."

Wyatt had raised his standard at Maidstone and dared to issue a proclamation protesting against the Spanish marriage. His army, the Council learned, to everyone's alarm, was five thousand strong, a match for the royal forces.

There were ashen faces around the council board when news came that he was marching toward London.

"There is panic in the City," Paget warned.

"Madam," said Oxford, "we have tried to raise the men of Kent to oppose him, but in vain. Now he has taken Rochester Bridge and commandeered your ships that lay anchored in the Medway, seizing their arms and ordnance. He may attack London by land or river."

Mary strove to hide her fear. She was the Queen. She was supposed to show courage and leadership, not shrink from her duty like a coward. "We will meet the threat when it comes," she said calmly. "Have Suffolk, Carew, and Wyatt proclaimed traitors in London. Let it be known that they have raised evil-disposed persons to my destruction and that Suffolk's purpose is to advance the Lady Jane once more. Offer a great estate to anyone bringing Wyatt to justice. You, my lord of Norfolk, shall march into Kent with the London trained bands to suppress these rebels."

"With pleasure, Madam," barked the Duke. He might be eighty, but he was a war-hardened veteran and hot to defend the right.

"Your Majesty might consider moving to the safety of Windsor," Paget suggested.

"No," said Mary. "My place is here. I will remain at Whitehall until the crisis is over. But I do wish you would address the urgent matter of providing me with a bodyguard."

Paget fell to his knees. "Madam, I have spent two weeks recruiting men, and I cannot do everything myself. But I will see to it."

She relented, and thanked him.

Some councillors felt that she should ask the Emperor for military aid.

"No," she said again. "I would not have him think me unable to deal with the situation, in case he has doubts about sending his son to a lawless country. And the arrival of an Imperial army on these shores would only confirm my subjects' worst suspicions. No, my lords, we must fall back on our own resources. Have London fortified. I have not forgotten how its citizens welcomed me as their Queen, and I have no doubt that I can count upon their loyalty now."

The lords did not look so sure.

Gardiner had received conflicting intelligence about Elizabeth's activities. She was either provisioning Ashridge against a siege, or she was moving to Donnington Castle. Whatever she was planning, Mary was anxious to have her where she could keep a watchful eye on her, and wrote a letter commanding her to come to court, saying she feared that Elizabeth might be in some peril if any sudden tumult should arise.

The messenger sped off, and was soon back. "The Lady Elizabeth is too ill to travel," he informed her. Mary did not believe it.

"I fear that her reluctance to come to court is proof enough that she is involved in the conspiracy," she said to Renard, who nodded grimly.

Her suspicion appeared to be confirmed when Gardiner had de Noailles's postbag seized on its way to Dover, and a copy of Elizabeth's last letter to the Queen was found in it. Everyone concluded that she was secretly intriguing with the French. Appalled at her sister's conduct, Mary ordered that her portrait be taken down from the gallery, but could do no more for the present, because events were gathering momentum. She would deal with Elizabeth later.

There was encouraging news to begin with. The people of the west had not risen in rebellion, and Sir Peter Carew had fled to France. Suffolk had tried to take Leicester, but been successfully resisted. He had withdrawn to Coventry, only to find its gates closed against him. His few supporters had abandoned him, and he had gone to ground. Crofts had made no move.

The news from Kent, however, was frightening. Norfolk had attacked Wyatt's host at Rochester, but hundreds of his men had deserted to the rebels, declaring they would never submit to the rule of proud Spaniards. Many others had fled, leaving behind, for Wyatt to seize, their guns and the money given to the Duke to finance the expedition. Norfolk's remaining troops were now staggering wearily back into London, their coats torn and ruined, and without arrows or string to their bows. Mary saw a tattered band of them from her window, and the sight turned her heart to ice, for nothing now stood between Wyatt and the capital.

The Council sent troops under Sir Edward Hastings to deal with the insurgents, but he was soon back. Mud-spattered and exhausted, he lurched into the presence chamber and threw himself to his knees before Mary.

"Your Majesty, forgive me, but when I met the rebel host at Gravesend, I did not have sufficient men to halt them, so I tried to parley with Wyatt. He bade me demand that you surrender to him your person and the keys of the Tower. Naturally, I refused, and I have ridden here at speed to warn you of his intentions."

Mary was bristling with outrage. How dare this rebel dictate terms to her!

Greatly agitated, she sent for Renard, and told him how serious the situation was. "And my Council have still not provided me with a bodyguard!" she seethed.

"Yet they are doing their utmost to raise men to fight for your Majesty," he reminded her.

"I can trust no one!" she cried.

At that moment, Gardiner burst in. "Forgive the intrusion, but your Majesty will be heartened to know that the gates of London have been closed and are carefully guarded, and the drawbridge on London Bridge has been raised, and great guns positioned next to it. For that is the way Wyatt will come."

"It cannot be long now before he is here," Mary said, trying to keep calm.

"A deputation from the House of Commons has arrived, Madam," Gardiner told her. "They wish to wait upon your Majesty."

"Send them in," she commanded, and seated herself in her chair of estate.

They knelt humbly before her, but the speaker's tone was bold. "We come to beg your Majesty to reconsider your decision to marry the Prince of Spain."

Mary stared at them, knowing that she ought to reprimand them for their presumption, but she held back, for she knew that it was crucial to retain their love and loyalty. She could sense Renard's alarm.

"I cannot do that," she replied. "I am bound by a treaty and by my own inclinations. But I assure you that my marriage will never interfere with your liberties."

She dismissed them, registering the dismay in their faces, then turned to Renard. "Rest assured, I consider myself his Highness's wife. I will never take another husband; I would rather lose my crown and my life."

It was essential to show a firm spirit and outward serenity. And it might be to her advantage if she made a personal appeal for support to the Londoners. The councillors begged her to consider her safety, but she paid them no heed.

That afternoon, wearing her crown and her robes of state, she rode to the Guildhall, having summoned the Lord Mayor and aldermen to meet her there. Word of her coming had gone before her, and huge crowds had packed the great hall. Smiling and bowing to left and right, she passed through them and ascended the throne. She had not prepared any speech, but she knew what she wanted to say. It came from the heart.

"I am come in person," she began, "to tell you that which you already know; that is, how traitorously and rebelliously a number of Kentishmen have risen against myself—and you." She looked down on the sea of frightened, anxious faces, and saw that the people were hanging on her every word.

"I am your Queen," she continued, "to whom, at my coronation, when I was wedded to the realm, you promised your allegiance and obedience. My father, as you all know, possessed the same regal state, which now rightly is descended unto me, and to him you always showed yourselves most faithful and loving subjects; and therefore I doubt not but you will show yourselves likewise to me."

Softening her tone, she smiled at them. "I say to you, on the word of a prince, that I cannot tell how naturally a mother loves her child, for I was never a mother; but certainly, if a prince and governor may as naturally and earnestly love her subjects as the mother loves her child, then be assured that I, being your lady and mistress, do as earnestly and tenderly love you. And I cannot but think that you as heartily and faithfully love me, and so I doubt not that we shall give these rebels a short and speedy overthrow."

She had them with her; the atmosphere had lightened. Yet she must address the matter that most worried and vexed them. "As for my marriage, I have not, for my own pleasure, chosen where I fancied, for I am not so desirous that I need a husband. Indeed, I thank God I have hitherto lived a virgin. But if, as my ancestors have done before me, it may please God that I might leave some fruit of my body behind me to be your governor, I trust you would not only rejoice, but also know that it would be to your great comfort. And, on the word of a Queen, I promise you that if it shall not be clear to all the lords and commons that this marriage shall be for the great benefit of the realm, then I will abstain from marriage while I live."

She rose, drawing herself up to her little height. "I am minded to live and die with you, and strain every nerve in our cause, because your fortunes, your goods, your honor, your personal safety and your wives and children are all at risk. If you bear yourselves like good subjects, I will stand by you, for you deserve the care of your sovereign lady. And now, good subjects, pluck up your hearts, and like true men face up against these rebels, and fear them not, for I assure you I fear them nothing at all!"

After the merest pause, the crowd erupted in a wild ovation. Caps were thrown in the air, and some people were weeping. It was evident that their loyalty to their Queen was greater than their aversion to her chosen husband. Mary herself felt tears welling up, knowing that she had won over public opinion.

"Oh, how happy we are, to whom God has given such a wise and learned Prince!" exclaimed an impressed Gardiner, as she descended the steps.

"There never was a more steadfast lady than your Majesty," murmured Renard, those handsome eyes gazing at her admiringly.

After that, men came flocking in their thousands to fight the rebels. It was as well, because Wyatt's army, now thought to be seven thousand strong, was advancing steadily. But it was halted at Southwark, where the citizens had been working through the night to make London Bridge impassable. Wyatt had to content himself with sacking the Priory of St. Mary Overie on the Surrey shore, and nearby Winchester Palace.

Nonetheless, London was in tumult. The Lord Mayor ordered that every man must stand at his door, to be on watch for the rebels. The Queen's speech was being read out by heralds in every part of the city to inspire courage in the citizens. Some were running around in panic, the women weeping in fear, pulling their children and maids into their houses, and barring the doors. People were donning armor as shops were shut and boarded up.

Fear and alarm were tangible in Whitehall Palace, too. Armed guards thronged the Queen's presence chamber, while her ladies wept and wailed, wringing their hands in terror, convinced they were going to be raped or murdered. But Mary kept a cool head. She had ordered that she be informed of every development.

"Place your trust in God," she urged those around her. "If He is for us, who can be against us?"

Her councillors pressed her to have the Tower guns fired across the river at the rebels, but she refused to allow it. "We cannot have the innocent people of Southwark killed!" she protested. Evidently Wyatt had anticipated that his forces might be bombarded, because he marched them upriver toward Kingston. There he crossed the Thames and moved back along its northern shore to Tyburn, outside the city walls.

When news of his advance reached Whitehall, the Council issued every member of the royal household with arms and begged Mary to make her escape by river.

"No!" she told them. "I will tarry to the uttermost. If I were a man, I would be in the field in person!" She took up a position at the window in the gallery over the Holbein Gate, calmly ignoring the tumult in the palace, the slamming of doors and the running and shrieking of her women. There was no sign as yet of Wyatt's army, but it could not be long before it appeared. The Earl of Pembroke and Sir Humphrey Clinton had been dispatched to St. James's Park with ranks of cavalry to bar its way. It was frustrating not knowing what was happening, but an hour later, Gardiner joined Mary at the window.

"Madam, there has been a brief skirmish, but it is said that Wyatt's men are exhausted and reluctant to fight. Many have deserted. He himself has taken a small detachment off in the direction of Charing Cross."

Mary's heart skipped a beat. He was so close! Her women started wailing again, and their cries were echoed in other parts of the palace.

Suddenly, several guards burst into the gallery. "Your Majesty, get down!" roared their captain. "They are shooting arrows into the palace precincts. All is lost! You must get away!"

"No!" Mary cried, staying where she was. "I am not moving one foot out of my house!" She marveled that she was so calm; such courage must be a gift from God.

"Fall to prayer," she told everyone, "and I warrant you we shall hear better news soon." So saying, she led her women to the chapel and sank to her knees.

"Wyatt is taken!" Gardiner was standing at the chapel door, looking disheveled but triumphant.

Mary rose to her feet and curtseyed to the crucifix on the altar. "Praise be to God, for He has worked another miracle." Behind her, the women were weeping with relief.

"He was taken at Temple Bar," Gardiner related, as they walked to the council chamber along galleries crowded with courtiers all eager to congratulate the Queen. "He'd been cut off by Pembroke's force from the rest of his army and was trapped. He just gave himself up, meek as a lamb. His followers have been rounded up and arrested."

"Have him taken to the Tower," Mary commanded, feeling a little faint. The ordeal had taken its toll of her, but she would be all right in a few moments.

It was obvious that her councillors had been thoroughly frightened.

"Madam," Paget said, as she faced them at the board, "we feel we must point out that this rebellion is the result of your being over-merciful at your accession. In future, you must harden your heart and show your subjects that you are not to be intimidated, because your leniency has almost cost you the throne."

At any other time, Mary would have bridled at such presumption, but her councillors, to a man, had just amply demonstrated their loyalty, and she knew they had her interests at heart.

"I will take your advice, my lords," she said. "Never again will I show clemency to traitors. I will not cease to demand of the law that it strike terror into those who venture to do evil. Nor will I tolerate heresy in my realm any longer, for we have seen how it can lead to seditious plots against me."

Unswervingly, she agreed that the leaders of the revolt should suffer death as an example to other would-be rebels.

When the meeting ended, she summoned Renard and told him of her resolve.

"They are right," he declared. "It is no longer the time to exercise mercy. Your Majesty should proceed firmly against all heretics from now on. It is fitting that you intend to exact such a fearful vengeance." He paused. "I urge you also to rid yourself of other persons who might become a focus for rebellion. I mean Lady Jane and her husband."

Mary was about to say no, very firmly, for she had given her word that she would not harm them, but then she remembered that she had sworn never again to be merciful to traitors.

Renard had seen her hesitate. "Madam, did you know that Jane's father declared for her during the rebellion?"

"Yes," she said, "but she cannot be blamed for that. She was miles away, and not involved in his treason."

Renard was implacable. "Madam, as long as Jane lives, she will prove a thorn in your side. Your councillors are of the same opinion; I have talked to many of them. And I have to tell you that the Emperor will not permit Prince Philip to come to England until she is removed."

That news fell like a blow.

"Then," Mary said, choked, "it seems I have no choice, for nothing must be allowed to jeopardize the alliance between our countries."

Renard gave a somber smile. "You have made a very wise decision, Madam, and demonstrated true statesmanship. His Imperial Majesty will be most impressed."

Ruthlessly quelling her conscience, Mary gave orders that the sentence passed on Jane and Guildford be carried out two days hence, then steeled herself to sign the death warrants, giving orders that the condemned couple be told to prepare themselves. She tried not to imagine how it must feel to be told—in the springtime of your life—that you were to die imminently. She was the Queen and must harden her heart.

Nevertheless, she could not sleep that night. She could *not* send that young girl to her death, she could not! And then, just before dawn, a way out presented itself. If Jane could be persuaded to embrace the true faith, she would not only save her soul, but could never again be a focus for Protestant dissidents.

First thing in the morning, Mary sent the learned Richard Feckenham, Abbot of Westminster, to offer Jane a reprieve in return for her conversion to the Catholic faith. He was a kind old man, and if anyone could move her, it would be he.

She sat at her desk in deep agitation, unable to concentrate on the state papers before her, which had piled up during the rebellion. It was afternoon before Feckenham returned.

"Madam," he said, looking pleadingly at her, "I think I am making some progress with the Lady Jane. If you would agree to postpone the execution for three days, I believe I can bring about a change of heart in her."

Mary was suffused with relief and gladness. Another soul won for Christ! She could see herself explaining to Renard and her councillors that this was a significant development, and that the right and only course was to spare Jane the axe.

"If you succeed in your holy mission, I will let her live," she told the abbot, who hastened back to the Tower.

When he had gone, Mary learned that Jane's father, Suffolk, had been discovered hiding in a hollow tree in his hunting park in Warwickshire, and was being brought south to London. All the rebel leaders had now been rounded up. She sat reading the reports and the confessions as the room grew chill and the February dusk closed in. She had just risen to add a log to the fire when Abbot Feckenham returned. She knew from his sad demeanor that it was not good news.

"I fear the Lady Jane is too steadfast in her beliefs to abandon them," he said wearily. "She treated me as if I was Satan come to tempt her. Alas, I can do no more, Madam."

"You have done your best," Mary assured him sadly. "We have both tried to save her, but she has sealed her fate. We can do nothing now but pray for her."

"The Lieutenant of the Tower told me that, unlike Jane, Lord Guildford Dudley is in a state of collapse, and weeps and rails against his fate. He has begged to say farewell to his wife, and I said I would pass on his request."

"I grant it," Mary said. "I will send the order to the Lieutenant and tell him that the executions are to be carried out on the morning of the twelfth of February. Guildford shall suffer on the public scaffold on Tower Hill. Jane, on account of her royal blood, shall die on Tower Green."

"I promised her that I would accompany her to the scaffold," Feckenham said. "She agreed, for I think she has conceived a fondness for me, yet she is adamant that there will be no last-minute conversion."

"Nevertheless, your presence will be a comfort to her," Mary said, suppressing the urge to cry.

When the morning of the executions dawned, she arose feeling ragged, for she had not slept again. Pulling on her night robe, she knelt at her prayer desk and prayed for Jane's soul, remaining there until the dread hour had passed. By then, her handkerchief was sodden.

She was dressed and composed when Feckenham arrived.

"The Lady Jane died bravely," he said. "It was over in an instant. I am sure she knew nothing about it."

Mary crossed herself. "God rest her soul. And thank you, Father Abbot, for your kindness."

Still feeling shaky, she sat in council that morning, for there was much business to be done, yet it was hard to concentrate. Only when she heard Gardiner mention the Lady Anna of Cleves did she give the lords her full attention.

"Madam," Gardiner said, "we have received information suggesting that the Lady Anna was privy to the plotting of the rebels and intrigued with her brother, the Duke of Cleves, and the King of France to help the Lady Elizabeth gain the throne."

Mary could hardly believe it of placid, amiable Anna, but the councillors laid before her letters hinting at her involvement.

"We ask your Majesty's permission to wait on the lady and question her," Gardiner said.

"Very well," she replied, "but I cannot believe she would do such a thing."

They regarded her almost with pity, as if she was being a foolish woman to ignore the possibility of treachery, and she was tempted to remind them of their own treason in supporting Lady Jane.

"The Lady Anna is close to the Lady Elizabeth, is she not?" That was Paget.

"She is close to me, too," Mary said. "But go and question her, to satisfy yourselves."

"Thank you, Madam, we will," Gardiner said. "Alas, there is the more pressing matter of your sister to be dealt with."

"Indeed," Mary replied. "She is still at Ashridge, still pleading sickness."

"I propose that some of us wait upon her there with two of your Majesty's physicians, to determine whether she is as sick as she claims to be."

Mary nodded. "A very wise course to take, for I feel certain that she was somehow involved in Wyatt's rebellion."

The lords murmured their agreement, to a man.

"Instruct the doctors to take my own litter with them and bring her to court if, in their professional opinion, she can be safely moved."

"Then there is the matter of Courtenay," Arundel said. "He is guilty of treasonable negligence in failing to help prevent Wyatt's forces from entering London. He should be behind bars."

Mary duly signed the warrant for his arrest they handed her. "Let him be imprisoned in the Tower," she ordered. "And have Lady Exeter banished from court." She could not be seen to be consorting with the mother of a traitor.

The two deputations set off later that day. Watching from a gallery as they rode out of the courtyard, Mary turned to Renard.

"You too believe that Elizabeth is implicated?" she asked.

"I do," he replied vehemently. "And this illness she pleads—could it be that she is with child by Courtenay?"

Mary stared at him, shocked. "I hardly think so . . ."

"It is what people are saying. If your Majesty thinks that is far-fetched, you should be aware that Messire de Noailles is putting it about that she is ill because you tried to poison her."

"I beg your pardon? How dare he say such a thing of me? I will demand his recall!"

Renard shook his head. "That, Madam, would be to give his spoutings a credence they do not deserve."

When the lords returned from their visit to the Lady Anna and asked to see the Queen, they appeared more disgruntled than relieved.

"We got nothing out of her," reported Gardiner. "She stated she has no knowledge of these affairs and has had no contact with the Lady Elizabeth since the coronation, and that she would never do anything to jeopardize the favor that your Majesty shows her. She maintains that she is your loyal subject and will ever remain so."

"Maybe she is. After all, there is no good evidence to the contrary."

"All the same, we cannot clear her of suspicion," Gardiner said, "and so it would be wiser if your Majesty withdrew your favor while we keep her under surveillance."

Mary sighed. They had her in a corner again. She did not want to freeze out Anna, but it was probably wise to do so for the present. After all, she had a far bigger problem on her hands.

The Ashridge deputation reported that the physicians had diagnosed bad humors in Elizabeth's water, yet pronounced that she was able to travel to court. She had protested that she would not be able to endure the journey without imperiling her health, but the lords had insisted, and she was now making her way by slow stages to London, apparently complaining all the way. Mary did not envy those accompanying her; she was aware of how difficult Elizabeth could be.

She knew that her councillors—and Renard—wanted her to deal with her sister as she had dealt with Lady Jane.

"Madam," Renard declared, his tone urgent, "I fear that the Emperor and Prince Philip will never have any peace of mind until two more heads have fallen, those of the two people most able to cause trouble in your realm. You know who I mean. Only when those traitors have been removed will your Majesty need have no fear for your crown."

Gardiner was also pressing Mary to proceed against Elizabeth. "By ridding yourself of her, you will be showing mercy to the whole commonwealth."

When Mary shrank from what he was suggesting, he rounded on her, never a man to mince words. "This is foolish! Have Wyatt rigorously questioned, and I guarantee he will reveal the Lady Elizabeth's involvement in his conspiracy."

"Let it be done, then," Mary muttered, stung by his anger. "What news of Courtenay?"

"He has admitted nothing, even when brought face-to-face with Wyatt, except that a servant of his had gone to France without his permission—a likely story, Madam."

Mary was inclined to agree with him. "Have him questioned again."

Chapter 32

1554

Elizabeth had arrived at Whitehall. Immediately, Mary dismissed most of her sister's attendants and refused her plea for an audience, sending to say that she must first be examined by the Council concerning her recent conduct. For now, she was to remain in her apartments, isolated from the rest of the court and heavily guarded.

"I will not see her," Mary told her dear cousin, Margaret Lennox, who was visiting court and providing some light relief in these dismal days. It occurred to Mary that Margaret would make an admirable queen and a worthy successor to herself—she was a staunch Catholic, of impeccable lineage, and had two healthy sons—and she began to toy with the idea of setting aside Elizabeth.

"You've put her in rooms below mine," Margaret said, her eyes twinkling mischievously. "Let's give her a small taste of the discomfort she has caused you!"

Over the next few days, she turned one of her rooms into a kitchen, so that Elizabeth would be continually disturbed by cooking smells and the noisy banging and crashing of pots and pans. Margaret was unrepentant—and gleeful. Perhaps scenting a crown, she began seizing every opportunity to denigrate Elizabeth to Mary and report every snippet of gossip that tended to confirm her guilt.

As a lesson to would-be traitors, Mary ordered that a hundred and more of the common rebels be hanged, and that their bodies be displayed on gibbets at every street corner in London.

"It's terrible out there," Susan reported, after visiting her goldsmith in Cheapside. "Everywhere I look, there are rotting corpses, and the stench is dreadful."

Mary hardened her heart. "But it was necessary, my dear. And I have shown mercy in some cases." The wives of four hundred rebel soldiers had come to Whitehall, beseeching her to pardon their husbands. She heard them out patiently, then decided that a grand gesture was in order. Ordering that the condemned men be brought into the courtyard of the palace with halters about their necks, she graciously pardoned them. She would never forget the joy on everyone's faces.

"I've pardoned far more men than I have condemned," she reminded Susan. "I've spared Lady Wyatt, although there can be no question of my showing mercy to her husband."

She wrote to the Emperor, informing him that the rebellion had been successfully suppressed. *I trust therefore that my rule is now established more firmly than ever, and that the alliance with my lord the Prince can be concluded.* England, she was telling him, was perfectly safe for Spaniards.

Then Renard told her that Philip had begun to assemble his fleet at La Coruña and to gather his household. She would be married soon after Easter!

In the meantime, there were traitors to be dealt with—and Elizabeth. Suffolk was attainted and beheaded. Immediately, Pembroke had Lady Katherine Grey's marriage to his heir annulled. Feeling sorry for the girl—she was just fourteen—Mary brought her to court and showed great favor to her and her hunchbacked sister, another Mary, named after herself. It was as well, because less than a month after the execution of her husband, the Duchess of Suffolk remarried.

Her bridegroom was her low-born master of horse, Adrian Stokes. Not only was he a poor match for a princess of the blood, but he was also, at twenty-one, half Frances's age. To add to the scandal, it turned out that the marriage had been necessary because the bride was pregnant. Mary received the newly wedded pair, but she would not allow Frances's daughters to return to her care, sending them instead to live under the guardianship of her formidable old friend, the Dowager Duchess of Somerset, at Hanworth.

Early in March, Mary was betrothed to Philip in the Chapel Royal at Whitehall. Count Egmont, representing the bridegroom, knelt with her before Bishop Gardiner, who was officiating at the ceremony.

On her knees in front of the Holy Sacrament, Mary solemnly declared, "I call upon God to witness that I am marrying Prince Philip, not out of any carnal affection or desire, but for the honor and prosperity of the realm. I call upon all here present to pray that God will give me the grace to accomplish the marriage, and that He would look upon the union with favor." She rose, and the Count placed on her finger a ring sent by the Emperor, which made her feel quite emotional. Turning, she displayed it to her watching councillors.

It was accomplished. The betrothal was binding on both her and Philip. It troubled her, though, that she had received no further word from him, apart from his signed agreement to their marriage. Not one word of love or anticipation. But maybe, now that they were affianced, he would feel it appropriate to write to her.

The Council was making every effort to uncover evidence incriminating Elizabeth. Wyatt and Crofts had been interrogated, but would not—or could not—give anything away.

Gardiner was fuming. "Wyatt told me that even if I resorted to torture, I could not make him reveal anything about communicating with the Lady Elizabeth."

"It sounds, then, as if there is something to reveal," Mary said tersely.

"Indeed, Madam. And when he was racked, he did admit that he had contacted her twice, once to warn her to leave London for her own safety, and once to advise her that he had arrived at Southwark."

"And did she respond?" Mary's tone was sharp.

"On the first occasion, according to Wyatt, she sent her gentleman, William Saintlow, to thank him and say she would do as she thought fit. But when we questioned Saintlow, he stoutly denied it and declared he was a true man, both to God and his prince. Lord Russell has confessed to having delivered letters from Wyatt to Elizabeth, but we can find no trace of them, or any proof that she responded. And there is no evidence that she sent or gave Messire de Noailles the letter found in his postbag."

"It seems we have come to an impasse," Mary sighed.

"All we can hope for now is a confession from Wyatt at the last," Gardiner harrumphed.

As usual, Mary sought Renard's advice, meeting him in her privy garden on the first warm day in March.

"Without proof of her complicity, there is no case against my sister," she told him. "Yet I am certain that she was involved with the rebels."

He regarded her perplexedly with those beautiful eyes. "Your Majesty, I cannot understand why you and your Council are so at pains to find direct proof. She has been accused by Wyatt of communicating with him, mentioned by name in the French ambassador's letters and suspected by the councillors, and it is certain that the enterprise was undertaken for her sake. If you do not seize this opportunity of punishing her and Courtenay, you will never be safe."

Mary sank down on a lichen-spotted stone bench, spreading her hands in dismay. "Our law does not inflict death on those who have committed no treasonous act. There is no certainty of her guilt."

Renard huffed. "I am sure it will be uncovered, if she is pressed hard enough."

"Like you, Gardiner insists that the removal of Elizabeth is essential, yet even he admits there is as yet no case against her."

Renard was shaking his head.

"Sit with me," Mary invited, and when he joined her, she fleetingly wondered if it would feel as good to have Philip so close to her. "My sister's character is just what I have always feared it to be. Even though I am in favor of having her indicted for treason, it would be inadvisable to institute criminal proceedings against her at this stage, for it might well precipitate another rebellion. I must go carefully. I hope that you and the Emperor can understand that."

Renard nodded, yet she could strongly sense his dissatisfaction.

She debated long and hard with her councillors as to what she should do with Elizabeth. Both she and they were convinced of her guilt and felt that any opportunity she might have to do mischief must be forestalled. Some favored keeping her under house arrest deep in the country.

"And which of you will be her custodian?" Mary asked.

There was a long silence.

"It seems that no one wants so dangerous a person under his roof," Gardiner observed. The idea was abandoned, and it soon became clear that the lords were bitterly divided in their opinions and unable to find a solution.

"We must make a decision," Mary insisted. "I am to leave for Oxford shortly, and it is essential that Elizabeth be placed in safe custody in a place where she can wreak no mischief."

"Where better than the Tower?" Gardiner said. "While she is there, she can be questioned further about her activities."

Several councillors shouted him down, so vehemently that it gave Mary pause for thought. They were having an eye to the future, she realized, and anticipating that if she herself died—perhaps in childbirth, perish the thought—Elizabeth would be their queen; how then would she deal with those who had urged her imprisonment?

But Gardiner was adamant, and by sheer force of will, he won the argument. Mary gave the order for Elizabeth to be arrested and taken to the Tower, with the proviso that she be dealt with fairly.

Renard expressed his deepest satisfaction, and he was even more gratified to learn that Elizabeth was to be questioned by the Lord Chancellor and nineteen lords of the Council before she left White-hall. Mary authorized Gardiner to warn her that she would incur the severest penalties if she did not admit her guilt and throw herself upon the Queen's mercy.

"But, Madam," he reported afterward, "she firmly denied that she had done anything worthy of reproach, saying she could not ask mercy for a fault she had not committed. She begs an audience with your Majesty, for she says that she has only to come face-to-face with you to convince you of her innocence."

"No," said Mary. "Tell her I am about to leave London, and that it is my pleasure that she go to the Tower while the matter is further examined."

"She was horrified," Gardiner said, after he had broken the news to Elizabeth. "I think she believes her imprisonment portends a similar fate to that of her mother and Lady Jane Grey. She still denies having had any involvement with Wyatt, and trusts that your Majesty will be more gracious to her than to send her to so notorious and doleful a place as the Tower. And there we left it."

Mary steeled herself to remain firm. Forget that motherless little girl who once clung to you, she admonished herself; forget the love that was once between you!

That night, she watched from her window as a hundred soldiers were set on watch in the gardens of Whitehall, ready to be on guard when Elizabeth was escorted to the Tower on the morrow.

The next day, the councillors informed her that when they came for Elizabeth, she had been in great distress, and had desperately deployed delaying tactics. She had begged them to wait for the next tide, and when her request was refused, she had asked if she could write a letter to the Queen, then took so long about it that they missed the tide anyway.

Pembroke handed the letter to Mary. It was full of protestations of innocence and emotional browbeating and contained nothing to make her change her mind. Anger rose in her. "And you were all taken in by these ruses?" she raged. "Writing such a letter to a sovereign would never have been allowed in my father's time. I wish he could come back, if only for a month, and give my councillors the rebuke they richly deserve! See to it that she goes to the Tower in the morning, without fail!"

She was not surprised when they told her that Elizabeth had refused to enter the Tower; crying and proclaiming her innocence, she had sat down on the cold, wet flagstones above the watergate and would not move. Plainly, she thought she would never come out of the fortress alive.

"But we finally managed to persuade her to go with the Lieutenant to the Queen's lodgings," Paulet, the Earl of Winchester said, with no little relief.

"That will be punishment enough," Mary murmured. "Her mother was held there." What ghosts haunted those rooms? she wondered. "Inform the Lieutenant that she may walk along the walls, as far as the Beauchamp Tower, as long as she is escorted by five attendants."

But the Lieutenant's superior, the Constable of the Tower, forthrightly expressed his concern at the freedoms permitted the prisoner, so Mary withdrew Elizabeth's privileges. She was not to have pen or paper, and was forbidden to communicate with anyone. When Elizabeth complained that being confined to her rooms was affecting her health, the Constable permitted her to take the air in the Lieutenant's walled garden, escorted by an armed warder. He reported that she was in a fever of anxiety as to what was going to happen to her, and was living in mortal fear of being executed.

A deputation of ten councillors headed by Gardiner went to the Tower to question her. They told Mary they had got nothing incriminating out of her, and she could see from their demeanor that some were uncomfortable about keeping her imprisoned.

Renard, however, was still pressing Mary to put Elizabeth and Courtenay to death. "While the Lady Elizabeth lives, it will be very difficult to make things safe here for the Prince," he protested, seated across the table in her closet. "I cannot recommend his Highness's crossing to England until every necessary step has been taken to ensure that he is not in danger."

Mary burst into tears, appalled at the prospect of losing Philip. "I would rather never have been born than that any harm should be done to his Highness!" she cried.

"Then, Madam, do what must needs be done!" Renard was implacable.

"Very well! Elizabeth and Courtenay will be tried before the Prince arrives, I promise it. As a precaution, he should bring his own doctors and cooks, just to be on the safe side."

As soon as the ambassador had left, she regretted giving him that assurance. If there was no evidence for a conviction, her councillors would never agree to such a trial, not in their present mood.

It was now the end of March, and Paget had begun to assemble Philip's English household. But Renard insisted on interfering, and a heated dispute arose, for the councillors were insisting that this was their responsibility, not his. Renard subsided, seething.

Still there was no word from Philip.

The Council continued to debate what was to be done with Elizabeth.

"She should be executed, in the interests of your Majesty's security," Gardiner barked, but was shouted down.

"Her guilt is by no means established!"

"There is no case against her!"

"I agree with my Lord Chancellor," Mary said, "but I will consult my senior judges."

They too advised her that there was no evidence to justify a conviction.

Back at the council board, Gardiner urged that Elizabeth be at least disinherited.

"No!" erupted Paget and several others. "Let her be married abroad to a friendly Catholic prince. And let Courtenay be freed. His friends are pressing for his release and pardon, and he has committed no overt act of treason."

* * *

"I see that your Majesty will not proceed against either the Lady Elizabeth or my lord of Devon," Renard said, disapproval radiating from him. "What will you do with them now?"

"I haven't decided." Mary stood fretting in the mocking sunshine, the April breeze stirring a stray lock from her hood. She could not bring herself to set Elizabeth free. She was still convinced that her sister had had some dealings with the rebels. The rejoicing of the crowds when Wyatt exonerated her on the scaffold had demonstrated how popular she was. Such popularity could be dangerous.

They walked in silence along the riverbank toward the orchard, courtiers falling back and making obeisance as the Queen approached. But Mary moved on unseeing.

"Your Majesty seems preoccupied," Renard said.

"Yes. I am grieved that Parliament has thwarted my attempt to revive the old heresy laws. The lords are much exercised by the issue of church lands; they fear that a Catholic revival will threaten the continued tenure of those who were granted ecclesiastical property after my father dissolved the monasteries. And Paget seems to be on a mission to undermine my plans. He knows I am in favor of reunification with Rome, but he has deliberately stirred up feeling in Parliament against it."

"Your Majesty should have him arrested!"

"For speaking his mind in a debate? No, but I have made it plain that he is not welcome at court, and he has gone home." Mary paused, gazing out across the river toward Lambeth Palace. "I should take heart from the fact that a thousand spectators jeered at Cranmer, Latimer, and Ridley when they were taken from prison to enter into debate with a panel of Catholic theologians, whom I sent to change their opinions. For three days they labored, getting nowhere, so they have denounced the three as heretics and excommunicated them. But, thanks to Parliament, there is no law under which heretics can be condemned to death, so they have been sent back to prison."

"In time, your Majesty's will must prevail," Renard said.

"Yes, but for now, as I am constantly being told, I have to go cautiously!" Mary flared.

* * *

The councillors were still deeply divided over what to do with Elizabeth. What one advised, another opposed. There was no justification for keeping her in the Tower, they said, but Mary insisted that it would not be honorable, safe, or reasonable to receive her at court.

"The best course is to have her held under house arrest in a secure place in the country, where she can be kept under surveillance," she told the lords. But, as before, no one wanted the responsibility of being Elizabeth's jailer. The silence lengthened until Sir Henry Bedingfield held up his hand.

"My father was jailer to your Majesty's mother, and so I will repay the debt by keeping custody of the Lady Elizabeth," he said, not looking too happy about it. The lords hastened to agree to the appointment, clearly mightily relieved. Mary thought Sir Henry perfect for the task, being a conscientious soul with a rigid sense of principle and duty, and a man of little imagination who would not be swayed by the caprices of a flirtatious young woman.

"It might be best to send her to the north, where most people are Catholics," Gardiner suggested. "Pontefract Castle is a secure stronghold."

Several lords opposed the idea, and eventually the decision was made to send Elizabeth to the ancient royal manor of Woodstock in Oxfordshire. As far as Mary was concerned, she could not be dispatched there quickly enough, for she wanted her out of the way before Philip's arrival. It was not just her own security she feared for. She was not having her much younger sister flaunting her striking looks and coquettish manners before Philip, prompting him to contrast them with her own fading charms; nor did she want her pleading her case with him and arousing any sense of chivalry he might possess.

Early in May, Bedingfield rode out to the Tower at the head of a hundred soldiers in armor to take charge of Elizabeth. Mary watched them go, relieved to have the problem of her sister taken care of at last. An hour or so later, there were sudden bursts of cannon fire from farther along the Thames. What was that? Surely the appearance of a heavily guarded Elizabeth had not provoked another rebellion?

Alarmed, she sent guards to investigate, then waited for what seemed like ages for their return. No, it was no uprising, the captain informed her; just a salute from the German gunners of the Hanseatic League on the Steelyard wharf as the Lady Elizabeth passed in her barge. Mary stiffened in outrage. How dare they!

Gardiner arrived, his hawk-like face suffused with anger. "She's making a triumphal progress of it!" he hissed. "Crowds have come running to the banks to see her, all cheering and waving."

Mary felt chilled to her bones, and a wave of jealousy slapped her. If Elizabeth chose, she could have them in the palm of her hand.

As the days went by, Mary simmered as she read the reports. Elizabeth was making the most of her time in the public eye. All along the route to Woodstock, the story was the same. The country folk had come flocking with their blessings and their simple offerings: cakes, wafers, and bunches of herbs or flowers, which they tossed into the litter, or into the arms of the Princess's attendants, who could not carry all the gifts she was given. Church bells had been rung to celebrate Elizabeth's release from the Tower, and Mary was gratified to read that Sir Henry had had the offenders clapped in the stocks. His letters showed that he was flustered and irritated by the attention paid to his charge. He had clearly done his best to ward off well-wishers, but with little success. For all his authority, he could not punish everyone who cried out, "God save Your Grace!" as Elizabeth passed, although he would clearly have liked to.

Mary exhaled in relief when she heard that her sister was safely confined at Woodstock, and she did not doubt that Sir Henry had done the same. She sent instructions that he guard his prisoner closely and treat her honorably. When she walked in the gardens, he was to accompany her. Mrs. Ashley had been dismissed, and her other servants were to be thoroughly vetted, and watched at all times in case they carried messages. There was to be no cloth of estate above her chair when she dined, nor was she permitted to write or receive any letters. Her laundry was to be searched for hidden messages. Unsuitable books were to be banned. If Elizabeth had any requests, these must be referred to the Council for approval. Mary knew she could rely on Sir Henry to follow her orders to the letter.

* * *

Nothing had been proved against Courtenay, but Mary still saw him as a menace to her security, and at Gardiner's suggestion, he was placed under house arrest at Fotheringhay Castle.

With both Elizabeth and Courtenay safely out of the way, and the memory of Wyatt's rebellion receding into the past, Mary's realm was relatively tranquil, and she began to look for news of Philip's arrival. It was now May; surely she would not have to wait much longer? Nothing now could prevent their union, and she was in a fever of impatience for the coming of her prince. She was tense and snappy, even fretting about the weather.

Preparations in England were well advanced. Philip's household was complete; the insignia of the Order of the Garter were being prepared for him; a party of noblemen were on their way to Spain to greet him; and a fleet was now patrolling the Channel in readiness to escort his ships to Southampton.

But after that brief note when the marriage treaty was drawn up, Mary had still not received a single letter from him, and Renard was clearly embarrassed at such unforgivable discourtesy. She wondered if he had prompted Philip when a letter—couched in disappointingly correct terms—did finally arrive in the middle of May. However, with it came three costly gifts: a beautiful table diamond in a rose-petal setting, which had belonged to the Prince's mother; a necklace containing eighteen flawless diamonds in a filigree setting; and an enormous diamond from which hung a matchless pearl called "La Peregrina," both suspended from long gold chains. This last Mary favored above any others. Immediately, she hung the diamond around her neck, admiring its sparkle as she peered into her mirror. All would be well. Such gifts betokened a willing, bountiful heart and the promise of future happiness and wedded bliss.

Early in June, the Prince's Spanish household sailed into Southampton in a fleet of one hundred and twenty-five ships. Upon receiving the news, Mary left Whitehall for Winchester, where her wedding was to take place. She met the head of the household, the stately Marquess de Navas, at Guildford and expressed the greatest delight at Philip's letter and gifts.

"His Highness will be with your Majesty in two weeks," he informed her, causing her heart to soar and flutter wildly. What would

Philip think of her? Would she please him? Was that mysterious business in the marriage bed so terrifying?

The next day she traveled to Farnham, where she took up residence in the castle belonging to the bishops of Winchester, there to await the summons to Winchester to greet her bridegroom. Her happiness was such that she could even feel warmth toward Elizabeth, and had her portrait rehung in the gallery. Yet she stopped short of setting her at liberty. She did, however, grant Elizabeth's request to write to her—and then wished she hadn't. For the letter was insolent and haughty, couched in the most disrespectful terms; she had addressed Mary as "you" rather than "your Majesty," and protested against the treatment she had received, denying that she had ever deserved it.

When Mary had calmed down, she wrote to Sir Henry, telling him categorically that Elizabeth was not to write to her again. Elizabeth had begged an audience with her, but Mary did not deign to reply. Let her stew!

By 9 July, Mary had waited at Farnham for three weeks, and still Philip had not come. The officers appointed to his service had been staying at Southampton at great expense, and his new household was now running out of food, not to mention patience. It troubled Mary deeply, and the delay left her imagining all the disasters that might have befallen him. In some agitation, she moved to the Earl of Wiltshire's palatial house at Bishop's Waltham, two miles from Southampton, and waited there, growing ever more anxious.

At last—God be praised—they brought her word that Philip had landed at Southampton, having endured a rough voyage.

Mary could not wait to see her future husband. She listened avidly to the messengers who reported that as the Prince had stepped onto English soil in the rain, he had been greeted by a salute of cannon fire, serenaded by her minstrels, and presented with the white horse richly caparisoned in crimson velvet and gold she had sent him.

"Did he like it?" she asked eagerly.

"His Highness was delighted with it," she was told, and she smiled when she heard that Philip had been formally welcomed to

England by Gardiner and Sir Anthony Browne, accompanied by virtually the entire peerage of the realm. Crowds had gathered to see him—people had been trampled underfoot in the crush, but no one had been seriously hurt.

"The Prince exerted himself to be courteous and amiable," Gardiner informed Mary that evening, after she had waited up late, eagerly awaiting his return. "When he had given thanks for his safe arrival in the church of the Holy Rood, we escorted him to his lodgings. At the banquet we hosted in his honor, he gave a speech, saying he had not left his country to augment the greatness of his power, but because God had summoned him to be your Majesty's husband, and he would not refuse His divine will. As long as we are faithful subjects, he will be our good Prince. The people applauded him, and they cheered even more when he accepted a glass of good English beer, which he seemed to enjoy. Then he turned to his Spanish nobles and told them to forget all their old customs, for henceforth they must live like Englishmen."

Mary had been hanging on his every word. Philip had certainly made a good beginning. But she could hardly ask Gardiner, a celibate churchman, the things a woman wanted to know. Was the Prince as handsome as his portrait? Had he spoken warmly of her? Did he seem excited at the prospect of their marriage? Well, she would find out soon enough!

"Take this ring," she said, drawing a diamond from her finger. "Pray take it to his Highness in the morning, as a gift from me. Tell him I look forward to meeting him at Winchester."

Chapter 33

1554

Gardiner had put Wolvesey Palace, his episcopal residence near the cathedral, at Mary's disposal, and seen that everything was in readiness for her arrival. She found it hard to settle into her lodgings, for she was crazy with impatience for Philip's arrival. The time seemed endless. But then, late one evening, when she had given up all hope of him coming that day and was about to retire to bed, Renard came to tell her that he was on his way.

"Quickly!" she cried, beckoning to her ladies and maids, and sped to her bedchamber, where she had them dress her in a gown of black velvet with a high neck and a silver underskirt, and loaded herself with jewels. She had been planning her attire for this moment for weeks, and knew she looked the best she was ever going to look.

She made herself walk calmly to the long gallery to await Philip's arrival, and stood there surrounded by her ladies and the councillors and courtiers she had hurriedly summoned. When she heard footsteps approaching up the stairs, her heart leaped and she almost ran to the door, then suddenly she was face-to-face with her future husband.

He was a vision in a suit of white kid with a surcoat embroidered in silver and gold and a hat with a long plume. He was even more handsome than his portrait. He had a princely face with a broad forehead, gray eyes, a straight nose, and a manly bearing. His hair and beard were fairer than in his painted image. He was well proportioned in body, although shorter than she had imagined. She could not hide her delight in the sight of him.

"Welcome, your Highness," she said joyfully, speaking Latin, for she spoke it better than Spanish, and she knew that Philip knew no English.

"Your Majesty!" He bowed.

Modestly, feeling herself flush, she kissed her own hand before taking his, but he smiled and kissed her on the mouth in the English fashion, making her feel quite dizzy. Then he took her hand and led her through to her presence chamber, where they seated themselves on the thrones beneath the canopy of estate, their courtiers standing at a respectful distance.

"I trust you have recovered from your voyage," she said, unable to take her eyes off him.

"Indeed, your Majesty. The warmth of my welcome banished all infirmity."

"And your father, the Emperor—is he in good health?"

"He was when I left him, thank you."

"I hope that the lodgings made ready for you have been satisfactory?"

"Very satisfactory."

They carried on exchanging courtesies for a while, until Mary realized that she was doing most of the talking. Nervousness was driving her on, and she knew that, as the person of higher rank, it was up to her to set the pace in the conversation. But she could not seem to turn their talk to more important, personal matters, for she did not know how. They were to be married, and yet it had not been mentioned. And there was so much she wanted to say to him.

Soon, she was running out of pleasantries, so she was grateful when Lord William Howard stepped forward. "Your Highness's coming has been most eagerly anticipated here," he told Philip, also speaking in Latin, and smiling at Mary. "The day you have both longed for is fast approaching. It will be a wedding and a bedding such as we have not seen these long years."

"Indeed." Philip returned the smile, but Mary sensed a certain stiffness in his manner. Of course, the Spanish were very formal, and he might not appreciate such bluff sailor's humor.

Lord William was undeterred. "You have a fair bride there, Sir. I'll wager you'll warm her bed well enough!"

Mary felt the heat rising in her face. She dared not look at Philip.

But he ignored the jest. "Permit me to introduce my gentlemen to your Majesty," he said, and beckoned them forward. When she had received them all, she returned the compliment and led Philip into the next room, where her ladies were waiting to meet him. They curtseyed, but he raised them in turn and kissed them all on the lips.

He then turned to Mary. "I have good news for your Majesty. I heard today that my father has ceded to me the kingdoms of Naples and Jerusalem. He has done this so that I might go to my wedding as a monarch in my own right, on equal terms with your Majesty."

There was polite applause from the lords present, as Mary smiled at him. "May I be the first to offer my congratulations—your Majesty!" she said. He beamed at her, and there was warmth in his smile.

All too soon, it was time for him to leave, for the hour was late, but Mary insisted on detaining him a little longer, asking him about his new kingdoms, and wondering if he would ever take her to see them. She would have dearly loved to visit the holy places in Jerusalem—if she could ever get away from her state duties for long enough. But Philip had never been to either realm.

"Maybe your Majesty would teach me some words of farewell to say to your English lords," he said. Touched, Mary whispered the words in his ear, then he rose, bowed to her, and said, "Good night, my lords all." It was obvious that he had made a good impression.

Mary barely slept that night. Her mind was in a whirl as she thought back over her meeting with Philip. Had he been as pleased with her as she was with him? She could not fault him on his courtesy, but she had sensed a certain aloofness. There had been no feeling of intimacy, no mention of their marriage and no attempt at wooing. But what did she know of such matters? Probably it was not the Spanish way to speak of such things before the wedding. Once they were married—once they were bedded—it would all be different.

The next morning—the eve of their nuptials—she sent Philip a gift of two magnificent suits to wear at the ceremony. One was particularly splendid, having a surcoat of cloth of gold with the roses of England and the pomegranates of Spain delineated in gold beads and seed pearls, and eighteen buttons fashioned from table diamonds. She hoped he would wear that one.

That afternoon, Philip came again to Wolvesey Palace, where they sat in the East Hall and chatted. Mary asked him about Spain, and he asked her to explain the English customs he needed to learn. They spoke of her mother, and of his, and for the first time he let down his guard a little, for loss was something they had in common. Mary felt more relaxed in his company today, and Philip seemed more animated, smiling at her a lot.

Everything was going to be all right.

The crowds were out in force, cheering loudly, as Mary, nervous yet excited, arrived at the west door of Winchester Cathedral. Her stiff gown of purple cloth of gold flared out elegantly as she walked, and her jewels glittered in the July sunshine. Behind her came Margaret Douglas, bearing her train, and the Marchioness of Winchester, followed by a great procession of Privy Councillors, peers, and ladies.

The choir was cool, hung with tapestries and packed with people craning their necks to see her. At the crossing, a circular wooden platform draped with purple had been erected. Here, Philip joined her, having arrived earlier and waited in a side chapel. He was wearing not her favorite of the outfits she had given him, but the other one, a full-length robe of cloth of gold lined with crimson satin and banded with crimson velvet and pearl buttons, and it suited him excellently. He smiled at her.

Accompanied by the Marquess of Winchester and the earls of Pembroke, Derby, and Bedford, they ascended the steps and knelt to be shriven by Bishop Gardiner. Then Winchester, as the senior peer, took Mary's hand, on behalf of the nation, and gave her away, presenting it to Gardiner, who laid it in Philip's outstretched palm and proceeded to conduct the marriage ceremony in both Latin and English. Philip placed on Mary's finger a plain ring of gold she had chosen for herself because that was how maidens had been married in the old days. She was filled with exaltation when Gardiner pronounced them man and wife, and there was a great shout of acclaim from the congregation.

"God send you joy!" people cried.

Gardiner then announced that the Emperor had ceded the kingdoms of Naples and Jerusalem to Philip, who was now, by virtue of his marriage, King of England. There were more cheers.

With Derby and Pembroke, bearing swords of honor, going before them, Mary and Philip walked hand in hand through the choir to the high altar beneath a canopy of estate borne by four knights. High Mass was celebrated by Gardiner and five other bishops with due splendor, the office being sung by the pure voices of the Children of the Chapel Royal and the cathedral choir, accompanied by the majestic sound of the organ. Mary could not take her eyes off the Sacrament; her heart was full of gratitude to God, who had brought her through so many tribulations to this day.

Trumpets sounded as the Mass ended, and Garter King of Arms solemnly proclaimed the rulers' new titles. Then the King and Queen, still holding hands, left the cathedral and walked under the canopy of estate to Wolvesey Palace, where the nuptial feast was served in the East Hall, which had been hung with cloth of gold and silk.

Seated at the high table with her new husband and Bishop Gardiner, and somewhat overwhelmed by the occasion, Mary noticed that while her food was served on gold plates, Philip's arrived on silver ones. Of course, the kitchen staff had not known of his new titles; all the same, she hoped that neither he nor the Spaniards present had taken offense. She smiled at him, and he smiled back, showing no sign of displeasure, then she tried to eat some of the rich food, as minstrels played and the royal heralds distributed alms for the poor.

Afterward, there was dancing, and Philip led Mary out in a German dance; he was not a natural dancer, being too stiff and reserved, but she enjoyed herself, having loved to dance all her life.

The hours sped by, and soon it was nine o'clock and time for supper. Mary and Philip retired to their separate lodgings to eat, but if she had had little appetite earlier, she had none now. The moment was fast approaching when the great mysteries of marriage would finally be revealed to her, and she was full of trepidation. Would it be painful, as some women had hinted? And would it be embarrassing? It was all right for Philip—he had been married before and knew what to expect. She just hoped she would not make a fool of herself. She shrank from the prospect of the public bedding ceremony and had insisted that only a few select courtiers be present. She would not allow anyone to see her in her night-rail, in bed with Philip. Her modesty would never permit it.

Supper was finished, and it was time to proceed to the bridal chamber that had been prepared for them. Mary was shaking so much she might have been going to her execution. Still wearing her wedding dress, she left her lodging, followed by her ladies and her chosen guests. On the door of the bedchamber, placed there by order of Gardiner, was a plaque bearing a Latin verse: "Thou art happy, house, right blest, and blest again, that shortly shalt such noble guests retain."

Philip was within, awaiting her by the great bed. The covers had been folded down and rose petals sprinkled on the pillows. The room was ablaze with candles and the lattice window was open, letting in a pleasant summer breeze. Mary stood by Philip and waited as Gardiner blessed the bed and prayed that they might be fruitful. Then he and the guests discreetly withdrew, leaving her alone with this man she scarcely knew.

She wished now that she had let her women undress her and put on her night robe, for she had never undressed herself in her life and knew that all the unlacing and unpinning was beyond her. But Philip had moved closer and was untying her oversleeves.

"Allow me to be your tirewoman, Mary," he murmured. It was the first time he had addressed her by her Christian name.

He had done this before. Of course he had: he had been married, for goodness' sake! How had he been with Maria of Portugal? Loving? Disengaged, as he seemed to be now? But his hands were gentle and his voice soft.

"There is no need to be afraid," he said. "The marriage act can be very pleasurable."

Her cheeks burned. He was pulling her sleeves off now and laying them gently on a chest. Next he unlaced her bodice, his breath warm on her bare neck. By all that was holy, he wasn't going to strip her naked, surely? She would die of shame!

When he had taken off her gown and let her kirtle fall about her ankles, leaving her standing there in her shift, she made a bolt for the bed, climbing in and pulling the covers up to her chin. Philip gave a chuckle, then got in beside her.

"Come," he said, pulling her toward him. "We have an heir to make for England!"

It hadn't been as bad as she had thought. She was surprised the next morning to find that she had fallen asleep quickly afterward, but then it had been a long and emotional day. Philip had been patient with her, had taken things slowly. She had been slightly outraged when she realized what he was going to do to her, but tried to relax, reminding herself that he was her husband, whose will she must obey. There was some pain, making her cry out, but Philip kissed her and gentled her before venturing further. Then she was half terrified, half excited by the violent momentum of what was happening, and afterward a little shocked by the messiness of it all. But after he had kissed her again and gone straight to sleep, she had felt a sense of triumph. She was a wife now, a fulfilled married woman, initiated into the mysteries of love; it was as if she had gained stature overnight.

The clock chimed six. Birds were singing outside the window, and Philip was lying there looking at her.

"Good morning, Mary," he said, and took her in his arms again. "We must not leave these things to chance. It is well to make the most of our opportunities."

It was far less painful this time, but when it was over, she realized that he had spoken no word of love the whole night. She was just wondering if it was actually the wife's part to do so when he rose from the bed and reached for his night robe. She quickly averted her eyes from his nakedness.

"I have work to do," he told her. "I will see you later, Mary. I bid you farewell."

Her ladies were clearly surprised to find her alone when they came to dress her.

"The King has many demands on his time," she told them, fighting down her disappointment at his sudden departure. How could he have been so dispassionate after the intimacies they had shared?

She would not be appearing in public today, so she decided to lie in bed a little longer and read. But presently there came a knock on the outer door. It was an usher, saying that Philip's Spanish nobles had come to call on the Queen. The ladies looked shocked, and Susan marched out.

"My lords," Mary heard her say, "it is not honest to call on a bride just after her wedding night. It is the custom in England that a Queen remains in seclusion until the second day following her marriage."

"Señora," one said, "in our country, it is traditional to greet our monarchs in bed on the morning after a royal marriage."

Susan obviously could not understand them, so she shooed them away like naughty children and barred the door.

Mary smiled. If she had wanted evidence of Philip's care for her feelings, that was it. He would have known about the Spanish custom, yet he had chosen to spare her modesty and follow the English way. *That* was why he had left her so soon!

Too restless to stay in bed any longer, she rose and let the women dress her, then sat down to write to her father-in-law, the Emperor. *Thank you for allying me with a prince so full of virtues that my realm's honor and tranquility will certainly be increased. This marriage renders me happier than I can say, as I have discovered in the King my husband so many virtues and perfections that I constantly pray God to grant me grace to please him and behave in all things as befits one who is so deeply bound to him.*

Philip came to her again that night and was as considerate as he had been before, and this time she began to feel, in the core of her body, some tingle of response, so startling that she drew back, fearing what might happen if she let the sensation build. She might faint—or even die! But he was pressing on heedlessly to his climax and the moment was lost anyway. She wondered if she was pregnant already.

She emerged from seclusion the next day to a week of triumphs, banquets, singing, masques, and dancing. She and Philip dined in the East Hall beneath the new cloth of estate bearing their combined arms, and danced in the presence chamber. When Philip was not attending to business or learning how English government worked, her lords showed him the local sights, and he put himself out to get to know them all. He and Mary conversed constantly about the important task of reconciling the English Church to Rome. At night, they were lovers.

Their marriage had begun admirably, she reflected. For the first time since she was ten, when her father's eye had first lighted on Anne Boleyn, she was truly happy. One day, she plucked up the courage to tell Philip that she loved him, and was thrilled when he smiled and kissed her hand. She wished only that he would say it to her.

She knew it must be difficult for him to give place to his wife in matters of state. He must know that he wielded only as much power as she would permit, which men would normally find intolerable and dishonorable, so she tried to defer to him in most things, and ask his advice, and very soon she realized that she was looking to him, rather than Renard, as her chief confidant. It was reassuring for her to have someone of equal rank to counsel her, after having to struggle alone and deal with her troublesome, squabbling councillors. But there were awkward times when she disagreed with Philip's wishes, and would argue the point and follow her head, for she was the sovereign here, after all. She knew this was not the usual behavior of a wife and that she should obey her husband without question— but what was a ruling Queen supposed to do? In her position, she could not be expected to conform as other women did.

She wrote to Cardinal Pole, asking for his advice, for she did not want any bad feeling between herself and Philip. But his reply was unequivocal. *Madam, I exhort you to pray for the King, for he is a man who, more than all other, in his own acts, reproduces God's image.*

Oh, dear. If she had hoped to find support there, she must think again. And she supposed that other men would say the same. As for her women, even the opinionated Margaret Lennox, they made it clear that they were reluctant to interfere between husband and wife.

It was becoming obvious that Philip preferred to be attended by his Spanish household, which was causing resentment among the courtiers. Yet the councillors would not intervene, because many were hoping that he would reward and advance them for their support of the Emperor, or help them pay off old scores against each other. Mary was helpless in the face of such united indifference.

The honeymoon period ended sooner than she would have liked, because she felt obliged to resume her duties as sovereign, which left her little time to spend with Philip. They now saw each other only when they dined in public, or sometimes in the evenings, when she would play the lute or virginals for him, and at night. There seemed never to be enough hours in the day for all she had to do, and the strain told in headaches and palpitations.

"You seem to have difficulty in controlling your councillors," Philip observed one evening.

Mary's head was throbbing. She had had a hard afternoon, trying to stop the lords quarreling about foreign policy, and had unburdened herself to Philip, thinking he would comfort her.

"Are you saying I am no stateswoman?" she snapped.

He shrugged. "Only that you should be firmer with them. We would not tolerate their squabbles in Spain."

"Well, this is not Spain!" she retorted, feeling miserable because they were quarreling for the first time.

"You are the Queen and should be obeyed," he replied evenly, "but they keep you in a corner. I wonder if you are aware of the poor state of this kingdom's finances."

Mary flared. "Of course I am."

"Your realm is bordering on bankruptcy, and what are your councillors doing about it? Nothing useful that I can see. But do not worry. I am making immediate arrangements to secure loans from Spain to fill up your treasury."

Mary could have cried. She had upbraided him when he was only trying to help her.

"I am sorry," she said. "I did not mean to be unkind."

Philip reached across the table and took her hand. "It is forgotten."

Chapter 34

1554

S ir Henry Bedingfield had written to the Council, having clearly been badgered to distraction by Elizabeth. She was begging for her case to be reconsidered and wished to be a humble suitor for the Queen's mercy.

"Her Grace asks either to be tried, or for liberty to come into your Majesty's presence," Gardiner told Mary, "which she says she would not desire if she did not know herself to be innocent before God."

Mary was in no mood to think about Elizabeth now. It was the end of July, and the court was about to leave Winchester to make a leisurely progress east toward Windsor. She was looking forward to a few days' hunting there with Philip, but they both caught heavy colds and had to stay indoors. As soon as they were better, Mary installed Philip as Sovereign of the Order of the Garter. Ever anxious to please him, she presented him with a jeweled dagger to mark the occasion. It occurred to her that he seemed much happier than when they first met. It was all down to their marriage, she decided.

In the middle of August, Mary and Philip rode across London Bridge and were welcomed into the City by bursts of cannon fire. This was the new King's state entry into the capital, and the civic authorities had spared no expense. Lavish pageants were performed at intervals along the streets, some on sites where gibbets had recently stood, and free wine ran from the conduits. The people were out in vast numbers—Spaniards or no Spaniards, the citizens always loved a holiday—and Mary was pleased to hear them cheering her husband. Philip appeared delighted with his welcome, and the people looked equally thrilled when he distributed generous largesse.

At the end of the day, they arrived at Whitehall. Numerous wedding gifts awaited them there. They wandered along the tables set out in the great hall, admiring the displays of costly presents, and were especially overjoyed with the tapestries embroidered with gold and silver from the Emperor, and a gold-and-silver portable organ, encrusted with jewels, from the Queen of Poland.

Philip made his first priority asking the reduction of his unwieldy household.

"They are all hanging about with nothing to do," he complained. "I should not have brought such a vast retinue. I had no idea that your Council would furnish me with so great a train. Renard should have kept me better informed. I'm asking my father to recall him."

A few weeks ago, Mary would have been horrified at the very idea, but it was becoming clear that Renard and Philip resented each other's influence over her, and she did not want to be a buffer between them. She would be very sorry to lose Renard, who had been such a support to her, but Philip must come first.

To her surprise, however, the Emperor refused to be deprived of the services of an ambassador who understood English affairs so well, so Renard stayed, and Mary resigned herself to playing mediator.

Philip tried to solve the problems in his household by delegating personal services to his Spanish courtiers and formal ones to his English attendants. This caused jealousy on both sides, sparking bitter complaints and rivalries. Mary tried to ignore it all; she had enough on her hands.

And then Philip asked when he was to be crowned.

"I would hope," he said, leaning forward across the supper table, "that it will be as soon as possible, to emphasize my regal status."

Mary wished he hadn't put her on the spot. His request was quite reasonable, but she knew—and so should he—that their marriage treaty did not provide for him to be crowned.

"I will speak to my Council," she said, but when she did, the lords showed little enthusiasm.

"Your Majesty is the sovereign and he the consort," Gardiner said. "King Henry did not have all his consorts crowned."

Mary reported the conversation to Philip, who did not hide his displeasure. She felt for him. He was doing everything he could to win the affection and respect of her subjects, deferring to English customs and being lavish with gifts and rewards to those who served him well. He had such a way with her nobles that many now thought highly of him. And it was being made clear to Mary, in various subtle and not so subtle ways, that most men at court saw him as the real power in government.

Even though he had no formal authority, she did her best to ensure that he was involved in state affairs, as befitted his dignity and rank, yet she was not always willing to play a subordinate role, and she sensed that Philip was dissatisfied about this. But he had to remember that she was the Queen.

She was finding, however, that marriage suited her. She had put on weight and looked comelier; there was a becoming blush in her cheeks. Her court had become livelier, as a result of the entertainments she kept commanding. She loved nothing better than to dance with Philip, dine à deux, or watch plays with him. She spent a fortune on entertaining.

However, it was fast becoming clear that while Philip had won some popularity with the nobility, he and his Spaniards were hotly resented by the majority of Mary's subjects. Some protested that they were being made to feel like strangers in their own land, and that their Queen appeared to care nothing for them. Knives were drawn at court almost daily, as both sides sought to settle private scores. There were bitter rivalries in Philip's household, and the Spaniards were always complaining that they were being fobbed off with inferior lodgings, overcharged in shops and taverns, and insulted or jostled in the streets. They hated the weather, the food, and even the women.

"I know, I know," said Philip, holding up his hands, after Mary had explained the problems. "I have made every effort to silence any

Spaniard who insults your subjects. But the problem is not always of my people's making. In London, they have been robbed and attacked. The friars in my train are too terrified to go out, because a mob tried to strip them of their habits and crucifixes."

"I am deeply sorry for that," Mary replied. She was horribly aware that the English were invariably the aggressors. She had ordered that anyone robbing or murdering a Spaniard was to be hanged, but that had not stopped the rioting on the streets. And the last thing she wanted was for Philip and his countrymen to be driven away.

She turned to him with tears in her eyes. "It is a matter of great sorrow to me when any of my subjects mistreats a Spaniard. If anyone in your train feels unsafe, they may stay in the palace, where they will be well guarded."

She discussed the matter with her ladies, then immediately wished she hadn't, for Susan said, "Many of the Spaniards are praying that your Majesty will soon be with child, so that the King can go to the Low Countries to fight the French."

Mary caught her breath. Philip go abroad? "He would never do that," she said. "His place is here, with me. And we have a great task ahead of us."

It was true. Now that her marriage had been accomplished, she was ready to turn her attention to fulfilling the duty God had laid upon her, which would be the greatest work of her life and the crowning glory of her reign—reconciliation with Rome.

Philip looked over her shoulder as she sat at the desk in her closet, writing a directive to the Council in which she commanded that Cardinal Pole be summoned from Italy to carry out an inspection of the English Church.

"I am going to order that heresy be rooted out and that the old laws against it be revived. I will have offenders burned so that others might be saved." She looked up, expecting to see Philip looking warmly approving of such firm measures. Instead, he seemed alarmed.

"Mary, I urge you to tread warily and use moderation," he said. "If the people think they are being persecuted, they will blame me, and the present situation is bad enough as it is."

Mary stared at him. "My dearest, there is a sacred mission to be accomplished. I will not be deflected from it."

He walked around the desk to face her, his gaze intent. "Mary, I beg you to think again. Do not allow Cardinal Pole to come to England until he has made it clear that he will not demand the return of church property."

She sighed. It was sound advice; that issue had to be resolved. Pole would have to wait. But not for long, she hoped.

She steeled herself to respond to Elizabeth's pleas for an audience. Granting her wish was out of the question, but she assured her sister that, although she thought her complaints somewhat strange, Elizabeth need have no fears that she had been forgotten. *We are not unmindful of your case,* she wrote to her. And there she left it, because events overtook her.

The consultation with her doctors had been excruciatingly embarrassing, but she emerged from it elated. "Summon the King!" she ordered her ladies, hugging her news to herself, joy welling up in her.

"I am with child!" she cried, the moment Philip appeared, and was overjoyed to see his triumphant smile. "We are to have an heir. God has smiled on our marriage!"

She could not believe it. Secretly she had feared she was too old for motherhood. But her courses had ceased, her breasts and abdomen had swollen, and nausea assailed her most mornings, making her feel sick to her stomach. It was the culmination of all her hopes. "It has to be significant that this has happened when our reconciliation with Rome is imminent," she said, as Philip took her in his arms and kissed her.

"We shall hold a ball to celebrate!" he announced. "And I must write to my father to tell him the happy news. My dear, you are not to do too much. You must rest and think of the babe. I am here to shoulder the burdens of state for you."

He was as good as his word. Seeing him exercising greater authority, his Spaniards were gratified; and both they and the English courtiers were united in their excitement about the coming heir.

*　*　*

Mary sent Renard to meet Cardinal Pole in Brussels and give him a letter, in which she told him it would be in everyone's interests to abandon any idea of restoring church property as it would jeopardize England's reconciliation with Rome. The Cardinal agreed, whereupon Philip was happy for him to proceed to England.

In November, Mary issued a proclamation requiring all her subjects to submit to the Legate's authority, but was dismayed when it sparked anti-Papist complaints and a new flood of Protestant propaganda tracts.

"We must cut out these cankers lest they infect my people," she demanded of her Council. Fortunately, when Parliament assembled that month, it was packed with sound Catholics who were raring to push through her proposed religious reforms. Clad in matching robes of crimson edged with ermine, Mary and Philip went in state to Westminster for the opening ceremony. As they rode through the crowded streets in an open litter, Mary was overjoyed to hear the people cheering. She was three months gone with child now and feeling so much better. Already, she was unlacing her gowns. What delighted her most was Philip's evident happiness at her condition. He was no longer stiff and diffident, but warm toward her and confident in his new authority.

Once Parliament was in session, Gardiner tried once more to introduce a bill disinheriting the Lady Elizabeth, but Paget blocked it on the grounds that the birth of an heir to the Queen would neutralize her sister anyway, and that to disinherit the Princess now might well have an inflammatory effect upon the people. Mary's child was expected in the middle of May. Naturally, she was apprehensive about something going wrong, for childbirth was hazardous, especially for older mothers. It was only prudent that Parliament pass a Regency Act, settling the government of the realm upon King Philip in the event of the Queen dying and leaving the throne to an infant heir.

Now there was talk of marrying Elizabeth to a safe Spanish nobleman, or even Philip's nine-year-old son, Don Carlos.

"No," Mary said, quite emphatically. Sending Elizabeth to Spain with suspected heretical views would expose her to the unwelcome interest of the Inquisition.

"You might consider marrying her to the Duke of Savoy," Philip suggested. "He is one of my father's best generals."

Mary was resting in her chair, her feet propped up on a footstool. She smiled at him. "I like that idea."

The Duke was duly sounded out, and arrived from Savoy uninvited, with impressive speed.

"He is not well off," Philip murmured, watching their visitor alight from his horse in the courtyard below. "That is why he is eager to secure a wealthy English princess as his bride."

"He might have waited for an invitation!" Mary laughed—she was laughing a lot these days. "But we ought to tell him that Elizabeth is under house arrest."

They explained that as gently as they could to the Duke, when he presented himself at court, but he looked most put out and made it clear he wanted nothing to do with one who might be tainted by treason. Soon afterward, he went home, leaving them once more with the problem of Elizabeth.

On 20 November, for the first time in twenty-three years, Cardinal Pole set foot in his native land, the first Papal legate to come to England since Cardinal Campeggio had arrived a quarter of a century before to try the Great Matter. Mary sent a deputation of councillors to receive him with great ceremony, and he proceeded along the Thames by barge to London.

Mary could not contain herself; she was filled with elation and triumph. She had gone in person with Philip to Parliament to give the royal assent to the bill reversing the Act of Attainder passed against the Cardinal under her father, so that it would be law when he arrived in the capital. The next day, to her utter joy, she felt the baby move for the first time.

The weather was chilly and overcast when the Cardinal arrived at Whitehall, to be welcomed by Philip and brought to Mary. She was waiting impatiently to receive him in the long gallery, and at the sight of him she was quite overcome with emotion, for when she caught sight of his crucifix, her child moved inside her, as had the unborn John the Baptist when his mother greeted Our Lady.

"Hail Mary, full of grace, the Lord is with thee," said the Cardinal, raising a hand in blessing as Mary curtseyed low before him in respect for the Church he represented. Then he knelt before her, but she and Philip hastened to raise him. "It was the will of God that I should have been so long in coming," he said. "He waited until the time was ripe."

"My child leaped in the womb at your Eminence's arrival," she told him.

The Cardinal beamed. "Blessed art thou among women and blessed be the fruit of thy womb."

She blushed at being compared with the Queen of Heaven.

They led him into a private chamber, where wine was served, and conversed for a while about their plans for the Church. Pole had aged. Mary remembered him in his twenties, when he had been young and handsome and she had hoped she might one day marry him. How differently things had turned out. Now he was a lean man in his middle years with gaunt features and a long gray beard. There was no mistaking that he was of the old royal blood of England, and she thought of his mother, dear Lady Salisbury, whom he so much resembled, and who would have been so proud to see this day.

Mary had ordered that Lambeth Palace, the London residence of the archbishops of Canterbury, be made ready for the Cardinal. It had been standing empty since Cranmer's arrest. It was her intention that, once Cranmer had been deprived of his see by the Pope, Pole would be her next archbishop.

She had commanded that the *Te Deum* be sung in churches in London to give thanks for the Legate's safe arrival in England. At the end of November, another service of thanksgiving was held in St. Paul's Cathedral for the quickening of the heir. Until the birth, every Mass celebrated in England was to contain a prayer that God would send the Queen a son.

On the same day as the service in St. Paul's, Mary and Philip rode to Westminster to hear the Legate address both houses of Parliament. Seated on twin thrones beneath a cloth of estate, they watched Gardiner present him to the Lords and Commons. "He has come from the Apostolic See in Rome upon one of the weightiest causes that ever happened in this realm," he told them.

The Cardinal rose from his chair and spoke in a firm, authoritative voice. "We should rejoice in England's long tradition of devotion to the Catholic faith, and in the Queen's miraculous triumph over her enemies and God's preservation of her; and we should give thanks too for King Philip's Christian reputation, and my mandate from his Holiness the Pope." His gaze ranged over the packed chamber. "I come not to destroy but to build. I come to reconcile, not to condemn. I come not to compel, but to call again. All matters of the past shall be as things cast into the sea of forgetfulness."

Mary's heart sang. She searched the faces of the people and saw that they looked reassured.

That night, in honor of the Legate, there was a lavish masque at court depicting the feats of Hercules. It was followed by a tournament with canes instead of lances, arranged by Philip, who took part and performed well, looking splendid in silver and purple. Mary smiled radiantly as she presented the prizes.

The next day was a very special one, for it was the day on which Parliament repealed King Henry's Act of Supremacy. The stage was now set for the public act of reconciliation that would return England to the Roman Catholic fold.

On the afternoon of St. Andrew's Day, Mary and Philip seated themselves on their thrones in the presence chamber at Whitehall, which was brilliantly lit against the November gloom by numerous torches. They watched as Gardiner led the members of both houses of Parliament to the dais and presented a petition asking them—as two people unsullied by heresy or schism—to intercede with the Cardinal that the realm might receive absolution for its disobedience and be reunited with Rome.

"We are very sorry and repentant of the schism and disobedience committed in this realm against the See Apostolic," Gardiner said. "We beg to be received into the bosom and unity of Christ's Church."

Cardinal Pole stood, and the entire company, apart from Philip and Mary, fell to its knees before him. His voice sounded loud and clear. "In the name of the Pope, I welcome the return of the lost sheep; and I grant absolution to the whole kingdom; which I hereby receive back into the mother Church."

Mary could not stop herself from weeping for joy. She exulted as the Lords and Commons murmured, "Amen! Amen!" Many burst into tears and embraced each other.

"From henceforth," the Cardinal announced, "this date should be celebrated as a new holy day, the Feast of the Reconciliation."

It was the supreme moment in Mary's life, the triumph that made all her past sufferings seem worthwhile. Now her conscience was at peace: she had done what God had called her to do and fulfilled her destiny. And let her not forget Philip, who had worked hard behind the scenes to bring about this happy reconciliation and ensured that her wishes were implemented by Parliament. To him, she owed a great debt of gratitude.

The next day, Philip attended High Mass in St. Paul's Cathedral, and when he returned, Mary was thrilled to hear that the church had been packed with worshippers.

"Bishop Gardiner preached to the people at Paul's Cross," he related. "His text was 'Now we must arouse ourselves from sleep.'" The words sent a shiver through Mary. "The Legate conferred on Gardiner the power to grant absolution, and you would have been amazed to see hundreds of people kneeling in the cold to receive it. A sight to see it was, and not a cough was heard."

Mary was gratified to see Pole embarking with a vengeance on the task of purifying the English Church. She did everything she could to support him. They got on as well as ever, and she began to rely heavily upon his advice. Next to Philip, he was now the man she trusted most. If only he would not keep making remarks about how unfit women were to rule! And he was clearly not happy with church property remaining in secular hands.

Yet it was becoming clear to both him and Mary that it was not going to be possible to turn the clock back in every respect. People had given up celebrating saints' days and going on pilgrimage; they couldn't do that anyway, because the monasteries, chantries, and shrines were long gone; and there remained few relics of the saints to replace those lost when the altars were stripped. But these things were not of prime importance. Mary's objective was to restore the spiritual values of the true Church, and to create a climate in which they could flourish.

It was her fervent desire that heresy should be entirely eradicated from her realm, and at last Parliament, fired with the spirit of reconciliation, showed itself willing.

"We must make an example of the heretics to deter others from adopting their pernicious beliefs," Gardiner declared, as they sat at supper one evening.

"I detest heresy in any form," Philip said. "In Spain, I championed the Inquisition and presided over its Acts of Faith, in which the sentences passed on heretics are carried out."

"Very commendable, Sir," Pole said. "If heresy is rooted out, my task of reforming the Church will be made easier."

"This transformation cannot come soon enough," Mary said fervently.

"Yes, but to achieve great ends, we must sometimes go cautiously in the beginning," Philip said. "Reform takes time, would you agree, my lord Cardinal?"

Pole looked thoughtful. "Your Majesty speaks good sense."

Mary looked askance at them both. This was no time for caution, not if true religion was to be restored. One must be a soldier for Christ, full of courage and decision. She did not doubt that when it came to it, both Philip and Pole would be filled with the proper zeal.

A week before Christmas, Parliament passed an Act granting bishops the power to investigate cases of suspected heresy and hand over those found guilty to the secular authorities for burning at the stake. Each execution was to be authorized by the Queen's writ. The property of a convicted heretic would then automatically revert to the Crown.

It was an awesome responsibility, and Philip and Gardiner both urged Mary to proceed with caution.

"Of course I will," she told them. "I am not a cruel person. Every heretic will be given a chance to convert. One chance. Yet it is my Christian duty, as sovereign, to make lapsed heretics suffer a foretaste of hellfire in this world, so that at the last they can repent and be saved. If I fail in that duty, I will surely incur God's wrath and displeasure. And I know you agree with me, my Lord Chancellor, that the burnings will act as a deterrent to others. Let the Act be implemented with due rigor, especially in London, where Protestantism has taken root more deeply than elsewhere. Be diligent in seeking out and punishing heresy."

"I will, Madam," Gardiner assured her.

"I know I am doing the right thing," she said to Philip later, when they were alone in her chamber, sharing a flagon of steaming aleberry in front of the fire. "I am a merciful princess, but I will not show my customary mercy to anyone guilty of offenses against God. Nor will I allow others to show lenience."

Philip nodded. She knew he was concerned about the new law, doubtless wondering if public feeling against it might rebound on him.

"I admire your resolve," he said at length. "I know you will not shrink from the task ahead of you. But I do urge you, Mary, to exercise caution."

That Christmas was one of the happiest of Mary's life. There were splendid celebrations at court, culminating in a moving service in the Chapel Royal, in which the King's choristers joined the Queen's, creating such an angelic sound that Mary thought she might be in Heaven itself. And her heart soared when she heard the Mass that Thomas Tallis, a talented member of her Chapel Royal, had composed for her, which was entitled "Unto us a child is born" in honor of the coming heir.

Less than five months to wait now.

Chapter 35

1555

The elation Mary had felt at Christmas had deserted her by January, when she began to feel very ill. The doctors assured her that the child was thriving inside her, yet she felt so poorly that she was unable to write more than a brief note in response to one of the Emperor's solicitous letters. To make matters worse, Philip was growing restive, and she was terrified that, having done his duty in England and got her with child, he might leave her. He was making no secret of the fact that he was anxious to depart for the Low Countries to fight the French. It would be his first campaign, his first opportunity to gain prestige in the eyes of the world.

Mary was devastated to think that he might leave before their child was born, and her distress only made her feel worse. As the date of her confinement drew ever nearer, her fears increased. To add to her other anxieties, she could not forget that, at thirty-nine, she was rather old to be bearing her first baby. And if the birth was to be a difficult and dangerous one, she needed her husband near at hand.

"You will not go to war yet?" she implored him, sitting up in bed wrapped in furs and feeling thoroughly miserable. "I need you here!"

Philip sat on the bed and took her hand. "My father may need me more than you do."

She burst into tears. Her condition was making her so emotional. She ended up crying and railing at him every time the subject came up. She could not help it, yet she knew that she was stretching his patience to the limit. If she carried on like this, she would drive him away—and that would further undermine her health, when she most needed her strength. And yet, Philip *was* her strength; if only she could make him understand that . . .

Renard, arriving for an audience one morning, found her in floods of tears after yet another wrangle with her husband, who had stalked off, asking what had happened to the woman who had shown such resolve over the Church.

"Your Majesty!" he exclaimed. "Why so melancholy?"

Weeping, Mary told him of her fears.

"We cannot have this!" he declared. "This is a time when your Majesty should be cherished. I will speak to the King!"

"No, don't," Mary protested feebly, but Renard was bowing himself out.

If he took it upon himself to admonish Philip, he might only make matters worse, for Philip did not like him anyway and resented his influence.

She waited for the sky to fall. But Philip said nothing. He was kinder to her. There was no more talk of leaving England.

The first heretic to be burned was John Rogers, a married priest of St. Paul's Cathedral who had published pamphlets inciting people to overthrow the Queen and the Papists, and then brazenly, in the presence of the Council, denied the Real Presence of Christ in the Mass. He went to the stake at the beginning of February. Gardiner told Mary afterward that the crowd at Smithfield had been angry to hear that Rogers had been forbidden to say goodbye to his wife and eleven children, who had cried out words of comfort as they watched his sufferings, which had been dreadful.

Mary hardened her heart and tried not to think about what burning actually meant.

"He was offered a pardon if he recanted, even as he approached the stake, yet still he persisted in his heresy," she said defensively. "He chose to die."

When she signed the writ for the execution of John Hooper, Bishop of Gloucester, she ordered him not to address the spectators or portray himself as a martyr.

"His death was terrible," Gardiner reported. "He burned for three quarters of an hour. I will spare your Majesty the details."

"He could have spared himself," murmured Mary, shuddering.

In March, five Protestants went to the stake in London and one in Colchester. All died bravely.

Mary, now great with child, had been convinced that the sight of heretics dying a dreadful death would deter others from straying from the path of righteousness. She had not been prepared for a public outcry.

"Madam, the protests are so vociferous that I fear there could be another uprising," Renard told her, looking deeply concerned. "Far from converting heretics, these burnings are having the effect of hardening their resolve and inflaming their anger against your Majesty. The bravery of those who have died has inspired many; they are calling them martyrs. Their courage is making others think that their beliefs are worth dying for."

The reports received by the Council confirmed the truth of this. It seemed there was no shortage of men and women ready to speak out against the burnings.

"We're having to sentence unprecedented numbers of wretches to the pillory," Paget informed Mary. "Many are spreading lies and sedition about your Majesty and your Council."

"Then they must be silenced," Mary declared.

She withdrew to her bedchamber for her afternoon rest, but there was Philip at the door, fretting about public opinion.

"This clamor will rebound on me!" he warned. "I need to distance myself from what is going on."

"But I need your support!" Mary cried.

"Better a husband at your side than one driven away," he retorted, and left her.

The next day, Susan told her that the King's confessor had preached a sermon in the Chapel Royal, condemning the burnings. Mary was furious.

"You could show me some loyalty!" she stormed, when Philip joined her for dinner.

"What of your loyalty to me?" he flared. "I warned you of what might happen, and now people think it is me and my people who have made you consent to this new legislation, when I have tried all along to urge moderation!"

"We are doing God's work, Philip! No one said it would be easy."

"I don't think you know what you're doing," he flung at her, and walked out.

She had just dried her tears when Gardiner arrived, requesting an audience.

"I have just spoken with the King," he said.

"Not you, too," Mary said wearily. Gardiner had been in favor of reviving the heresy laws, but was now clearly having second thoughts.

"Madam, the people are sickened by the burnings," he persisted. "They are producing the opposite effect to that which we intended. Could I not persuade you to resort to other methods of punishment? Cruelty serves no useful purpose."

Mary sighed. "Some might say we ought to be cruel to be kind; that it will ultimately lead to more souls being saved. But I will consult the Cardinal and the Council."

They all expressed the view that Philip and Gardiner were being too mild and gentle toward people who were guilty of a great atrocity against God. Some were zealously eager to continue with the burnings.

"And I have to say I think they are right," Mary told Gardiner, who subsided, defeated. "We have to remain strong, my Lord Chancellor. Please ensure that the bishops are not tardy about bringing heretics to justice, or lenient with those who leave it too late to recant. Only this morning, I had to send a rebuke to the Sheriff of Hampshire for sparing a heretic who recanted as soon as he felt the heat of the fire."

She would not waver in her resolve. She saw her duty clear, even as Philip warned her that, having come to the throne on a tide of popularity, she was losing the love of many of her subjects. There was no denying what government agents were saying. The people were now reviling her, and not all were Protestants.

Her dismal mood worsened when yet another plot to marry Elizabeth to Courtenay and make them King and Queen, this time fomented by the brother of Messire de Noailles, was discovered. Not again! Renard observed that the kingdom would never be at peace while Elizabeth and Courtenay lived. Mary fretted over that, but she knew that Elizabeth could not have been involved, for she was too closely guarded.

In addition, with her confinement now just two months away, and everything being prepared in readiness, she had other matters to consider.

"I will remain in England until after our child is born," Philip told her, as if he was conferring on her a great favor. Thwarted of satisfying his need for military glory abroad, he devoted himself to planning a series of tournaments at court, but Mary did not attend them because she could not bear to watch him risking his life in daring exploits in the lists.

"You must not worry about Elizabeth," he said one afternoon, returning from the jousts to find Mary in a distressed state after being hectored by Renard to take some decisive action in regard to her sister. "Why not send her and Courtenay abroad to places where they can be kept under supervision? She could go to Brussels and he to Rome."

Mary brightened at that. But when she proposed it to her councillors, they warned her that exiling Elizabeth now, at such a sensitive time, might provoke another rebellion, and she was forced to abandon the idea.

"I urge your Majesty to disinherit the Lady Elizabeth," Gardiner demanded, but Philip was against it.

"Mary, if—God forbid—you die in childbirth, and your child with you, the King of France will press the claim of his daughter-in-law, the Queen of Scots, to your throne, and that is the last thing I and my father want. If Mary Stuart succeeds, England would become a French dominion and we would lose all the strategic advantages we have gained by our alliance."

Mary understood his position all too well; she just wished he hadn't sounded so dispassionate about the prospect of her dying. It chilled her to think that he believed it to be a possibility; it was what she feared herself. If she died, Elizabeth would succeed, and the realm would revert to heresy. Everything that she had accomplished would be undone.

Philip drained his glass and fixed his gaze on her. "Married to some foreign prince, Elizabeth would no longer be a threat. But let us defer any decision on her future until after you are confined. Bring her to court so that we can keep an eye on her until then."

All Mary's instincts warned her to say no, but she could see that he was once more giving her good advice, and she did not want another wrangle over whose will should prevail. But it occurred to her that he might be looking to establish a good working relationship with Elizabeth in case she did become Queen. It was understandable. If she looked upon him with gratitude as the person who had rescued her from confinement, he might obtain her goodwill and so preserve the Anglo-Spanish alliance. Yet it made her go cold to think of him planning for a future in which she no longer existed.

He drained his glass. "Sir Henry Bedingfield has reported that the Lady Elizabeth is a good Catholic, which leads me to hope that her conversion is genuine."

"That is my constant prayer," Mary said. "My kingdom must go to a Catholic heir. Very well, I will summon her to court."

"You might also pardon Courtenay. Then he can be sent on a diplomatic mission to the court at Brussels, where he would be under my father's supervision. That would get the other embarrassment out of the way."

Mary agreed to that, too, reflecting that, in an instant, Philip had solved a problem that had been plaguing her since she came to the throne.

In Easter week, Mary and Philip moved to Hampton Court to await the birth of their child. Mary was well into her eighth month of pregnancy and expected to be confined around 9 May. Taking to her chamber with all due ceremony, she bade farewell to her courtiers and retired into the privacy of her apartments for the forty days of her confinement. No man other than her husband, her chaplain, and her physicians would be admitted, and her ladies had taken over the duties normally performed by male officers of the household.

Everything was ready for the baby's arrival. In the Queen's bed-chamber stood a sumptuous cradle covered with an embroidered counterpane; Latin and English verses had been carved in the wood and read: "The child which Thou to Mary, Lord of might, hast sent, to England's joy, in health preserve, keep and defend!"

Swaddling bands and wrapping cloths were laid away in a chest in readiness, along with four smocks for Mary of the finest Holland cloth trimmed with silk and silver braid at the neck and wrists, with breast binders and extra blankets. She and her ladies had stitched a beautiful bedcover and matching headpiece for the bed in which she would be delivered. Midwives, physicians, nurses, and rockers had been engaged and were already in residence, while the great ladies of the realm had arrived, ready to sit with their mistress and be her gos-sips when her hour was upon her.

In the birth chamber, the midwives had assembled the equipment they would need, and tables, benches, and bowls had been set there for their use, as well as bottles of scented water to sweeten the air during the delivery.

Mary was becoming increasingly anxious, and her fears were exac-erbated by more news of protests against the burnings in London. To reassure her, Philip summoned men to reinforce the guards already on duty and ordered that the watch take extra precautions in the city by recruiting more members and patrolling the streets continuously through the night.

But Mary still had to face the ordeal of childbirth. Her doctors shook their heads at her poor appetite.

"Madam, you eat so little that you cannot possibly provide both yourself and your baby with adequate nourishment."

Yet, try as she might to force herself to take some food, Mary could not get it out of her head that her mother had lost five of her eight children, and feared that history might repeat itself. Oh, if only the babe could be safely born! She longed to hold it in her arms. She would cherish and love it as no child had been loved before. Her breasts were already leaking milk in anticipation and her stomach had swollen to an enormous size. The infant was still moving, although it was not as active now. It must be here soon.

Elizabeth had arrived at Hampton Court. Philip brought the news as Mary was resting on her bed.

"I arranged for Sir Henry to bring her by a back entrance, and she is lodged in apartments near to my own and those of Cardinal Pole. Sir Henry seemed rather pleased to be relieved of his duties as jailer, and has already left for his house in the country."

Mary gave a wry smile. "It must have been no easy task keeping watch on my sister. Elizabeth can be cantankerous when she pleases. I shall not receive her yet. First, I have to know if she really was involved in Wyatt's rebellion. Pray send Gardiner and some of the councillors to her. Tell them to inform her that even if she confesses to it, I will be good to her."

But Elizabeth vehemently maintained her innocence. A second visit by the councillors failed to move her, and Gardiner sent to inform Mary that nothing further was likely to be obtained from her.

"I marvel that she should so stoutly stand by her innocence!" Mary exclaimed, making Jane Dormer start as she sprinkled rose water on the bedclothes. It was hot, and the bedchamber, with its heavy hangings that covered all but one window, was becoming intolerably stuffy. "My sister is inordinately stubborn," Mary said. "I will not set her at liberty until she has told the truth."

She gave orders that while Elizabeth might receive visitors, she was not to leave her rooms.

"I intend to see her," Philip announced. Mary was horrified. Here she was, fat as a great beached whale and looking every one of her thirty-nine years, and he was going to meet with her twenty-one-year-old sister, who well knew how to work her wiles on men. Not to be borne!

But Philip insisted and, with bad grace, Mary gave in. She sent a curt message to Elizabeth, ordering her to wear her finest robes and prepare to receive the King.

The meeting took place in private, and while it was in progress, Mary could not sit still. She knew she would not be able to bear it if

Philip was drawn into Elizabeth's snares. She could not control her jealousy. It did not help that when he came back, he was full of how amenable Elizabeth had been, how upset she was to think that Mary had such awful suspicions of her, how adamant she was that she was innocent of any wrongdoing.

"And you believed her?" Mary asked.

"I do," he said. "She cannot confess anything if there is nothing to confess. She is very different from you, my dear. She does not see things in black and white. There is a subtlety in her."

Mary was outraged. That he should compare her to her sister! And imply that she too should be subtle!

She could not help it. "I'll wager you thought her fair and beautiful into the bargain!"

He gaped at her. The flush creeping over his cheeks told her all she needed to know. It was as she had feared. Elizabeth had played the coquette and contrived to ingratiate herself with him—and he had fallen for it. Mary could have howled.

Too late, he sat beside her and took both her hands. "You are making a fantasy of nothing," he said. "You know why I think it is necessary to foster good relations with your sister. There is nothing more to it than that."

She wished she could believe him. She wished she could send Elizabeth far away and never have her at court again.

She let him kiss her. Almighty God, she prayed, let me be delivered of a healthy son. Everything in her kingdom depended on it. If the good Lord was pleased to grant her a safe delivery, Philip would cleave to her again and all would be well between them.

Letters announcing the birth had already been prepared by the royal clerks. Mary's ambassadors had instructions to convey the happy tidings to foreign courts as soon as the child was delivered. To hearten her, and relieve the tedium of waiting, Susan arranged for three beautiful infants to be brought to the palace. One of the mothers had given birth only a few days previously; she was a woman of low stature and mature age, like Mary, yet she declared she was out of danger and feeling well and strong. Mary was much encouraged to hear it.

At dawn on the morning of the last day of April, she was awakened by the sound of church bells ringing. After a while, they ceased. Later, she learned from her ladies that it had been prematurely circulated in London that she had been delivered of a prince, and the citizens, always glad of an excuse for a celebration, had declared the day a holiday, shut their shops, lit bonfires, and set tables laden with meats in the streets, while the city authorities had laid on free wine for all, and the clergy had gone in procession around the city giving thanks.

"But the child is not due for another nine days!" she cried. "Let that be known! The people must stop their celebrating." It was tempting fate, she feared.

The ninth day of May came and went, with no sign that the child was about to make its appearance.

"It is nothing to worry about," the midwife said briskly, seeing Mary fretting. "Very few babies arrive when they are expected, and many are late."

"It is not unusual to be a week late," she said, seven days later. And then, later still, "I have known children to be born a month after they were due. I think your Majesty has miscalculated the dates."

By now, Mary was distraught. The child was twelve days overdue, and she was sure she had got her dates right. But of late she had noticed a worrying symptom. Her belly did not seem so swollen. The doctors told her that this was because the baby had moved down toward the birth channel, ready to be born. "It will not be long now," they reassured her. "We expect labor to commence any day now."

Mary could not shake off her despondency. Was God punishing her for not rooting out heresy with sufficient rigor? Heaven forfend! In a panic, she sent a written order to all her bishops, commanding them to step up their efforts to search out and punish offenders.

She tried to calm her agitation by frequent perambulations of her privy garden, the midwife having advised that walking could bring on her pains. It alarmed her that she was no longer dragging herself along, but stepping down the path in something approaching her former sprightly gait. But the doctors were adamant that everything was progressing well.

Philip's face told her otherwise. "No sign of the birth being imminent?" he kept asking, frowning.

"No, but I am certain that I muddled my dates," she told him. "The physicians now say that the birth will take place in two days."

Philip did not look convinced. Neither, to be honest, was she. And now even the midwife seemed concerned, although she was obviously putting on a cheerful face. At the end of May, when Mary asked if she really was with child, the woman seemed overly emphatic that she was.

Mary was beside herself. She was spending long hours alone, sitting silently brooding on cushions on the floor of her chamber with her knees drawn up to her chin, staring at the wall, a position she could not have achieved two weeks before. Had the child died and withered inside her? The notion terrified her, for how would it be born? She could not bear having people around her, even Philip. Heaven only knew what they were all thinking—and what the world at large was saying. She burned with humiliation. What if she was not with child? And if not, what was wrong with her? How would she ever live with the loss of her hopes, let alone the shame of it?

She dared not confide her fears to Philip, for she was in terror that he would leave her and go to the Low Countries. She was painfully aware that he was itching to be off fighting the French, and that he would depart for the Netherlands the moment the baby was safely born. The way he had been acting, a single hour's delay seemed to him like a thousand years. When news reached England of the death of his grandmother, Mary's aunt, Queen Juana, who had been shut up in a convent for decades on account of her madness, Mary panicked, lest he return to Spain. He had hardly known Juana, yet he ordered the courtiers to put on mourning, and everyone was plunged into black. Now he had retired to his apartments to remain in seclusion until the late Queen's obsequies were over.

"I will put off this mourning for the joy of the delivery of my son," he'd told Mary before he disappeared.

And then—a miracle, praise be to God! On the last day of May, Mary felt the first pains of labor. There was a flurry of activity as the midwives and maids ensured that everything was ready. Walking up and down, waiting for the next pang, Mary could sense everyone holding their breath in anticipation. But in the afternoon, the pains came less frequently, and by suppertime they had ceased altogether.

She had never felt so despondent. The doctors tried to cheer her.

"Do not fret, Madam. It's just a minor miscalculation. The nine months will not be up for another week." Did ever babe tarry so long to arrive?

Philip was growing ever more impatient. And it worried Mary that he had begun putting pressure on her to receive Elizabeth. Did he think she was going to die?

"No!" she said. But he did not cease his persuasions.

"It would be politic—and the best thing for this kingdom—if you ceased being at odds with your heir."

"This is my heir!" Mary cried, pressing her belly.

"And Elizabeth will be *his* heir," Philip reminded her.

"God grant that he grows up to father children," she said fervently. But she capitulated in the end.

That evening, she sent Susan to fetch Elizabeth and sat waiting, her heart pounding in her chest. Was that the babe she felt kicking? It must sense her nervousness. She was dreading this meeting. Too much bad blood had flowed between her and her sister for them ever to be truly at peace with one another. But Philip was with her, concealed behind a tapestry. The knowledge gave her strength.

The door from the back stairs opened and Susan entered, carrying a torch aloft.

"The Lady Elizabeth, Madam," she said, and vanished.

And there was Elizabeth, a pure vision in white, looking petrified. With one graceful movement, she fell to her knees and burst into tears. "God preserve Your Majesty! You will find me as true a subject of Your Majesty as anyone, whatever has been reported of me."

Mary looked beyond her, unwilling to meet her eye. "If you will not confess any offense, but stand stoutly to your innocence, I pray God that you are speaking the truth."

"If it is not, I desire neither favor nor pardon at your hands," replied Elizabeth with passion.

It was not the firm denial Mary wanted to hear. "Well," she said coldly, "you still persevere stiffly in your denial; doubtless you think you have been wrongly punished?"

"I must not say so to your Majesty," Elizabeth answered humbly.

"But you will to others?"

"No." The girl's lip trembled. "I have borne the burden, and I must continue to bear it, but I humbly beseech your Majesty to have a good opinion of me, and to think me your true subject, as long as life lasts."

Mary paused. "God knows the truth," she murmured. Then she rose and looked down on Elizabeth. "Well, I shall have to trust you, so be at peace. You may have your liberty and take your rightful place at court." She knew it was what Philip wanted her to say.

Elizabeth's face lit up radiantly. "Your Majesty will not have cause to regret the mercy you have shown me," she said fervently. "I ask only to serve you."

Mary nodded, extended her hand to be kissed and dismissed her.

Philip emerged from his hiding place. "You have done a good day's work, Mary," he smiled.

"I wish I could see it that way," she replied. "I will never trust her again."

"I think you will be pleasantly surprised," he countered. "Now, I think it is time you went to bed. You need your rest."

When, shortly afterward, three of Elizabeth's servants and Dr. John Dee, the astrologer they had consulted, were arrested for having conspired to cast the horoscopes of the King, the Queen, and Elizabeth herself, Mary regretted having given her sister her freedom. Had Elizabeth tried to discover what the future held for her? Surely she would have known it was treason to forecast the sovereign's death? But before the accused could be questioned, one of the servants who had informed on them fell down dead, and the other was suddenly struck with blindness. The news chilled Mary to the bone. Had someone used sorcery to ensure that the charges would be dropped? And where was Elizabeth in all this?

Keeping to her lodgings. Rarely venturing into the court. Attending Mass like a good Catholic. Oh, she was too clever by far!

Chapter 36

1555

It was an unseasonably cold, rainy summer. In the muddy fields the corn had failed to ripen, presaging a bad harvest and the prospect of famine in the coming winter. Many matters of state were of necessity being deferred as Mary waited out the days at Hampton Court, unable to deal with any business except that connected with God's work until her child was safely born. Reports of the appearance of a rash of scurrilous placards libeling her in London and protests at the sickening spectacles at Smithfield seemed to belong to another world.

Gardiner wrote a memorandum warning her that wild rumors were circulating, some claiming that she was dead, or that she was not pregnant but mortally sick, and even that King Edward was alive and about to emerge from seclusion and return to the throne. *What is most concerning is that many speak with deep affection of the Lady Elizabeth, and a printed prayer to be said at her accession is being circulated.*

Philip laid down the paper and frowned. "I do not like the mood of the people."

"The Council is sending Pembroke at the head of a small force to keep order in London," Mary said, frightened that Philip might leave her and go abroad to escape the escalating situation—and the court, which was becoming a very unpleasant place to be. So many people were packed into the palace that the privies were becoming disgusting. The air was fetid, and tempers were short. The tension between the English and Spanish courtiers was at a boiling point, and fights and squabbles were breaking out at the slightest provocation. Some had led to bloodshed, something her father would have punished severely, but she had not the will.

Early in June, Mary was awakened by angry shouts and chanting. She rose and pulled on her night robe, and was about to have her women summon the guard to find out what was going on when Philip burst into her bedchamber without ceremony.

"Your Majesty, my ladies, you must stay here and bar the outer door. A riotous mob of hundreds of young Englishmen is advancing on the palace. They are at the main gates with their swords at the ready to slay any Spaniard who dares venture forth. I have ordered the guards to drive them away, but they are resisting. For your own safety, stay here!"

He was gone, leaving Mary and her attendants looking fearfully at each other. Had Mary not been with child, she would have defied him and faced the mob, for she remembered well how she had pacified and won over the Londoners before Wyatt's rebellion. But she was helpless, and she had all to do to calm her ladies.

After an anxious hour, Philip returned. "The knaves have been overcome. There was a nasty skirmish, and I am sorry to report that a dozen men lie dead. I addressed the miscreants sternly and ordered them to go home and keep the peace. Given the current climate, I dared not punish the offenders harshly."

Mary was relieved that the nasty incident was over, but worried that the hotheads would think Philip weak. Had they withdrawn only to plot a more ambitious assault on Hampton Court? But the Council were two steps ahead of them, sending men after them, who discovered that they were indeed intent on returning and arrested the ringleaders.

When Mary's baby showed no sign of being born on 6 June, the doctors conferred, frowning, questioned her closely, then pronounced that the birth would now take place around the 24th. She could have wept. Had she not waited long enough? By her reckoning, she was now nearly ten months pregnant.

"The doctors can't be right," she complained to her midwife. "Sometimes I wonder if they know what they are talking about."

"All is proceeding normally," the midwife soothed. "Your Majesty is worrying unnecessarily."

"You don't think I'm too old to be bearing a child?" Mary asked anxiously.

"Not at all! Many women older than you have borne healthy children. Your Majesty's own grandmother, Queen Isabella, had a child at the age of fifty-two, I'm told."

Mary wasn't so sure about that, but she did accept the midwife's theory that she had simply muddled her dates. Given her history of irregular courses, it made sense. Nevertheless, to be on the safe side, she asked that the clergy go daily in procession through London, praying for her safe delivery, and that similar intercessions be made each morning at court. Over the ensuing days, she watched from her window as the councillors and courtiers processed around the courtyard, chanting prayers and doffing their bonnets when they caught sight of her. She was feeling much better now, and less worried.

In the middle of June, she had another false alarm, and noticed that her women looked skeptical when the midwife assured her that it heralded an imminent birth. Peering in her mirror, she was perturbed to see that she no longer looked pregnant, and again wondered if she was with child at all. The expressions on the faces of those around her were untroubled, but it was as if they were wearing masks. When she asked if they thought anything was amiss, they quickly denied it.

On 24 June, with no sign of labor, the physicians admitted that they had been two months out in their calculations, and that the child was not due for another eight or ten days. Not more waiting! Mary was just about climbing the walls in frustration. She had been confined for so long that her chamber felt like a prison—a smelly, stuffy one.

July came in. Nothing happened, yet she did not abandon hope. The palace was now unbearably hot, stinking and filthy, and everyone feared an outbreak of plague. The doctors and midwives were still assuring Mary that she had got her dates wrong, but they now spoke with less conviction. When they announced that the birth might not take place until August or September, she found it very hard to believe them. Her figure was back to normal. To take her mind off things, she had started attending to official business once more and walking in her garden. The midwife stored away some of the items prepared for her confinement, saying they wouldn't be needed yet.

But I *am* pregnant, I really am, Mary kept telling herself, and sent instructions to her ambassadors abroad, commanding them to deny any report that she was not with child. Because that was what everyone must be saying—and what Philip, she feared, was thinking.

It was now late July. Her pregnancy had lasted eleven and a half months. All she could do now was pray for a miracle to show that God was smiling upon her. She spent hours on her knees, her prayer book open at the page of prayers for women with child. It was blotted with her tears.

When her courses returned in August, she had to face the bitter fact that there would be no miracle. Shutting herself in her bedchamber, she lay on the bed and wept for hours. Then she got up, pulled some of the lovingly sewn baby clothes from the chest and held them to her cheek, thinking of the infant who would never wear them. When she emerged late in the afternoon, pale and drained, she asked Susan to dismiss the midwives and the nursery staff, and to send for Philip.

"I am not with child," she told him, her voice breaking.

"I am very sorry," he said, his face impassive, although she could detect his disappointment, for he had very much wanted a son and heir. "You must not distress yourself. Did you lose it?"

"I don't know!" she wailed. "My belly just began to subside. My milk dried up, and I was no longer feeling any movements. I just don't understand it."

She was longing to throw her arms around Philip and cling to him for comfort, and was hoping that he would hold her, but he went away to talk to her doctors. When he returned, he seemed more sympathetic.

"It seems there are times when women want a child so much that they believe they are to have one."

"But the signs I had—they were real!"

"No one can explain that, Mary. But the good news is that there is no reason why you should not bear a healthy child."

Not if you go away to war, she thought desperately.

Suddenly, Philip smiled at her, that slow, almost grave smile she had come to love. "When your courses cease, we must try again. I should like to leave you pregnant before I go to war."

"And I should dearly love to be pregnant," she said, although her heart was dying inside at the prospect of his absence.

She made no public announcement. When she emerged from her chamber, she resolutely ignored all the inquiring faces around her and left Hampton Court with Philip for the royal hunting lodge at Oatlands. Elizabeth retired to a house not far away, at liberty now to choose for herself where she went. No doubt everyone would be treating her with a new deference, given that her eventual succession was now more likely. But, Mary assured herself, all was not lost. She *would* bear a son! God would surely grant her this favor.

At Oatlands, she resumed her normal routine, granting audiences and putting a brave face on her bitter disappointment and humiliation. She never referred to her calamitous confinement, and when de Noailles made a sly reference to it, she cut him dead.

They had not been at Oatlands a week when Philip rode off to Windsor for a few days' hunting. Many members of his household had already left for the Low Countries, and Mary knew he was desperate to join them. Yet he sent to say that he would join her at Hampton Court. There was no mention in his letter of going to war.

It felt unsettling to be back in the palace that had so recently been the scene of her misery and crushing disappointment, but Philip was coming and she must put on a brave face for him. She knew enough of men to understand that they did not like clingy, mournful women.

But when he arrived, and they were finally alone together in her bedchamber, she could see that he was tense. She rose and poured him some wine, then joined him on the window seat.

"Mary," he said, swallowing, "I hope you understand, but my duty to my father obliges me to leave England for the Low Countries without further delay."

She could not help herself. All the emotion she had been suppressing for so long rose in her like a tidal wave. Bursting into noisy tears, she flung herself at his feet and clutched his hands.

"No! No!" she wailed. "Don't leave me! How will I live without you? Oh, Philip, my darling, do not go! Please, I beg of you!" She thought she had tasted the depths of despair at the abandonment of her hopes for a child, but she had been mistaken: this was far worse.

He put his arms around her. "Do not weep, Mary! Please calm down." He shook her shoulders gently. "Oh, God, help me!" he groaned despairingly. He tried to pull her up, but she was crying so hard that she could barely move, so he slid to the floor beside her. "Mary, listen! I will be gone for six weeks at the most. The campaigning season will be coming to an end soon." He reached out and brushed the tears from her cheeks.

She rounded on him. "Your place is here with me, not fighting your father's wars against the French!"

"Mary, we've been through this—"

"And don't lie to me about coming back in six weeks. You're only saying that to mollify me."

He drew back at that, once more the stiff Habsburg prince. "Are you saying I'm a liar?"

"No!" she cried. "But you ought to put me first!"

"Mary," he said, rising, and speaking as if to a naïve child, "you should know, as a ruling Queen, that monarchs must put their political obligations before their personal inclinations. You knew when we married that I would be needed from time to time in my father's dominions. He is ailing, and he will require my presence more and more now. One day I will be king of Spain and will be needed there. You will have to live with that."

She glared up at him, stumbling to her feet and hating him for having made her abase herself before him. "I am not a fool. I know all that. But I have just been through a terrible ordeal. My kingdom is divided. I need an heir. Your place is here right now."

He spread his hands. "Mary, I've told you—"

"What of love?" she cried. "If you loved me as I love you, you could not bear to leave me!"

"My feelings cannot come into it," he said, flushing.

"Get out!" she ordered. "Do as you please. Board your ship and leave England. See if we miss you!"

He gave her a foul look and was gone.

"Susan!" she yelled. Susan came running.

"Yes, Madam?"

"Take the King's portrait down from that wall and put it in a cupboard."

Susan looked nonplussed, but she must have heard the quarrel. Without a word, she lifted the picture from its hook and took it away. As soon as she had gone, Mary sank down on the bed and wept.

Two hours later, as she lay wakeful, Philip appeared at the door. "I cannot leave you like this," he said. In one bound, he crossed the room and gathered Mary into his arms. "Listen, dearest. I will leave most of my household here to prove to you that I will be back in six weeks. I am truly sorry that I must go, but I am urgently needed now to fight the French."

Mary felt tears welling again, but for now it was enough to be in Philip's arms. He was in a difficult position, she understood that, but if he had been as gentle with her earlier, she might not have quarreled with him.

"I'm sorry I reacted the way I did," she murmured against his shoulder. "I should be grateful that you have remained with me for so long. You know there is nothing in the world I set so much store by as your presence. I do believe you when you say your absence will be brief. Please forgive me."

"There is nothing to forgive," he said, and kissed her.

Later, when he had claimed her again after months of abstinence, and they lay quiet together afterward, she wishing that it could always be like this, Philip turned to her. "Mary, when I'm gone, will you ensure that, as heiress presumptive, Elizabeth is treated with respect, and show her some affection? You do not need any more conflicts at this time, especially not with her."

Why had he had to ruin such a precious moment? It was painfully obvious to Mary that he was storing up favor with Elizabeth for when she became Queen. Jealousy welled in her, but she made herself promise to take his advice. He was right, after all; there were sound political reasons behind it.

He was leaving everything in as good an order as he could. During her confinement, he had reorganized the Council, making it more efficient and smoothing over the deep divisions that had caused such disruption, to the extent that the lords were now united in most things.

"And I have instructed Cardinal Pole to look to your welfare and that of your realm," he told Mary, piling up his books for packing. "He will advise you and your Council on all major issues."

She was grateful for his care for her and her kingdom, but she could not help wondering if she was being relegated to the role of a figurehead. She had long suspected that Philip—and her councillors—thought that, as a woman, she had no understanding of statecraft. Well, she would soon rectify that!

Late in August, Mary and Philip left Hampton Court and rode through London toward Greenwich. It was her first public appearance since her confinement. As she was borne through the streets in an open litter, with Cardinal Pole riding at her side, people cheered, bringing tears to her eyes, for she had feared that her popularity had been lost. Some ran after her, shouting for joy. Yet there were others who pointedly refused to doff their caps, either for their sovereigns or for the ceremonial cross that was borne before them. Their stares were hostile. Mary was relieved when they reached Tower Wharf, where they boarded their barge.

Elizabeth was also on her way to Greenwich, but in a small boat with a lesser retinue. Mary had feared that if her sister traveled by road, there would be demonstrations of loyalty and affection for her, and that she could not have borne.

At the end of August, the entire court assembled to witness Philip's departure. That morning, Mary had urged him to agree to her accompanying him as far as Dartford, or even Dover, but—probably envisaging more tearful scenes—he had dissuaded her.

"I will be back in time to open Parliament in October," he said. "Let us say farewell in private. May God have you in his keeping, Mary, until we meet again." He bent forward and kissed her lightly on the lips.

She had envisaged being locked in a loving embrace. Longing for just one word of love, she took his hand. "Goodbye, my dearest husband. I will pray for you daily and look forward to your return."

Hand in hand, they left the palace. At the top of the great staircase, Mary formally bade Philip farewell, then watched him descend lithely through the crowds of courtiers to the landing stage where the ship that would take him as far as Gravesend lay at anchor. She managed to stay smiling, but she was grieving to the core of her being. Yet she could not, within sight of such a crowd, make any demonstration of emotion unbecoming in a Queen.

Miserably, she watched Philip leap aboard the ship and fixed her eyes on him as he stood on the deck. Only when the last of his gentlemen had kissed her hand and departed after him did she hasten indoors to a window in the gallery, where she sat down to watch the ship sail. Now she did weep, and bitterly, not caring who saw her. But then—oh, joy of joys—Philip turned and caught sight of her at the window. Waving his hat, he blew her a kiss. She waved back, the tears streaming down her face, and sat there, watching and weeping, until he had sailed out of sight. Then she hurried to her closet and wrote him a letter, expressing her love and loss as best she could.

After Philip's departure, the court seemed a gloomy place, as dismal as if this were a time of mourning, which, in a way, it was. Mary felt utterly desolate without him and spent hours sobbing in her bedchamber, when she wasn't on her knees praying for his safe return. She took comfort only in writing every night to him, telling him her news and begging to be assured of his health. To escape the pain of separation, she threw herself into her royal duties with such a vengeance that Cardinal Pole warned her to have a care for her health.

She did not listen. There were too many things to be done. The Council might be more efficient now, thanks to Philip, but her kingdom was divided, and protests against the heresy laws had yet to be quelled. She kept her lords incessantly occupied, laboring hard herself at official business and counting down the days until she and Philip would be reunited.

Although Pole was not a member of the Council, he was constantly at hand to advise and console her. She had always valued his opinion and now came to seek it before she made decisions. She assigned him apartments near her own, so that he might comfort her and keep her company during the long, lonely evenings. He would have been a good husband if God had not decreed otherwise, she reflected. But she could never have loved him as she loved Philip.

Elizabeth had stayed at court, and although Mary did not delight in her presence, she suffered it for Philip's sake. He wrote frequently, often reminding her of his advice to treat her sister with kindness and respect. Mary made herself receive Elizabeth graciously and tried to show her favor, but she struggled to conceal her distrust and her jealousy. Whenever they met, they spoke only about agreeable subjects, never touching on anything likely to be contentious.

Elizabeth behaved with circumspection, accompanying Mary to Mass every day. Yet when Elizabeth began a three-day fast, for which the Pope himself would grant her remission for her sins, Renard warned Mary that she was doing it for pragmatic reasons, which Mary had suspected herself. It seemed that the court had divined the Queen's mood, for most courtiers still deemed it best to shun Elizabeth's company.

Philip had arrived safely in Brussels, but the news was not good. The Emperor was ailing, worn out by the strains of ruling his great empire; already, he had begun to transfer power to his son, preparatory to abdicating. Philip was now also regent of the Netherlands, his Aunt Mary having resigned from the office. Mary wept at the realization that when Charles abdicated, Philip would be ruler of Spain, the Low Countries and Burgundy; it followed that he would hardly have time to spare for visiting England. Quaking, she thrust the thought away.

And now here was Renard, craving an audience, and come to tell her that he was to return to Spain, at his own request. The Emperor and Philip had given their consent.

Mary was not surprised. Since Philip had made it clear that he resented her reliance on Renard and that he did not like him, she had distanced herself from the ambassador, and she sensed that he, no fool, was aware of that.

"I am not to be replaced, Madam," he told her. "His Majesty feels he can rely on his friends on the Council to keep him informed of English affairs and represent his interests." The expression on his face told her just what he thought of that—and he was right, for since Philip had gone, the councillors had been dismissive of his policies and his wishes. Still, she would not comment on that. Smiling, she gave Renard her hand to kiss, and later presented him with a gift of gold plate.

"This is to thank you for your good service to me and your master. May God go with you." He bowed, and she watched him leave, aware that she would miss his sound advice.

At the end of September, England suffered the worst rain and floods in living memory. Men and beasts drowned, houses were flooded, and the harvest was ruined. Mary's heart went out to her subjects, but there was little she could do to help. She knew what some were saying: that it was God's judgment on her for the burnings, of which there had been eighty so far. That was patently unfair when she was doing God's work.

She was also preoccupied with a stream of requests from members of Philip's household to join him in the Netherlands. To her dismay, his Spanish grandees were leaving England every day, which made her wonder fearfully if they thought he had left her for good. Her fears increased when she learned that some had taken his personal possessions, and deepened further when she found out that he had settled all his debts to his English creditors and dismissed the crew of a ship that had been waiting to bring him back to her.

Worst of all, he was replying less and less frequently to her letters, and when he did, he wrote no comforting words of love, saying only that he had a fair hope of seeing her soon. She found this increasingly hard to believe. Her days were fraught with worry, her nights a torment.

"I have not received a letter from the King for a week!" she confided to Susan, weeping bitterly. Susan could only hold her comfortingly, but neither she nor anyone else could give Mary the assurance she so desired, that Philip loved her and would return to her.

At length, a letter did come. Excitedly, she took it to her closet, closed the window to shut out the howling gale outside, and broke the seal. Then she stared at it, the words dancing before her eyes. Philip was demanding to be crowned.

If only she could grant his request! But he must know she could not authorize his coronation without the sanction of the Council or Parliament, and as the councillors were none too keen on the idea, she would be obliged to wait until Parliament met. Philip wrote again and again over the next weeks, accusing her of not trying hard enough on his behalf, and making it painfully clear that he would not be returning to England until his request was granted *and* he was assigned an honorable role in the government of the kingdom—to which he must surely know he was not entitled under the terms of their marriage treaty. In the middle of October, he wrote to the Council expressing his regret that he would not after all be able to return in time to open Parliament. Soon afterward, he wrote once more to Mary, asking her to arrange more members of his household to be sent to join him. In grief, she did as he asked.

To add to her misery, she learned from her ambassadors at the Imperial court that Philip seemed to be enjoying himself in the Low Countries. He was attending hunts, banquets, and weddings, dancing until the early hours of the morning with notable beauties and sometimes moving on to another glittering function. Mary strove to hide her distress.

In Oxford, the Protestant bishops Latimer and Ridley had been condemned to death for denying the Real Presence in the Mass. Archbishop Cranmer had been tried on the same charge, although his case had been referred to Rome for a decision.

Mary sat in her closet, the warrants before her. Outside her window, a storm was raging. It seemed that the rain would never cease. She sighed. She had not forgotten Ridley's past kindness to her, but she could not pardon such a dangerous heretic. Summoning her resolve, she took up her pen and signed the orders for the burnings, then scribbled a letter to the Sheriff of Oxford, commanding that Cranmer be made to watch, in the hope that he would recant his heretical beliefs.

"If he can be brought to repent," Cardinal Pole had advised her, "the Church will derive no little profit from the salvation of this single soul, for many others will follow his example."

After the executions, Mary's councillors expressed concern. "The bishops died bravely," they informed her, their faces grim. "As they were chained to the stake, Latimer bade Ridley be of good comfort, for, he said, they would be lighting such a candle in England as he trusted would never be put out. He died quickly, but Ridley burned for three quarters of an hour."

Mary shuddered to think of his agony; agony he had suffered by her order. But she must not falter; human frailty must not deter her from her holy purpose.

"Ridley has not been the only one to endure such torture," Gardiner said sternly, looking worried. "This wet weather has resulted in prolonged ordeals for several heretics. I fear that the courage of Latimer and Ridley has inflamed public opinion."

"The outcry against the burnings has intensified," Paget added. "There have been many violent demonstrations."

Mary sat stiffly in her chair. "We must not be daunted. The burnings must go on until every last heretic has been removed from this kingdom."

"But Madam," Gardiner said, "in some cases your officers and parish priests have been overzealous. They have sent to the stake poor, ignorant folk who could not recite the Lord's Prayer or did not know what the sacraments were. There was a dreadful case in Guernsey. A woman gave birth as she was burning, and the executioner cast the child back into the flames."

There were indrawn breaths around the board.

"He far exceeded his remit," Mary said stonily.

"Some executions have been grossly mismanaged by incompetent executioners," Petre put in. "We've had several reports of the kindling being damp, which causes prolonged suffering. It is no wonder that there are demonstrations."

"Make sure there are more guards present to stop the onlookers from comforting or praising the heretics," Mary ordered. "And order the sheriffs to see that the fires are laid with dry kindling."

"That will not be enough, Madam," Gardiner barked. "In the minds of your subjects, the Catholic cause is increasingly becoming identified with brutal persecution. There are those who look to your sister as their savior. Many want you to call a halt to the burnings and send the Spaniards home, for they blame Spanish influence for the new heresy laws."

"It grieves me to hear these things," Mary said, shaken by these revelations, yet refusing to be deterred from her sacred mission. "I firmly believe that the hearts of my people have been hardened by heresy and that more examples must be made to bring them to their senses. The Protestants are enemies of the state and must be ruthlessly eradicated. It is they who are inciting rebellion."

Gardiner frowned. "We hear what your Majesty says, but it might be advisable, while public feeling runs so high, to have heretics executed in private."

"No!" she snapped, banging her hand on the table. "The burnings act as a deterrent."

Seeing the skepticism in their faces, she stood up and swept out, having said her final word on the subject.

When Elizabeth asked for leave to go to her house at Hatfield, Mary gratefully granted it, bidding her a cordial farewell and presenting her with gifts. Later, she regretted letting her go, for she heard that her sister had received a rapturous welcome on the road, and that church bells had pealed for joy at her coming. She felt the bitter gall of jealousy rising in her throat . . .

She took the precaution of setting spies in Elizabeth's household, determined that no one could come or go, and nothing be spoken or done, without her knowledge, for she had no cause to trust her sister. But the reports all stated that Elizabeth attended confession and

Mass regularly and spent much time at her studies. Oh, she was clever!

Mary opened Parliament in solitary splendor, wishing that Philip was occupying the empty throne beside her. To her dismay, Gardiner suddenly fell ill and had to be lodged in Whitehall Palace, as he was too weak even to be carried just along the Thames to Winchester House. They did not always agree on everything, but Mary felt bereft without his strong support, which she desperately needed, for Parliament was in a stubborn, rebellious mood. She dared not raise the matter of Philip being crowned. Instead, she wrote to him, saying she hoped to defer a decision until after Parliament had been dissolved, and then, with the aid of those peers who supported him, grant his request.

So dangerous was the mood of Parliament that when, in November, several members proposed the extradition from their safe havens abroad of those Protestants who had left England without permission, there was uproar in the Commons. Mary, who fervently agreed with the motion, had hurriedly dissolved Parliament, but ordered that those who had opposed the measure be imprisoned in the Tower.

Things were going from bad to worse. The Council next uncovered several mysterious plots both at home and abroad to have Mary assassinated and Elizabeth set up in her place. Mary was horrified, and so, apparently, was Elizabeth herself, who bombarded her with letters in which she protested her loyalty and passionately denied that she had had anything to do with these conspiracies. Mary found it hard to believe her. It seemed she was surrounded by enemies, she, who had only ever intended good.

She mourned deeply when Gardiner died in November.

"As a royal servant, he was unmatched," she told her councillors, sitting before them in deepest black.

Philip wrote to propose Paget to succeed Gardiner as Lord Chancellor, but Mary chose Nicholas Heath, Archbishop of York, although it soon became apparent that he possessed few of his predecessor's qualities. Thus she found herself turning increasingly to Cardinal Pole as her chief adviser. The Council resented this, and before long, the old divisions resurfaced, for there was no one strong enough to hold the lords in check. How Mary wished that Philip was there to control them!

She was desperate to have him home. In a frenzy of anxiety, she wrote to break the news to him that, given the mood of the government and people, there was little likelihood of his being crowned in the near future, and sweetened the physick by sending with her letter some of his favorite meat pies, prepared specially by her cooks. When his reply came, she held her breath, hardly daring to read it—and it was as bad as she had feared. While his chief desire was to please her, he had written, his honor would only permit him to return to England if he were allowed to share the government with her. He was now the absolute ruler of the Low Countries, and to accept a lesser status in England would be unbecoming to his dignity.

Mary knew there was nothing she could do. She swallowed her misery and struggled on alone with her mounting problems. In an atmosphere charged with her fear of conspiracies and secret intrigues, she hardly knew whom she could trust. When she looked around and carefully considered the people about her, there seemed barely any who had not injured her or who would not fail to do so again, were the opportunity to present itself.

In December, news came that the Pope had excommunicated Cranmer, formally deprived him of the archbishopric of Canterbury, declared him guilty of heresy and commanded that he be delivered to the secular arm for punishment. He had also named Cardinal Pole as the new archbishop. But then came the sting. Mary was painfully aware that his Holiness had no love for the Habsburgs, or for a queen who had married one of them, and her agents abroad now warned her that he had just signed a secret treaty with France against Spain and the Empire. The news plunged her into fresh misery. The last thing she wanted, or needed, at this time was an open rift with Rome.

Shortly before Christmas, the last members of Philip's household left England, to Mary's profound distress.

I am deeply sorry, she wrote to him, *for being unable to have you crowned, but I am encompassed by enemies, and I know it would be impossible to accede to your wish.*

When he replied, she feared he was testing her again, for he was now asking for English support against the French. To grant that would endanger her throne, for she could not contravene the terms of their marriage treaty. Nor could she afford to alienate the Pope. A deadlock had been reached. The truth was staring her in the face. Philip would only return to her if she could give him everything he was asking for—which she dared not do. She might be his wife, but she was first and foremost the Queen.

Chapter 37

1556

Throughout the Christmas festivities at Greenwich, Mary had been aware that her gloomy mood had cast a shadow. Now they were hardly into the new year, but the news was relentlessly dismal. The rains and bad harvests of the summer and autumn had led to food shortages and famine. She arranged for relief to be given to the poor, and took measures against those despicable people who were hoarding grain.

Kneeling in her oratory, she begged God to lift these burdens from her people. But she knew in her vitals that she and her realm were being punished because she was not stamping out heresy with sufficient rigor. Back in her closet, she gave the matter much thought, then summoned the Cardinal.

"Until now, heretics have always been given the opportunity of recanting," she said.

"That is correct, Madam, and if they do so, they are reprieved," he confirmed.

"We are being too lenient," she declared. "Once a heretic, always a heretic. And as few people are benefiting by example, I have decided that, in future, the sheriffs must not offer condemned heretics this choice. Furthermore, my wish is that those who show sympathy toward heretics suffering execution are themselves to be arrested."

The Cardinal's lean features tautened. "Madam, you know you have my support in your great task, but these are radical measures and may only incite the people further."

"I am not doing this for the sake of my popularity," she reminded him. "We have to save souls for God!"

When the Emperor finally abdicated that January, Philip and Mary became King and Queen of Spain, the Netherlands, parts of Italy, and the Spanish colonies in the Americas. Mary had expected Philip to become Holy Roman Emperor, too, but the German electors chose his uncle, the Archduke Ferdinand.

She was in despair, knowing that there was now little likelihood of her seeing Philip soon. He seemed to have lost all interest in England, save for protecting Elizabeth's interests, which only made Mary more jealous of her sister. She kept writing to him, begging him to return to her so that their marriage might bear fruit, but all she got were meaningless promises and demands for men for his army.

"The marriage treaty expressly forbids it," Paget said forcefully, when she consulted the Council. "Even if it did not, England is in no financial state to contemplate a war, especially in support of the interests of a foreign power."

Mary fought to stem her tears. She would not cry in front of her councillors. She could not say to them that she doubted Philip would return to her if she did not give him what he wanted. And she doubted too that they would care.

Her misery increased when she learned that Chapuys had died in Savoy. She had not heard from him for some time and had wondered if he was ill. She had the disloyal thought that, had it been possible for her to marry him, he would have been a kinder husband than Philip; he would not have abandoned her. She wept for what could never have been and for her loss. The world seemed an emptier place without him.

On the morning of her fortieth birthday, she looked in her glass and saw a sad, aging woman whose face was scored by sadness and disappointment. Her countenance, although still pink and white, was heavily wrinkled, and she was thinner than ever. How could Philip love her now? She was aware, too, of her worsening eyesight. Hours of writing to him by candlelight in the small hours of the morning had caused that. But what was she to do? She could not sleep these days—four hours was the best she could manage—and the only way to calm her night terrors was to pour out her heart to Philip on paper. Then, when she did sleep, she was tormented by sensual dreams, in which he was making love to her. Waking up and realizing he wasn't there was dreadful.

She seemed to spend her days weeping, sighing, and raging against her people. She could not rise from the depths of her melancholy. She had even thought of taking her life, but knew she could never do so, for suicide was a mortal sin and she would never see God if she committed it. Instead, she decided to withdraw as far as she could from public life and live quietly, as she had done for the greater part of her life before she became Queen. In future, religion would be her chief consolation.

She had taken to attending Mass nine times a day. When, to mark her birthday, they brought to her forty victims of the "queen's evil," the dreaded scrofula, to receive her healing touch, she kissed their sores with ecstatic devotion. It was suggested that she go on a progress through her kingdom to restore her popularity, but she refused, not only because she shrank from the prospect, but also because it would place too great a financial burden on her subjects. And she could not shake off the underlying fear that her reception from those subjects would not be a warm one. Yet her ladies were always praising her for her kindness and consideration. They knew her for the person she truly was, and she wished, how she wished, that her people could see her that way, too. For although her policies might seem harsh to them, they were for their good, which was all she had ever intended.

She had intended to be a merciful princess, but she could not show mercy to the heretics, and she certainly did not intend to be merciful to Cranmer, whose offenses were such that she could never bring herself to forgive him; this was the man who had declared her parents' marriage null and void and herself a bastard. Willingly, she signed his death warrant. The next she heard, he had recanted his beliefs. But she refused to spare his life, for he had seduced so many into heresy by his heretical policies and his prayer book. He must be told to prepare for death at the stake.

Afterward, they told her that he had publicly reaffirmed his Protestant faith. As the flames were lit, he had plunged his right hand into them, saying it should be the first part of him to burn, as it had so offended God by signing his recantation.

Mary was chilled to hear that. Would his courage in the face of a terrible ordeal be a more potent inspiration to others to cling to their subversive opinions?

On the day after Cranmer suffered, Cardinal Pole was consecrated archbishop of Canterbury. Mary knew she could rely on him to pursue and punish heresy.

It was Pole who came to her that month and broke the news that another conspiracy had been uncovered.

"It's the Dudleys again, Madam."

"No!" Mary's throat tightened in horror; she was struggling to draw breath.

"It has come to your Council's attention that Sir Henry Dudley, cousin to the late Duke of Northumberland, has been in France raising an invasion force with the intention of landing on the Isle of Wight and marching on London. His conspiracy was far-flung and dependent on too many people. One of your own officials was involved, but he came to me and confessed all. We have therefore been able to arrest twenty others, who are being interrogated as we speak."

Mary listened, speechless, as the Cardinal read out a list of those under suspicion.

"Many have connections to my sister," she faltered. "John Bray is her neighbor at Hatfield; Sir Peter Killigrew is her friend; some of these others are her servants. Do you think she herself is involved?"

Pole frowned. "So far, nothing has been said to incriminate her. But Messire de Noailles is up to his neck in it."

"What can we do? Can I expel him from the realm?"

"Your Majesty might do well to consult your Council."

The councillors were all for deporting the ambassador, but they were preempted by King Henri, who swiftly recalled him. Henry Dudley escaped arrest, too, because he was still in France. The ramifications of the plot seemed endless, though, and Mary was deeply troubled. It seemed as if the whole fabric of her government was crumbling, and that her authority carried little weight. She could not help seeing treason everywhere; she could not even trust her councillors or her personal servants.

I need your presence more than ever, she wrote in anguished vein to Philip, and instructed her ambassador to ask him to say frankly when he purposed to return, and if she should continue to maintain the fleet she had kept waiting in readiness to bring him home. *Urge him to comfort me by his presence and remind him that there is no reason yet to despair of his having heirs,* she concluded, worrying that she might soon be past the age for bearing children.

But Philip sent to say that it was necessary for him to remain in Brussels for the present because the King and Queen of Bohemia were expected for a state visit. Mary could have screamed in exasperation when she heard this, but she replied that the royal guests would be most welcome in England. She received no reply. Undeterred, she dispatched Paget to Brussels with letters and rings for Philip and his father—Paget, who was dear to the King and very subtle, and whose words might carry some weight. She waited in suspense for a letter, and was overjoyed when Paget wrote that Philip had been pleased to see him and eager to know that she was in good health. Wonder of wonders, he had assured Paget that he hoped to return to England in a few weeks' time.

Mary's heart overflowed with happiness. The long, lonely months of waiting would soon be at an end. How deeply she had felt the solitude in which her beloved's absence had left her. But soon, her chief joy and comfort in the world would be restored to her, and her unspeakable sadness would be at an end.

So far, none of those accused of involvement in the late conspiracy had mentioned Elizabeth. Her servants were questioned, but denied all knowledge of the plot, declaring that Elizabeth bore only love and truth toward the Queen.

At the beginning of June, Mary sent Lord Hastings and Sir Francis Englefield to Hatfield on the pretext of apologizing to Elizabeth for any disruption caused by the removal of her servants. They took with them a diamond ring from Mary, who would have liked to have Elizabeth herself questioned, and even sent to the Tower, but dared not do either without Philip's approval. She had sent a special courier to ask him for it, for now that he was coming back to her, she would do nothing contrary to his will.

Philip absolutely vetoed any move against Elizabeth. *I pray you send her a kind message,* he replied. *Be loving and gracious to show her that she is not hated, but loved and esteemed by your Majesty.*

Eager to please him, Mary forced aside her suspicions and invited Elizabeth to court. She was relieved when her sister politely declined. It occurred to her that she could send her own trusted servants to Hatfield to replace those of Elizabeth's who were being questioned. They could keep an eye on her sister. Their presence in her household would not only set Mary's mind at rest, but prevent Elizabeth's enemies from accusing her of subversive activities. Surely Philip would approve of that! Elizabeth certainly did, and thanked Mary for her kindness.

Philip was ill. In a panic, Mary sent to him daily to ask how he was progressing, agonized because he could not join her as planned. Yet even when he had recovered, he did not come. She was both crushed and furious. Her hand shaking, she wrote to his father, asking him to send her husband back to her.

The July sunshine seemed to mock her. She could take no pleasure in it, or in anything else. She feared she was sliding into a depression from which she might never emerge, and spent most of her time shut up in her apartments. Sleep still eluded her; dark circles had appeared under her eyes. Her waking hours were spent in tears or in writing pleading letters to Philip.

Terrified that some new conspiracy might be astir, she filled the palace with hosts of armed guards, saw only those few councillors whose loyalty she had no cause to doubt, and permitted just Susan, Jane Dormer, and three other trusted ladies to enter her chamber and attend to her personal needs. At times, she could not help raging against her ungrateful subjects—and against the new French ambassador. To her chagrin, King Henri had sent Messire de Noailles's malicious brother, of whom she had good cause to be suspicious, for he had already plotted against her.

At his first audience, after she had gritted her teeth and welcomed him to England, he regarded her with exaggerated sympathy. "Ah, your Majesty, please accept my commiserations for what is happening in Rome."

Bewildered, she asked, "What *is* happening in Rome?"

"Your Majesty does not know? Then forgive me for being the one to tell you that the King your husband has applied to the Pope for an annulment of your marriage."

Her heart gave a massive jolt and she felt faint. It could not be true! She would have heard of it through the usual diplomatic channels. But what if Philip had approached his Holiness in secret and someone at the Papal curia had leaked the news? Oh, this was terrible! Did she not have enough misery to cope with?

"Mere rumor," she said dismissively, recovering herself, "and I marvel that anyone gives credence to it." Smiling, she dismissed de Noailles, then sought the privacy of her chamber.

Cardinal Pole was proving a great support. He was a good listener, and she always felt she could unburden herself to him. When she visited him at Canterbury that July, she poured out her fears and frustrations about Philip.

"But I am intent on enduring my troubles as patiently as I can," she said, as they strolled in the gardens in the sheltering shadow of the great cathedral.

"Alas, it is the lot of women to wait at home, as St. Paul enjoined," the Cardinal said. "The husband's part is to get, the woman's to keep."

"But we are not villagers," she said gently, "and Philip's wars are not my wars. His place is here with me. England needs an heir. I have lost count of how many times I have told him this."

"But he is coming, Madam. I am sure he will come. You must not fret."

She could not help it. By the time she returned to London, she had worked herself up into a fury at Philip's negligence. The first thing she did at Whitehall was order the removal of his portrait from the council chamber. Her councillors stared at her in astonishment, but she did not care. When the painting had been stood against the wall, she gave it a vicious kick and stalked out, almost running into one of her ladies on the way. "Why does God send evil husbands to good women?" she cried.

Alone in her bedchamber, she wept with mortification, ashamed that she had given way to such a base impulse in public. When she finally roused herself and sat down before her mirror, she caught sight of her reflection and gasped, for she looked dreadful, gaunt and haggard. How could she expect Philip to love her when she resembled an old harridan?

August was stiflingly hot. She could not tolerate the heat and stayed in her apartments for most of the time, not even attending Council meetings. Even with all the windows open, there was no breeze, and on several days she went about clad only in her smock. She was doing her best to eat a careful diet and look to her toilette, for Philip had finally written to tell her to expect him very soon. She wished she could believe it. A long year had passed since she had seen him, and she was sick to her stomach of this interminable waiting. She felt like screaming when her ambassador in Brussels informed her that, instead of hastening to her, Philip had left the city for fear of the plague and gone into the country.

September came in, and still he lingered abroad. But there was news of Courtenay, whose name had often been mentioned in connection with various conspiracies, though without any proof. Mary had rarely read such a tale of woe. He had gone to Venice from Brussels and behaved himself there. Unfortunately, having taken a gondola ride in the lagoon, he had been stranded by a storm and had to wait, soaked to the skin, until a ship rescued him. The experience had left him with a fever, and he had insisted on traveling to Padua, where there were excellent doctors in the university. As he made ready to leave, however, he had fallen down the stairs of his lodgings, and consequently found the journey very uncomfortable indeed. When Mary's ambassador greeted him in Padua, he had found him very ill with a high temperature and summoned two notable doctors, but Courtenay's condition had worsened, and now he was dead.

The ambassador had suspected poison. There had been rumors that Spanish assassins had been hired to kill him. Mary did not believe that. She was sorry for Courtenay, but relieved that this Plantagenet thorn in her side was no more.

"God has once again shown His justice," she told her councillors.

They nodded sagely, but their minds were clearly elsewhere.

"Madam, we are concerned that relations between Spain and the Papacy have deteriorated," Paget said.

Mary's first thought was that de Noailles's sly suggestion that Philip was seeking an annulment from the Pope could not be true.

"The King has done his best to avoid an open confrontation," she said.

"Alas, that time is gone. When he heard that his Holiness was aiding the French in their attempt to drive the Spaniards out of Italy, his Majesty ordered the Duke of Alba to invade the Papal states, sack their towns, and hang their garrisons."

Mary could not speak, she was so appalled. "This is not our quarrel," she blurted out eventually, "but it places me in an impossible situation. I do not wish to be on bad terms with my husband or the Holy See."

"There is no need to be," Paget soothed. "We urge your Majesty to remain neutral."

But how could she? She was married to Philip and duty-bound to support him.

Increasingly, she was feeling a chill wind blowing from the Vatican, as England's relations with Rome became more and more strained. Cardinal Pole was also grieved by the rift, and wrote begging the King not to make war on the Vicar of Christ. To Mary's dismay, Philip ignored him.

"I think it would help if I could discuss the matter with the King in person," the Cardinal told her, regarding her with deep compassion. "It is most frustrating that he is not here. Indeed, I am beginning to be incredulous at his prolonged absence. I do not wish to criticize, Madam, but I am concerned about you."

"I appreciate your kindness," Mary replied, feeling choked. If only Philip cared as much for her well-being.

They were at Croydon Palace, where the Cardinal kept a suite of apartments in readiness for her. Miserably, she returned to them, only to find her ladies staring aghast at some broadsheets that lay strewn around the presence chamber.

"We found them here just now, when we returned from Mass," Susan said.

"They're horrible." Jane Dormer was nearly in tears. "Don't look at them, Madam."

But of course, Mary had to, and was sickened, for they were the worst kind of subversive propaganda. She saw herself depicted as an ugly old crone suckling Spaniards at her sagging breasts, with the legend *"Maria Ruina Angliae"* encircling the picture. It was shocking to be portrayed so cruelly.

Dear God, Philip should be here! She could not go on shouldering her burdens alone.

Another appeal to his father might make all the difference. If he heeded anyone, it would be Charles. Ordering the women to have the offending broadsheets taken away, she sat at her desk, her pen flying across the page. *I wish to beg your Majesty's pardon for my boldness in writing to you at this time, but I implore you to consider the miserable plight into which this country has now fallen. Unless the King comes to remedy matters, not only I myself, but also wiser persons, fear a catastrophe. I am not moved by my personal desire for the King's presence—although I do unspeakably long to have him here—but by the good of my kingdom. I beg of you, urge him to come home to me.*

It was doubtful, she learned soon afterward, that Charles had ever received her letter, for he had already left the Low Countries and traveled to Spain, where he had retired into a monastery to spend his remaining days in prayer. Mary felt bereft. How cruel, at such a critical time, to be deprived of his friendship, protection, and advice.

But maybe someone had seen her letter, for in October, she was pleased to learn that Philip had sent some members of his household back to England. Her spirits soared. This could mean only one thing: that he himself would soon be with her. Her optimism increased when the first Spanish grandees began arriving in London. She only wished she felt better, but all that anguish she had suffered had taken its toll. When Cardinal Pole led the court in a great celebration of the Feast of the Reconciliation at the end of November, she was unable to attend.

Yet she was happy, and in this new, buoyant mood, she even found in her heart some warmth toward Elizabeth. She decided there was no longer any reason to keep her under close surveillance, and informed her agents that their services were no longer required at Hatfield. At the same time, she allowed Elizabeth's own servants to rejoin her household.

Philip wrote to say that he was again considering the Duke of Savoy as a husband for Elizabeth. *It would be advisable to marry her to a Catholic prince. The Duke's inheritance has been seized by the French; he might be more amenable now to a match. And he would never allow Elizabeth to show friendship to King Henri, or attempt to restore the Protestant religion in England.*

Mary read this with mixed feelings. It was an ideal alliance, yet why did Philip have to make it so obvious that he was planning ahead for when she herself was dead?

She summoned Elizabeth to London to discuss the proposal. Judging by the state in which she arrived, riding through London with a great company in velvet coats and chains, her sister was also looking to the future. It was so easy to win popularity when you were the heir—and so hard to keep it when you had to make difficult decisions as a monarch.

There was no official welcome, although Mary received her as graciously and affectionately as she could. They sat together by the fire in her privy chamber, Mary noting the becoming cut of Elizabeth's black velvet gown, which showed off her slender figure and flaming red hair to advantage. Oh, to be blessed again with youth! Beside her sister, she felt old, dumpy, and overdressed in her purple gown and profusion of jewels.

Presently, when they had caught up on their news, Mary brought up the subject of a match with Savoy.

"No!" cried Elizabeth, and burst into tears. "I have no desire for a husband. I would rather die!"

Mary was moved to see her so distressed, and puzzled at her vehemence, but she was determined that Elizabeth should accept Savoy.

"Could you not bring yourself at least to consider it?" she asked.

"No, Madam, I will not," declared Elizabeth. "I *cannot.*"

"Perhaps you should go now to Somerset House, where I have had lodgings prepared for you, and calm down," Mary said. "We will talk another time."

When they met again early in December, Elizabeth was as adamant as ever that she would not marry Savoy. This time, Mary lost patience with her.

"The marriages of princes are not a matter of personal inclination," she seethed. "You are my heir, and you will marry to my advantage, without complaint! I have had enough of these histrionics."

"You can't make me!" Elizabeth flared.

"I am your Queen!" Mary cried. "You are bound to obey me. Or would you rather I have you disinherited by Parliament?"

"You would not dare!" Elizabeth countered, the hooded eyes glittering. The mask had fallen away now.

"I most certainly would." Mary's blood was up. "Margaret Douglas would make an excellent queen."

"Not that termagant!" Elizabeth spat. "Parliament would never allow it. Our father specifically excluded her line from the Act of Succession and his will."

"What Parliament makes, it can unmake," Mary reminded her. "And if you carry on like this, I will send you to the Tower to cool your heels. Don't force me to it! In fact, I think it best if you go home to Hatfield."

Elizabeth started laughing at her. "We both know, Sister, that the King would never allow you to do either of those things, and nor would Parliament."

"Get out, before I have your head, and be damned to Philip!" Mary screamed, and Elizabeth made a hasty exit.

She would disinherit her! She would, Philip or no Philip! In a determined mood, she hastened to her library, where she began searching for precedents. She wrote to him, telling him what she planned to do, saying she was going to seek legal advice. His reply came winging back. She was to do nothing of the sort, but she must insist that Elizabeth marry Savoy. There could be no question of disinheriting her sister; she must instead acknowledge her formally as her heir. But that was a prospect from which Mary now shrank.

She was still brooding over how to proceed when Cardinal Pole came to her. "Madam, I bring grave news. I have learned from my contacts in Rome that the Pope is refusing to deal with any matters concerning England because he believes you to be as guilty of offenses against the Holy See as the King your husband. He has said that you both deserve to be excommunicated."

Incensed and horrified, Mary leaped to her feet. "This is intolerable! I have always been a true daughter of the Church. I am leading what amounts to a crusade to stamp out heresy in this realm. And this is how his Holiness treats me! Well, I think it is time that England joins Spain in what I now realize is a just war."

When she wrote to Philip of her fury toward Rome, it was what he had clearly been longing to hear. There was a new warmth in his letters, and before long, secret agents were moving between him and Mary on a daily basis. By Christmas, most of his household had returned to England to await his coming. In an ebullient mood, and trying to quell unworthy thoughts that he was just using her to gain a victory, Mary moved her court to Greenwich. At Philip's request, she swallowed her pride and invited Elizabeth, who was to remain at court until his return. She had no room in her heart now for jealousy. Instead, she gave generous gifts of plate to her sister. All she could think about was her imminent reunion with her husband. Her heart was singing with joy.

But there was little else to rejoice about. The kingdom was seething with discontent. It caused Mary much distress to realize that her subjects blamed her for it, and that her popularity had declined still further. When she thought of the tide of affection that had brought her to the throne, she could not help but cry. But three bad harvests in succession, and rising unemployment caused by the enclosure of farmland under her predecessors, were not her fault. It horrified her that many of her subjects were dying of malnutrition and starvation; her treasury was all but empty, yet she did all she could to help them. Even so, people were seeing the ills that were befalling the kingdom as God's judgment on her; and it was no secret that many were looking to Elizabeth as their deliverer. Dear God, Mary prayed, let me bear just one child, just one heir for England, so that my great work may be carried on, and that the people may see that You really do smile upon me, and that the measures I have taken have always been for the common good.

Yet still the heretics proved stubborn; still the burnings continued. Mary could hardly bear to face the fact they were not working as a deterrent.

"Ensure that my officers act more rigorously in punishing offenders," she instructed her Council, refusing to acknowledge the dismay in their faces.

Chapter 38

1557

In January, King Henri broke the truce he and Philip had signed, and mounted an offensive on the Habsburg city of Douai. Hearing of this, Mary summoned her Council and demanded that England go to war with Spain against the French, as she had promised Philip she would. The lords were horrified.

"It is not possible, Madam!" Paget thundered. "We cannot afford a war. This quarrel does not involve us, so why should we impoverish this kingdom to support the interests of a foreign power?"

"Might I remind your Majesty that England is not bound by treaty to support the King in his wars," Arundel cut in, and there were vehement growls of approval.

Mary consulted Cardinal Pole, but he was at one with the Council.

What did they expect her to do? Her duty was to support her husband.

Her mind was made up for her when she received a letter from Philip making it quite clear—although it was not worded so bluntly—that his arrival in England would be dependent on her promising to declare war on the French. Aware that she was being offered an ultimatum and devastated at the realization that she her-self meant so little to him, she promised to do all she could to persuade the Council to agree. They must agree! It was the only thing that would bring him back to her. Besides, declaring war was her prerogative.

The lords looked at her as if she was mad when she told them of her decision.

"Does your Majesty wish to bankrupt your kingdom?" Paget asked.

"It will not come to that," she said. "I am confident that, together, England and Spain will be victorious. And think what a great victory would do for morale in this land."

She left them then, refusing to listen to any arguments. She gave orders for the building of new ships to reinforce her navy, but stopped short of declaring war yet, fearing that it might be a step too far in the face of such vehement opposition.

But then, at last, came the news for which she had waited eighteen long months. Philip had left Brussels. He was on his way.

Twelve days later, having been informed that the King's ship had docked at Dover, Mary was waiting at Greenwich, pacing the gallery and trembling with anticipation. She had done her best to look comely for him, donning her richest gown and even allowing Susan to apply a little color to her cheeks. She was looking as attractive as she would ever look, and praying that all would be well between her and Philip, and that he was coming home for good.

The clock chimed five. He would be here soon!

When the guns sounded a salute, she ran to the window, her heart thumping alarmingly. There was the royal barge pulling in at the landing stage. Picking up her heavy skirts, she ran from the gallery, down the stairs and out into the open air, then passed between the ranks of courtiers to where Philip stood on the landing stage, magnificent in black velvet embroidered in gold. Heedless of the onlookers, she threw her arms around him and kissed him heartily, reveling in the feeling of his manly body pressed to her heart. All around them, people were cheering and crying, "God save the King and Queen!"

When she finally let him go, he was gazing at her amusedly. "Well, Madam, I did not anticipate such a warm welcome!" he de-

clared, raising her hand to his lips. If he found her unappealing, he
gave no sign. Together, hand in hand, they turned and walked toward
the palace. But when they reached the great doors and Mary turned
to acknowledge the ovation of the crowd, she saw at once that only a
small retinue had disembarked in Philip's wake—and froze. For that
made it abundantly clear that he did not intend to stay long in England.

He made his purpose plain over supper that evening. He was here
chiefly to discuss joint strategies for the war with France, and to
conclude Elizabeth's marriage to the Duke of Savoy. Mary sat there,
waiting in vain for one word of love or affection, or even an acknowl-
edgment of her support for him. The delicious dishes she had ordered to delight his palate tasted like sawdust. Unable to eat, she
laid down her knife and fork. It evidently did not concern Philip
that her councillors were opposed to England going to war on behalf
of Spain, and she dared not tell him that she herself would have preferred not to pursue the Savoy marriage.

The next day, she gave orders that all the bells in London were to
be rung in celebration of the King's return and *Te Deum*s sung in
every church. At Richmond, she organized a splendid festival in
Philip's honor, to which Elizabeth came, arriving in a royal barge
bedecked with flowers. The King and Queen then rode in state to
Whitehall, with Elizabeth at their side. Her sister's presence evoked
a resounding response from the Londoners, and Mary struggled to
keep the smile on her face. She could not wait for Elizabeth to return
to Hatfield.

No sooner had she departed than Mary and Philip welcomed to
court his bastard half-sister, Margaret, Duchess of Parma, and his
cousin, Christina of Denmark, Duchess of Lorraine. Philip met them
at Whitehall Stairs and escorted them up to the presence chamber to
be presented to Mary. She peered with interest at Christina, who, at
the age of sixteen, had been proposed as a bride for her father, King
Henry, but had astounded everyone by refusing, declaring that if she
had two heads, one would be at his Grace's disposal. Looking at this
beautiful, spirited woman, Mary could well imagine it!

The purpose of the ladies' visit was to collect Elizabeth and escort
her to Savoy for her marriage to the Duke. But Mary had decided

that the marriage could not go ahead. Braving Philip's evident anger, she was adamant that her sister could not come to court or receive the duchesses at Hatfield. In private, she told him that she needed more time to persuade Elizabeth to frame her mind to the match.

She was deeply uneasy about the presence of the fair Christina at her court, having noticed her husband's admiring glances. She had long feared that he might fall in love with another woman, and as she watched him dancing with the Duchess and becoming animated in her company, she burned with jealousy. Yet she could not complain, for were these not the normal courtesies due to visiting royalty?

She was not feeling well. She was still sleeping badly, and she had a persistent toothache. She had expected her melancholy to be cured by Philip's arrival, but she continued to feel low. In the privacy of her chamber, she gave way to tears, for this was not proving to be the second honeymoon she had happily anticipated. In confidence, she consulted her doctors, who ordered that she be bled from the foot to relieve the evil humors in her blood, but it made no difference; in fact, it left her looking pale and emaciated.

She could not fault Philip for being inattentive, however. He visited her bed regularly, as aware as she was that producing an heir was vital. But the process, far from being an act of love, was brisk and efficient, and it always left her wanting more. At least, she begged God, let her conceive a child!

If her barrenness was a constant sorrow to her as a woman, in a queen it was a reproach, a sign that God had withdrawn His favor from her. No one seemed to believe it was possible now for her to have children, and day by day, she saw the diminishing of her authority and the respect it should have commanded. She worried constantly about the succession. It was vital to the stability of the country that this question be resolved, yet she could not bring herself formally to acknowledge Elizabeth as her successor.

"It is anathema to me to think that the bastard child of a criminal who was punished as a public strumpet might inherit my throne," she confided to Philip one night as they lay in the darkness.

"But Parliament has named her your heir," Philip murmured. "She is in a strong position."

Thanks to you! She nearly said it. He had protected Elizabeth from the first.

"She has the love of the people," he went on relentlessly.

"They do not know her!" she hissed. "She is proud and haughty. She knows she was born of such a mother, yet she does not consider herself of inferior degree to myself. She prides herself on our father and I'm told she says she resembles him more than I do. It is an intolerable insult, especially when one considers that she might not be his daughter at all!"

"You don't really believe that, do you?" Philip asked wearily. "She looks remarkably like King Henry in his portraits."

Mary rounded on him. "Why do you always champion her?"

"I think it politic to keep her sweet."

She was about to make a tart retort, but she did not want to rile Philip or sound shrewish. What she dreaded more than anything was that he might leave her again. She could not bear to contemplate another separation.

She turned to him, reaching out her hand and laying it on his. She longed for him to take her in his arms again, to whisper words of love and share with her that special intimacy they had once enjoyed. But he was already asleep.

Philip had not been in England a week before he began to put pressure on Mary to declare war on France.

"You promised me you would," he reminded her.

"I know," she said, panicking inwardly, for she knew she faced stubborn resistance from her councillors, who remained hotly opposed to England becoming involved. "There are many things to be taken into consideration."

Philip glared at her. "If you let me down now, Mary, I might as well go back to Brussels. And if I do, I will never return."

"No!" she cried, agonized at the thought. "I will insist. I vow it."

She summoned her Council and, in Philip's presence, set out the arguments in favor of war. They listened gravely, but asked for time in which to consider the matter. Two days later, she entered the council chamber and knew from their long faces that their answer would not be what she wanted to hear.

Paget, as usual, acted as spokesman. "Madam, England cannot, and should not, become involved in a foreign conflict."

She flung every argument she could think of at them, growing increasingly agitated and desperate. Without their support, she could hardly declare war. But they were immovable.

She dared not look at Philip. She could not face his anger. After the meeting, he took her aside.

"I am sorry, truly," she babbled. "I need more time to persuade them."

He looked at her skeptically. "See them one by one, in private. Persuade them of the necessity for England to go to war. Threaten them with death or the loss of their goods and estates if they do not consent to our will."

Terrified that he would abandon her if she refused, she made herself do as he bade her. She did not like making threats, and she feared to alienate her councillors, but Philip must come first.

In April, she bowed again to his demands and summoned Elizabeth to court, knowing that Philip had every intention of forcing her to marry the Duke of Savoy.

"I can take her back to Brussels when I leave," he had said, striking fear into Mary's heart.

But Elizabeth once more flatly refused to agree to the marriage. She knew that the Council would never allow him to take the heir to the throne abroad, even if she or Mary wished it.

"She will obey," Philip told Mary, "especially when I tell her that you will acknowledge her right to succeed if she accepts Savoy."

Mary shrank from doing that, yet she need not have concerned herself, for Elizabeth persisted in her refusal.

"I'm sure the Duke would be happy to come and live in England with you, for he has no lands of his own," Philip told her, beginning to lose patience.

Elizabeth looked desperately at Mary.

"I do not think this is the right match for her," Mary said.

Philip glared at her. "Well, I do, and if you support her in her obstinacy, you will be failing in your duty of obedience to me."

Mary felt winded. "Very well," she murmured. She turned to Elizabeth, who looked like an animal caught in a trap. "You have heard what the King says."

"No, I will not do it!" Elizabeth cried. "You can't make me."

"It's true," Mary said. "Neither of us can make her marry against her will."

But Philip was adamant. "You can command her to do as she is bid. You are the Queen."

It was Mary's turn to look desperately at Elizabeth. "You heard his Majesty. Will you not obey him, for my sake?"

"I am sorry, Madam, but I do not wish to marry at all," Elizabeth declared, "not even if I were to be offered the greatest prince in all Europe." Torn between relief and fear of what Philip might do, Mary dismissed her before he could say anything.

"She will marry Savoy," he growled, when Elizabeth had gone.

"Just let her come around to the idea," Mary urged. She knew she was only playing for time.

Later that month, she visited Elizabeth at Hatfield, and was royally entertained. Together, they watched a bear-baiting and a Latin play performed by the boys of St. Paul's School. Then Elizabeth played flawlessly on the virginals. Mary found she was enjoying herself. United in their opposition to the Savoy match, she and her sister were closer than they had been in years.

When she returned to court, she was relieved to say farewell to the two Habsburg duchesses. But Philip was still in a dark mood. Then Mary had word that Anna of Cleves was mortally ill. Greatly saddened, and feeling guilty that there had been a distance between them after that nastiness with Wyatt's rebellion—how could she ever have believed that Anna had been involved?—she placed the palace of Chelsea at her stepmother's disposal. It lay in a healthy rural location by the River Thames, and Anna could gaze out on its beautiful gardens, which would be looking their best at this time of year. Mary would have liked to see her, but was informed that she was too ill to receive visitors.

At the end of May, Philip burst into Mary's closet. "The Pope," he seethed, "has excommunicated me!"

Mary stared at him in horror. "No. No!"

"That's not all." He drummed his fingers on the desk, a habit he had when angry. "He has recalled all his legates, including Cardinal Pole, from my realms and dominions."

Mary's hand flew to her mouth. Excommunication—what every Christian dreaded. She tried to gather her thoughts and think what it would mean to Philip to be cast out from the Church and condemned to eternal damnation. He could not go to Mass, make confession, or receive any of the sacraments. If she bore him an heir, he could not attend its christening. If he died, his body would lie unburied. He could not be crowned. In her anguish, she realized that she would have to choose between the obedience she owed her husband and that which she must render to Christ's vicar on earth.

And then she saw that God had shown her a way out of her cruel dilemma. England would now be forced to take sides; there could be no question of her remaining neutral. It was a heartbreaking decision, but her love for Philip won out.

"We will declare war!" she said, rising. Philip's eyes met hers. At last, they were as one.

She harangued her councillors into submission. She and Philip wrote to the Pope, protesting at his treatment of Cardinal Pole, whom he had now deprived of his legatine status, and reminding him of all the good work the Cardinal had carried out in the cause of the Church. They warned his Holiness that without Pole, the Church's welfare in England would be severely endangered. The Council wrote in similar vein, wishing to avert a war, as did the Cardinal himself. Everyone thought that Paul would give in to pressure and restore him as legate. The councillors, however, were still proving stubborn in regard to going to war.

"The King will finance it out of his own funds," Mary assured them. They looked mutinous. But divine providence played into her hands when news reached her that one Thomas Stafford, a sprig off the Plantagenet tree, had invaded Yorkshire. It was a minor incident, easily dealt with—until the Council received intelligence that the French had backed it. Nervous and angry, the lords backed down, and in June, Mary declared war on France. That same day, she sent a herald to the French court to throw down the gauntlet before King Henri.

A jubilant Philip immediately plunged into preparations for an offensive, enthusiastically supported by young English noblemen eager for military glory and—in the case of pardoned offenders such as Henry Dudley, Sir Peter Carew, and Sir James Crofts—the chance of rehabilitation. The fleet was placed on battle alert, having been augmented on Philip's orders with two new ships, the *Philip and Mary* and the *Mary Rose,* named after King Henry's famous warship, which had sunk off Southampton twelve years ago. True to his word, Philip sent to Spain for another fleet of ships and chests full of gold to defray the government's expenses. He was here, there, and everywhere, making ready, and Mary felt he had gone from her already, for she knew that when the Spanish ships came, he would sail away to war.

But she also understood it was crucial that he go. The Pope had ignored her pleas, failed to restore Cardinal Pole, and appointed in his place Friar William Peto. Mary knew Peto well, for he had been her mother's confessor, and her own when she was a child, and he had chosen exile after openly preaching against her father's Great Matter. He had returned to England when she became Queen, and was now living in quiet retirement in the restored convent of the Observant Friars at Greenwich. She suspected that he was no more keen on becoming Papal legate than she was to have him replace the Cardinal, whose counsel she would miss sorely.

Friar Peto was a devout man, but he was now over eighty and losing his wits. In her fury at his appointment, Mary refused to allow Paul's nuncio to enter England. To her mind, the Pope was giving every sign of being motivated entirely by vindictiveness and envy, qualities that rode ill with his role as Christ's earthly representative.

She summoned the Cardinal. "I will not allow you to leave England," she told him. "You have not yet received your papers of re-call, so you cannot be accused of disobedience to the Holy See. And I have ensured that those papers will never reach you."

He looked doubtful, for he was a good man, an upright man. But he agreed to stay. The next they heard was that the Pope had ap-pointed Peto a cardinal; but Peto refused the honor and returned his red hat to Rome.

On 20 June, the returning Spanish fleet was sighted in the Channel, and Mary watched with a heavy heart as preparations for Philip's departure began in earnest. All too soon, it was time for him to leave.

They left Whitehall early in July and traveled down to Dover. On the way, they stayed overnight at Sittingbourne and Canterbury, and each night they shared a bed, hoping to conceive an heir—and Mary prayed for some word of love while there was still time. But when his duty was done, Philip had other things on his mind.

"It is vital that Elizabeth be married without delay to Savoy. Just think what might happen if she took a husband of her own choosing. It could convulse the whole kingdom into confusion, so do not tarry in this matter."

"I hear you," Mary whispered. "I will do my best." But she would not press the matter. She did not know how she would even function when Philip was gone.

Chapter 39

1557

It was not worth going to bed. In the small hours, Mary had her women dress her in her most becoming gown, the purple velvet one with the gold embroidery. She wanted Philip to take with him the memory of her looking her best. He was waiting for her, impatient to be away. It was approaching three o'clock. They processed down to the quayside, where his flagship was waiting, and then it was time. He looked at her, as if remembering that she was there, then took her in his arms and kissed her. She clung to him, unable to let go, aware that she might never see him again. There were so many things she wanted to say, yet her tongue seemed to be tied—and, in truth, she had not the courage, for she feared he might not reciprocate in kind, and that was the last thing she needed.

"God keep you," he said, and kissed her lips.

"May He bring you safely home to me," she murmured, finding her voice. "I pray He sends you a speedy victory."

She watched, fighting back tears, as he boarded the ship, then stood there as the anchor was raised and it sailed in stately fashion away into the night.

A week later, Mary was signing orders for the burnings of yet more heretics when Paget informed her that Philip had summoned his entire Spanish household to join him. With a sinking heart, she realized that he had no intention of returning to her soon. Maybe he believed that this war would not be over quickly. Well, she could deal with that, for it needed to be fought. It was her suspicion that he might not come back that tormented her.

One thing cheered her. He had left his confessor, Father Fresneda, to comfort her—or so she thought. But when it soon became clear that the man had instructions to persuade her to carry out Philip's wishes, she felt desperate, and then angry.

"No, I will not acknowledge the Lady Elizabeth as my heir!" she snapped. "She is neither my sister nor the daughter of King Henry." She was not sure that she still believed that, but it effectively killed off any arguments.

"But, Madam, at least show favor to her, for the sake of peace within your realm."

"No," Mary said. "She is born of an infamous woman who greatly outraged the Queen my mother, and myself."

She dismissed Fresneda, then burst into tears of distress, for resisting Philip would certainly not bring him back to her. She wrote to him, explaining that while she had listened to all his arguments with a true and sincere heart, she knew she was in the right. *That which my conscience holds, it has held these twenty-four years*—as long as Elizabeth had been in the world.

Fresneda persisted. He was eloquent and learned, and frequently got the better of Mary in arguments, but still she would not change her mind. Even when Philip wrote to complain of her continuing obstinacy and made it clear that he was extremely displeased, she held her nerve, thinking it fortunate that his attention would soon be diverted away from English affairs.

In July, the Council received a dispatch from England's ambassador at the Vatican, warning that the Pope, believing that Cardinal Pole was a secret agent acting on Philip's behalf, had trumped up a charge of heresy against him and would have him arrested as soon as he set foot in Rome. Pole was summoned and looked aghast when he heard that.

"It is reported that your close associate, Cardinal Morone, was apprehended in May by the Inquisition on a charge of heresy," Paget informed him, as Mary looked on, appalled. "The Pope then made it clear that he believed your Eminence to be guilty also."

"He knows he has no good reason for recalling me," Pole said. "This false charge of heresy has but given him a pretext for doing so."

"But he has instructed the Inquisition to proceed against you."

"This is preposterous!" the Cardinal exploded. "It is true that I have openly supported reform within the Church, but my orthodoxy has never yet been called into question, nor have I ever given any cause for it to be."

"It seems the Pope believes that you are working secretly on the King's behalf to destroy him."

"In truth, I fear his Holiness is losing his mind!" Pole exclaimed. "I shall send one of my clerics to plead my case with him."

Mary herself wrote to Pope Paul, expressing her indignation and disbelief that he had taken such action against the Cardinal. *He has given your Holiness no cause for offense and has a record of outstanding and distinguished service to the English Church. He does not deserve to be recalled in such a manner.*

In a militant mood, she sent Pembroke with a force of seven thousand men over the sea to Philip, who had laid siege to the town of Saint-Quentin in northern France. Soon afterward, she learned that his forces had routed a French army sent by King Henri to relieve it. The news sent her hurrying to her oratory to give thanks. Victory would be Philip's. She knew it in her bones.

Her joy turned to sorrow when she heard that Anna of Cleves had died. Filled with remorse, she gave orders that Anna be buried in Westminster Abbey with great ceremony, and commissioned one of her countrymen to come to England and fashion an elaborate tomb.

Philip had stormed into Saint-Quentin and captured it. In England, Mary again gave heartfelt thanks to God for his miraculous victory and prayed that it would increase his popularity with her subjects.

There seemed little sign of that, however, even after news of his seizure of other towns and fortresses filtered across the Channel.

What happened next, she learned only piecemeal, her heart in her mouth at every turn. The Pope, furious to see Philip triumphant, had denounced him, whereupon Philip had ordered the Duke of Alba to march on Rome and force the Holy Father to make peace. Acting on the King's instructions, the Duke had knelt at Paul's feet and begged his pardon for having invaded his territories, giving the Pope no choice but to accept Philip's terms. An uneasy peace had been negotiated, and Mary ordered that *Te Deum*s be sung in London. By October, Pembroke's valiant English troops were on their way home, and Philip's army was seeking out winter quarters. It did not look as if he would be coming to England.

Feeling desolate, Mary was further dismayed to learn that Paul had refused to drop the charges against Cardinal Pole and ignored the anguished letters she sent him. He seemed to have persuaded himself that Pole was a secret Lutheran and had for years been involved in a treacherous conspiracy against the Church. Yet, for reasons known only to himself, he stayed his hand and did not press any charges against the Cardinal.

"He has probably realized that I would never allow you to go to Rome to answer them," Mary told Pole.

He regarded her sadly. "I wish he *had* pressed charges, Madam, because for the rest of my life, the fear of heresy proceedings will hang over me."

She took his hand. "Do not let that distress you, dear friend. The world knows the truth of it, and I will be your protector."

It was now nearly six months since Philip had left, months in which Mary's courses had become erratic and then dwindled to nothing. When she finally confided in her ladies, they asked her if she could be with child.

"It's not unheard of for a woman to bleed a little in the early stages," Susan told her.

It began to dawn on Mary that she might be right. She waited a while, and still there was no blood. When she felt her belly, her fingers detected a slight swelling. Joyously, she embraced the truth. She was with child! God had vouchsafed her this great gift, and this time He would not fail her. And if anything was going to bring Philip home, this would.

When she announced that she was truly with child, she told everyone that she was absolutely certain of her condition. Congratulations were showered on her, although she could detect skepticism in a few faces, for doubtless some thought there was no child at all, and that she was deluding herself, like the last time. So she made it known that she had very sure signs of pregnancy. By her reckoning, the babe would be born in March.

Philip replied quickly, expressing his satisfaction at the news. *It has given me greater joy than I can express to you, for it is the one thing in the world I have most desired, and which is of the greatest importance for the cause of religion and the welfare of the realm. I therefore render thanks to Our Lord for this mercy He has shown me.*

His response was not as loving as Mary had hoped for. Possibly he too entertained private doubts, or thought it a ruse to make him return to her. But I *am* with child, I *am,* she told herself, studying her reflection in the mirror. She still looked slender, yet beneath the stiff skirts she could feel the babe growing. She was counting down the weeks until March.

1558

That winter witnessed the escalation of an epidemic of influenza that quickly spread across the land, taking numerous souls in its wake. It had swept in from Europe the previous year, having brought many to their long home. Sufferers had strange aches, pains in the head, and fever. Mary's doctors were very concerned, because the illness was known to lead to miscarriages, so she took their advice and kept to her lodgings as much as possible.

The cold season had also brought a natural lull in the fighting abroad, and she was hoping that the spring would see a decisive victory and an end to the war. She was shocked when, early in January, Susan shook her awake in the depths of night and told her that her councillors were insisting on seeing her. Her heart missed a beat and she thought she felt the babe flinch in her womb as her bleary-eyed ladies dragged on her furred night robe and brushed her hair.

The lords were waiting in the presence chamber, their faces grave. "Your Majesty, we apologize for disturbing your rest, but the French have mounted a surprise attack on Calais and taken it."

Mary felt faint. "Blessed Mother of God, not Calais? These are the heaviest tidings to England that ever was heard of." Calais had been the last remaining bastion of the Plantagenet Empire in France and had been in English hands for over two hundred years.

She sank down on her throne, burning with humiliation. That Calais should be lost under her watch was intolerable. It was hard to grasp the news, harder still to imagine the reactions of her subjects. For the rest of her life, she knew, she would remember this as the worst failure of her reign. And it was her fault, for had she not defied her councillors and involved England in her husband's war, it would never have happened. It would be she, justly, who would bear the blame.

She hardly dared look the lords in the eye, fearing to read reproach or worse there. "Is there nothing that can be done?" she asked. "Surely we have the resources to recapture the town?"

"We will look into that immediately, Madam," said Paget, but she could tell he was not optimistic. And indeed, in the morning, as she had feared, it became apparent that England did not have the where-withal to reclaim Calais. Her weakness would be exposed for all Christendom to see.

Catastrophic as it was, the loss of Calais was not the only evil afflicting the land. Despite the first good harvest for years, which put an end to the famine, the kingdom was in a desperate state.

"I have never seen this realm weaker in strength, money, men, and riches," Paget addressed Mary across the council board, almost accusingly. "I love my country and countrymen, as your Majesty knows, but I am ashamed of them both. We are seeing nothing but crime, treason, rioting, heresy, bankruptcy, and disease, and now we have lost our only stronghold abroad. Madam, your subjects are dispirited and exhausted. Justice is not executed. The people are out of order. They protest against the heresy laws. All things cost dearly. We are at war with France and in conflict with the Scots. The French King threatens this realm. There is no steady friendship abroad."

Mary stared at him, aghast at such an outburst. Yet it was all true. But how had these things come to pass, when she had striven always to do the right thing and meant nothing but good to her people?

"What can we do to make things better?" she asked.

"Put an end to this ill-advised war," he replied firmly. "The King did not lift a finger to save Calais, so why should we fight his wars for him?"

Mary would have liked to protest, for the last thing she wanted to do was tell Philip that she had ordered England's withdrawal from the war, but she knew she was standing on unsolid ground.

It was a relief therefore to receive a letter from him informing her that he had actually done what he could to avert disaster in the limited time available. *The French attacked so suddenly,* he explained. *I cannot express the sorrow I have felt for the loss of Calais.*

As the news spread, Mary was vilified. Arundel slapped on the council board a seditious pamphlet that described her as an utter destroyer of her subjects, a lover of foreigners, a traitor to God and her country, and a persecutor of saints. Her eyes widened.

"Who wrote this? And who published it?"

"Alas, Madam, we do not know. There are many such broadsheets."

"Tell my officers to redouble their efforts to track down the offenders. I will not tolerate such calumnies!" Mary was finding it hard to suppress the pain the unknown libeler had caused her.

The epidemic was still raging, the death toll still rising, giving the Protestants cause to say that it was a plague sent by God to punish the Queen for her sins. Mary was brooding upon this when the Count de Feria was announced. Philip had sent him to England formally to congratulate her on her pregnancy. He was a swarthy, bustling little man, who had a disconcerting habit of staring at her belly, making her feel uncomfortable.

It was not long before she deduced the real reason for his coming.

"My master asks that your Majesty send more men to France," he said, to her consternation.

She quickly recovered herself. "I will discuss the matter with my Council. All that matters to me is that his Majesty returns to me victorious, and soon."

Her condition was making her feel ill. It was not like last time, which was how she knew that she really was with child. She felt sick at odd times and her stomach was now quite distended. The infant was quiet, although it moved gently from time to time, and she could feel it, a hard lump inside her. Truth to tell, she was over-whelmed by all her troubles and the strain of her royal duties. Her court was rife with squabbles, her councillors divided by dissensions, and there was only herself to control them all—yet she was in no fit state to do so.

She could have done without Elizabeth visiting the court at the end of February. She received her graciously enough, and was touched when her sister presented her with her a layette of baby clothes she had made herself. "For your little knave," she smiled. "I had to come. I want to be here when he arrives."

Mary wasn't sure that she wanted Elizabeth nearby, but she could hardly send her away now.

March came in and she took to her chamber to await the birth of her child. They told her that Friar Peto had died. Cardinal Pole was carrying on as before, but she was dismayed to hear that his health was failing and that he was too weak to assist her in the burdensome task of governing England. It could not have happened at a worse time.

Philip wrote regularly, always asking solicitously after her health. He urged her to make her will, just to be on the safe side. It fright-ened her; was he again thinking that she might die in childbirth, as he had before? March was all but over when she had the will drawn up. And still her babe had not arrived. She was beginning to feel worried.

She bequeathed her kingdom to the heirs of her body, designating Philip regent if she died before their child came of age. *I leave to my husband my chief jewel, the love of my subjects, with the jewels he gave me at our marriage.* He and Pole were to be her executors. She concluded with a long list of generous bequests, in which she remembered the London poor, destitute scholars, and prisoners.

April came in, breezy and chill, and the days dragged on with no sign of her going into labor. Meanwhile, the King of Sweden dispatched an envoy to England offering his son, Eric, Duke of Finland, as a husband for Elizabeth. Mary sent to ask Elizabeth what she thought of the proposal. Back came the reply: Elizabeth had no desire to marry anyone at all; she wished to remain a virgin.

Mary wondered if this proceeded from maidenly modesty; it was hard to believe that her sister did not want to wed, especially if some honorable match were to be offered her.

When Philip learned of the King of Sweden's approach, he wrote to complain that Mary was supposed to be promoting the match with Savoy; it was time, he said, that she reconsidered her objections to it. Yet she would only agree to lay the matter before Parliament, knowing that the Lords and Commons would not sanction a forced marriage. But the cool tone of Philip's letter had distressed her greatly; it was unkind of him to be bothering her with this quarrel right now. Tears filling her eyes, she wrote to him: *I beseech you in all humility to put off the business until your return. For otherwise you will be angry with me, and that will be worse than death for me, for I have tasted your anger all too often, to my great sorrow.*

Philip ignored that, and Mary, upset and offended, continued to express interest in the Swedish proposal. It was now May, and although her belly was still swollen, she had started bleeding, and wondered if she had miscarried. The doctors said not, yet they could not explain what had happened; but there would be no child.

She had to summon all her reserves of Christian resignation to counter her bitter disappointment, but it was hard, desperately hard. She had the empty cradle taken from her bedchamber at once, being unable to bear the sight of it. She could not stop crying. She would never bear an heir now, she feared. She had lost Philip for good.

Ill though he was, Cardinal Pole took it upon himself to give Philip the news. To Mary's heartfelt surprise, she received a loving letter from her husband, apologizing for not having been able to come and see her as he had hoped, and saying how impressed he was by her bravery. *I have asked Cardinal Pole to cheer you in your loneliness,* he ended. So he did understand how unhappy his absence made her.

She could take little comfort in his words. They were not enough. She had moved to Richmond, thinking a change of scene might be the best thing, but she was sinking helplessly into a depression so terrible that she could not leave her chamber and lay unmoving and withdrawn in her bed. She felt weak, but she could not sleep. This was more than her usual bothersome ailments. Her physicians said it was natural for a woman whose hopes for a child had just been dashed to feel melancholy, but that was little comfort to Mary. In her misery, she imagined that everyone was against her. When she did finally drag herself out of bed, she called for a breastplate for protection, fearing that someone might try to assassinate her.

Not even Philip's letters could lift her spirits. She felt a deep sense of failure. When she died, Elizabeth would succeed her, and she knew in her bones that her sister was a heretic at heart. It was hard to come to terms with the fact that her great work would die with her. If only she could leave her throne to Margaret Lennox, or even Katherine Grey. But she knew that neither her Council nor Parliament would wear that, and certainly Philip would not.

She could not forget the loss of Calais. But her profoundest grief was the absence of her husband. How could he be so far away when she needed his presence so desperately? She had hoped he would be home before now, but he kept saying that affairs of state were keeping him from her. *I have greatly desired to come, and I know it would have given both of us much happiness had I been able to do so.*

The warmth in those words left Mary hopeful that he would soon return to her, and she gave orders that a fleet be kept waiting in readiness to escort him across the Channel, and that lodgings on the road between Dover and London be prepared for him.

Then she learned, to her annoyance, that Count de Feria had been visiting Elizabeth, who had returned to Hatfield. What had been his purpose? And what had they been discussing? It troubled her. Yet the likeliest explanation was that he had been told by Philip to persuade her to accept the Duke of Savoy. Although it had been most remiss of him to go to Hatfield without her permission, she dared not risk alienating Philip by complaining.

What really jolted her, though, was a letter from her husband in which he suggested that she make Elizabeth give an undertaking to uphold the Catholic faith when she became Queen. Did he think that she herself was dying? She knew that he had all along had an eye to what might happen afterward, and that he had been storing up credit with Elizabeth for when the time came. It hurt deeply. It made her feel redundant and of no consequence.

She could not bring herself to name her sister as her heir.

Chapter 40

1558

In August, Mary left Richmond and moved to Whitehall. Soon afterward, she began to suffer from an intermittent fever, which she feared might be influenza, for the epidemic had lasted all through the cold, wet summer. She was also bringing up a lot of black bile, and it troubled her that she could still feel that hard lump in her stomach, the lump she thought had been a baby. It had not diminished; in fact, it had grown bigger, and she was too terrified to consult her physicians for fear of what they might tell her.

She was still signing the orders for the burnings, which continued to take place in London and elsewhere. Heretics were being steadily rooted out, and yet heresy seemed to be flourishing.

The Bishop of London came to see her. She did not like Edmund Bonner—for all his heartiness, there was a coarseness about him—yet he was zealous in his pursuit and punishment of heretics, a zeal that had led dissidents to call him "Bloody Bonner."

He was not looking zealous today. In fact, he looked frightened.

"Your Majesty, I must tell you that the tumults at executions are increasing, putting myself and the secular officers at risk. I beg you to order that the burnings take place early in the mornings, before people are about."

"No, my lord Bishop," Mary cried. "How could they then be a deterrent?" And she sent him about his business.

She returned wearily to her desk, feeling a little sick, and looked at the latest list of those who had suffered burning. By her reckoning, nearly three hundred had died in the past three years. If only the Protestants had not clung so stubbornly to their false beliefs. They had cost her much of her popularity—and Philip, too, for the heresy laws had long been associated with the Spaniards in the minds of the ignorant. It was an inescapable fact that many of those who had welcomed Mary to the throne with such enthusiasm now hated her. It was a bitter physick to swallow. No wonder she was finding it hard to escape the morass of her depression.

She determined, nonetheless, to take good care of herself, for Philip's sake, and by September, she was feeling better. She moved to Hampton Court, but had not been there long before the fever recurred, worse than before. Her doctors assured her that there was no cause for alarm—but they did not know about the mass that lurked in her belly.

Presently, she returned to London and took up residence in St. James' Palace, which her father had built for Anne Boleyn, but which had been not completed until after her death. No sooner had she arrived than she began to feel very ill indeed and was compelled to take to her bed.

Lying there, feeling like death, and too unwell to care what happened to her, she watched the doctors as, one by one, they took her pulse, checked her water, and felt her brow, then retired to huddle together in the antechamber to discuss their findings. When they returned, she could read the despair in their faces. Yet they continued to assure her that her malady was not serious, and that it would actually help to relieve the old autumnal sickness that had troubled her all her life.

Soon, she did feel better, but then the fever took hold once more and she suffered violent convulsions. The black pall of melancholy descended again. She lost the will to recover. In her moments of clarity, she wondered dispassionately whether she was dying. Had it not been for her kingdom and Philip, she would have embraced death.

News of the Emperor's passing made her feel infinitely worse. She had regarded him as a second father, and now he was gone.

When her ladies told her that Philip had been sent for, she knew that her illness was grave. Yet the weeks passed, and still he did not come, explaining that he was detained by official business. He would be with her as soon as he possibly could.

The lords of the Council came to Mary's bedside.

"We urge your Majesty to name your successor," they demanded.

"No," she said weakly. She did agree to make a codicil to her will, ordering that Philip should have no further involvement in the government of the realm after she was gone, and asking him to be as a father, brother, and friend to the next sovereign. Yet she avoided saying who that sovereign would be.

When she lay back listlessly after making the effort to sign the codicil, Jane Dormer came to her, all golden curls and blushes, to tell her that she and Count de Feria had fallen in love. "We wish to marry, Madam, and we crave your blessing," she asked, her eyes shining.

How could Mary resist? It was heartening to see Jane so happy.

"I will be loath to lose you," she said, taking the young woman's hand, "but you deserve a good husband, which I am sure the Count will be. He is a perfect gentleman whom I hold in great regard. I shall look forward to your wedding, and hope to be there, although I would ask that you delay it until the King's return."

Jane willingly agreed, and Mary wondered for the thousandth time if Philip ever would come back. It grieved her to think she might never see him again. She really must make an effort to get better.

Her councillors were clearly growing increasingly anxious about her. Early in November, they prevailed upon her to recall Parliament. She was well enough to discuss its agenda with them, although she felt so sick and weak that she could not talk for long. It was that which convinced her that she was dying, and when the lords all trooped into her bedchamber the next day, she knew they had come to press her to name Elizabeth her successor. Feeling terrible, she gave in and uttered the words she had resisted saying for so long.

"Very well. Elizabeth shall be Queen after I am gone. I ask only that she maintains the old religion and pays my debts," she stipulated, although she knew that her successor was not in any way obliged to comply with her wishes. But Philip would be pleased with her decision, which was to be conveyed to Elizabeth at Hatfield.

Mary sent Jane Dormer there to ensure that Elizabeth swore to uphold the ancient faith and see that the provisions in her will were faithfully carried out. She was praying that her sister would make that vow, but then she became confused, and the next thing she knew was that she was waking up with Susan beside her and it was broad day. She must have slept through the night.

But no. "You've been asleep for three days, Madam," Susan murmured gently. "Shall I make you comfortable. Let's raise you on those pillows. I'll fetch some rose water and sponge you down."

"Three days?" croaked Mary, dazed. She could still feel the dead weight of her illness. "What has been happening?"

"Your physicians asked to be informed when you woke up, Madam."

"Send them away. I know they can do no more for me. I am in God's hands now."

Susan did not demur. She took Mary's hand in both of hers and held it tightly.

"I am dying, am I not?" Mary whispered.

Tears filled Susan's eyes. "I fear so, Madam."

"Thank you for your honesty. Everyone else has been assuring me I will get better soon, but I am not a fool. I have not been in this world for nearly forty-three years without learning how to spot a dissembler. Yet they mean well. It's a relief not to have to keep up the pretense."

They sat in silence for a while, still holding hands, then Susan spoke. "Count de Feria has been asking to see your Majesty."

"Tell him I will receive him, but make me presentable first."

When he came in, his face told her how ill she looked.

"Your Majesty, I bring a letter from the King."

He laid it on the counterpane, but Mary was too weak to pick it up and read it.

"What does it say?"

He read it out. Philip had written lovingly, saying how sorry he was that she was so unwell, and how he longed to be with her. He would come soon. Yes, she thought, but you will be too late.

She summoned Jane Dormer, and was moved to see how Feria's face lit up when he saw his betrothed. They looked radiant together. That could have been her and Philip, Mary thought, had they been closer in age and not divided by war.

"I am sorry for having delayed your marriage," she said, "but I give you my blessing." Sighing, she signaled to Jane to take a velvet box from the table and hand it to the Count. "Pray take this ring to the King, as a sign of my undying love." She saw that Jane was silently weeping.

"Do not distress yourself, child," she murmured. "I am going to meet my God, and I am not afraid."

The next day, however, she felt a little better and was able to force herself up against her pillows to do her duty to God and sign a warrant for the burning of two heretics. It might, she reflected, be the last she would authorize. When she was gone, she knew, Elizabeth would not punish heresy. The knowledge was bitter gall in her mouth.

After that, she felt herself drifting in and out of consciousness. When she woke to see her ladies weeping, she raised a hand to attract their attention.

"You must not mourn for me. I am having the most wonderful dreams in which I see little children like angels playing before me and singing pleasing notes, which gives me more than earthly comfort." It was, she was sure, a foretaste of Heaven.

Every day, Mary had Mass celebrated in her bedchamber, and derived her greatest comfort from it. She hoped that the Cardinal, who was lying sick to death at Lambeth Palace, not a mile away, was being similarly comforted. They were consoling each other with loving messages.

But there were other times when she awoke in tears and could not stem them, lying there impervious to the attempts of her ladies to comfort her. One afternoon, some of her councillors arrived to find her sobbing.

"Your Majesty, why are you so sad?" they asked her. "Is it because the King's Majesty is gone from you?"

"That is one cause," she whispered, "but it is not the greatest wound that pierces my oppressed mind. When I am dead, you will find Calais lying in my heart."

Some of the lords looked as if they would weep with her.

She made a final effort to persuade Elizabeth to preserve the Catholic faith. She sent her a message exhorting her to honor her dying wishes. She had done everything in her power to ensure it, and now all that was left was to pray that God would direct her sister along the right path.

It was dark when she awoke. Something had changed. She felt lightheaded, weightless, as if she was fading. Weakly, she summoned her ladies.

"I am about to meet my Maker," she told them, although they had to lean close to hear her. "Always remain steadfast to the true faith." They swore they would, some of them sobbing openly. "Do not weep," she said. "I go to a better place, where all suffering is at an end."

She asked that her priests come to celebrate Mass, and was able to make the responses clearly.

"I pray," she said aloud, "that the weakness of my flesh be not overcome by the fear of dying. Grant me, merciful Father, that when death has shut up the eyes of my body, the eyes of my soul may still behold and look upon Thee."

At the moment when the Host was elevated, she shuddered with emotion and bent her head forward. The last thing she saw, before the light took her, was the image of her Savior and Redeemer on the crucifix that lay on her breast. Soon, she would behold Him in His glorious body in Heaven. Her heart leaped with joy, and then stilled.

Author's Note

Mary I has become a controversial figure among historians. Since I published my nonfiction book *Children of England: The Heirs of Henry VIII* (*The Children of Henry VIII* in the United States) in 1996, much research has been done on her, and new biographies have been published, focusing on her achievements. Gradually, in recent years, I have become aware of new opinions emerging, and that there has been a concerted attempt to rehabilitate her reputation. Some historians now hold quite passionate views on the subject, and their assessments have become the received wisdom of our day.

When I came to write this novel, however, and revisited my own research, I found that I could not entirely support this new view. Yes, it is important to credit Mary for her achievements, the greatest of which was her successful taking of the throne that was rightfully hers. No one could doubt her courage or her presence of mind. Against tremendous odds, she overcame an attempt to replace her with her cousin, Lady Jane Grey, and emerged triumphant, to a roar of popular acclaim.

Legally, Mary was England's first queen regnant. The 1544 Act of Succession, passed under her father, Henry VIII, settled the succession to the throne on his children, Edward, Mary, and Elizabeth and their heirs. If they all predeceased him, "the King's most excellent majesty, for default of such heirs as be inheritable by the said Act, might by the authority of the said Act, give and dispose the said Imperial crown and other the premises by his letters patents under his great seal, or by his last will in writing signed with his most gracious hand, to any person or persons of such estate therein as should

please his Highness to limit and appoint." The Act did not confer
that same authority upon Edward VI, whose deathbed "device" of
1553—aimed at safeguarding the Protestant settlement by setting
aside his sisters and leaving the crown to Jane—had no force in law;
even if he had had that authority, such a device did not supersede
Letters Patent or a will, and had no power to overthrow an Act of
Parliament. Thus Jane's accession was illegal and she had no right to
the title of queen. The people rallied to Mary because they wanted to
see the lawful heir restored.

Mary encouraged trade. Her financial reforms bolstered mercantile
enterprise, which in turn led the government to receiving more taxes.
She increased England's naval strength, founded hospitals, and took
steps to improve the education of the clergy. She afforded relief to the
poor during the bad harvests of 1555–6 and the influenza epidemic
of 1556–8, and took measures against those who hoarded grain.

These were all sound and beneficial acts, but I think Mary's fail-
ings far outweighed them, and that the traditional view of her is
closer to the truth. The loss of Calais was "the heaviest tidings to
England that ever was heard of." Mary herself saw it as the worst
failure of her reign. It was she who bore the blame, for people said
that had she not agreed to involving England in her husband's war in
the first place, it would never have happened. To make matters worse,
it quickly became apparent, not only at home but also abroad, that
the kingdom did not have the resources to even attempt to recapture
Calais. England's weakness was therefore exposed for the world to
see, and the morale of her people plummeted.

The loss of Calais, catastrophic as it was, was not the only evil to
afflict the kingdom. In 1558, Armagil Waad, one of Edward VI's
former councillors, reported: "The Queen is poor, the realm exhausted, the nobility poor and decayed. The people are out of order.
Justice is not executed. All things are dear. There are divisions among
ourselves, wars with France and Scotland. The French King is be-
striding this realm. There is steadfast enmity but no steady friendship abroad." The Queen was vilified in seditious pamphlets as "an
utter destroyer of her own subjects, a lover of strangers, and an unnatural stepdame both to these and to thy mother England." It was
said that she was a traitor to God and her country, a promoter of

idolatry, and a persecutor of saints. (In the novel, these words, and those below, have been put into the mouth of Paget.)

In 1560, Sir Thomas Smith, Secretary of State under Edward VI, recalled: "I never saw England weaker in strength, money, men and riches. As much affectionate as you know me to be to my country and countrymen, I assure you I was ashamed of them both. Here was nothing but fining, heading, hanging, quartering, and burning, taxing, levying and beggaring, and losing our strongholds abroad. A few priests ruled all, who thought to make all cocksure."

Mary was not politically astute, a fact of which her councillors and foreign ambassadors were clearly aware. They saw her as weak and indecisive. She could not control Parliament, which sometimes opposed her. Her religious reforms were too radical, and she implemented them too quickly, ignoring the concerns of her advisers. For her, the crowning achievement of her reign was reconciling the English Church to Rome, yet it backfired on her, for 1555 saw the election of Pope Paul IV, who was virulently anti-Spanish and at odds with Mary's husband, Philip of Spain, which was a setback to the Counter-Reformation in England.

The elephant in the room, as far as modern assessments go, is the Queen's persecution of Protestants, which earned her the enduring epithet "Bloody Mary." From 1555 (when she revived the old heresy laws) to 1558, between 284 and 313 people were burned at the stake by her order. Revisionists correctly point out that this was a small number compared to persecutions for heresy in Europe, and that other Tudor monarchs also sent heretics to the stake: Henry VIII burned 55 and had many other felons executed (claims that he put between 52,000 and 70,000 people to death in his reign are grossly exaggerated), while Elizabeth I burned 9, although she had 183 Catholics hanged, drawn and quartered for treason. It has been argued that no one has called them "Bloody Henry" or "Bloody Elizabeth."

Yet while Henry, Mary, and Elizabeth all acted in the interests of preserving legitimacy and the integrity of the religious settlements they established, Mary was perceived to be doing so under the influence of her foreign husband, Philip of Spain, which her xenophobic subjects found intolerable. The marriage was deeply unpopular and sparked Wyatt's rebellion. While Mary showed great courage and presence of mind in rallying the Londoners to oppose him, she had ignored the groundswell of public opposition to the marriage that had led to the revolt, opposition that was underpinned by serious concerns. We might applaud her for wishing to ally herself to a powerful prince and providing for the succession, but her marriage to Philip has been called her most significant failure. Repeatedly disregarding ongoing vehement protests against it showed poor judgment, for there were justifiable fears that such a union would drag England into fighting foreign wars for Philip, which was what actually did happen, culminating in the disastrous loss of Calais. It was in the interests of preserving the Spanish marriage alliance that Lady Jane Grey was beheaded. In this, Mary had little choice, for it had been made plain to her that her marriage could not go ahead while Jane lived. But in arresting and imprisoning Elizabeth, who had played no part in Wyatt's rebellion, and against whom no evidence was found, she let jealousy and suspicion cloud her judgment.

She chose a husband who represented everything Englishmen hated. Philip was heir to Spain, a land that had nurtured the Inquisition, with its persecutions and public Acts of Faith that witnessed heretics being sent to their death. It has been claimed that the Protestant Edwardian settlement had not fully taken root and that the burnings in England were not as unpopular as has generally been assumed; yet if that was true, why did Philip and Lord Chancellor Gardiner, both of them hardliners, urge Mary to exercise caution? Why did even "Bloody Bonner" beg her to have the burnings carried out early in the morning to avoid demonstrations? Why, in the light of public protests, did Mary's councillors debate whether they were necessary and effective? And why was Elizabeth's Accession Day, which marked England's delivery from the persecution, celebrated right up to the middle of the eighteenth century? That alone shows the strength of feeling against Mary, and it is notable that it was first celebrated after the Pope had excommunicated Elizabeth and authorized loyal Catholics to assassinate her. People did not want to go back to the bad old days under a Catholic monarch; they did not want foreign interference in England.

Mary could have halted the burnings, but she did not. She persisted doggedly in her chosen course. In this, as in everything else, she was single-minded and determined, acting on instinct and principle. She personally signed the warrants that sent human beings to a dreadful death. Her motives have been outlined in the novel, and I believe that she was set on putting the clock back to the happy certainties of her childhood. We cannot doubt her sincerity. She truly believed she was ridding the world of those who could put others' souls at risk, and that she might save those of the heretics in the process, hoping that a taste of the hellfire to come would make them recant at the last. Yet, paradoxically, she eventually deprived them of their one chance to recant.

It has been said that John Foxe's *Acts and Monuments,* or "Book of Martyrs," published under Elizabeth I and placed in churches, was largely responsible for Mary's bloody reputation. Yet it authentically chronicled, in horrific detail, the burnings, which many of Elizabeth's subjects would have remembered; and it reflected public revulsion against them.

Mary's policy failed. It did not eradicate heresy; it created martyrs; it showed her subjects that the Protestant religion was a faith worth dying a horrible death for. England was not, as a nation, entirely happy in its reconciliation to Catholicism. We can only guess what might have happened if Mary had lived longer. Almost certainly, the burnings would have continued, as they had up until a week before her death. The numbers sent to the stake did not decrease significantly as her reign progressed.

When Mary died, Londoners joyfully celebrated her passing and the accession of Elizabeth I, whom they looked upon as their deliverer. Mary had left England in what her successor would describe as "a sad state," reduced to the status of a minor power on the edge of a Europe riven by religious and political strife, and prey to the ambitions of the two major international monarchies, Spain and France. There was no money in the English treasury because much of it had gone to finance Philip's foreign wars, and the country had been stripped of its arms and munitions, while its chief defenses and fortresses were ruinous. Had war come, England could not have defended itself.

"Certainly," wrote a Spanish observer in 1558, "the state of England lay now most afflicted." Internally, there was dissension and dissatisfaction. Many had lost confidence in the government, which was in debt to the tune of £266,000—an enormous sum in those days. The people of England, having lived through a quarter-century of Reformation and Counter-Reformation, were now divided by deep religious differences. Count de Feria, Philip's ambassador in England at the time of Queen Mary's death, claimed that two thirds of the population was Catholic; he may have been exaggerating, but the fact remained that London, the seat of court and government, was aggressively Protestant and influential in public affairs. Where London led, the rest of the country eventually followed.

Today, opinions of Mary are polarized. When I ran a competition on Facebook to suggest a subtitle for this novel, one person was adamant that it should be "Bloody Mary"; another hoped that I would not use that title.

I have enormous personal sympathy for Mary as the child of a broken marriage and, later, a woman fighting for the right to practice her religion. She was eleven when her parents' marriage started to fall apart; I was eleven when my parents split up. In each case, there was another woman involved, whom I loathed as much as Mary loathed Anne Boleyn. In each case, the breakup was complicated and painfully drawn out. My father did not spare me the emotional traumas from which he should have protected me, and the same could be said of Henry VIII's treatment of Mary. My mother was as staunchly loving and supportive of me as Katherine of Aragon was of Mary. Like Katherine, she was threatened with prison if she defied my father. I understand Mary's nervous reactions, and why she always wanted to put the clock back; I reacted in a similar way, having suffered lifelong anxiety as a consequence of what my father did, and I frequently hark back to the safe, happy world of my childhood, which seems like a golden age in retrospect.

My own experiences therefore inform this book. I can understand how the Great Matter impacted on Mary. I would not now define myself as a victim, but that was nevertheless what I was—and what Mary was. And both of us, I feel, eventually rose above it.

But there, with her accession, my sympathy for Mary evaporates. As a novelist, it was hard to identify with her as queen, hard to make her sympathetic. If she comes across as the opposite, and even as pathetic, it's because that is how I see her. I have tried to look at things from her point of view, but I cannot go against what the historical evidence is telling me—and this book is based closely on the historical record. My characterizations of historical figures and the interactions between them are underpinned by the rich contemporary sources of the period.

The cause of Mary's death has been much debated. It has been suggested that she fell victim to the influenza epidemic, or that she had ovarian or uterine cancer. There simply isn't enough evidence to reach a conclusion. But when I was invited to the opening of the Queen's Diamond Jubilee Galleries in the triforium of Westminster Abbey, I was intrigued to see that the body of Mary's wooden funeral effigy had finally been reattached to its head, the only part of it that had hitherto been on display. What struck me was the great mound of the stomach, like a pregnant woman's. And it was that which gave me my storyline.

As ever, I should like to thank my wonderful publishers, Headline in the UK, Australasia, and Canada, and Ballantine in the United States; my commissioning editors, Mari Evans and Susanna Porter; my editorial director, Frances Edwards; and the fantastic teams who ensure the smooth transition of my book from a Word document to the bookshops. I want to thank especially my indefatigable publicist, Caitlin Raynor, for her amazing support, and my editor, Flora Rees, for her exceptional creative input and sensitive enhancement of the text.

I would like to express my thanks also to the readers, media people, bloggers, librarians, event organizers, Facebook friends, and Twitter and Instagram followers who buy, promote, and review my books, or post lovely comments online; and to my fellow historians and friends for all the helpful, insightful discussions and—in Mary's case—arguments! I am profoundly grateful to you all.

Warmest thanks, as ever, go to my agent, Julian Alexander, who has been such a wonderful mainstay and inspiration over the past thirty-four years, and to my daughter, Kate; her husband, Jason; my cousin Chris; my uncle and aunt, John and Joanna; and all my very special family and friends for the kindness and encouragement you give me. And to my beloved husband, Rankin, who passed away as this book was in the final stages of production, my most profound gratitude and affection for the devoted support and strength he gave me over fifty-two years. May you rest in peace, darling, knowing that you leave only love behind.

Dramatis Personae

The Princess Mary, only surviving child of Henry VIII and Katherine of Aragon; later Mary I, Queen of England

Henry VIII, King of England, Mary's father

Katherine of Aragon, Queen of England, Mary's mother

Francis, Dauphin of France, eldest son of King Francis I

Charles V, Holy Roman Emperor, King of Spain, Mary's cousin

Margaret Pole, Countess of Salisbury, Mary's governess

Arthur, Prince of Wales, Mary's deceased uncle, older brother of King Henry VIII and first husband of Katherine of Aragon

Ferdinand and Isabella, joint sovereigns of Spain, Mary's maternal grandparents

Isabella, Juana (later Queen of Castile), and Maria, Katherine of Aragon's sisters

Reginald Pole, later Cardinal, son of Margaret Pole, Countess of Salisbury

Christopher Columbus, Italian explorer and navigator

Philip the Handsome, King of Castile, husband of Juana, Queen of Castile

Isabella of Portugal, mother of Isabella, wife of Ferdinand

Father Richard Fetherston, Mary's tutor

Cardinal Thomas Wolsey, Mary's godfather and King Henry VIII's chief minister

Amata Boleyn, Lady Calthorpe, Mary's first governess

Margaret, Lady Bryan, Mary's second governess

Dr. Thomas Linacre, Mary's first tutor

Juan Luis Vives, Spanish educationist

Sir Thomas More, humanist scholar, later Lord Chancellor

King Arthur, mythical British monarch

Francis I, King of France

Garter King of Arms, herald

Thomas Manners, Lord Roos, later 1st Earl of Rutland

Sir Thomas Boleyn, courtier and ambassador, later 1st Earl of Wiltshire

Henry Fitzroy, 1st Duke of Richmond and Somerset, bastard son of King Henry VIII

Margaret of Austria, Regent of the Netherlands

Edward IV, King of England, Mary's great-grandfather

Henry Pole, Lord Montagu; Geoffrey Pole; Arthur Pole: sons of Margaret Pole, Lady Salisbury

Isabella of Portugal, Holy Roman Empress, wife of the Emperor Charles V

St. Thomas Aquinas, thirteenth-century philosopher and theologian

Henri, Duke of Orléans, second son of King Francis I; later Henri II, King of France

Eleanor of Austria, Queen of France, wife of King Francis I and sister of the Emperor Charles V

Pope Clement VII

Anne Boleyn, maid-of-honor to Katherine of Aragon, later Lady Marquess of Pembroke; later Queen of England; second wife of King Henry VIII

Pope Julius II

Cardinal Lorenzo Campeggio, Papal legate

Gertrude Blount, Marchioness of Exeter, friend of Katherine of Aragon

Martin Luther, religious reformer, founder of the Protestant religion

Eustache Chapuys, Imperial ambassador to the court of King Henry VIII

Henry, Prince of Wales, and six other children, all deceased; Mary's siblings

Henry Percy, Earl of Northumberland

William Warham, Archbishop of Canterbury

John Fisher, Bishop of Rochester

Jane Seymour, maid-of-honor to Katherine of Aragon and Anne Boleyn; later Queen of England; third wife of King Henry VIII

William Blount, Lord Mountjoy

Thomas Cromwell, Principal Secretary to King Henry VIII; later Lord Privy Seal, Lord Cromwell and 1st Earl of Essex

Thomas Cranmer, Archbishop of Canterbury

Master Hayward, Lady Salisbury's messenger

Charles Brandon, 1st Duke of Suffolk, husband of King Henry VIII's sister Mary

Thomas Howard, 3rd Duke of Norfolk

John Longland, Bishop of Lincoln

The Princess Elizabeth, daughter of King Henry VIII and Anne Boleyn

Catherine de' Medici, wife of Henri, Duke of Orléans; later Queen of France

Duke of Urbino

Nicholas West, Bishop of Ely

Anne Boleyn, Lady Shelton, Mary's governess

Sir John Shelton, her husband, governor of the Princess Elizabeth's household

Alice, Lady Clere, Anne Boleyn's aunt

Sir Francis Bryan, courtier, son of Margaret, Lady Bryan

Dr. William Butts, physician to King Henry VIII

Dr. de la Saa, physician to Katherine of Aragon

George Boleyn, Lord Rochford, Anne Boleyn's brother

Stillborn son of King Henry VIII and Anne Boleyn

Jane Parker, Lady Rochford, wife of Lord Rochford

Henry Parker, Lord Morley, her father

Margaret Beaufort, Countess of Richmond and Derby, Mary's paternal great-grandmother

Sir Henry Norris, Sir Francis Weston, William Brereton and Mark Smeaton, Anne Boleyn's alleged lovers

Sir Edward Seymour, older brother of Jane Seymour; later Lord Beauchamp, 1st Earl of Hertford, 1st Duke of Somerset and Lord Protector of England

Mary, Lady Kingston, wife of Sir William Kingston, Constable of the Tower

Sir Thomas Wriothesley, later Secretary of State and Lord Chancellor

Janie, Mary's fool

Sir William Sandys, the Lord Chamberlain

Katherine Champernowne, later Mrs. Ashley, governess to the Lady Elizabeth

Susan Clarencieux, lady-in-waiting to Mary

Thomas Tonge, Clarencieux King of Arms, her husband

Edward, Prince of Wales, later King Edward VI; son of King Henry VIII and Jane Seymour

St. Edward the Confessor, King of England

William Fitzalan, 11th Earl of Arundel

Dr. John Chamber, physician to Henry VIII

Robert Aldrich, Bishop of Carlisle

Cuthbert Tunstall, Bishop of Durham

Lancaster Herald

Sir Thomas Seymour, later Lord Sudeley, brother of Jane Seymour

Blanche Herbert, Lady Troy, governess to the Lady Elizabeth

Christina of Denmark, Duchess of Milan, later Duchess of Lorraine

Marie de Guise, later wife of James V, King of Scots, and afterward Queen Regent of Scotland

Hans Holbein, "King's painter"

Father John Forrest, former chaplain to Katherine of Aragon

Mother Jack, Prince Edward's wet nurse

William I, Duke of Cleves

John III, Duke of Cleves

Anna of Cleves, Queen of England, fourth wife of King Henry VIII

Amalia of Cleves, her sister

Mrs. Sybil Penne, nurse to Prince Edward

Henry Courtenay, 1st Marquess of Exeter, cousin of Henry VIII

Henry Pole, his son

Edward Courtenay, his son, later 1st Earl of Devon

Philip of Bavaria, Duke of Palatinate-Neuburg

Mary Howard, widow of Henry Fitzroy, Duke of Richmond and Somerset

Lady Margaret Douglas, Mary's cousin, later Countess of Lennox

Margaret Tudor, Queen of Scots, her mother, and sister of King Henry VIII

Katheryn Howard, maid-of-honor to Anna of Cleves; later Queen of England; fifth wife of King Henry VIII

Agnes Tilney, Dowager Duchess of Norfolk, her grandmother

Catherine Willoughby, Duchess of Suffolk, second wife of Charles Brandon, Duke of Suffolk

Maria de Salinas and William, Lord Willoughby de Eresby, her parents

Katharine Parr, Lady Latimer, later Queen of England; sixth wife of Henry VIII

Sir Nicholas Carew, courtier

Stephen Gardiner, Bishop of Winchester

Dr. Richard Cox, tutor to Prince Edward

Juan Esteban, Duke of Najera, Spanish envoy

William Parr, 1st Earl of Essex, brother of Katharine Parr

Desiderius Erasmus, Dutch humanist scholar

Francis van der Delft, Imperial ambassador to the court of Henry VIII

Nicholas Ridley, Bishop of London

Henry Howard, Earl of Surrey, son and heir of the Duke of Norfolk

Lady Jane Grey, Henry VIII's great-niece

Lady Katherine and Lady Mary Grey, her sisters

Anne ("Nan") Stanhope, wife of Edward Seymour, Duke of
Somerset

John Dudley, 1st Earl of Warwick, later Lord President of the
Council and 1st Duke of Northumberland

Temperance, daughter of John Dudley, later Duke of
Northumberland

Sir William Paget, Privy Councillor

Father Matthew Parker, chaplain to Katharine Parr

Sir Robert Rochester, Mary's comptroller, later a Privy Councillor

Sir Francis Englefield, Mary's chamberlain

Sir Edward Waldegrave, Mary's steward

Jane Dormer, maid-of-honor to Mary

Edmund Bonner, Bishop of London

Sir Anthony Denny, courtier

Joan Champernowne, his wife, sister to Katherine Ashley

Mary Seymour, daughter of Katharine Parr and Thomas, Lord
Seymour

John Rochester, a priest

Sir Richard Rich, Lord Chancellor

Sir William Petre, Privy Councillor and Secretary of State

Dr. Hopton, Mary's senior chaplain

Robert Ket, rebel

John Knox, religious reformer

John Hooper, Bishop of Gloucester

Hugh Latimer, Bishop of Worcester

Dom Luis of Portugal, Duke of Beja

Albert II, Margrave of Brandenburg

Mary of Hungary, Regent of the Netherlands

The Lord Lieutenant of Essex

Jehan Scheyfve, Imperial ambassador to the court of King
Edward VI

Jean Dubois, secretary to Francis van der Delft, Imperial ambassador to the court of Edward VI

Henry, Mary's groom

Master Merchant, brother-in-law of Jean Dubois

The Imperial Admiral and Vice Admiral

Master Schurts, friend of Sir Robert Rochester

Prince Philip of Spain, son and heir of the Emperor Charles V; King of Naples and Jerusalem; later husband of Queen Mary I and King of England; King Philip II of Spain

Dr. Mallet, Mary's chaplain

The Sheriff of Essex

Dr. Barclay, Mary's chaplain

Frances Brandon, Marchioness of Dorset, later Duchess of Suffolk, Mary's cousin and mother of Jane, Katherine and Mary Grey

Henry Grey, 3rd Marquess of Dorset, later 1st Duke of Suffolk, her husband

John de Vere, 16th Earl of Oxford

Anne Radcliffe, lady-in-waiting to Mary

Sir Anthony Browne, Master of Horse

Sir Anthony Wingfield, Privy Councillor

William Cecil, Secretary of State

An unnamed chaplain of the Lady Mary, called "Dr. Hall" in the novel

Lord Guildford Dudley, son of John Dudley, Duke of Northumberland, and husband of Lady Jane Grey

William, Lord Herbert, husband of Lady Katherine Grey

William Herbert, 1st Earl of Pembroke, his father

Sir Nicholas Throckmorton, courtier

Sir John Huddlestone, Catholic gentleman

Bridget Cotton, Lady Huddlestone, his wife

Alice, Lady Burgh, Mary's friend

Master Raynes, Mary's goldsmith

Lord Robert Dudley, son of John Dudley, Duke of Northumberland

Sir Henry Bedingfield of Oxburgh Hall

Sir Edmund Bedingfield, his father

Sir Richard Southwell

John Bourchier, 2nd Earl of Bath

Henry Radcliffe, 2nd Earl of Sussex

Sir Edmund Peckham, cofferer to Edward VI

Thomas, Lord Wentworth

William Fitzalan, 12th Earl of Arundel

The Gentleman Gaoler of the Tower

Jane Guildford, Duchess of Northumberland

The Duke of Northumberland's apothecary

A female quack

Simon Renard, Imperial ambassador to the court of Queen
Mary I

Elizabeth Stafford, Duchess of Norfolk

Antoine de Noailles, French ambassador to the court of Mary I

Pope Julius III

Anne Bassett, Mary's maid-of-honor

Catherine Brydges, Lady Dudley, courtier

Maria of Portugal, first wife of Prince Philip of Spain

Don Carlos, son and heir of Prince Philip of Spain

Edward Stanley, 3rd Earl of Derby

Sir Edward Dymoke, the Queen's Champion

Matthew Stewart, 4th Earl of Lennox, husband of Lady Margaret
Douglas

Sir Thomas Wyatt, rebel

Sir Peter Carew, rebel

Sir James Crofts, rebel

Sir Edward Hastings, later Lord Hastings, military commander

Sir Humphrey Clinton, military captain

Richard Feckenham, Abbot of Westminster

Sir John Brydges, Lieutenant of the Tower

Adrian Stokes, master of horse to Frances Brandon, Duchess of
Suffolk, and her second husband

Lamoral, Count Egmont, proxy for Prince Philip of Spain

William Saintlow, the Lady Elizabeth's gentleman

Francis, Lord Russell

William Paulet, Earl of Wiltshire and 1st Marquess of Winchester

Sir John Gage, Constable of the Tower

The Marquess de Navas, head of Prince Philip's household

Lord William Howard, half-brother to the Duke of Norfolk

Elizabeth Seymour, Marchioness of Winchester, sister of Jane Seymour

Catherine of Austria, Queen of Poland

Emmanuel Philibert, Duke of Savoy

Thomas Tallis, composer of the Chapel Royal

John Rogers, heretic

Father Fresneda, King Philip's confessor

The Sheriff of Hampshire

Francis de Noailles, brother of Antoine, later French ambassador to the court of Queen Mary I

Mary's midwife

Dr. John Dee, astrologer

Perotine Massey, Guernsey heretic

Nicholas Heath, Archbishop of York and Lord Chancellor

Pope Paul IV

Ferdinand of Habsburg, Holy Roman Emperor, brother of Charles V

Sir Henry Dudley, rebel

John Bray of Hatfield, neighbor of the Lady Elizabeth

Sir Peter Killigrew, friend of the Lady Elizabeth

Anne of Bohemia, Holy Roman Empress, wife of the Emperor Ferdinand I

Margaret, Duchess of Parma, half-sister of King Philip II

Thomas Stafford, rebel

Friar William Peto, Mary's former confessor

Bernardo de Fresneda

Cardinal Morone, friend of Cardinal Pole

Fernando Álvarez de Toledo, 3rd Duke of Alba

Gómez Suárez de Figueroa y Córdoba, Count de Feria, Spanish envoy

Gustav I Vasa, King of Sweden

Eric, Duke of Finland, his son, later Eric XIV, King of Sweden

Various nobles, Privy Councillors, gentlemen of the privy chamber, Esquires of the Body, courtiers, knights, Members of Parliament, chamberlains, household officers, heralds, royal servants, clergymen, monks, clerks, Yeomen of the Guard, Gentlemen Pensioners, Barons of the Cinque Ports, ambassadors, envoys, Constables of the Tower, envoys, lawyers, physicians, Masters of the Revels, musicians, children, and choristers of the Chapel Royal, Lords of Misrule, painters, grooms, ushers, messengers, ladies-in-waiting, maids-of-honor, midwives, admirals, soldiers, sailors, mayors, civic officers, citizens, merchants, common people, apprentices, boatmen, whores

About the Author

ALISON WEIR is the *New York Times* bestselling author of *The King's Pleasure, The Last White Rose,* and the novels in the Six Tudor Queens series: *Katharine Parr, The Sixth Wife; Katheryn Howard, The Scandalous Queen; Anna of Kleve, The Princess in the Portrait; Jane Seymour, The Haunted Queen; Anne Boleyn, A King's Obsession;* and *Katherine of Aragon, The True Queen.* She has also written numerous earlier novels and historical biographies, including her ongoing series, England's Medieval Queens.

alisonweir.org.uk
alisonweirtours.com
Facebook.com/AlisonWeirAuthor
X: @AlisonWeirBooks